Terror in the Skies:

A Moment in Time Christian Thriller

Alana Terry

Note: The views of the characters in this novel do not necessarily reflect the views of the author, nor is their behavior necessarily condoned.

www.alanaterry.com

Contents

Terror in the Skies

Alana Terry

Christian Books Today

CHAPTER 1

IF YOU WERE TO look at me in passing and see my bright blue hair, you might guess I was some kind of art major with a decided bleeding-heart complex. Well, you'd actually be pretty close. Except instead of art, it's theater.

My name is Willow Winters, which if you had any reservations before about my slightly bohemian tendencies earlier, you can assure yourself that your first impression wasn't mistaken. With me it's what you see is what you get. Promise.

It's kind of funny, really. I'm an only child, and so you'd think I'd be more used to being the center of attention, except I'm not. If I had friends who were of marrying age or inclination at this stage in my life, I'd definitely be the *twice a bridesmaid* type or however that saying goes. In fact, even in my theater roles I'm almost always thrown into a critically important albeit nevertheless supporting part.

Fine by me. Fewer people to let down if you mess anything up.

I'm just the blue-haired second fiddle. That could be the name of my autobiography, I swear. Except now I'm stepping into the spotlight. Because it's time for me to tell my own story. My own way.

Are you ready?

Let's go.

It's so funny. Until I moved out here to the East Coast, I didn't think that being from Alaska was any different than being from, oh, say Montana or Georgia or any of the other forty-nine states in the union. But people kind of geek out here when I tell them where I'm from, so I guess I'll go ahead and start there.

Yes, I'm from Alaska. No, I don't ski cross-country to travel from one town to another, nor have I ever seen or spent the night in an igloo. I live an hour away from the nearest grocery store, and my town only has about three hundred people living in it. (Drop that down to a hundred and fifty in the winters if you count the snowbirds.)

Because I'm from Alaska, I'm going to say a few things differently than you. When I talk about going outside, I'm talking about leaving the wonderful beauty of Alaska and venturing out to the Lower 48. (That's the contiguous United States if you're not familiar with the phrase.) A snow machine is what everyone else in the States insists on calling a snowmobile, and breakup season has nothing to do with romantic relationships and everything to do with melted ice and snow.

Because I'm an Alaskan, I'm more than comfortable processing a moose (even though I'm most decidedly vegan), snowshoeing for five or ten miles a day, and using an outhouse. No, I don't drive a team of sled dogs around (although my nearest neighbors do). Yes, I have running water at home (although we have to haul it in on the back of my dad's truck). Yes, I've seen the northern lights, made fireweed jelly, and driven over potholes big enough to drown a beluga.

So, now that we've gotten those preliminaries out of the way, it's time for me to tell you about my most recent trip back home. It's time for me to tell you about the closest I've ever come to dying, and how that experience ultimately saved my life.

CHAPTER 2

I NEVER HAD SIBLINGS growing up (yes, I know I mentioned that before, but bear with me). Mom and Dad were already fairly old by the time I came around. Having both come from academic lifestyles in the past, they were ready to retire rural, and they brought me along for the ride.

I didn't feel lonely growing up. We had goats, sheep, several dozen chickens, and acres of woods to explore. There was never a shortage of things to do, since my parents were one-hundred percent devoted to subsistence living. By that I mean summers were spent growing all the food we'd need for the winter; falls were filled with canning, blanching, and freezing; and if we couldn't buy or make or grow it local, we learned to do without.

Books were the only exception, and after years of conscience wrangling, my dad even bought himself an e-reader when I was in high school.

Life was simple. Organic. Predictable.

And then I moved to the East for college. It wasn't a surprise, really. Even though nobody from my hometown had ever been accepted to a school like Harvard before, it was tacitly understood I'd be heading toward the Ivy League. My summers spent at camps and enrichment programs all across the country were meant to broaden my horizons and puff up my resumé. Harvard was happy to have me, and as excited as I was to taste the freedom of city living, Alaska has always been and always will be home.

Don't get me wrong. College is fine. I like my classes, I have some awesome friends in the theater department, and I've been cast in quite a few interesting productions already. I've got a great roommate, if you can handle living with a neat-freak bookworm. Seriously, though, Kennedy's amazing. It's kind of an unlikely friendship if you ask me, and since she's going to end up playing a decent part in my near-death experience, I suppose you should get used to hearing about her now.

Kennedy's one of those people you just don't forget. If I'm second fiddle, she's sitting pretty in first chair. Super smart, studious, classic type-A personality. It's a small wonder we shared a dorm room our first year of college without killing each other. But that's just what we did, and we managed not to kill each other with such alarming talent that we decided to go ahead and do the same thing all over again for our sophomore year.

Which brings me to the present.

Or actually to about three months ago.

Winter break.

Kennedy, my oh-so-studious roommate, was coming home with me for the semester holiday. Meet the family. Learn to milk goats, all that fun stuff. Kennedy's a typical city girl, so I thought it would be a blast to offer her that very first taste of rural living.

Fast-forward to day one of winter break. Kennedy had been studying herself sleepless (like normal) to get through all her finals. As for me, two of my classes just had final projects. The others were papers, not all that different than the ones I'd been writing all semester. So basically, Kennedy and I had both made it through another term. It's just that I managed to do it without aging myself a decade and losing a cumulative total of three days of sleep in the process. But that's neither here nor there.

Our first flight to get home was going to take us from Boston to Detroit. Fairly standard, I suppose, as far as airplane trips go. From Detroit on to Seattle, Seattle to Anchorage ... Yeah, getting anywhere when you're from Alaska is a royal pain. Not to mention the fact that even once we landed in Anchorage, we'd still have a five-hour drive ahead of us to get home to Copper Lake. Kennedy's a pretty seasoned traveler. City girl, like I said, all that jazz. Between the two of us, we've probably circumnavigated the world a good number of times if you were to throw our miles together. All that is to say that neither of us was green when it came to flying.

Which is why neither of us had any clue when we boarded that plane how close we were about to come to death.

CHAPTER 3

HAVE YOU EVER SEEN someone die before? I know, I know. Morbid question. Too disturbing. I grew up on a farm. I already told you that. So you can guess that I'm not too squeamish when it comes to blood, birth, the circle of life, all that jazz.

Except I'd never seen a human die. Not until I got on that flight with Kennedy.

I'd certainly never seen anyone murdered. But I'm getting ahead of myself.

Let's see ... This is the first time I've tried to lay out any of the things that happened to me in any kind of logical order. It's a lot harder than I imagined. I guess I should just start at the beginning.

Kennedy and I were seated in the back of the plane. I mean the very back. And a few weird things happened right at the start. Well, maybe not totally weird as far as traveling goes, but looking back, they all added up.

So first of all, this Mennonite family got on board. You wouldn't know it if you've never lived here, but Alaska has quite a lot of Mennonites, especially when you get toward Palmer and Wasilla. Most people know the area because that's where Sarah Palin's from. You've heard of her maybe? Fun fact: Jewel is also from Alaska, but that's a less well-known piece of trivia unless you're one of her fans.

So anyway, this Mennonite family came on board. Nothing all that surprising about that, at least to me. If I remember right, this guy in front of me had some kind of problem with them.

Made a joke about the Amish not being allowed to fly in airplanes, something ignorant like that. Sadly, not too different than what you might expect.

They seemed like a really nice family too. Quiet kids. Mom was reading to the younger ones if I remember right. But then these two men with Middle Eastern clothing and features came on board. They were sitting toward the front of the plane, but I watched the Mennonite husband and wife exchange a look. I don't have to describe it to you exactly, do I? You know what I mean don't you?

The look.

And then the wife told her husband she had a bad feeling about the flight, and she wanted to get off. I was expecting him to tell her everything was fine. Maybe she hadn't flown much in the past and got nervous. Maybe she'd just watched a documentary recently on 9-11 and hadn't read the memo that not all people of Middle Eastern descent are terrorists. Who knows?

But instead of calming his wife down, the husband called over the flight attendant. Her name was Tracy. Now, think about how many flights you've been on. Not just this year or this decade even, but over your whole life. On a single one of them, can you remember any of the flight attendants' names?

I didn't think so.

But Tracy is a woman I will never forget.

Never.

Except I'm getting ahead of myself again. First we need to go back to the Mennonites. The husband told Tracy he and his wife were uncomfortable and wanted to get their family off the plane. At this point, I expected Tracy to say something like, "Oh, we're perfectly safe here, you have nothing to worry about. Is this your first time flying with us?" If we were ten or fifteen years in the past, she'd probably have offered to give all the kids little wing pins. You remember those, don't you?

Well, that's not what Tracy said. She was very polite and very professional and told them that if they wanted to get off the plane, that was totally their right. So of course that obnoxious man in front of me started complaining about delays, but it happened very quickly and smoothly. One minute they were on the plane. The next minute they were off.

At the time, I'll go ahead and admit it, I thought it had everything to do with racism and xenophobia and that Mennonite woman not wanting to be on a plane with two dark-skinned men wearing turbans. Looking back, I wonder if it was God's way of warning them. I think about that family sometimes. Think about those kids. Did their parents tell them what almost happened?

And what about the parents? Do they feel survivor's guilt? Or maybe some sort of arrogant smugness that they had the good sense to get off that plane? I'll probably never know, but that doesn't mean I don't wonder.

There's a lot of things I wonder about the other victims on that flight. Like Tracy. What did she think about helping that family deboard the plane? Did she think they were being paranoid? Did she begrudge them the extra few minutes of time it took to get them and their luggage back to the terminal? Was she thinking about paperwork she'd have to fill out to explain the change in the passenger list?

Or maybe she wasn't thinking about them at all. Maybe she was thinking about her two children back home. Or where she'd spend the night once we landed in Detroit. I've read everything I could find about Tracy online, but it still doesn't give a good sense of who she really was. But I think about her escorting that family off the flight. Wonder if she herself had any sort of inkling. Any sort of intuition.

What does a flight attendant do when they don't feel safe on a flight? They still have to do their job, right?

Which is exactly what Tracy did. Exactly what she'd still be doing right now in fact if things hadn't taken such a terrible, terrifying turn.

CHAPTER 4

So I'm going to come right out and say it. I met a guy on the plane. Nothing serious. Nothing that would've led to anything. But I guess now's just a good a time as any to explain to you where I was spiritually when I got on that flight.

Which was dead.

Spiritually dead, I mean.

My roommate Kennedy was really the first Christian I'd met who wasn't entirely mean-spirited, hypocritical, and judgmental. In fact, her faith made a really positive impression on me. Not that I was looking for a new religion to try on. I was quite comfortable at the time with my blend of agnostic spiritualism with a few borrowings from Eastern thought, meditation, enlightenment, all that jazz. I was adamantly against organized religion, and other than that I was quite happy to live and let live.

Kennedy was the best kind of Christian friend to have because she wasn't ever shoving her beliefs down my throat. I'd come home on the weekends drunk or high or whatever, and she wouldn't give me a sermon. I asked her about it later, and she said her dad always told her it was wrong to expect non-Christians to act like Christians, which is smart advice if you ask me.

Anyway, back to the flight and this guy I met. He was a teacher. Math, if I remember right, and we got to flirting. We even did a little chair hopping. Kennedy moved over so he and I could sit together. It was really nice of her, now that I think about it, and kind of rude of me. But anyway, I spent a while talking to Mr.

Math Babe (not that he was a total babe; I just forget his name at the moment). Which goes to show you what I said before, that this was a typical flight. We were all doing our thing, waiting to eventually land in Detroit. When you think of how much traveling Kennedy and I still had to do to get all the way out to Copper Lake, we'd really just started our trip.

And things were pretty uneventful for the first couple hours. Math Dude was making jokes. Suggesting we get some drinks during my layover in Detroit. The guy in front of us continued to be rude and obnoxious. Kennedy struck up a conversation with this old white-haired retired missionary lady ... It was about as typical as flights get, if not a little chattier than normal.

And then I saw something.

No, it wasn't the two Middle-Easterners. But wouldn't that be a fine setback for the case against racial profiling? It was this big guy in a Hawaiian shirt sitting toward the front of the cabin. Now that I think about it, I couldn't even tell you what it was about him that got my attention. I'm a people-watcher, I guess. Comes from all my time in the theater. Studying people's quirks, memorizing their body language, all that jazz. But there was something about this guy that made me uneasy right from the start.

Maybe it was that gaudy Hawaiian shirt, but there was more to it than that. He was on the flight with this teen girl. I suppose if you were to glance at them real quickly you would have assumed it was a dad traveling with his daughter. And hey, it wasn't too long since I was that age myself. I totally get not wanting to buddy up to your old man, especially in public.

But this was different.

When I looked at them together, I sort of knew they weren't the right fit. Has that ever happened to you? Like once my dad totally embarrassed everybody involved when he starting chatting it up with this middle-aged man at the Anchorage theater. And yes, striking up a conversation with a complete stranger is totally something my dad would do. As would assuming that the young, pretty woman sitting beside him was his daughter and not only making that assumption but saying so out loud.

Hello?

They were obviously a couple, and I knew that from the start, but I couldn't explain to you how I figured it out right away and good old Dad didn't. Well, it was the same thing on the plane. I looked at that middle-aged, balding man, looked at the teen girl he was traveling with, and I knew they weren't right. I kept watching them, kept trying to figure out what it was about the way they were sitting together that creeped me out.

Knowing what I know now, I almost wish I'd said something sooner. But who could tell if that would have helped? Anyway, I kept watching this couple that certainly wasn't a romantic couple and almost certainly wasn't related if I were to trust my instincts. But what was I supposed to do? Just walk up to the flight attendant and tell her that some old guy on the plane was weirding me out?

So I was keeping half of my attention on those two and half of my attention on my roommate. Mr. Math Babe had moved back to his old seat to work on grading papers or something, so it was just Kennedy and me. Talking about what?

They say that when you're in the midst of intense danger, your brain focuses in on the smallest, sometimes most random details. A kind of protective measure so that you can avoid that particular danger again, I suppose. Honestly, you'd have to ask my roommate about that. She's the science nerd. But you'd think, given everything that was about to happen, my conversation then with Kennedy would somehow be forever seared into my memory.

Except it isn't.

I'd like to think that we had some heavy, weighty discussion about God, the afterlife, anything. But like I said, Kennedy and I didn't usually talk religion. At all. She's quiet. Unassuming in her I'm-going-to-study-until-three-o'clock-in-the-morning-and-ace-all-my-tests overachieving kind of way.

My best guess? We were talking about things like how excited I was for Kaladi Brothers coffee once I landed back in Alaska and whether or not I thought I'd take Math Babe up on his offer for drinks at the airport.

Sometimes I hate how frivolous I can be. I mean, if I'd had any idea what was about to happen, if I had any clue how close I'd come that day to spending an eternity in hell ... Sometimes I want to grab Kennedy by the shoulders and shake her and demand, "Why didn't you tell me sooner?" Except now that I'm a Christian myself, I totally get it. It's not like you get saved and all of a sudden have this unavoidable urge to convert the whole world. Or maybe you even have the inklings of an urge, but you talk yourself out of it. *I don't want to scare him away. I don't want her to think I'm judging her. I don't want them to assume I'm some kind of closed-minded, religious nut-job weirdo.*

I get it. I really do. But it's sobering, too. Because back when I was convinced I was going to die, I was scared out of my mind. Scared that maybe I wasn't good enough for heaven after all. It's only by the grace of God I'm alive today. Except now I'm going to remember the lessons I learned on that flight. I'm not going to take my days for granted anymore. I'm not going to be so flightly that all I care about is getting drinks with some cute math teacher.

And I'm going to thank God every day that he forgave me for my sins and saved me from an eternity of fire and terror. Because I've tasted enough fire and terror in this life alone. I certainly don't want it chasing me into the afterlife.

I'm saved now. And I thank God for that. But it's terrifying to think of how close I came to the end without knowing him at all.

How close I came to dying with no hope or chance of salvation whatsoever.

CHAPTER 5

WHILE KENNEDY AND I were wasting our time talking about nothing at all significant, I was still eyeing that big man in the Hawaiian shirt and the teen he was with. At one point, he leaned over and said something to her, and she pulled away. It happened so fast I can't be certain I actually saw it, but I could have sworn he yanked her by the hair.

That's when I finally did tell the flight attendant. Tracy. The one whose name I'll never forget. The one whose family background I've checked online a hundred times to see if there's anything more to learn about her.

Mother of two. The family's trying to stay out of the public eye (yeah, good luck with that), but one picture from a family vacation has been all over the press. It's Tracy and her kids, out camping in the woods somewhere. She was married too, so I kind of assume her husband was the invisible man behind the camera. And they look so happy. So happy and healthy.

So alive.

I told Tracy that this man pulled that girl's hair back. Mentioned that she looked super uncomfortable with him. I don't know if this is where your mind goes or not, but I immediately started to think human trafficking. It's absolutely ridiculous how many Americans are convinced that sort of stuff doesn't happen in their own backyards. I'm pretty sensitive to it. As a feminist, even as a halfway decent human being, there's no way I can stand for any sort of enforced slavery. It's terrible. And absolutely disgusting if you ask me how many smug suburbanites sit in their comfortable middle-class privilege and assume that any girl — any *child* — who's subjected to rape, violence, and exploitation on an hourly basis must *like* the life she's chosen.

So yeah. You probably don't want to get me started on that. But that's exactly where my mind went. Strange man flying across state borders with a teen girl who's obviously uncomfortable with him? No, I'm not paranoid to have worried that's what was going on.

I didn't tell Tracy all of my suspicions. You'd be proud of me. I spared her the lecture, the statistics, the stories of trafficked girls I've read online. But I did tell her about how that man pulled her hair and yanked her head back. I was sort of thinking she'd poo-poo it away, but she was actually very professional about the whole thing. "Thanks for bringing this to our attention," and "we'll definitely keep our eyes on them," that sort of thing. It's nice to have your concerns validated.

And then we waited.

Except what we thought we were waiting for was the plane to land in Detroit.

I'm so ashamed to think that after I brought up my observations to Tracy, my biggest concern was whether or not I'd join Math Babe for drinks. We had several hours' layover, but I didn't want to ditch Kennedy or make her feel like the third wheel. It's kind of funny since she's the one who not only saved my life that day but also introduced me to the Lord, but at the time, I still felt like I was the one who was looking out for her.

She was real sheltered growing up. At least in some ways. Private all-girls' school. Paranoid, safety-addicted father breathing down her neck. Stay-at-home mom baking cookies every day of the week. That sort of thing. It could have been any upper-class American suburb, except the only difference was it was overseas. You should have seen my face last year when I learned my college roommate grew up as some missionary kid. I was totally convinced she'd be this backwards, socially incompetent child who wore Catholic school-girl uniforms (and I'm not talking about the Halloween party kind, by the way). So I was pleasantly surprised to discover just how normal Kennedy actually was. If spending five hours a day studying for a test that's still two weeks away can ever be considered normal.

The point I'm trying to make is I felt like it was my job on campus to look out for Kennedy. She had this whole international city chic thing going on, but in other areas she was totally clueless. Like the first time one of my theater friends and I decided to medicinally help ourselves reach a state of deeper relaxation (if you get what I'm saying), Kennedy came back to our room a few hours later and seriously had no idea what the smell was. She asked me if I had put on some new kind of perfume. I should point out that I'm doing my best to give up that sort of thing now that I'm a Christian, but I'm not going to lie or pretend that I didn't come from a pretty hard partying background.

I actually used to pity Kennedy for being so up-tight. Thought it was my job to teach her how to let her hair down (both metaphorically as well as literally). I thought she was sheltered and naïve for her beliefs. And I'll go ahead and admit that I teased her sometimes. It was all in good nature, I should mention. She never got angry. Never fought back. On the other hand, she didn't do what some Christians might have done and made the practicing of her faith that much more obnoxious just to spite me.

No, she kept on living her quiet, Christian life, never realizing how closely I was watching. Never realizing that with each passing week my respect for her grew more and more.

Never guessing that when I came face to face with death on that doomed flight to Detroit, it was the God she served so quietly and steadfastly that I'd call on to come and rescue us both.

CHAPTER 6

OKAY, SO THIS IS admittedly a little bit of a sidetrack, but can someone please explain to me why the majority of Christians today seem so against environmental progress? I mean, I see how your faith will impact your politics when it comes to things like abortion. I totally get that.

But seriously? When did conservative Christians decide to leave the environmental debate up to everyone else to fight over? Doesn't God in the very first book of the Bible put humans in charge of taking care of the earth? Hello?

I've only been a Christian for a few weeks now, and I know there's still a ton I need to learn. I also know that my specific political leanings may not line up a hundred percent with the majority of evangelical Christians, and that's fine with me. I figure that God's judging me based on how much I actually meant it when I asked him to forgive my sins as opposed to how I'll choose to vote in the next election.

But I'm not off my soap box yet. I just need another minute. (And yes, this totally does tie into my near-death experience on that doomed flight to Detroit. I'll get there.)

Did you know that one of the biggest reasons I never even dreamed of becoming a Christian myself was because I thought I'd have to dye my hair back to its natural brunette and start voting for the other guys? Seriously. That's honestly what I thought Christianity was. That's why I'm saying I'm so glad God doesn't judge me based on which box I check when I go to the polls.

I already told you how upset I get about human trafficking, but now I need to talk for a minute about environmental justice. I took a whole course last semester, and I'm pretty well studied up on it.

Did you know that if you go up to a typical pastor and say, "Hey, do you know what environmental justice is?" you're likely to either get a blank stare or some kind of tirade about how global warming is a hoax? But that has nothing to do with environmental justice.

You want a living example? Take the Flint water supply. There's lead in the pipes and no way to fix it. Apparently, it would cost far less to relocate the entire Flint community than to figure out which pipes are leaking lead and poisoning Flint's children (and adults).

That's bad. I'm pretty sure we can all agree on that no matter where we lie on the political spectrum. Right?

But there's more. This isn't just about clean water. This is about class distinction. Because what are you going to do if you're a professional working in Flint, making a multi six-figure income a year and you find out the water there is poisoning you and your family and nobody's going to do anything to fix it?

You move.

Worst case scenario? Maybe your house forecloses (because who's going to buy land in Flint?). So your credit score takes a hit. But you've got the money, the resources, and the savings account to start over.

Good-bye, Flint. Hello water supply that isn't going to kill you.

Easy as pie.

Now imagine you're an immigrant single mother. You're working two jobs just to put food on the table because your income's just high enough you don't qualify for food stamps and just low enough that you can't afford anything. You've got three kids. Those kids have to eat. The baby needs diapers. Oh, and since you're working all the time, you have to pay for all that baby formula.

The problem? The water you're mixing with your baby's formula will eventually kill her.

So what are your options? Well you can buy bottled water. Except oops. That costs more money than you have, and you're already diluting your formula to make it stretch and worried that your baby's health might suffer as a result. Besides, even if you give her purified water to drink, what happens when she needs to wash her hands or take a bath? She's still soaking in poison through that soft, porous skin of hers.

So maybe you wait for the government to come and fix things. After all, poisoned drinking water certainly should fall under the category of a national emergency. Except the government's uncomfortably silent on the matter. I wonder why that is. Could it be because those with the loudest political voices have already taken their trust funds and their retirement accounts and moved away?

Back to choices then. Because after all, this is America. The land of freedom. You have the right to live anywhere you want. Don't need the state's permission to move to a new town.

Except how are you going to afford a moving van? Or a safety deposit on a new apartment? And what about the fact that you're too busy working your two jobs just to keep the kids from starving that you literally can't start over?

And so you stay. And each and every time you fill up that baby's bottle, even though you're using a filter and hoping that will help even just a little, you have to wonder if while nourishing your daughter, you're also killing her.

Slowly. Methodically.

Because this is what happens when you're poor and voiceless and living in the land of the free.

Am I off my soapbox? I suppose for now. But I just had to get that off my chest.

Going back to what happened on that flight, there's absolutely no excuse for murdering an innocent victim in cold blood. No reason anyone should stand up and shoot a flight attendant execution style.

Nor is there any reason whatsoever in which it is justified to tamper with a flight carrying hundreds of people. People who are going to die because of your callous decisions.

Sometimes when I wake up from nightmares, the sound of gunshots reverberating in a stark airplane cabin in my ears and the scent of smoke in my nose, I'm tempted to hate the men who did this.

Except I can't.

I can't hate them because — even though I could never justify their actions — I understand exactly why they felt this act of homegrown terrorism was the only solution to their plight.

CHAPTER 7

BEFORE GOING ON, I'D like to apologize to you for my little mini rant back there. Probably wasn't one of my finest moments, I'll be honest. But I've read some of the news articles involving the crash lately, and a lot of people are asking those kinds of questions.

If things were so bad in Detroit, why didn't they just leave?

Why'd they hijack a flight with hundreds of innocent passengers on it when they could have just telephoned their state representative?

I've made myself a promise not to go off on another tirade. Suffice it to say that comments like these really get under my skin. If I were slightly less self-aware, I might even wonder if this was a case of Stockholm syndrome. If I'm sympathizing with the terrorists who nearly killed me for some twisted psychological reason or other.

But I'd been studying what was going on with Brown Elementary School over there in Detroit for months. I already knew which side of the aisle I was on.

Nearly losing my life to a couple desperate, deranged terrorists didn't change that.

Not at all.

But I suppose I'm getting ahead of myself.

Kennedy's the one who should tell you about the letter. She was the one who got it, but it completely confirmed every disgusting suspicion I had about that man in the Hawaiian shirt and the girl he was with.

Everything except for the trafficking angle, at least.

I didn't see it happen, but Kennedy got up to use the bathroom. She had to go to the front of the plane because there just so happened to be a man planting a bomb in the lavatories in the back. Of course, none of us knew it at the time. We just thought he'd fallen on the wrong side of an argument with a taco truck on his drive to the airport.

I keep trying to remember what I was doing when that girl reached out to Kennedy for help. It's not like I thought it was my duty to stare at my roommate as she walked all the way up the aisle just to use the bathroom on an airplane. Truth be told, I was probably wasting time on my phone. Or maybe touching up my makeup since we were now less than an hour away from Detroit, and I was still seriously considering taking a quick detour to go on a date with Math Babe.

I heard the man yell first. And I looked up and saw him shouting at Kennedy. The girl he was with, the teen I'd had my eye on, was terrified. I wouldn't even say she screamed for help. It was more like a squeal. Like something you'd hear from a dying animal.

Everything's a little fuzzy in my mind as I recall it. Maybe because it was so shocking. Or maybe because watching someone yell at your roommate and hearing a terrified teen screaming, "Help, I've been kidnapped," isn't as traumatizing as nearly dying in a fiery plane crash.

But there I go again getting ahead of myself.

The girl was screaming. Kennedy stood there dazed, not that I can blame her. I doubt I'd have had any sense to do anything different. A man in a suit jumped out of his seat in an instant. The air marshal. The hero coming to save the day.

The girl kept shouting, "He's kidnapping me," the air marshal got the Hawaiian shirt dude in handcuffs, and everyone lived happily and safely ever after.

I wish.

Because as it turned out, the main point of the whole scene was to get the air marshal to reveal himself. Couple quick moves — I don't even remember them they were so fast — and the air marshal was knocked out. The guy in the Hawaiian shirt grabbed the officer's gun, gave it to this other man who was in on the entire thing, and we were officially hostages.

There's this type of therapy where you go back and relive traumatizing events, but you do it in this almost dreamlike state where you're in control of the outcome. So you can go back and revisit the moment of terror and give it any ending you want. I haven't been to any actual psychologist or anything, but I've tried this little technique on myself from time to time, and here's my favorite out of all the happy ending scenarios I've come up with.

First of all, who comes to the rescue but Math Babe? (I've started to feel awful I've forgotten his name, so in my imagination I call him Raul.) Raul jumps out of his seat, halfway graded math papers flying everywhere. "Stop!" he shouts in a deep, husky voice. And then there's this fairly exciting but totally one-sided scuffle, the end result of which is both hijackers knocked out and bloody. Passengers cheer. The air marshal wakes from his beauty sleep, his assailants are bound and tied, and we all land safely at the Detroit airport where Raul and I share extravagant tapas and wine.

End of story.

Pretty good one, isn't it?

I was somewhat proud of it.

But of course, if that's what really happened, I wouldn't have become a Christian. Which leads me to a question I've been wrestling with for weeks. Did God *cause* our plane to get hijacked because he knew that experience is what it would take to wake me up and bring me to my senses? What about the people who died? What about that poor kidnapped girl?

The more I think about it, the more I hate the thought that God wanted the plane to crash just so my soul could be saved. I mean, I'm already dealing with enough survivor's guilt as it is. I'm just going to leave it at I have absolutely no idea. Maybe I'll ask Kennedy's pastor or something. He seems to have all the answers, which is just fine because I'm still so brand new to this whole Christian thing and can't be expected to know it all.

So then. We've covered the somewhat uneventful beginning of the flight. I've told you about Hawaiian Shirt and his partner beating up the air marshal and knocking him out. I've given you my thoughts on the politics that led up to the terrorist attack.

So now I guess it's time to dive into all the details of what happened next.

CHAPTER 8

General had the air marshal's gun. And I have no idea why he took to calling himself *General*, but he did. His name's not what's important. What mattered is he had the gun. Which meant from that moment on, he was the one calling all the shots.

I'll go back to that first minute or two. It's hard to describe the absolute chaos in the cabin. Like you could literally feel the fear and confusion in the air. I think that's what he was counting on. Because seriously. Let's do the math. One gun. How many bullets could that be, right? I mean, it wasn't like it was this big automatic assault rifle or anything. It was just your ordinary, run of the mill pistol. What's that, like six bullets? And how many of us passengers? Several hundred, right? It's not like he could have killed us all.

But what do you do when someone starts yelling and calling himself General and waving a gun around in a crowded airplane cabin? You freeze up, you turn off your brain except the one tiny fraction of it that's necessary for your survival, and you do whatever he tells you to do.

Which is exactly what we did.

General ordered us to get out our phones. He wanted us recording everything he had to say, his big manifesto. And maybe it doesn't come as a surprise to you after my tirade a little bit earlier, but General was a dad concerned about his children's safety.

We're back to Michigan and environmental justice. I'm telling you it's a real thing. If someone's willing to execute innocent bystanders and crash an entire airplane, you'd better believe it's a thing.

A very serious thing.

Brown Elementary School. That's where General's kids were enrolled. Detroit's dirty little secret. And by dirty, I mean it in both the literal and nuanced sense of the word.

Dirty because there was arsenic in the soil, which at one point had been a dumping ground for a pharmaceutical tech company. The area was so toxic, grown men on the construction crews were landing in the ER. Now I don't care who you are. I don't care if you hate environmentalists and think that vegans and Greenpeace are minions of the antichrist. But seriously, who would ever be okay with building an elementary school in a hazardous waste zone?

Now obviously I'm not saying that the answer to this debacle would be to kidnap a girl, knock out an air marshal, and take over a plane. That's just lunacy. But the inciting event? The anger and the injustice? I'm all over that.

General took his good old time telling the cameras all about how unfair it was, how the superintendent was to blame, how Detroit had miserably and egregiously let down its children. And you know, if it weren't for the fact that he'd just hijacked our airplane and was waving that gun around, I might have felt more inclined to give him a good old-fashioned *amen* or two.

But obviously none of that goes through your head when you see a crazy man waving a gun around. You're not thinking about those poor kids in Detroit whose health is jeopardized on a daily basis just to save the district a couple extra bucks. You're not feeling the frustration of these parents who are mostly working class, immigrant, and minority families who lack the political clout to stand up for their kids.

No. You're staring at that gun. Wondering what would happen to the cabin pressure if it went off. Wondering if the metal hull of the airplane was built to be bulletproof. Wondering if it would be scarier to die in a plane crash or by gunshot wounds.

Hoping he doesn't notice you. And then when you get your wish, that means you're left to feel both relieved and guilt-ridden for the rest of your life because he's turned his wrath on someone else.

CHAPTER 9

"WHAT'S YOUR NAME?" THE General asked.

"Tracy," she answered. And I wanted more than anything to look away, but I was too scared of the uncertainty. I had to watch.

He asked if she had children. That's how I knew about her two kids even before I saw their family photo in the news.

"Would you like to see your children again?" General asked. Tracy nodded. And in that moment she stopped being a flight attendant. She stopped being an airline employee. This was a woman. A fellow human being. A mother with children she loved, with teeth that rattled, with a voice that cracked as she answered General's questions.

She could have been any of us.

She could have been me.

General wanted to make sure all the cameras were still rolling, that we were all streaming our images and footage to the news-frenzied masses down on solid ground.

Wanted to be sure that everybody knew the exact reason for this woman's death.

"It's the superintendent's fault," he said. "He now has two orphans on his conscience."

And he pulled the trigger.

I don't remember screaming, but I'm sure I must have. Everyone did. Because even though we saw the gun, even though we identified the crazed rage in General's eyes, we couldn't bring ourselves to believe he would actually do it. That he would actually kill that flight attendant.

"You have five more minutes, Mr. Superintendent," General told the cameras. Five minutes until what? Another one of us died?

If you haven't been in a cabin full of terrified passengers and a man bent on terrorizing you all, you maybe would expect me to behave differently. To think differently. I already told you I wasn't a Christian at this point in my life, but I'd lived with one for over a year and kind of knew the basic tenets. Love your neighbors. Pray daily. Ask Jesus to forgive your sins.

And maybe you'll expect me to jump in now and say that's just what I did. Dropped to my knees. Told God I was a sinner. All that jazz.

But while General was waving around his gun and pacing up and down the aisles, I wasn't thinking about God or heaven or my sins or my need of a Savior. Do you know what I was thinking?

That the dead woman lying crumpled in the aisle could have been me.

And that in order to survive, I needed to make myself far more inconspicuous than how I normally appear. For the first time in my life, I cursed my obsession with dying my hair. Who would want to stand out in a situation like this?

But stand out I did. And when General's five-minute timer buzzed, his eyes locked onto mine, and he strode deliberately toward the back of the cabin and stopped right in front of me.

CHAPTER 10

"STAND UP," HE TOLD me, and I obeyed because apparently that's what your body does when someone's waving a gun at you. Someone who's just shot another woman not ten feet away from where you are.

I stood up.

"Come here," he told me.

So I did.

"What's your name?"

It's funny because as he was asking me all these questions, I could only think about one thing. *Kennedy will be traumatized if she has to watch me die.* Of course, any and every one of us on that flight were already traumatized. You don't have to know a murder victim to feel terrified in a situation like this.

But my mind was on Kennedy. On how goodie-goodie she always was, and look where it got her. On a doomed flight, forced to watch while her blue-haired roommate got executed.

General was still talking to the video cameras. Going on and on about how none of this was his fault, how he didn't want to hurt anybody but this was the only way he could get the people of Detroit to take him seriously.

And I think I prayed. I say I *think* I prayed because it wasn't anything formal. It didn't start with *Dear Jesus* and end with *Amen.* In fact, if I had to relive that moment in pristine detail, I'm pretty sure my prayer only consisted of one single word.

Please.

"You don't want to die, do you?" General asked me. I assume I shook my head or gave him some sort of response because he frowned as if he actually felt sorry for me. He let out his breath. "I wish I didn't have to kill you." Somehow as I stared at the tip of his gun pointed straight at me, I had a hard time believing him.

"Your hair's blue," he told me, as if I might not have realized.

"I know."

"You some kind of punk girl?" General asked.

"No." And unless you've had a conversation with a terrorist holding a gun at you with dozens of cameras recording your upcoming execution, you have no right to tell me that hair color is a strange topic of conversation when you're about to literally get blown to hell. To me, it felt just as natural as standing there waiting to die.

"You know those dyes have chemicals in them," he told me.

"I only use all natural." Looking back, I too can see the absurdity of the conversation, but when I mentioned all-natural, he locked eyes with me. And for a second, I saw a man and not my own executioner.

Then the moment passed.

"I'm sorry about what I have to do," he said, except he wasn't talking to me. He was talking to the cameras. The cameras all pointed at me waiting to record my death.

I hoped my parents weren't watching.

When I relive this event, why I try to get to that state where I can recreate the moment when General decided it was time to pull the trigger, I picture a lot of different plausible scenarios, all of which result in my survival.

Of course there's Math Babe rushing up from behind, tackling my assailant, and saving the day. I'm a self-proclaimed pacifist, but more often than not, this scenario ends with Raul (aka Math Babe) shooting General square in the head. Often I stick around to watch an epilogue, and sometimes it involves a doctor jumping up and declaring Tracy the slain flight attendant was still alive, thank God, and sometimes it involves Raul and me walking hand in hand beneath a gorgeous Detroit sunset after a lovely evening of tapas.

One of my personal favorites is when I stretch out my hand, and with some super skilled ninja moves, I disarm my would-be assailant to the sound of thunderous applause from the rest of the cabin. I never actually kill General in this particular daydream of mine, but I like to remind him that I'd be well within my rights if I did.

We land in Detroit, and an army of hot twenty- and thirty-year-old SWAT men in super tight combat gear showing off each and every one of their well-defined muscles barges in, congratulates me on saving the flight, and holds a celebration on the ground that more often than not involves more tapas.

But it's only in my daydreams where I'm saved by myself, a handsome math teacher whose name is possibly Raul, or a couple dozen SWAT men. The true story is that I was saved by a little old granny lady with a head of white hair and enough courage to put all the heroes of the Bible combined to shame.

CHAPTER 11

GENERAL HAD JUST APOLOGIZED to the cameras, regretting that he had to shoot me, when this little old lady stood up and told him, "Put that gun down, sonny." And it wasn't so much that she dared to talk back to General, who probably weighed three times as much as she did, but it was the boldness with which she addressed him that seemed to tilt the entire axis of power in the cabin.

General gave a little chuckle, but I could tell by his face he was thrown off. "Who are you?" he demanded, and she smiled at him sweetly and answered, "You can call me Grandma Lucy. And I'm here to save this young woman's life."

I'd never been at the wrong end of a handgun before, and I'd certainly never witnessed some ninety-year-old grandma try to talk down a raving terrorist, but sometimes truth really is stranger than fiction.

"If you need a hostage," Grandma Lucy said, her voice as calm and patient as if she'd been discussing the roses in her garden, "why don't you take me instead?"

I hadn't expected General to look even more thrown off than he already did, but his expression at Grandma Lucy's words proved me wrong.

"If you shoot me," Grandma Lucy explained as if she were reciting Bible stories to a class of first-graders, "you'll still get your point across, and you won't have to worry about murdering someone so young and scared. As for me, I've been ready to see my Jesus for the past fifty years."

She stood squarely between me and the gun, stuck out her chest, and waited.

I'd like to tell you about how I came to my senses, realized how selfish it would be to let this tiny four-foot-tall grandma take a bullet for me, but I was too stunned. I couldn't move. Couldn't think. Couldn't talk.

Surprisingly, Grandma Lucy suffered from none of these problems.

"But before you kill me," she began, "there's something I'd like to tell you. Something your audience might be interested in hearing."

He sneered at her. "Yeah? What's that?" I could tell he was growing impatient.

Grandma Lucy's voice rose in both volume and conviction. "That Jesus Christ is the risen Savior of the world. He is my shepherd, my redeemer, my healer, and my coming king. If you kill me, my soul will leave this broken jar of clay and enter into the presence of God. And since you're doing me such a great honor, I want to return the favor."

What was going on? Was she just stalling? And how in the world was it working? Who was this old white-haired lady? Was she a martyr, some kind of miracle worker, or was she just insane?

And then, believe it or not (did I mention before that truth is stranger than fiction?), this Grandma Lucy lady stretched out her hand, raised it to General's forehead (I'm surprised she could actually reach that high), and she started to pray for him.

After everything happened, once the plane crash-landed and we all got evacuated, I looked for Grandma Lucy. Nobody was supposed to leave triage. Once we got our injuries taken care of, we had to answer all kinds of questions from the authorities.

But nobody knew where Grandma Lucy went.

I'm a little embarrassed to admit it, but I'll just go ahead and come right out and say it. Sometimes I've wondered if she was really some sort of angel sent to distract General. Because while she was praying and General was focused on her, Raul (remember Math Babe?) and a couple other passengers managed to rush him from behind. I swore to the feds doing the interviews later that I heard the gun go off, but apparently my mind must be filling in blanks because nobody else recalls anything like that, and there were no stray bullets anywhere in the cabin.

Go figure.

It just goes to show that I really can't trust my memory at this point in the story because what I remember most vividly is a gunshot, a whole bunch of screams, and a scuffle that was over before I even realized I was still alive. General was subdued. The captain came on and assured us we were just a few minutes away from landing.

The nightmare was over.

That's what we all wanted to believe at least.

But really the terror was just beginning.

CHAPTER 12

YOU EVER KNOWN ONE of those people who just always seem to have bad luck? Or maybe now that I'm a Christian I shouldn't attribute it to luck, but I think you probably get what I'm saying. People who have one bad thing happen to them after another until you want to scream to the universe on their behalf, "Haven't they been through enough?"

I've met quite a few people like that in my day. Kennedy's one of them, actually. It seems like at least once a semester she's getting into some kind of terrible trouble or danger. For being the kid of such a safety-paranoid father, she sure has managed to find herself at the wrong place at the wrong time more often than I would care to count.

Well, that's how I'm guessing we all felt on the plane after Raul and a few other brawny passengers managed to get General and his Hawaiian-shirted partner subdued. You'd think by that point, with the hijackers bound and the plane just minutes away from touching down, we could start to let out our breaths. Thank God (or the universe or luck or whatever) that we were safe.

Except we weren't.

Because General and Hawaiian Shirt weren't exactly working alone. And that dude who kept making a nuisance of himself in the back lavatories all through the flight was a Detroit electrician with just enough skill to know how to cause some major damage. This is another case where memories fail, because I'm certain the shouting came first, but others insist it started with the fire alarm going off.

Either way, the back of the cabin was on fire. Smoke began pouring out of the lavatories.

While General had been marching around the cabin with that gun of his, the passengers had remained eerily silent. Now, all that terror we'd been bottling up snapped, and it was complete chaos. I heard later that the paramedics had to treat more people for injuries related to trampling than smoke inhalation.

It was madness. Madness and unceasing terror as everyone raced to the front of the cabin.

I would have joined them. I tried to join them. But someone knocked me down from behind. I have no idea who it was. By this point, the smoke had grown so dense so quickly I could scarcely see anything. I was relying entirely on feel.

And then I stumbled. A woman's high heel stomped on my hand. I cried out, but there was no way to hear anything over the screams of the passengers and the drone of the fire alarm.

Get up, I told myself. *You didn't survive a near-execution just to get yourself trampled to death when you're only a few minutes short of landing. Get up.*

Except I couldn't. There were too many people. Too many bodies. I couldn't stand. Couldn't breathe. Someone stepped on my back. No more air in my lungs. I couldn't even cough out the smoke I'd just inhaled.

And that's when I knew it had happened. My luck had finally run out.

I really was going to die.

CHAPTER 13

YOU EVER READ ANY of those stories about people who swear they nearly died and went to heaven? Then they were resuscitated and survived and came back to tell the whole world about their experiences? Apparently Christians are kind of divided when it comes to stories like that. I guess some people think it's all hocus-pocus, maybe even the work of demons (although I really can't understand why a demon would try to convince someone they were in heaven, but that's neither here nor there). Other folks get all into it, write their bestselling books, earn their millions.

I honestly don't know where I fall on that spectrum. I've already told you that I've only been a Christian for a couple of weeks. Seriously, I'm still trying to figure out what to do with myself on a Friday night now that I'm not allowed to go out and party, so I'm probably not the best person to ask about convoluted matters of faith and theology.

All I can tell you is what happened to me.

And that's basically the reason I'm saved now.

I was stuck. I couldn't move. I don't know if it was my injuries from getting stepped on or what. Maybe it was even a literal demon holding me in place, trying to kill me before I had the chance to turn my life around. I seriously don't know.

But I couldn't move. Each time I budged, something caught around my neck. Like something was trying to strangle me.

I was going to die.

And do you know what I thought about? Well it certainly wasn't tapas. Or Mr. Math Babe. Or how terrible Kennedy would feel once I was dead.

I thought about my family. Wondered if they were following the news already or if they were blissfully waiting for their only child to come home, never suspecting the life was seeping out of my pores with every second.

But more than anything? I thought about that little old lady. Grandma Lucy. The one who stood ready to take a bullet for me.

There are people I'd probably die for. My parents, for one thing. Maybe even Kennedy if it ever came right down to it. Underage victims of human trafficking? I'd be willing to risk my life if I knew it could save them.

But this little old lady stood up for me. Told that deranged General she would take my place.

I suppose if you were looking in from the outside, maybe you'd think it made evolutionary sense, in that cold, calculated Darwinian way. Grandma Lucy was old. Had lived her life. Had passed on her genes, blah, blah, blah. And here I was. Young. Healthy. Strong.

So she was willing to trade places.

But there was more to it than that. I wish I could explain to you what I heard in her voice. Wish I could describe the intensity. You ever watch those superhero movies? There's a common trope in a lot of them. This old lady with wicked awesome supernatural powers. The kind who can heal you with a touch or strike fear into villains five times their size.

That's the kind of power I sensed in Grandma Lucy when she stood between me and that gunman. An unmistakable, never before experienced *power*.

I was agnostic basically my entire life, but I always believed in something divine. Something beyond what science can explain or the eye can see. But I'd never experienced it until that moment. And do you know what it was I felt pouring out of Grandma Lucy?

Love.

She loved me.

Not in the way some do-good Mother Theresa-esque kind of saint would feel warm and fuzzy toward all humanity. This was far more personal.

Far more powerful.

Grandma Lucy loved me. Enough to die in my place, even though she didn't even know me. Some people look at my dyed hair, my couple extra body piercings, and they write me off as some kind of edgy weirdo. Once at the bookstore I even had a mom tell her child, "Don't make eye contact with her." So yeah. I may not be part of a marginalized minority in any real sense of the word, but I certainly have experienced my share of prejudice. Of being written off as "other."

But Grandma Lucy saw past all that. It was like she was seeing the real me.

Me, Willow Winters. A scared young woman who only wanted to get home to her mom and dad.

And she was willing to die in my place.

She'd already saved my life once. I knew that much. I can't recall a single word she said in her prayer while she was staring at that gun, ready to take that bullet meant for me, but I can tell you the power I felt behind her words.

In another culture, another religious era, she might have been called a shaman. A spiritual healer. A miracle woman.

Instead, she was just Grandma Lucy. The most powerful woman I've ever encountered.

Thinking about her gave me hope, and that's all I had to cling to as I lay on that cabin floor, smoke burning my lungs, stinging my eyes, draining the life out of me. Grandma Lucy loved me enough to save me.

And she hadn't done that so I could die here alone.

CHAPTER 14

AT ONE POINT I ended up passing out. Because apparently that's what your body tends to do when you're stuck in a smoke-filled airplane cabin. You know how I was talking about near-death experiences, Christians claiming to go to heaven, all that jazz?

None of that happened to me.

But *something* did.

I'd like to say I had a dream because that puts it into a neat little easy-to-define category that everyone can relate to. I mean, who hasn't ever had a dream while they're asleep?

Except I really couldn't call it that. Not while maintaining any sense of literary integrity. Imagine a dream that's even more real than the physical world. Where the moment you're in it everything flips around and you realize that the world you've always called real is actually the dream and you've never been truly awake until that very moment.

Then imagine that love isn't just some esoteric emotion or a word you use to describe how you feel about your family or your dog or your favorite vegan tapas bar. Imagine that in this real world, the one that makes everything you've ever known seem like the dream, love is an actual, tangible force. And that force is pouring into you, like the most powerful waterfall you could ever imagine, except instead of drowning it makes you feel like for the first time in your entire existence you're actually alive.

And part of you doesn't want to wake up and go back to the real world because this power you feel is so tangible, but you also know you're not ready to leave the dream yet. There's more you have to do.

If you can picture all of that, and if you have what could be called the most active imagination out of every human who's ever lived, you might be able to grasp at least the smallest fraction of what I experienced.

And then the feeling was gone. The dream was done.

And all that was left was terror and fear and pain.

And smoke. So much smoke ...

CHAPTER 15

BETWEEN THE TIME I passed out and woke up in the Detroit hospital, I have literally no recollection, and so I'm free to make up whatever turn of events I'd like.

My initial go-to is that once we landed, Raul rushed to the back of the cabin, frantically screaming my name until he found me. He knelt down, swooped me up, and raced me off that plane, shouting, "This woman needs a medic!"

Other days, I kind of like the idea of Grandma Lucy walking off that plane (she's totally fine as I envision the scene in my head because she's got some kind of Holy Spirit bubble surrounding her that kept the smoke out and the oxygenated air in). Once she gets onto the tarmac, she kneels down, thanks God for his protection, and senses with powerfully divine intuition that I'm in trouble. At which point she prays for God to send a couple angels to get me off the flight, and these heavenly beings are quick to comply.

It's also quite possible that my rescue was far more mundane, that the first-responders who were on the scene when we made our descent into Detroit were simply doing their job. Which doesn't make my survival any less miraculous or my saviors any less heroic.

Now, if this were a little Christian novel I was writing, if I were relying on fiction instead of hardcore, actual fact, I'd probably wrap things up with me on my knees in a hospital room, folding my hands together, praising God for his salvation and begging him to forgive my sins. At which point, I'd probably commit my entire life to becoming a missionary in Africa, taking selfies with a bunch of orphans, all that jazz.

Well, I hate to let you down, but I've got to tell things like they are.

Yes, I experienced my first real taste of divine intervention and heavenly power on that flight. No, I will never forget that sense of love that poured into my soul after I passed out.

But that doesn't mean I turned my life around the second I woke up in the hospital. Even now, weeks after my conversion, I really couldn't say my life's been *turned around*. Turns out this whole Christian walk is a lot harder than it looks, and it took me quite a while before I was ready to actually bend the knee to Christ (figuratively, I should say; I never actually got down and knelt, which Kennedy as well as her pastor assure me isn't required for salvation).

The other thing you probably wouldn't expect me to talk about right here is the nightmares I still have about that flight. Sure, I can joke all I want about getting rescued by Math Babe Raul or irresistible SWAT teams in their kick-butt, bullet-proof gear. But more often than not, my dreams are about being stuck in that smoking cabin, realizing I'm not going to make it out alive, knowing that I'm not ready to die.

I guess that just goes to show that even when God swoops down and literally saves you out of the pit of hell, sometimes it still takes a little while before you're ready to acknowledge him.

After our rescue, I spent my entire semester break in Alaska with Kennedy thinking about what happened to us. Asking her questions about what it would mean if I actually were ready to become a Christian. And she wasn't pushy. Wasn't over-zealous to get me to sign on the dotted line. I think she knew I needed to figure all this out in my own time and in my own way.

I was so scared of flying back to campus after all we went through (we were both basket cases on that flight back to campus, truth be told), that I made my first bargain with God. If he gave me that same sense of power and love and protection out on the flight back to campus, I'd spend the upcoming semester studying the Bible and deciding for real if I was ready to get serious about this whole Christianity thing.

Well, there wasn't anything nearly as dramatic as when I'd passed out in the cabin, but I wasn't quite as scared as I expected I'd be either. I guess I can say God met me halfway.

So I did the same for him.

Kennedy and I started doing this Bible study together some nights when we were both in our dorm room and she didn't have her nose buried in her books. I found a couple preachers online I liked and began listening to their podcasts. It was right before Valentine's Day if I remember correctly that I told Kennedy I was ready to go ahead and jump into the Christian life. At the time, I really didn't know what that meant, and to be honest, I'm not sure that even now I do. Like I said, I don't have a clue when it comes to debates about theology or all that jazz. What I do know is that I was saved by God, first physically on that flight and then spiritually just a few weeks ago.

Took me long enough, some believers might say. But I didn't want to jump into something one minute only to decide a few days or weeks later it wasn't going to work out. I knew that if I wanted to commit, I needed it to be serious.

Am I serious about my faith now? I think so. Like I said before, I've given up partying, at least the aspects of that lifestyle that are inherently sinful. That's a pretty big deal for someone like me. And I'm studying my Bible with Kennedy. We're praying together too. It's like we're an old married couple saying our bedtime prayers before lights out. Sometimes I feel bad that I wasn't instantaneously turned into Miss Sunday School Goodie-Goodie like Kennedy right away, but I suppose everybody matures differently, right? At least that's the excuse I'm telling myself.

Sometimes, I'm a little embarrassed that it took something so drastic as getting my flight hijacked, witnessing a murder, and nearly dying to get me to accept Jesus. I mean, some people hear the gospel once and decide to be saved. And I'll be the first to admit that the survivor's guilt is awful. I may not be the best at praying yet, but I do pray for poor Tracy's family every time I think about her.

Maybe one day I'll look up her two kids and tell them how brave their mom was. How much she loved them. How she didn't want to leave them.

But for now, I'm still covering the basics. Trying to remember to read my Bible each day. It still doesn't make sense how I could have done so many sinful things and I only had to pray once for God to forgive me, so I'm spending a lot of time confessing right now. Just in case I forgot some things the first time.

I think about Kennedy, about how mature she is in her faith. Then I compare that to Grandma Lucy, who I never did manage to find after our plane landed. It can be overwhelming at times, realizing how much I still have to learn. How far I still have to go.

But I guess that's part of the Christian journey. One step at a time. And maybe what matters isn't whether or not you're taking baby steps or giant leaps as long as you're headed in the right direction.

I certainly hope so at least.

My name is Willow Winters. I'm a theater major. Airplane hijacking survivor. Blue-haired second fiddle.

And now, by the grace of God, I'm saved.

Refined by Fire

Alana Terry

Christian Books Today

CHAPTER 1

LOGAN AIRPORT

Meredith found an empty seat at the gate and sat down with a weary sigh. She still couldn't believe the past 24-hours had really happened. That after fifteen years of service, of pouring her blood and sweat and tears into her ministry, it had come to such a crashing end.

Maybe it couldn't have been helped. She'd seen the handwriting on the wall a few years ago, hadn't she? But still, she'd founded Living Grace. Who would have thought it would carry on without her? Could it carry on without her?

Time would certainly tell.

She watched holiday travelers bustling past her gate, men and women and children off to Christmas dinners and vacations with grandparents. Meredith didn't have any close relatives. The ministry had been her family.

Which made what she'd just gone through akin to divorce.

No, not divorce. More like watching your child torn away from you, knowing how helpless you were to intervene.

Maybe she'd feel differently if she'd been asked to resign as a result of some kind of sin issue or scandal. No. The board asked for her resignation and showed her a copy of the press release that would come out Wednesday. *Because we feel God has called us to walk down different paths* ... It made it sound so holy, so righteous.

Well, some things couldn't be changed. Meredith refused to become a victim. She'd already decided to allow herself exactly two days of pity. That was all. And then she was moving forward.

She didn't have any other choice.

Just a few more hours until she was back home. Back in her cozy Grand Rapids condo, where she planned to heat herself up some hot chocolate, bury her feet in her favorite slippers, put on some nice, relaxing worship music, and allow herself a good cry. Until then, she planned on holding it all together.

After all, she had a plane to catch.

It felt strange sitting here. How many times had she flown in and out of Boston to meet with the Living Grace board? How many days out of the past fifteen years had she spent in the air? Meredith thought back to the prayer she prayed when she was in her twenties, dreaming of a speaking career, ministering to Christian women. Meredith asked God for the chance to preach to women in all fifty states. Well, she had that checked off her bucket list. And quite a few foreign countries too. In the past fifteen years as the director of Living Grace Ministries, she'd spent thousands of days away from home. Weeks away from home.

Years away from home, if you were to add up their cumulative effect.

And all for this.

She didn't want to get bitter. She didn't want to be angry. She promised herself not to allow resentment to take root in her wounded soul. In spite of how betrayed she felt, in spite of the terrible, sinful mistake she knew the board had made, she had to be the bigger one. The mature one. The forgiving one. And maybe once she got home, soaked away her sorrows in a scalding hot bubble bath, she'd feel more gracious. Right now, she had to resist the urge to whip out her phone, log onto social media, and tell the entire world what just happened.

But she wouldn't. Before she told her followers that she was stepping down from Living Grace — a fancy way of saying she was fired — Meredith had to give herself time to heal. Get over the initial shock of it all. Technically, she wasn't allowed to mention her resignation until Living Grace put out their press release next week, which gave her time to prepare. Quite gracious of them, Meredith thought. Really living up to their name.

Come on, Meredith told herself. *You're the bigger woman. You don't need to get bitter.*

Her stomach growled as passengers scurried by. When was the last time she'd eaten? Usually when she traveled, she wouldn't think twice before treating herself to something fancy. A mocha that cost five times its worth. A seafood salad at an actual sit-down restaurant if she had a long layover. And why not?

Why not, indeed?

And now it was time to pinch pennies again, just like she had in the early days when Living Grace's headquarters doubled as her studio apartment. She had her salary covered through the end of May. Something told Meredith the board of directors expected her to fall to her knees in gratitude when they mentioned her severance. And sure, it was better than nothing. But even though she wasn't destitute yet, she couldn't find the appetite for a twelve-dollar muffin or fifteen-dollar fruit salad. The five bucks she'd just spent on a bottle of water felt like enough splurge for one day.

Flights were getting canceled left and right, the result of a big snowstorm across the US. It was scheduled to hit Michigan the worst by tomorrow evening, but Meredith planned to be sequestered in her home by then, safe, sound, and warm.

What would it feel like to wake up tomorrow without several dozen items on her to-do list? Her assistant, Angie, would spend the next few days canceling all Meredith's upcoming speaking gigs. Apparently Living Grace saw fit to demand her resignation but were magnanimously willing to keep Meredith's assistant employed. Oh, well. Nobody could blame Angie. Four kids, Christmas right around the corner ... Angie needed her job.

Which was the irony of it all, really. Because this was never a job to Meredith.

It was her life.

And she loved every minute of it.

"Excuse me."

Meredith glanced up in surprise at an old woman with white hair. "Yes?" Meredith's smile was automatic.

"I'm sorry to bother you, but I saw you sitting here and just had to come introduce myself." The petite woman reached out a wrinkled hand, which was surprisingly soft and warm when Meredith shook it.

"My name is Lucy Jean," the woman said, "but I insist on being called Grandma Lucy. And I am such a fan of yours. Our ladies' Bible study just finished your series on Ruth, and I was so blessed by the words of wisdom and encouragement you had to share."

Meredith was used to being recognized out in public. How long would it take for the world to forget she'd ever existed?

She thanked the old lady, feeling a spark of actual, genuine gratitude. After the discouragement of yesterday's board meeting, Meredith's spirit soaked up Grandma Lucy's kind words like a parched desert floor.

"Is this your flight?" Grandma Lucy glanced at the sign in the terminal. "You're on your way to Grand Rapids?"

Meredith nodded.

Grandma Lucy squinted at the sign above the check-in counter. "Looks like you have a little time. Can I buy you a cup of tea? My treat."

Part of Meredith wanted to decline. By this time next week, Grandma Lucy and all the ladies in her Bible study would know about Living Grace. Would know that Meredith had lost her job, her position, her ministry.

But Grandma Lucy's smile was so genuine and sincere. So different than the expressions of her former friends who'd faced her in the board room yesterday. Meredith sighed and grabbed the handle of her carry-on. "You know what?" she said. "I'd love something to drink. Thank you so much for asking."

CHAPTER 2

Flight 219, Three hours later

Meredith stared wide-eyed at the man with the gun in his hand. This couldn't be happening. She wasn't even supposed to be on this flight.

Her ears still rang with the sound of gunfire.

"Five minutes until another hostage dies," Bradley snarled, stepping over the passenger he just shot.

Before she grew Living Grace to the point where she could actually draw a salary from her work there, Meredith had made a living for a few years as a Christian counselor. She knew rage when she saw it. She knew instability.

She knew just how dangerous this man was.

The fact that they were flying thirty thousand feet above ground made the experience all the more harrowing. Visions from September 11 flashed through her mind. Those poor passengers. The moment of impact playing over and over again on the news in a never-ending loop.

Through her work with Living Grace, Meredith had counseled hundreds of women through loss, divorce, grief. Lately, she'd felt particularly burdened for women struggling with anxiety.

"Remember the Lord is always with you," she'd tell them. "His word promises that we have nothing to fear."

Nothing to fear. Those women probably should have just laughed in her face. Instead, they'd clung to Meredith's words. Praised her for bringing them such a sense of encouragement and hope. Meredith was a speaker and teacher, a women's leader. At least, she had been until yesterday.

It was funny, in a sad and pathetic sort of way, how when she'd boarded this flight — the flight she wasn't even supposed to be on in the first place — she'd been broken and lost at the prospect of going through life, earning a living while no longer serving as the president of Living Grace. Three hours earlier, it was the most dejected she could remember feeling in years.

And now what did it matter? What did any of it matter — the board meeting, their decision to demand her resignation, the cowardly, averted gazes of men and women she'd previously considered her closest friends and allies ...

There's nothing like staring down the barrel of a loaded gun to put things into perspective.

Meredith didn't know what was going to happen to the passengers on board her flight. Didn't know if she would be the next hostage shot or if the plane would manage to land without anyone else getting hurt.

What she did know was that her concerns about her future sounded ludicrous now.

What did it matter if you lost your job if you'd end up dead the following day anyway?

If she survived this ordeal, maybe she'd be grateful for the mindset shift it provided.

If she survived ...

CHAPTER 3

LOGAN AIRPORT

"So, what topic can I tell the ladies in my Bible study to expect from you next?" Grandma Lucy asked as she sat across from Meredith at a noisy café booth.

Meredith gave Grandma Lucy a cautious smile. "I really don't know what I'll be working on." That much was certainly true. Meredith felt guilty, sleazy somehow, since she couldn't mention the fact she was no longer working or writing for Living Grace. According to the paperwork she signed with the ministry's attorney, a woman she herself had hired, Meredith wasn't allowed to mention her resignation until next week's press announcement. Still, the omission in her conversation with Grandma Lucy felt cowardly somehow. Like she didn't have the courage to admit the truth.

Grandma Lucy gave her hand a squeeze. "Well, the Lord is sure to guide you, isn't he? But let me ask you something." She reached into her back pocket and pulled out a small-sized New Testament. "This came up in our discussion of Ruth." She flipped through the pages. "You said that in First John, the Bible tells us that ..."

Her words were interrupted by a buzz from Meredith's cell. Was it the board calling to say they'd changed their mind? Of course it wasn't. But still, Meredith's heart raced until she pulled out her phone and read the text.

"What is it?" Grandma Lucy asked, glancing up from her Bible. "Is everything all right?"

Meredith put her phone back in her purse. "Yes. My flight's been delayed. That's all."

"It's that snowstorm, isn't it?" Grandma Lucy shook her head slowly. "You know, I woke up this morning with a feeling, a premonition if you will, that something about today's flight wouldn't go exactly as planned. So I said, *okay, Lord, if that's how you want it to be, that's how it's going to be*, and that's the most I spent worrying about it. Then my niece back home called to tell me how bad the weather is. Guess the schools have already announced they'll be closed tomorrow. Don't want to take any chances. A lot of the flights are being delayed. So I just told God that if he doesn't want me on my scheduled flight, I'm fine taking any old plane he feels like putting me on. I figure, what's the worst that can happen? The flight attendants sit me next to someone who needs to hear about Jesus, right?"

Meredith tried to return the old woman's chuckle. Tried to keep her brain engaged in the somewhat meandering conversational turn.

"I should probably head back toward my gate soon," she muttered, half distracted. "I want to be close in case they make any announcements."

"Of course, dear." Grandma Lucy's smile warmed Meredith's aching heart. She reached out and grabbed her hand. "You truly have a gift and an anointing, and I'm blessed that I got the chance to meet you in person. Here. let me take a picture. My niece is a big fan of yours, too. She'll be tickled pink to find out we had a cup of tea together."

Meredith smiled for the selfie as Grandma Lucy wrapped her up in a strong embrace. "May God bless you and keep you and preserve your spirit until the day of Christ," the old woman declared in Meredith's ear.

Meredith felt awkward returning such an intimate blessing and instead gave the old woman one last little hug before saying goodbye. As she made her down the terminal, she wondered what Grandma Lucy would think when she heard the news that Meredith had been fired. She couldn't dwell on that now, though. She had to get to her gate. Everything was changing all around her. Her life, her future, her ministry. It made sense that even her flight itinerary would get rearranged.

She walked up to the ticket booth. "I just got a text that the flight's been delayed," she said. "Is there any word on when it's going to be rescheduled?"

The man behind the counter shook his head, barely looking up from his computer screen. "Have a seat, and we'll be making announcements as soon as we know anything."

As soon as we know anything. May as well be the name of this chapter in Meredith's memoir.

She found a quiet seat near the window. Outside, the Boston sky appeared perfectly clear. Hard to imagine from this vantage point the massive storm front moving across the country. She'd hoped to get back home to Grand Rapids in time to buy a few groceries and lock herself in for the next couple days, nursing her wounds in peace and privacy. Now she wasn't so sure about her plan.

Meredith let out her breath and loosened the strap of her heels. She was no longer the president of Living Grace, so maybe she wouldn't feel the need to get so dressed up when she traveled anymore. The next flight she took, she could show up in a jogging suit and tennis shoes. Maybe even throw her slippers into her carry-on if she wanted to make herself extra cozy.

Inside her briefcase was her half-edited manuscript that she was supposed to turn into her publisher next month. When she told her agent yesterday what had happened with Living Grace and asked if she should still focus on polishing up her project, the response she received was far from hopeful.

"Well, you could always get it edited *just in case ...*"

Meredith pulled out her draft, her sixth full-length book, not counting the dozens of Bible studies and workbooks she'd created in the past. Because it was so personal, this manuscript had been one of the hardest for her to write. When she felt God telling her to focus on this particular topic, she'd fought him for months. Cried, begged, worked herself into such a state she'd caught the flu and had to stay in bed for a full week.

And then she did what she told all her readers and all her Bible study participants and conference attendees and podcast listeners to do. She yielded her will to the Holy Spirit, embraced the work God had laid on her heart, and submitted to his calling. She wrote sixty thousand words even though she could have sworn every sentence would kill her.

When she gave her manuscript to her assistant to clean up, Angie told her it was the most powerfully moving writing she'd ever read. And dangerous too.

"You know some people aren't going to like this," her assistant warned her.

Meredith knew. But it certainly wouldn't be the first time her words had gotten Meredith in trouble. Just last year, she'd come under fire for a blog post she'd written urging pastors to stop guilting Christian wives to remain in dangerous and abusive situations. Based on the reactions of evangelical leaders, you might have thought Meredith was advocating cannibalism.

Did she feel ready to broach another controversial topic, especially one as explosive and personally traumatic as sexual abuse within the church? No. But Meredith had been talking to her audience for years about authenticity, and she'd finally found the courage to take her own advice and expose her deepest shame.

Her agent was hesitant at first. Said he wasn't sure the Christian community was ready to discuss this degree of sexual assault in such a candid manner. Would Meredith consider writing another women's Bible study instead?

But Meredith had insisted. And because her agent knew there were a dozen or more of his colleagues in the Christian market who'd line up to start bidding on her manuscript if he was stupid enough to reject it, he signed her on. "We may have to tone some parts down," he warned her, but she knew that in the end she'd have the final say. She was Meredith Crowley. Bible study leader, bestselling author, number one podcaster in both the Christian women and Christian living categories.

The story would get published how she envisioned it, and it would inspire and encourage hundreds of thousands of believers. Her work would open up the doors of communication, get Christian leaders and pastors and ministers talking about this dirty little secret the church didn't want exposed. With every other book she'd written, she'd enjoyed the unanimous support of the Living Grace board of directors. The same men and women who looked her in the eye yesterday and demanded her resignation were the men and women she'd called on the phone crying if she didn't think she could finish her manuscript. Through every book in the past, they'd encouraged her. Prayed for her. Supported her.

Losing your job was one thing, but what about being torn away from your entire family?

Meredith glanced at the clock. One of the tips she gave women who wanted to find more time to connect with God was to make the most of waiting periods. Recite Bible verses to yourself while you're standing in line at the grocery store. Get a Bible audiobook to listen to while you're in the car. If you find yourself with time to spare and not a whole lot to do, go to the Lord in prayer.

Meredith decided to take her own advice. She bowed her head and prayed.

CHAPTER 4

Flight 219

Dear God, I don't want to die.

It sounded so trite. So glib. Of course she didn't want to die.

But there was so much more to Meredith's prayer than mere survival instinct. And just like so many people who come face to face with death, Meredith found herself trying to bargain with God.

What about my next book, Lord? Think of all the victims it's going to help. All the people it's going to bless. Think of all the believers who need to read it.

As soon as she prayed these words, she realized how prideful she sounded. Did God need her writing? No. She tried a different tactic.

I don't want to die while my relationships with my old friends on the board are strained. Think how guilty they'll feel if they find out I was killed just the day after they fired me ...

No, that wasn't the right focal point, either.

Think about the women I've ministered to, God. All those women I've helped. I can't just abandon them.

The big man with the gun stomped back and forth in the aisle. Meredith tried to imagine how she'd react in a situation like this on her best days, when she was at her strongest spiritually, her most sanctified. She'd pray for him. That much was for sure. To take an entire plane hostage like this, he must be broken and hurting.

She would pray for him and everyone else on the plane. Pray for those who might not know Jesus yet. Ask God to give her the chance to tell them how to be saved.

That's what she'd do on her best day.

Which clearly wasn't today.

Today all she wanted was to erase the past few hours. Make it so she never stepped foot on this plane in the first place. All she wanted was to get back to Grand Rapids and nurse her aching soul in safety.

Today she wanted to live.

She wasn't ready to die.

CHAPTER 5

LOGAN AIRPORT

"Attention passengers for Flight 761."

Meredith glanced up from her Bible to listen to the announcement.

"Due to inclement weather, all flights to Grand Rapids have been cancelled until further notice."

Meredith's spirit joined the chorus of groans from the passengers at her gate. The snowstorm must be moving faster than the meteorologists had predicted. No rookie to changing travel plans, Meredith was on her feet in an instant and the first at the counter.

"Meredith Crowley," she stated for the attendant. "I'm trying to get back to Michigan."

The woman shook her head. "Everything's shut down because of the storm."

Meredith tried to keep her voice polite. Reassuring. Based on the size of the line forming behind her, this worker was about to deal with several dozen irate passengers. Meredith didn't want to make this any harder on her than necessary.

"What about flights to a nearby area? Is the Detroit Airport still open?" The last thing Meredith wanted to do was stay here in Boston. A detour through Detroit wasn't the worst-case alternative.

The woman smiled at her albeit without much patience. "You could go to the main airlines counter. That'll be your best bet if you want to try to re-route. Do you need directions there?"

Meredith shook her head and let out a sigh. Gone were the days when you could tell the ticket counter attendant where you needed to go and they'd print you up a boarding pass right there at the gate and offer you meal and hotel vouchers if you ended up delayed overnight. Well, Meredith didn't plan to stay in Boston overnight. In fact, she doubted she'd ever want to return to this city after everything she'd gone through in the past twenty-four hours.

Meredith thanked the agent, clutched the handle of her carry-on, and made her way toward the correct terminal. With the snowstorm now spreading like wildfire, she would probably have to carve her place in line with hundreds of others. She might do better to call the airlines directly. Maybe she'd do both.

"Miss Crowley! Miss Crowley!"

Meredith turned around and saw a woman running toward her. Journalist if you were to judge by the small hand-held microphone she was waving in her direction.

"Chelsea Harris, reporter for Channel 2."

Meredith wished she hadn't paused for the stranger.

"Do you have a minute? Can I ask you a few questions?"

"I'm actually headed to a different terminal." Meredith kept her voice curt, hoping the reporter would take the hint.

It didn't work. "I'll walk with you. Talk about a stroke of good luck. I'm on my way to report about the elementary school scandal in Detroit, but I've been following your story for quite some time now. My mom's a big fan of your Bible studies."

Meredith glanced at the young woman and suddenly felt every day of her age.

"My mom would never forgive me if I didn't stop and talk with you," Chelsea gushed. "My producer either. I just want to say how thankful I am that you're championing the cause of women's rights in the evangelical movement. Even my mom supports you one hundred percent, and she's about as conservative as you get."

Meredith did her best to sound polite. "Listen, I'm really thankful for your mom's support, but my flight just got cancelled ..."

"No problem." Chelsea swiped the screen of her phone and shoved it into her back pocket. "We can be totally off the record. But I just have to ask you how it feels to be one of the only women willing to speak up against the patriarchy in conservative Christian circles."

"That's certainly not what I set out to do." Meredith's mind was reeling. For the thousandth time in the past twenty-four hours, she reminded herself as well as the Lord that all she wanted when she founded Living Grace Ministries was create Bible studies to encourage Christian women. How in the world could a mission that simple become so controversial?

"I heard things have been a little rocky for you ever since you published that blog post on domestic violence last year. Is it true that some members of the board of directors asked you to take your original article down?"

When the board fired her yesterday, Meredith had told herself one silver lining she could find in the midst of her turmoil was that she'd no longer be a lightning rod for political controversies. Maybe she'd spoken too quickly.

"Listen," Meredith said, hoping not to come across as rude or impatient as she felt. "I'm actually not able to discuss my relationship with the board of Living Grace at this time." That much was true. Just a few more days, and this reporter could read all about Meredith's resignation in the press. "I want to thank you for your interest, and please tell your mother thank you for her support, but I really can't comment."

Meredith sped up her pace, but unfortunately, the reporter hurried along right beside her.

"Oh, I totally get it. Remember, we're off the record. Can I just say how happy I was to read your blog post last year to women in abusive relationships? You're, like, the first Christian leader I know who actually had the guts to say that it was okay for women to get a divorce."

Meredith paused long enough to brush a strand of sweaty hair out of her face. "Actually, I never advocated divorce specifically. I just encourage women in danger situations to take whatever steps were necessary to get themselves and their children to safety." Meredith had defended her arguments from last year multiple times on multiple platforms. Based on the new drama with the Living Grace board, her writing to defend and protect abused women felt decades old.

Chelsea shrugged. “Tomatoes, to-mah-toes, right?” She gave Meredith a wink. “I’m just glad someone came out and said it. I suppose you knew going into it the backlash it would cause.”

Meredith nodded, even though she couldn’t be in complete agreement with the reporter’s assessment. When she encouraged church leaders to stop telling battered women to overlook their husband’s explosive tempers, she guessed that some people might skew her words. She didn’t delight in ending marriages for any and every reason; she just didn’t want to see victims battered, bruised, or dead.

Meredith’s cellphone rang. Thankful for the chance to pull herself away from this awkward conversation, she excused herself, reached into her purse, and took the call.

CHAPTER 6

Flight 219

"Get out your phones," the gunman ordered. "I've got a message for the good folks down on the ground in Detroit."

Meredith wasn't supposed to be here. This wasn't her flight. If she hadn't been so eager to get herself out of Boston, she could have waited an extra day and flown straight to Grand Rapids in the morning. Was this God's way of punishing her for her impatience? A little overdramatic maybe.

"The people of Detroit have failed our kids." The hijacker wasn't saying anything new. Meredith and all the other passengers on Flight 219 had been listening to his tirade now for the past half hour. Of course parents wanted their children to have access to safe and quality educations, but who would go so far as to threaten innocent passengers on an airplane to make their point?

If Meredith hadn't just lost her job, she might have offered to pay the gunman off himself. "You want better schools? Great. So does everyone else. How many improvements would a twenty-thousand dollar check buy your kids?"

This was madness. Sheer madness. If God wanted Meredith to stop focusing on her own worries, he'd certainly made his point.

Okay, God, she wanted to say. *I've learned my lesson. You can land this plane now.*

The young mother in the seat beside her was clutching her son and crying. The little boy looked stunned. Meredith wished she knew something she could say or do to offer either of them the smallest ounce of comfort. She hesitated for a moment, then reached out and took the young woman's hand. The mother squeezed back so hard Meredith winced.

"It's going to be all right," Meredith whispered.

"He's only four," the mother sobbed. "My sweet, precious baby is only four." She clutched him closer against her chest.

"It's going to be all right," Meredith repeated, but then the gunman's cellphone beeped. He gave the passengers a sneer and announced, "Okay then. Time for someone else to die."

CHAPTER 7

Logan Airport

"Hi, Meredith," came the voice on the other end of the line. "It's me. Connor."

Connor. She'd wondered if he'd give her a call or if he, like so many others, was ready to put distance between himself and her.

Meredith let out her breath. Her hands were sweating more than she wanted to admit as she fumbled in her purse for her hands-free set. "Hi, Connor." She didn't try to mask the tiredness in her voice. Didn't try to put on a show to alleviate any guilt he felt. The two had been close once. Even dated a few times. Things might have gotten more serious if they hadn't both realized how significantly Connor's position as a divorced dad of two would compromise Meredith's ministry.

Connor sounded as weary as Meredith felt. "Listen, I just wanted to let you know how sorry I am. The board's decision ... it was far from unanimous."

"I know." It was nothing Meredith hadn't heard before. But if every board member who assured her their decision wasn't unanimous had voted in her favor, Meredith would still have her job. Her life. Her ministry. Still, she couldn't picture Connor voting against her. They'd known each other over fifteen years now, back when Connor was still working for that Christian publisher out of Grand Rapids. Back before Meredith had written her first Bible study, recorded her first video, signed her first publishing contract. They'd attended the same church, and Connor was the one who introduced Meredith to her literary agent.

"This may not be a good time," he began, "but I just wanted to see if there was anything I can do."

"That's kind of you." Meredith was ashamed of herself for mistrusting Connor in the first place. This whole situation had made her second-guess every friendship, every relationship, every ally she had. But she shouldn't have doubted him.

"I still know a lot of people in the publishing world," Connor said. "If you're looking for a new position ..."

Meredith remembered their very first dinner out. Connor's kids were still young at the time, and they'd had to postpone their date twice to accommodate his babysitter's fickle schedule. "What's your biggest dream?" Connor had asked over mediocre pasta. Meredith had told him about her vision to bring Bible-based workbooks and videos and books to Christian women around the world. She hardly knew him at the time, but he'd been so easy to talk to. So eager to hear what she had to say. Five minutes into their meal, and she'd divulge her entire mountain of dreams.

And he didn't laugh. Didn't question whether or not there was a market for more theology resources for women as opposed to topical studies on marriage or femininity or homemaking. He didn't mention how hard it was to break out into the publishing world, where an unknown woman with no audience and no platform would be more likely to get hired on as a cleaning lady for a publishing house than to receive a decent contract.

Instead he sat back in his chair in that carefree, comfortable way, smiled, and said, "You know, I have a buddy who's a literary agent. Let me see how hard it would be to get the two of you together for lunch."

And that was the beginning of Meredith's new life. Serving as the president of Living Grace was exhausting, rewarding, and more often than not as frustrating as it was exhilarating. Still, Meredith knew that she was one of the privileged few who got to wake up every day convinced that she was doing exactly the work she was made for.

What could be more satisfying than that?

She thought back to that first dinner with Connor. Wondered if she'd take him up on his offer to help if she knew where she would end up right now.

The answer was a resounding yes.

Meredith adjusted her headset. It was just like Connor to be looking out for her even now. Just like he'd done over fifteen years ago. *I have a buddy who's a literary agent. Let me see how hard it would be to get the two of you together for lunch ...*

And now he was basically offering her the exact same thing.

"That's really nice of you to offer," she told him on the phone. "I don't know what the plan is. My flight just got cancelled, and I don't know how I'm going to get home ..." Meredith recognized how close she was coming to tears and refused to let them fall.

"You're still in town?" Connor sounded surprised. Surprised and something else. What was it?

She cleared her throat and steeled up her voice. "But I appreciate the thought. Thanks so much for calling."

"Meredith, wait."

She stopped with her finger over the end call button, her heart racing in her chest. She told herself it was because she'd been walking so quickly to get away from that reporter just a few minutes earlier.

"Yeah?" She cleared her throat again. She had to sound strong. Strong and brave. Because Connor was a fixer, and if he got even the slightest sense that Meredith was broken ...

"I just wanted to tell you what a gifted teacher you are," he said. "And I know God has something great in store for your future. I'm convinced of that."

Meredith waited. For some reason she'd been expecting something else. Something more.

But the silence on the other line told her that Connor had said everything he planned to say.

"Thank you." She needed to end the call now, or she really would start crying.

"Have a good flight," Connor offered somewhat awkwardly. "Take care of yourself and stay safe."

"I'll try." Meredith sighed wearily. "I'll try."

CHAPTER 8

Flight 219

"I just want to go home." The little boy sitting beside Meredith started to cry. "I want to go home."

His mother rubbed his back and tried to shush him. Meredith understood her reaction. All the passengers were doing everything in their power to avoid catching the gunman's attention. Keep themselves as inconspicuous as possible.

"We can't go home yet," the boy's mom told him.

Meredith leaned over to him. "Hey, buddy, what's your name?"

"West." His voice was a tiny squeak.

"West?" She gave him a smile. "That's a great name. Do you like animals?"

He nodded, his eyes wide.

"Do you have any pets back home?" Meredith asked.

He gave another slight nod, and Meredith smiled. "What do you have? A dog?"

"A guinea pig," he answered proudly.

"A guinea pig?" Meredith repeated, glancing behind her to see if the gunman was getting closer. "Does he like to cuddle?"

West nodded.

"What's his name?"

West opened his mouth, but Meredith couldn't hear his response.

Passengers screamed. West's mother shrieked. Meredith's body tensed, and her ears reverberated painfully with the sound of gunfire. The hijacker had just claimed his next victim.

"Five more minutes," Bradley announced to the cabin. "Five more minutes, and then another one dies."

CHAPTER 9

Logan Airport

Meredith's life as she knew it was over. Which meant that before long she'd have to decide if she was going to take Connor up on his advice. Make some new connections in the publishing industry. Right now, she couldn't imagine doing anything other than writing, teaching, proclaiming God's word to women around the world.

But was that door shut to her forever?

On her best day, Meredith would give herself some kind of pep talk. Remind herself that there were many women creating online presences for themselves without a six-figure publishing deal backing them up. She could learn the ropes, take her writing and her inspiration and her videos and go indie. Maybe now was the time. Maybe this was God's way of moving Meredith forward.

So why did it feel like such a setback?

Yesterday's meeting was a shock, and yet not altogether a surprise. Still, she hadn't expected to lose her entire career in a single day. The final strike came a few weeks ago when Meredith brought up her memoir as a personal prayer request at the start of one of the weekly online board meetings.

"I'm writing about my experience of sexual assault in the church, and it's bringing up some difficult memories. I'd love your prayers."

Her request was met with silence until the chairman finally stated, "I thought you were doing that Bible study on Esther."

Meredith tried not to let her exasperation show. “Yes, I’m also working on my Esther study on the side, and the final manuscript is still on target to be finalized in this spring.”

“Well, I think you should focus on that.” Richard spoke with finality.

And Meredith expected the conversation to end there. She’d never needed Richard’s approval about what she wrote in the past, and she certainly didn’t need it now. It wasn’t until she received that email the following day, she realized Richard had gone behind her back. Talked to four of the six other board members and then drafted a letter *strongly urging* her not to write about such a heavy topic, mentioning that readers had come to expect Bible studies from her, not self-help manuals.

It wasn’t until Meredith asked her assistant Angie to scour all the Living Grace bylaws when she realized that yes, technically the board could vote to decide if one of her books should be published or not, even though her contracts had always been signed under her own name and were distinctive from her work with Living Grace.

She should have seen then the turn that the board was taking against her, but she still thought of herself as the leader of Living Grace, the ministry she’d started in her studio apartment with nothing but a desktop and a dial-up modem.

“Well, look who it is.” A familiar voice interrupted Meredith’s thoughts. “I had a feeling God would bring us together again.”

Meredith glanced over. It was Grandma Lucy, smiling up at her in genuine pleasure. “Did you find out about your flight?” she asked.

“The Grand Rapids airport is closed. I’m on my way to the ticket counter to see if I can get on a different one.”

Grandma Lucy smiled. “Well, if you don’t mind a quick detour to Detroit, that’s the plane they put me on. Flight 219. Still on schedule to take off on time. Maybe I’ll see you on board.”

Meredith smiled. “Maybe you will.”

CHAPTER 10

FLIGHT 219

Meredith was glad for her position in the front of the plane. Glad that so far, the violence had all taken place toward the rear. In the seat next to her, West was still clinging to his mother, but at least he didn't seem so panicked anymore. In fact, most of the passengers appeared to be suffering from a combined sense of shock and resignation. Ever since the last murder victim fell, the only noise to be heard over the drone of the engines was the gunman himself, who spoke loudly into a cell phone camera.

"You might be wondering why I've taken control of this flight. I wouldn't have to go to these measures if it weren't for the crimes the superintendent committed against my children."

Meredith was familiar with the uproar it had caused when the city of Detroit built an elementary school on top of toxic land. The school board cited budget cuts and overcrowding, making it out as if there were no other valid options. Meredith understood the father's emotions. She'd be livid if her children were sentenced to play on soil riddled with lead and arsenic. The conditions were so bad that several adult workers at the construction site had been hospitalized last summer.

Meredith would be unhappy if her kids were forced to attend school there. Unhappy, yes.

Willing to hijack an airplane and kill innocent victims?

Absolutely not.

Bradley continued spouting off about how the city of Detroit had left him no choice but to murder and take over an entire plane. Listening to his rage, Meredith realized her problems with the Living Grace board weren't quite as horrific as they initially seemed. After all, what did it matter that she'd just lost her job if she'd be dead in five minutes anyway?

She had one arm around West and was holding his mother's hand.

The little boy hid his face in his mother's chest. "We're going to be all right, honey," his mother told him. "We'll be home real soon. Safe and sound."

Meredith had a hard time focusing on what she was saying. Words like *home* and *safety* had become vague concepts, not actual, tangible hopes to strive for.

For now, it was just waiting.

Waiting for Bradley to finish his speech. Hoping that when his timer went off again, she wouldn't be the next one he chose to kill.

CHAPTER 11

Logan Airport

"Can I help the next customer in line please?"

Meredith stepped forward and handed the agent her ID and boarding pass. "I need to get to Michigan, and my flight was just cancelled."

The man clicked a few buttons on his keyboard and frowned. *Click, click, click.* "Looks like all flights are postponed to Grand Rapids due to the snowstorm."

"I understand that. I was hoping you could book me to some other airport nearby."

Click, click, click. The man's expression didn't change as he continued to stare at his screen. After a minute of typing, he finally said, "There's a flight headed to Chicago. Is that close enough?"

"Chicago? I guess if that's all there is," Meredith answered. The cost of a rental car and a tank of gas was probably comparable to the expenses involved in spending another night at a hotel here.

The agent frowned. "Looks like that flight's full."

Meredith tried not to let her impatience show. "When's the next flight to Chicago leave?" she asked.

"Let me check." *Click, click, click.* "There's a flight to Chicago taking off in an hour and a half, but it's departing from Terminal E."

"That's fine, I'll take it."

Click, click, click. "Unfortunately, that flight's full, too."

Meredith was ready to get home, however she got there, and then avoid traveling for at least the rest of the winter.

"Forget Chicago," she finally said. "What flights do you have heading to Michigan?"

"Michigan?" he asked as if he'd never heard of the state before.

"Michigan," Meredith repeated dryly.

Click, click, click.

"There's a flight to Detroit that still has one seat available."

"I'll take it." She just hoped he'd book it for her before another passenger grabbed it.

Click, click, click. "Would an aisle seat be okay?"

"An aisle seat would be fine," she answered hurriedly.

He pressed a few more buttons, printed up a boarding pass, and handed it to her.

"Here you go. Your one-way ticket on Flight 219, headed to Detroit."

CHAPTER 12

Flight 219

"The people of Detroit have failed our children," Bradley was saying. He still hadn't put his gun away, and Meredith felt her body inching as far away from him as possible whenever he passed her in his relentless pacing up and down the aisle. "If the superintendent and his board of crooks had actually done their jobs instead of selling out our kids to the lowest bidder, I wouldn't be forced to do any of this."

Meredith had already decided that if the gun pointed in her direction, she'd use her body to shield little West and his mother. Far better to lose her own life than sit by and watch a helpless child die. The resolve gave her a new burst of courage, a sense of control, however imaginary.

"Until the superintendent of the Detroit school systems or the governor of Michigan himself calls me on my personal cell," Bradley raged on, "one hostage will continue to die every five minutes. You have my word, and I promise you I always keep my word."

The threat sent a chill racing up Meredith's spine, but she'd already determined not to give way to fear. She had to be strong. Had to give West and his mother a sense of courage. In this situation it was the least she could do. Not much, but it was something.

Bradley pulled out his phone, looked at one of the cameras pointing straight at him and announced, "Thirty more seconds."

CHAPTER 13

Logan Airport

"Flight 219 headed to Detroit will begin boarding in fifteen minutes."

Meredith sat back in her chair. A young mother traveling with her son was asking the counter agent for an update on their seats. Her concerned tone made Meredith thankful to have her boarding pass in hand. Re-routing through Detroit would add a few extra hours to her day, but at least she'd spend tonight in her own home. Never had her own bed and her own pillow sounded so inviting.

Meredith's seat was toward the very front of the plane, meaning that she'd be one of the last called on to board. She decided to use that extra time efficiently. It was all fine and good to wallow in self-pity for short bursts of time, but then she had to be proactive. Proactive and positive.

She pulled out one of the notebooks she always traveled with, turned to the first new page, and wrote on the top *Things I can do after Living Grace Ministries*. She proceeded to stare at the journal for several minutes. When the blank page proved too intimidating, she decided to give herself a little more structure. She divided the page into three columns and wrote *Ministry*, *Career*, and *Totally Frivolous*.

The frivolous category was the easiest to fill. For years, Meredith had told herself she'd take music lessons. Soon, her column was spilling over with ideas like hiring a piano teacher, finding a singing tutor, even starting up ballroom dance classes and joining a gym. For a minute, she tried to decide if she wanted to add travel to her list, but she was starting to enjoy the thought of staying home for a while. Maybe she could even get herself a pet.

The other two columns proved more difficult to fill in. For almost half of her life, ministry and career had been one and the same thing to her, and she wanted to keep it that way if possible. But what did she know how to do other than writing and speaking? And how could she do either now?

Always practical, Meredith realized the bills had to get paid. She didn't live extravagantly, but she'd need a job to put food on the table, not to mention those music and dance lessons she was hoping to dive into now that she had so much extra time on her hands.

Maybe there was a church or a nonprofit nearby she could work with. Grand Rapids was full of Christian publishing companies and colleges, and with her old friend Connor willing to help her make new connections ...

She thought about the manuscript in her backpack. It had been over two decades since she'd been taken advantage of by a Christian leader she trusted, but she'd only started talking about her experience a few years ago. In that time, she'd realized how many other women around the world shared similar trauma, often at the hands of pastors and youth leaders. And just as horrific as the abuse itself was how eager churches were to cover up sin to avoid a scandal.

She stared at the blank columns on the page. Tried to decide if she could see her career going in a vastly different direction.

Decided that change wasn't always such a bad thing.

Start a ministry for victims of sexual abuse. Since she couldn't decide whether it fit best under the column for ministry or career, she wrote it down in both.

And for the first time that day, she smiled.

CHAPTER 14

Flight 219

Bradley broke out into a cocky smirk. "Time's up." He put his phone into his back pocket. "Let's see what else I have to do to get my point across."

Meredith steeled herself, ready to protect the young boy beside her and his mother if the gunman came anywhere near them. Instead, he made his way toward the back of the plane.

Was that a good sign? Did that mean Meredith was safe? Was she supposed to feel relieved?

Was she supposed to feel anything?

Meredith assessed her own mental state. It was a technique she'd taught Christian women for years. *God, right now I'm feeling* ... Then let your mind fill in the blanks.

She tried.

I'm feeling ...

I'm feeling ...

God, help.

It was all she could manage to pray, the nonverbal equivalent of a squeak or a gasp.

"Stand up." Bradley's voice was strong and echoed from where he stood in the back of the cabin. Controlled. Where did his presence of mind come from?

West's mom whimpered.

"It's okay," Meredith assured her, immediately recognizing the idiocy of her words. She squeezed the young woman's hand and repeated once more, "It's okay."

How could she say such a thing? How could she even think such a thing? *At least he didn't pick one of us*, Meredith told herself, remembering her resolve to protect West if she had to. She let out her breath.

God, I'm feeling ...

She looked around her. Everyone was staring at the back of the cabin. Everyone was focused on Bradley, terrified and unable to move. Wasn't that the whole point? Wasn't that why he'd managed to gain control of the plane so quickly? If someone could just mobilize everybody, if they could just do something ... But what?

God, I'm feeling ...

Bradley had the gun pointed at a young woman with her hair dyed in beautiful shades of blue. Meredith couldn't hear their conversation. Was that because they were too far away, the drone of the engine too loud? Or were her senses shutting down?

God, I'm feeling ...

She didn't want to look. Didn't want to see. Wanted to wrap her arms around the helpless boy, shield both of them from the terror that was palpable in the cabin. And yet whenever she tried to turn her body, tried to pry her eyes away, she couldn't. Like a frightening movie that's so intense you should have never started it to begin with. But once you get past a certain point you have to keep watching. Your mind won't settle until it knows how everything's going to end.

God, I'm feeling ...

And then she could hear Bradley's words again, rushing in over the roar of the engine, over her own pulse surging through her ears.

"The people of Detroit have yet another victim on their hands," he declared, holding the gun steady. "Your time is up."

Meredith squeezed her eyes shut. She couldn't watch. It took every nerve fiber in her body to keep her eyelids from flying open. She wasn't thinking about the mother beside her. She wasn't thinking about the little boy she'd vowed to protect. All she knew was that Bradley was about to kill yet another innocent victim, and there was absolutely nothing Meredith or anyone else on this flight could do to stop him.

God, I'm scared.

CHAPTER 15

Logan Airport

"Well, isn't this a blessing. I had a feeling I'd see you again."

Meredith glanced up from her notebook where she'd been feverishly jotting down ideas for her future, a future apart from Living Grace. The board might have taken away her job and her salary, but there were many other things that belonged solely to Meredith. Her network of Christian leaders across the country. Her contacts with influential donors who were using their financial blessings to advance God's work throughout the world.

Even though Meredith's primary goal had been and always would be to teach Scriptural truths to women, her time at Living Grace had also given her a crash course in organizational leadership that no MBA or advanced degree could offer.

Start a ministry for victims of sexual abuse. She stared at her notes, her numerous mind-maps, her lists of people she'd contact to recruit for her startup team. Maybe she'd even invite Connor to join the board.

She'd been so lost in her vision-casting and daydreaming that she was startled by the old woman's voice. She looked up in surprise.

Grandma Lucy.

Meredith forced her brain to shift from planning for the future to focusing on the present, and she returned Grandma Lucy's wide smile.

"May I?" Grandma Lucy gestured to the empty seat beside her.

Meredith moved her carry-on to make room for the old woman.

"So, you're flying to Detroit, then?" Grandma Lucy asked.

Meredith nodded. "I figured it's either that or wait around here. And I'm ready to get home." She felt the truth of her words the moment she spoke them. *Home*. Was there ever a sweeter sound to anyone's ears?

Home. Not so she could nurse her wounds. Not so she could count the friends who had turned on her. Betrayed her. No.

Home. So she could plan. So she could give life to this idea that was visibly growing on the page before her.

"Is that your prayer journal?" Grandma Lucy asked.

Meredith realized she'd kept her book open. She shut the cover. "Of sorts."

Grandma Lucy reached out and grabbed her hand. The gesture was too familiar and quite unexpected, and yet somehow Meredith didn't mind. In fact, the contact gave her comfort. Energy. Even more fuel for her newfound dreams. Who knew? Maybe she'd even invite Grandma Lucy to join her team of prayer support for her new endeavor.

"You know, I didn't want to be too forward when we were talking earlier." Grandma Lucy said. "But God's just been putting something on my heart and it won't stop. So I told him if I saw you again, I'd be sure to bring it up, and even if not, I'd find your contact information when I got home and write you."

Meredith waited. What was it the old woman wanted to say?

In her time as a public figure in the Christian women's ministry niche, Meredith had received several alleged prophesies from various individuals. Once a Christian warned her not to travel anymore because she'd had a terrible nightmare about Meredith trapped inside the cabin of a burning airplane. Another time someone wrote in to plead with Meredith to get a mammogram because God revealed to them that she would one day die of breast cancer. Which raised the obvious question: If she Meredith going to die of the breast cancer anyway, what was so urgent about getting herself checked out?

But Meredith was up to date on her health checkups, and she'd flown hundreds of times now without incident. These kinds of so-called words of God just went with the territory of being in the public Christian eye. And most of the time, even though she never took their warnings to heart, she was able to extend grace to the speakers. Surely they meant well.

Most of them. With a few of the messages she'd received over the years, Meredith had a harder time being that gracious. Like the pastor's wife who wrote an email to Living Grace Headquarters claiming that she'd seen a demon of lust clinging to Meredith's back.

Or maybe it was her neck. Meredith couldn't remember the finer details now.

Of course, some people didn't need to have a spiritual excuse to just be plain old jerks. In Angie's inbox sat three different canned responses ready to send to Christians, mostly men, who complained that it was sinful for a woman to teach the Bible. Of course, Meredith's studies were very obviously targeted to women, but that didn't seem to matter. Twice in her career, the board even forced Meredith to get the Grand Rapids police involved when hate mail turned a little too personal. Meredith knew her friends were overreacting but appreciated the fact that they looked out for her best interests.

At least they had at one point.

Meredith was skeptical when Grandma Lucy told her she had a message for her, but she knew that the old woman's heart was in the right place.

"After we met for tea," Grandma Lucy began, "I just felt this burning need to pray for you. And not only for you, but for Living Grace as a ministry. I don't know all the details, mind you, but I sense that you've taken some backlash for a few of your stances."

Some backlash. That was one way to summarize Meredith's relationship with her former board.

Grandma Lucy gave her hand another squeeze, stronger this time. "And I just wanted to tell you that he who began a good work in you will carry it on to completion until the day of Christ. Because you are a child of the Most High God. You are blessed by the Almighty with your name written down in the Lamb's book of life, with your forehead sealed with the symbol of God's favor. You are blessed, you are anointed, and you are God's chosen instrument to deliver his message to hurting women."

Meredith sat perfectly still, wondering if she was supposed to close her eyes or not. It was hard to tell if Grandma Lucy was praying or speaking directly to her. In a way, she was doing both at the exact same time.

"And I know that your road hasn't been easy," she went on. "The pathway of God's chosen servants is riddled with thorns and briars, but he is the God who lifts you up out of the miry clay and places your feet on a firm place to stand. He is the God who shields you with his protection so that the sun will not harm you by day, nor the moon by night. The Lord will keep you from all harm, both now and forevermore. He will watch over your coming and your going. He will shelter you with his love and carry you under his wings."

Now Meredith had an even harder time articulating what exactly it was that Grandma Lucy was doing. Was she preaching at her? Reciting Bible verses?

What she couldn't ignore, however, was the pounding in her chest, the swell of conviction and hope in her spirit.

"Heavenly Father," Grandma Lucy continued, this time addressing God directly, "I lift up my precious and anointed sister to you. I pray blessings to rain down on her head. I pray that whatever she touches will succeed. I pray that you will expand her territory, increase her ministry, and protect her from all harm. It's your Holy Word that says not even a sparrow falls to the ground apart from your will, that we are fearfully and wonderfully made to do good works, which you created in advance for us to do. It's your Holy Word that describes the deep love you lavish on us, calling us your children even though we are so unworthy."

Meredith didn't know if she wanted to cry or raise her hands up in the air and begin singing praises. How long had it been since she'd experienced the presence of the Holy Spirit like this? How many years had she spent teaching women about God's love and power without ever reaching out and grasping it herself? Had she gotten so busy, so caught up in teaching others that she'd neglected her own spiritual health?

Grandma Lucy wasn't close to slowing down. Meredith was vaguely aware of a few stares as the old woman's voice grew in volume and intensity, but she wasn't about to tell Grandma Lucy to quiet down. In fact, Meredith had a pretty good feeling that if she said anything right now, Grandma Lucy was too absorbed in her prayer to hear.

"It's your Holy Word that says you will restore the years the locusts have eaten. It's your Holy Word that promises all things work together for the good of those who love you, who are called according to your purpose."

Meredith wondered if the entire snowstorm happened for this one precise moment. If she couldn't get to Grand Rapids because God knew she needed this right here, right now — this inspiration pouring into her spirit, breathing life into her soul that had grown so weary.

"It's your Holy Word," Grandma Lucy proclaimed, "that compels us to come to you and cast our cares upon you, and that's exactly what we do, dear Lord. We cast our burdens down at your feet, praying they will be an acceptable and pleasing offering to you. We surrender our souls, our bodies, our very lives to you and your service, and we know that you are the God who promises to never leave us nor forsake us. You are the God who declares, *When you pass through the waters, I will be with you; and when you pass through the rivers, they will not sweep over you. When you walk through the fire, you will not be burned; the flames will not set you ablaze*." Grandma Lucy gave a slight gasp and let go of Meredith's hand.

Meredith wasn't sure what had happened. Why had Grandma Lucy stopped? Why was she staring at her like that?

"Did you say you have a seat on this flight?" Grandma Lucy demanded, as if she had no idea that she'd spent the past ten minutes boldly praying, breathing life and conviction into Meredith's battle-weary soul.

Meredith stared at her in confusion.

"Flight 219?" Grandma Lucy pressed. "Headed to Detroit?"

"Yes." Meredith leaned forward, trying to determine if the old woman was all right. Had her skin always looked so pale?

Grandma Lucy's voice, which had a moment earlier carried more hope and conviction than Meredith had experienced in all her years of ministry combined, was now faint and trembling.

"Dear Jesus," the old woman whispered, "Let this cup of trouble pass or we will all be lost."

CHAPTER 16

Flight 219

Even though Meredith hadn't been able to hear the entire exchange between Bradley and his next victim, the loud and confident voice from the back of the cabin now carried over every other sound in the plane.

"Let her go."

Meredith's breath caught in her throat when she recognized the voice of the speaker.

"I said let her go." Grandma Lucy was out of her seat now. Meredith forgot any of her former resolve. Forgot that she was supposed to focus on the child beside her. Forgot that she was supposed to keep her eyes closed. She remained twisted around in her seat and stared, transfixed, a hint or maybe an echo of the same sense of power she'd experienced when Grandma Lucy prayed over her in the airport gate now flying somewhere overhead in the cabin. If she could focus her attention just a little more, she could grab hold of it.

Keep some of that peace and conviction for herself.

"Sit down," Grandma Lucy ordered the young woman, who only a moment before had been staring at the end of Bradley's gun. The passenger didn't move.

"Sit down, child," Grandma Lucy told her again, her voice gentler this time.

Grandma Lucy turned her attention to Bradley. "If you need a victim that badly, young man, take me."

"You?" Bradley scoffed. "You're nothing but a shriveled up old woman."

"You're exactly right." Grandma Lucy straightened her back. Even though she couldn't have been more than five feet tall, Meredith could have sworn the old woman was staring down at the hijacker. "That's why if you want to kill someone, you kill me instead. Let that poor girl go. Can't you see how terrified she is?"

Bradley didn't take his eyes off Grandma Lucy. Neither did Meredith.

Her assailant stood at least a full foot taller than she was, yet Grandma Lucy managed to convey the impression that she towered over him.

"If you're so determined to take another life today, I'm more than ready to meet my Maker. One could say you'd be doing me a favor."

Bradley sneered. Meredith couldn't stop staring at Grandma Lucy. Was the old woman growing taller by the second?

There was a moment of hesitation. A pause. Was Bradley considering?

And then he raised the gun to Grandma Lucy.

No, Meredith wanted to scream. *No.* But she couldn't find the words. Couldn't even pray for the old woman. All she could do was watch.

"Before you shoot me, I have one small favor." Grandma Lucy's voice hadn't yet wavered once. How did she manage to sound so calm? She tilted her chin up. Glared at Bradley.

"What is it?" he asked. And whatever it was Grandma Lucy demanded of him, Meredith believed he would comply with her request. How could he do anything but?

"I want to pray for you."

He scoffed again, and Grandma Lucy silenced him with a stern glare.

"You will let me pray for you, and then you can do whatever you want with me."

Pray for him? What was she doing? What was she saying? What was this? Did Grandma Lucy mean to stall him? Was someone going to sneak up and grab Bradley from behind, tackle him to the ground while his attention was on this little old prayer warrior?

No. Nobody in the cabin was moving. If Meredith could have guessed, she would have said nobody in the cabin *could* move, not in the face of such conviction. Such boldness. The confidence that exuded from Grandma Lucy's entire being was nothing short of divine. Nothing short of miraculous.

Who was this old woman? An angel, maybe?

Meredith recalled the warmth of her touch when Grandma Lucy had grabbed her by the hand to pray for her at their gate. Not an angel. Then what?

And how in the world could Meredith call herself a Christian leader when she knew with certainty she'd never possess the undying faith that Grandma Lucy displayed with every defiant tilt of her head, every confident demand?

Grandma Lucy didn't wait for Bradley's permission. She lifted her hand up toward heaven and began to pray. Meredith held her breath. Any criminal in his right mind would shoot the old woman right now. He'd already killed before and was prepared to do it again. How hard could it be? And yet Meredith knew, just as certainly as she knew that if the plane's engines malfunctioned she and everyone on board would plummet to their deaths, that Grandma Lucy was safe. In the past, Meredith had prayed for God to shield other believers from harm, to put up a hedge of protection around them. Now, she was half certain that if she were to walk up to where Grandma Lucy stood and reach out her arm, she'd find Grandma Lucy surrounded by an impenetrable wall of divine power.

Grandma Lucy's prayer for Bradley was just as passionate, just as powerful as her prayer for Meredith at the gate.

"Father God, Savior of the world, our Creator, Healer, and Friend, I pray for this young man. I pray for all the hurts he's carrying around, Lord, all the confusion, all the pain and fear. I pray for your sweet and holy Spirit to minister to his yearning soul. God, show him that you are the way and the truth and the life and that no one comes to the Father except through your Son.

"I pray that every sin this young man here has ever committed would be forgiven on account of the blood shed for him when you sent your Son Jesus to die on the cross to take his place, to carry the punishment for his transgressions. Lord, you alone can forgive sins. You alone can take the pain that this man is feeling and turn it into something beautiful. Something glorious. And so I ask you to minister to his soul today, Father. Show him that salvation isn't found in guns or terrorism or fear. Salvation is found in no one else, for there is no other name under heaven given to men by which we must be saved. This is what we believe, and this is what we proclaim ..."

"Stop! That's enough." Bradley growled. The gun in his hand trembled as he took closer aim at Grandma Lucy's forehead.

The spell was broken.

Bradley pulled the trigger.

Meredith closed her eyes.

CHAPTER 17

Logan Airport

Sitting in the airport gate, Meredith's whole body chilled at the strange ending to Grandma Lucy's prayer. *Let this cup of trouble pass or we will all be lost.* What was that supposed to mean? Had God told Grandma Lucy about Meredith and her meeting with the board of directors? Had yesterday's board meeting been this so-called cup of trouble?

And what about the last part? *All will be lost*? Where was the hope, the conviction that had resounded so majestically in Grandma Lucy's words just moments earlier?

Meredith's phone rang. At first she wasn't going to answer, but Grandma Lucy's bizarre, piercing gaze made her uncomfortable. Meredith stood up, thankful for a reason to excuse herself. What had started as a monumental spiritual revelation had just as quickly and inexplicably morphed into one of Meredith's most awkward airport encounters to date.

She glanced at the caller ID then wheeled her carry-on a few steps away to she could have a little privacy to talk. "Hi, Connor." Ordinarily Meredith would have wondered why he was calling her so shortly after they had just spoken, but after meeting Grandma Lucy, she doubted much more could surprise her today.

"Hey." His voice sounded unsure. Uncertain. So different than the power, the divine confidence that infused Grandma Lucy's words a few minutes earlier. Meredith glanced back at the old woman, who was bent over in her chair now as if in silent, tormented prayer.

She looked away. No reason to focus on Grandma Lucy right now. Meredith didn't know why Connor was calling her but figured whatever it was deserved her attention more than an eccentric old woman waiting at an airport gate.

Connor cleared his throat. "So, I wanted to talk to you about something ..."

Meredith had figured as much when she saw his name land on her caller ID and waited for more. But what?

A slight cough. What was Connor trying to say? "Listen," he finally managed to get out, "I don't know if you've been paying much attention to the weather. I know you've had other things on your mind." His voice trailed off. Awkward. Embarrassed.

Meredith continued to wait.

"And maybe I'm the last person you want to hear this from ..."

Oh, great. Meredith gripped her cell. Was this the part where he confessed that he was the tie-breaking vote that got her fired? Was he calling to ask her forgiveness? To absolve his guilt?

"I'm really not sure you should be flying today. The Grand Rapid airport's closed ..."

"I've rerouted to Detroit," she interrupted. Meredith had no idea why Connor was so concerned about the weather in the Midwest right now, but at least she didn't have to talk about that final meeting with the Living Grace directors. "We'll be boarding in just a few minutes," she told him, glancing at the time. "It's fine."

"How are you getting from Detroit back home?" he asked. "The roads are all shutting down. It's a mess out there."

Meredith rolled her eyes. Had it been so long since Connor moved East that he forgot how efficient Michiganders were at weathering a little snow?

"I'm sure it'll be fine." Should she be touched that he was concerned for her or annoyed that even now a member of the board of directors was trying to give her orders? Telling her what to do? Meredith hadn't realized until now how many years she'd spent afraid to make any major decision. She'd gotten into the habit of calculating each step with how much mental energy it would take to get the directors to agree. How many ideas had she conceived in prayer times that she immediately discarded because she knew the board would never approve?

She was free from all that now. Connor and the others made that very clear at yesterday's meeting. She didn't have to submit to them anymore. Didn't have to weigh every decision she made against the group's opinion.

The gate attendant made an announcement.

"Listen," Meredith said, ready to wrap up this call, "I've got to go. We're just about ready to board."

"I still don't think you should get on that flight. It doesn't seem safe..."

Another announcement. Could Connor hear that on his end of the line? "They're calling us now," Meredith told him. "Thanks for checking in, but I've got to go."

"Meredith, wait ..."

She ended the call but continued to stare at Connor's name on her screen. What had that been all about?

"Flight 219 to Detroit, now boarding."

Meredith took in a deep breath. Finally decided that Connor's concern for her safety was probably remnant guilt for what happened at the Living Grace board meeting yesterday. It was kind of him to be concerned, but a classic case of too little too late.

Meredith gripped the handle of her carry-on.

She had a flight to catch.

CHAPTER 18

Flight 219

Silence.

Meredith's ears strained for the deafening burst of Bradley's bullet, for the sound of Grandma Lucy's body hitting the cabin floor with a thud.

Instead, nothing.

"His gun doesn't work," a passenger shouted.

Screams. Chaos. A young man with broad shoulders leaped up. Two others joined him, tackling Bradley to the ground.

The mother in the seat beside her screamed. Meredith focused her attention on West, wrapping him and his mother up in a bear hug so tight it was impossible to know if it was simply Meredith's body quivering or if they were all trembling in unison.

"Dear Jesus," she prayed out loud, "please keep us safe. Please keep us safe. Please keep us safe." There was nothing more she could say. Nothing more she could hope for.

Keep us safe. Keep us safe. Keep us safe.

Her whole body tensed. Each second, she expected to hear the sound of gunfire. The dying screams of Bradley's next victim. Each second, she wondered if the hijacker was making his way up the aisle closer to her. Closer to the young family Meredith promised herself to protect.

Keep us safe. Keep us safe. Keep us safe.

There was no other prayer appropriate for a time like this. Meredith might have led one of the country's most popular series of Bible studies for Christian women, but right now her prayer was no more eloquent than everyone else's on this flight.

Keep us safe. Keep us safe. Keep us safe.

West was crying, whimpering softly into his mother's chest. Meredith grabbed his hand and tightened her grip around them both.

Keep us safe. Keep us safe. Keep us safe.

Screams behind her. Terror in the cabin. It was impossible to tell who was yelling out of fear and who was hurt.

Don't turn around, Meredith told herself. All her energy was focused on the young mother beside her and her crying little boy. Protecting them. Shielding them.

Someone cursing. Bradley's angry yell.

Don't turn around. Meredith's heart pounded in her throat and she in turn could feel the hummingbird wings fluttering in the little boy's chest pressed up against her.

Keep us safe. Keep us safe. Keep us safe, she continued to pray.

And Meredith kept her eyes squeezed shut.

CHAPTER 19

TWO HOURS EARLIER

Meredith enjoyed having the aisle to herself, at least for now. Time to think. Time to breathe.

She wanted to get her mind back to the place where it had been before she encountered Grandma Lucy at the gate. Before Connor called and things got weird.

A ministry for victims of sexual abuse. Homes set up around the country. Compassionate Christian staff trained to offer support and counsel. The ideas had been flowing so quickly at the gate that Meredith could hardly keep her pen moving fast enough, but now she sat motionless and stared at the half-filled page in her journal.

A visionary at heart, Meredith had never been short on ideas. Never been short on dreams. She'd built up Living Grace from a vague idea to an international ministry known for its solid, Bible-based resources. Always looking to stretch herself out of her comfort zone, Meredith started blogging before half of Americans had signed up for a personal email account. Hers had been the very first podcast targeted specifically to Christian women, and her books had landed on several major bestseller lists. Even though Meredith recognized it was God's blessings and his grace that allowed her to achieve each of these accomplishments, she also knew her personality was simply wired to keep on growing, stretching, changing.

To never stop dreaming.

Which is what she'd been doing before Grandma Lucy interrupted her earlier. Dreaming about another ministry she could build from the ground up. Meredith would have never willingly stepped away from Living Grace, but maybe her resignation was God's way of forcing her down a new path. A path she would have never chosen for herself but was now looking forward to with a zeal and excitement she hadn't experienced in quite a long time. In a way the ministry she started had grown so large that the majority of her energy was focused on administrative duties instead of the real work she felt called to do. God had stripped all that away from her, which certainly wasn't easy, but maybe this was a pruning experience so she could be even more fruitful for the kingdom in the years to come. Meredith had always assumed she'd stay on with Living Grace until she died, but the truth was she'd grown complacent.

Maybe a change, a new project, a new calling was exactly what she needed.

So why had her ideas stopped flowing all of a sudden? Had her strange encounter with Grandma Lucy left her that thrown off?

"Excuse me. Can we get to our seats please?"

Meredith glanced up at the young mother who was holding onto her son's hand in the aisle.

"Excuse me," the woman repeated, stepping aside so Meredith could slip out of her seat to let the two pass. "Do you want the window seat, West?" the mother asked.

The boy nodded, wide-eyed.

Meredith and the mother exchanged pleasant smiles. "I'm Meredith."

The woman nodded. "I'm Justine."

Meredith smiled at the little boy. "And how old are you?"

West was too busy staring out the window to answer, watching the luggage as it got loaded into the belly of the plane.

Justine sat in the middle seat and gave Meredith one more smile as they reached for their safety belts at the same time.

Justine helped her son buckle up, and Meredith stared at her journal once more. Where had all her ideas gone?

"Do you want a drink from your water bottle?" While the young mother attended to her little boy, Meredith reached into her purse to pull out her phone. May as well check her emails one more time before she had to switch to airplane mode.

I'm worried about you.

She stared at the message. When had Connor texted her, and why hadn't she heard her phone beep?

Maybe you should stay the night here and fly home when the weather clears.

Meredith wasn't sure if she should be grateful or annoyed. What business was it of Connor's to begin with?

Just boarded, she typed back. Then to ease his concerns she added, *If the roads are really bad, I'll get a hotel in Detroit.*

There. That should calm his nerves. When had he gotten so concerned for her well-being, and where was all that protective zeal yesterday when she could have used it in the board room?

She picked up her pen and decided list out people who could help her begin her new phase of ministry. For the past fifteen years, Meredith was convinced that she was one of the few blessed believers fortunate enough to be working in a job that matched her passions and callings perfectly. Was it possible that Living Grace wasn't her final goal in life but merely practice for this new ministry God was laying out before her?

She couldn't remember the last time she felt so excited. So energized. Who knew that getting fired could end up so freeing?

I want you to call me as soon as you land. Let me know you arrived safely.

Connor again. Meredith knew that everybody handled guilt in different ways, but this exaggerated display of concern was starting to annoy her.

She typed a quick thanks then switched her phone to airplane mode. Beside her, Justine was pulling out a snack of Cheerios for her son, and Meredith turned back toward her journal.

Time for some more dreaming.

CHAPTER 20

FLIGHT 219

The cabin seemed to let out one collective sigh of relief when the captain announced their landing in Detroit. After a short scuffle following his gun malfunction, Bradley was subdued, bound with zip cords, stashed away somewhere in the back of the plane.

Meredith was safe.

She was going home.

Justine still gripped her son.

"You should probably make sure he's buckled in," Meredith told her gently.

Justine nodded, wiping tears from her eyes before tightening West's safety belt. "I just can't believe it," she breathed. "Just can't believe it."

"Mommy?" West's voice was squeaky.

"Yeah, buddy?"

"That was a bad guy, right?"

Justine let out her breath in what sounded like a half-laugh, half-sob. "Yeah. He was a very bad man."

"Will the police rest him?" he asked.

Justine nodded. "Yeah. They're gonna arrest him."

West leaned his head against his mother's shoulder and shut his eyes. "I wanna go home."

Justine responded by wrapping both arms around him. Meredith couldn't blame her. She'd only known the little boy for a few hours and felt like doing the same. If this was how she felt toward a small child she'd just met, how much more tender and loving did her heavenly Father feel toward her right now?

The thought left her feeling protected. Cherished.

But still far from safe.

Grandma Lucy's strange prayer at the gate. Connor's worried texts. Had God been trying to warn her? If Meredith hadn't been so busy worrying about her past and planning for her future, would she have heard his voice more clearly?

But what could she have done?

God had known. Even before Meredith sat down in this seat, God had known what terror was waiting for her. He knew when the Grand Rapids airport closed, when she stood in line to demand a different flight. All that time, had he been trying to keep her off this plane? Or was this part of his original plan all along?

On one of her recent podcast episodes, Meredith had answered a listener's question about prayer. Does it really change God's mind? The heart of the question, and one which Meredith had addressed hundreds of times phrased in hundreds of ways, was does prayer actually make a difference? Or does it just give believers peace and a connection to God during difficult times?

Meredith couldn't believe that prayer was simply for a Christian's benefit. There were countless examples in the Bible of God acting in direct response to his children's prayers. King Hezekiah recovering from what should have been a deadly illness. The angel of the Lord agreeing to Abraham's plea to save Sodom and Gomorrah if enough righteous souls could be found.

And yet God always knew the future. Always knew what prayers his children were going to pray and how he was in turn going to respond to them. In short, it was a mystery but one which left Meredith even more convinced of the need to pray than otherwise.

What if Grandma Lucy hadn't been so bold? Would Bradley's gun have gone off? Could that one prayer have saved Grandma Lucy's life? Or had Grandma Lucy only been aligning herself with facts that God had already decreed, with events the Lord had already set in motion?

Meredith would never have all the answers. But she was glad to know that others were praying for her. With Bradley's demands being streamed live from the cabin, there was no way other believers on the ground didn't know about the terror the passengers faced on Flight 219. Had Connor been watching the news? Had he been praying for Meredith specifically?

For a minute, she pictured him logging onto Living Grace's multiple social media accounts. *Please pray for Meredith, who is one of the passengers on Flight 219.* She imagined the thousands, maybe tens of thousands, of Christians praying for her.

Bring Meredith home safely. Help the other passengers. Be with them all, dear Lord.

But she'd never given Connor her flight information. All he knew was she was leaving Boston and landing in Detroit. Would that be enough? Did he know? Was he one of the Christians on the ground interceding for her right now?

And in the end, did it really matter if people were praying for her specifically? Of course, hundreds of thousands of people must know about their flight by now. Bradley's entire stunt had been to raise awareness to the situation at that Detroit school, and he'd forced dozens of people to record his tirades live on their phones. How many Christians were saying prayers for their safe landing at this exact moment? Those prayers couldn't be any less effective if they didn't mention the passengers by name, right?

"I wanna go home." West was crying in the seat beside her, and Justine was doing her best to calm him down even though she was still in tears as well.

It was time for Meredith to focus on others besides herself. She ran her hand on West's head. "You've been such a brave little guy," she told him.

Justine looked up at Meredith and smiled gratefully.

West's lower lip quivered.

"Do you want to know a story about some brave, brave men in the Bible?" Meredith asked. He nodded, and Meredith glanced at his mother to judge her reaction. Justine's expression didn't change, so Meredith went on. "Once there were three men named Shadrack, Meshach, and Abednego. They loved God very much, but the king they worked for was a wicked, wicked man."

"Like a bad guy?" West asked with wide eyes.

In spite of the adrenaline still surging through her body, Meredith found herself smiling. "Yes," she answered. "Like a bad guy."

He nodded sagely, and Meredith continued.

"The wicked king told Shadrach, Meshach, and Abednego that they should all bow down to a false god, but they knew the Lord didn't want them to do that. So do you know what the wicked king did?" Meredith hesitated, wondering if after the trauma they'd all just been through she should have picked a different story. She hadn't realized she was trembling until West's mom reached out and rubbed her shoulder, Justine now being the one to comfort Meredith.

Encouraged by the small gesture, Meredith tried to find a way to explain the next part in language that wouldn't sound too scary.

"Help!" A terrified shout from the back of the cabin interrupted her story. Meredith twisted herself in her seat to see what was happening. Had Bradley escaped his bonds?

"Fire!" The yell rang out at the same time as a piercing alarm deafened the passengers aboard Flight 219.

CHAPTER 21

MEREDITH HAD NEVER SEEN a crowd stampede before. There couldn't have been more than a couple hundred passengers on board, but every single one of them was clamoring to escape the smoke pouring from the back of the cabin. Shouts of *fire* and *smoke* and *help* mingled with pleas for divine intervention and screams of sheer terror. Every so often, someone cried out in pain as men and women trampled each other in a vain attempt to outrun the smoke and flames.

The problem was clear. There was nowhere to run. And yet Meredith was one with the crowd, throwing off her seat belt, trying to race forward, forward, forward, away from the black smoke.

"West!" she recognized the panicked sound of a mother screaming. Justine?

"West! Has anyone seen my baby?"

Oh, no.

Where was he? Where was Justine's little boy? He'd been right beside Meredith just a moment ago.

"West!" Meredith raised her voice to join the frantic mother's. She grabbed the shoulder of a man in a business suit. "A little boy," she panted. "There's a little boy missing."

The man looked at her with pity but then pried himself away from her grip and pushed his way through the frenzied crowd.

"West!" Justine's voice was shrill, a terrified screech that made Meredith's heart race in her chest.

God, please help us find him.

Her eyes stung, and the black smoke was surging closer, closer, closer …

Another scream as the plane lurched forward. This time it was Meredith. Meredith and every single other passenger on board the doomed flight.

"He's bombed the bathroom," someone shouted, and soon murmurs, shouts, and yells of *bomb* reverberated through every square inch of the smoke-infused cabin. A bomb? What did that mean? Bombs exploded, right? They didn't just burn. Did that mean the danger was yet to come?

And in the end, did it really matter? You could die from smoke as easily as from fire as easily as from an explosion. And of course, nobody would survive a crash from thirty-thousand feet. It was a morbid thought, but it was all Meredith could focus on.

"West!" Over the shouts of all the other passengers, Meredith heard Justine calling for her little boy.

Meredith felt like she was going to be sick. She tried to escape into one of the empty rows of seats when she heard a faint cough.

West?

She knelt down and scooped up the small form huddled beneath one of the seats. "Come here, West," she urged. "Come here. I'll help you find your mom."

He held onto the seat cushion and wouldn't let go.

"West!" Justine screeched from the other side of the aisle.

"He's over here," Meredith yelled before a coughing fit seized her own lungs. She tried again. "Over here." Her voice was so hoarse, she couldn't make herself heard.

"Mommy!" West was crying. Screaming. Coughing. At least he was under a seat. Away from trampling feet. Whether instinct or divine guidance, he was probably in one of the safest places he could be right now. Of course, if the plane crashed, nobody would be safe, but Meredith wouldn't think about that.

"I'll go get your mommy." She wasn't sure West heard her. Wasn't sure she had even heard herself. The smoke had reached the front of the cabin now. Nearly blinding. Meredith had to grope her way through throngs of sweating, screaming, crying passengers, pushing herself to the other side of the aisle where she heard Justine's voice clearer than all the others.

"West!"

"He's over here." Meredith grabbed Justine's arm when she reached the frantic mother and had to give a yank to get her to follow. "He's over here," she repeated and shoved her way, elbowing, pushing, pressing through the crowd to get Justine over to her son.

Dear God, Meredith prayed, *please don't let me step on anyone.* The thought sent a wave of fear and revolt crashing through her stomach. Meredith tried to find some place out of the way where she could be sick.

"Baby." Justine was on the floor by her son, who still refused to let go of the seat. It was probably a wise idea to stay low and out of the aisle. The plane lurched forward once more. Meredith knelt down by Justine who was cradling West in her arms and sobbing. She rubbed the young mother's back. Patted West's sweat-soaked hair. Wondered if reuniting this terrified child with his panicked mother was the last good deed she would accomplish before God ushered them all into the throne room of heaven.

CHAPTER 22

IT WAS THE ROCKIEST landing Meredith had ever experienced, and based on the smell in the cabin that mingled with the acrid smoke, she wasn't the only passenger who got sick.

Sirens. More clamoring. Meredith and Justine both used their bodies to shield little West from the passengers that jostled and tripped and fell into their row as everyone clambered to the emergency exits.

Passengers shouting. Rescue teams racing toward the injured. Meredith had to help a paramedic pry Justine's arms from around her son so they could both get carried off the plane.

Meredith didn't struggle when a woman grabbed her forearm. Her legs could scarcely support her weight, and she had to lean on her rescuer to the exit slide.

Her fall was broken by two men who easily hefted her onto a stretcher. She tried to tell them she didn't need it, but as soon as her lungs took in their first real breath of fresh air, she was attacked by a coughing fit that left her unable to speak.

Someone threw an oxygen mask over her nose and mouth, and she had the strange sensation that she was racing through space. The air was cold. Cold and crisp and miraculously, gloriously clean.

"You're safe now," a man told her. "You're going to be all right."

CHAPTER 23

Once the triage workers declared her healthy, the first thing Meredith wanted to do was get online. Let everyone know she was safe. But all the passengers were scheduled to complete interviews with federal agents and weren't supposed to post anything publicly before they were debriefed.

An entire hospital ward had been transformed into a temporary trauma unit. From what Meredith could gather, a few passengers with more severe injuries had been transported for intensive care, but everyone else was being monitored here. A miracle, perhaps, that everybody except Bradley survived their fiery crash landing. Meredith knew she should probably pray, but her spirit was too exhausted, let alone her body. Paramedics told her what symptoms to expect over the next few days. Many of the passengers were given freedom to leave after their debriefing but were still strongly advised to check themselves into area hospitals for overnight monitoring.

Meredith figured she'd skip that step.

All the carry-ons perished in the cabin fire. Meredith's purse, her ID, her phone. Maybe it was a symbol of starting over. Still, she thought God could have proved his point far less dramatically.

She didn't mind losing her suitcase. Her travel clothes. Her only regret was losing the journal with all her notes. But she could always start dreaming again. Planning again. Just not until after she got a full night of sleep and a chance to let her body recover.

Meredith had no idea what she expected survivors of airplane hijackings to feel like, but whatever it was, it wasn't this. Shouldn't she feel relieved? Grateful? Something?

God, I'm feeling ...

Hard as she tried, she couldn't put a name to it. Tired? Scared? Shocked?

God, I'm feeling ...

"Well, look who decided to drop out of the sky." Something about the jocular voice made her turn around.

Blink. "Connor?"

He smiled at her. She blinked again. What was he doing?

"How did you get here?" She glanced out the window in the distance. She was still in Detroit, wasn't she?

"Heard what happened," he said. "Got the last flight out. That snowstorm is just terrible."

Meredith tried to give a name to this particular emotion.

God, I'm feeling ...

Connor leaned down to hug her. Meredith hadn't realized she was so close to tears until after she soaked his shoulder. She pulled away, trying to feign a laugh.

"It's okay," he said. And she thought for a moment she knew exactly what he was talking about.

"Mommy, it's her!"

Meredith's heart skipped rhythmically at the cheerful sound of a little boy.

"West!"

The child leapt into her lap as his mother hurried up behind him, laughing and apologizing at the same time. Meredith's eyes locked with Justine's, and there was an instant understanding. Meredith stretched out her arms, and in the tearful three-way embrace that followed she lost all track of time.

"He kept saying he had to find you." Justine wiped her face, sitting down beside Meredith with West snuggling them both.

Meredith was so happy to see him safe and smiling she couldn't stop touching him. Holding him. Hugging him. Thankfully, both he and Justine seemed to understand perfectly her need for this human contact. While they were in the air, Meredith thought it was her job to be strong and protective for West and his mom. But maybe she'd had it all backwards. Maybe God seated them together because he knew how much Meredith would actually need the two of them.

"He wants you to finish the Bible story," Justine said.

Meredith gave a small chuckle. "Sure. I can do that." She smiled at West, noted how clean his face looked, how happy his expression. Sweet, angelic innocence like a balm to her soul.

Meredith cleared her throat. "Should I start from where we left off?" she asked.

West nodded.

"Well. Once the three men refused to obey the wicked king, he told his men to punish them." After all West had gone through, Meredith hated to give details about the fiery furnace, so she tried to gloss over that part as quickly as she could. She caught Connor's expression as he stared down at her, smiling, and she blushed, embarrassed to admit that in her joy seeing West and his mother safe and sound, she'd completely forgotten he was there.

"The men were thrown into a big fire." Meredith tested the words tentatively, wondering if they'd produce a flashback of terror. No. She was okay. So was West. She could continue.

"The fire was so hot, everyone thought the three men would get burned up right away, but do you know what? God protected them. He stood there in the fire with them and when they came out, they didn't even smell like smoke."

Smoke. Another trigger word. Meredith paused. No coughing spell. No echoes of terrified screams of passengers over the screech of the airplane fire alarm.

She was still okay.

And so was West.

Justine's cell rang. "That's Daddy." Her face lit up, and she set West on his feet. "Come on. Let's tell him we're safe."

Meredith watched Justine leading her son to a quiet corner. A calming peace settled over her heart.

"Make some new friends on the flight?" It was Connor. She hadn't forgotten he was there, not exactly, but his voice still startled her.

"Something like that," she answered.

He glanced at her awkwardly. "I'm glad you're okay," he said.

"Me, too."

He rocked back and forth on his feet. "So, what happens now?"

Meredith glanced at the time. She had no idea how long these federal interviews were supposed to take. All she really wanted to do was take a shower and go to sleep. Forget today had ever happened.

"I'm supposed to answer some questions," she told Connor. "There are agents here interviewing everyone."

He nodded. "What about after that?"

She shrugged. "I guess I find some place to clean up and get some rest." She cocked her head to the side. Why was he staring at her like that?

He took the seat next to her, which made it hard to know where to look. Straight ahead? At him? At his feet?

God, I'm feeling ...

He reached out for her hand. He felt so warm. So alive.

God, I'm feeling ...

"As soon as I heard about your flight," he said, "when you were up there in the air and I had no idea if you were going to survive or not, I realized something."

She waited. Was her heart racing because of the smoke? Because of the trauma? Or something else entirely?

God, I'm feeling ...

He cleared his throat. "I turned in my resignation to Living Grace." It wasn't the confession she expected.

"Really?"

Connor nodded his head. His eyes were so deep. Had she ever noticed them before? Deep pools of compassion.

God, I'm feeling ...

He was the first to turn away. "I just couldn't stay there after the way they treated you."

She blinked again. Wondered at the curious sensation in the back of her throat. Symptoms from the smoke inhalation?

God, I'm feeling ...

Connor let out his breath. Gave a nervous chuckle. "This shouldn't be as difficult as it is ..."

His eyes rose to meet hers once more. "You and I aren't working together anymore," he stated. "Not in any professional way, I mean. Which means that we ..." He let out a cough. Laughed at himself once again. Then leveled his gaze until she was certain she could see straight into the depths of his soul.

"Can I take you out to dinner?" he blurted. "I'll wait as long as you need. I'll stay here all night if we have to. Keep you company. Pray with you. I can't even imagine how terrified you must still feel. But I want to be here for you. Want to help you ..."

Her breath raced back into her lungs all at once, and she realized that the burning sensation in her throat wasn't from the smoke at all.

She blinked back tears. Glanced over Connor's shoulder to where West sat happily on his mother's lap, talking into a cellphone.

She took in a deep breath, stared into Connor's eyes, and finally she could give a name to that emotion she hadn't been able to identify before.

God, I feel hope.

And she'd never been more grateful to be alive.

Unreliable Witness

Alana Terry

Christian Books Today

CHAPTER 1

I DIDN'T MURDER MY husband. It's important to explain that from the very beginning. There are enough people in the world right now who think I'm a conniving murderess. I don't need you to be one more of them.

I didn't murder my husband. Which, now that I write the words out, now that I see them there on the page in front of me, they don't absolutely ring true.

You've heard of the unreliable narrator, I assume. It's a literary device. Meant to trick readers.

I read a book like that once. It was written like a detective novel, which to be totally honest, isn't exactly my cup of tea, but I was going through what you might call a rough spot and was willing to read anything I could get my hands on.

In this mystery, the narrator herself ended up being the villain, but you didn't find that out until the very last chapter. I saw it coming a mile away, mind you, but I went online to look at what the reviewers were saying, and most of them had been duped right up until the end.

I'm harder to surprise. Probably because I know just about every trick there is, every manipulative tactic, every method there is for twisting the truth ever so subtly until reality itself bends to your command.

I didn't murder my husband.

I want you to know that from the very beginning.

But I thank God every day that he's dead.

CHAPTER 2

JUSTINE HELD HER SON'S hand as they stood in line.

"How much longer?" West whined.

Justine tried hard not to snap. She'd made herself a promise to hold it together for her son. For West.

"This part can take a while," she reminded him, "but after we get through the line and go through the big machines, we'll find a spot by the window to look at the planes taking off."

As a toddler, West would have lit up at the idea of watching giant planes taxiing outside Logan airport. Now he was four and already jaded.

He shifted his weight from one foot to the other, yanking down on her arm.

Justine freed her hand and pulled out her cell, not because she had anything important to look at on her screen but because she needed to rest her nerves. It had been years since she'd flown anywhere. That was before she'd become a mother, and even those few short experiences hadn't been all that friendly to her anxiety. Now she had West to worry about, not only for his safety but also for her sanity and that of all the other passengers on their flight.

West was what his daycare teacher called "energetic," and Justine wasn't exactly looking forward to trying to keep her son entertained and quiet for the next five hours, especially not when she herself was so nervous about traveling.

West had been looking forward to this trip for months. During his four years on the earth, he'd never ventured beyond about a fifty-mile radius from their New England home. She wondered what he'd think about Detroit.

She wondered if he would hate it just as much as she did.

It wasn't exactly Justine's idea to head back to Michigan. When she moved away, she'd made herself a promise never to return, and up until now she'd remained true to her word.

Her husband and her therapist thought the trip was a good idea. A chance to get some kind of closure, maybe.

Or maybe the chance to tell her mother how much she hated her once and for all.

CHAPTER 3

I'M NOT SORRY THAT he's gone. I think it's important to get that out of the way. If I were to tell you all that he put me through ... oh, well. The jury didn't want to hear the details, and I assume you don't, either.

That's fine with me.

But I don't want you to think I'm terribly heartless. You can think of these pages as my confessions of sorts. I don't know. Maybe you'll burn them after you read them. That's fine with me.

As long as you read them first.

That's all I ask.

The jury didn't get to hear the entire story. I realize nothing I'll say here can change what already happened, but it's important for me to tell you that I'm sorry.

I'm not sorry he's dead, mind you, but that certainly doesn't prove that I'm the one who killed him. Did I think about it? Yes. Fantasize about it? Sure, but that's not breaking any law. You can't prosecute a woman for murderous thoughts. It's just not how things work in a free society. And yet here I am.

Here I am.

I didn't murder him.

I don't know if you're going to believe me or not. I don't blame you for hating me, for believing everything those newspapers wrote about me.

But I didn't murder him.

I loved him, in a sick and twisted way. I was lost without him. Entirely and utterly lost.

And I'm sorry for your sake that he's gone.

I didn't want to leave you so young. I didn't mean to abandon you like that.

But it wasn't my fault.

I've looked up details about the family that adopted you. Seem like nice folks. Salt of the earth kind of people. I hope they did right by you. I know it's too late now, but I would have liked the chance to thank them. For taking you in. For raising you right.

I wasn't ever planning on contacting you, but then I heard that your parents had passed. I was mighty sad to learn it, too. Here you are, barely in your thirties, and you've lost just about everyone.

I wish I could have changed things for you, but we've all got our own path to walk. Yours, I'm afraid, has been riddled with difficulties and pain, and for that I'm truly sorry.

You probably don't want to hear this from me, but I'm proud of you. Proud of the woman you've become, the mother I know you are. You love that boy. Trust me, I know it. And now that you're a mother yourself, I hope you can understand a little more fully why I did what I did.

How I ended up here.

That's why I'm writing you now. To tell you my side of the story. I know I might not be able to change your mind, but I want you to hear me out. Think about what I'm telling you. Then you can decide for yourself if that jury was right or wrong.

I want the chance to tell you my side of what happened. To assure you that I didn't murder your father. That's all I ask of you, Justine.

CHAPTER 4

"COME ON, MAMA," WEST prodded her leg as Justine fiddled with the strap on her boots. Why had she decided to wear her heels on a day like this? It wasn't as if she were trying to impress anybody back in Detroit.

Justine smiled apologetically at the elderly couple waiting to go through security behind her. She and West were holding up the line.

"Come on, Mama," West repeated impatiently.

When Justine's husband booked tickets for their flight, she'd been adamant she wanted to travel during the day. No red-eyes for her, thank you very much. Now, she wondered if she'd made the wrong call. Maybe if West was dead tired, he wouldn't act up so much.

She squeezed her eyes shut as she finally managed to wedge her foot out of her tight shoe. Steve was supposed to be here with her. She needed his support. It wasn't her fault that the partners thrust this case on her husband at the very last minute.

"Good thing we paid for travel insurance," was all Steve said as he logged onto the website to cancel his ticket.

She couldn't believe he'd abandoned her like this. And why had she let him, anyway? She didn't owe her mom this visit. When Steve told her he couldn't make it to Detroit, she wondered if this was God's way of warning her to leave well enough alone.

She couldn't understand why she let Steve talk her into flying without him. Didn't he know how nervous she got on airplanes?

No, she hadn't ever specifically told him she was scared of flying, but he must know by now. Wasn't that why he never suggested outlandish vacations in the Caribbean like so many of his colleagues at the firm took?

She should have put her foot down. Told her husband that there was no way on God's green earth she was going to travel alone with their four-year-old son, especially not to Detroit. No way she was going to subject their child to the ravings of a madwoman. Not that West was going to come within a ten-mile radius of his grandmother, but still. Steve should have known how impossible it would be for Justine to make this trip without him. Not just emotionally but logistically as well. Did he have any idea how many daycare providers she had to screen in order to find someone to watch her son while Justine went out to talk to Alice? What if he hated it there? What if the daycare was dirty? What if there was lead in the water or something worse? The entire state of Michigan was falling apart. One of Steve's associates had even been called to Detroit as an expert witness to discuss that school where they built a playground on toxic soil. That kind of thing was happening all over the state. And Steve thought it was a good idea for her and her son to spend four days there without him?

He was as insane as Alice.

She set her boots on the conveyer belt and waited her turn to step through the full-body scanner. West was young enough they let him go through the gate after a cursory once-over with the wand. In ten or fifteen years, on account of his skin tone alone, he'd be stopped, questioned, harassed when he wanted to travel. It was part of life he'd have to get used to soon. Her son didn't realize how lucky he was to be so young.

For now, everything was new and exciting. He grinned widely at Justine as he waited for her on the other side of the full-sized scanner. She hated the machine, hated to think about whatever radiation might be coming out of it. She held her breath, reminded herself that there was nothing to fear, and stepped through the machine.

"Wasn't that cool?" West jumped enthusiastically as Justine tried to put her tight boots back on without losing her balance.

"Yeah," she mumbled. "Real cool."

"Will we get to do it again before we get on the plane?"

She shook her head and answered mindlessly, “Not this time.”

Justine glanced at the TSA line, which had only grown longer in the half hour they’d been waiting. First hurdle past. A hundred more to endure before this ordeal was finally behind her.

CHAPTER 5

I DIDN'T WANT TO disrupt your life. I can only imagine you meant it when you told me in no uncertain terms that you didn't want to have anything to do with me.

I'm sorry, Justine. I really am. I wanted to be a good mother to you. I wanted to give you the life that you deserved.

It sounds bad of me to say, unnatural somehow, but I think you were better off with those rich folks who took you in. I know it wasn't easy. I'm sure growing up in the suburbs had its share of hardships, but it was a better childhood than I could have offered you.

I don't regret what I did, Justine. I only regret that it ruined any chance of having a relationship with you.

That's why I begged you to come and see me now. You probably don't know this. I made him promise not to tell you, but I've been writing to that husband of yours. The rich lawyer. He seems like a nice man, Justine. He really does. And I'm happy for you. For the life you've created and that little family of yours.

Your husband knows about my condition. That's the real reason I need to see you. Why it can't wait any longer.

I'm dying, Justine. Cervical cancer is no picnic even if you aren't serving a life sentence for murder.

I didn't want to tell you until I saw you face to face. But it can't wait. Doctors have given me a few more weeks, a month or two if I'm lucky. But given my track record, Justine, I don't put much stock into things like luck.

I told your husband. I didn't tell you. I was worried you'd think I was being manipulative. Conniving. But it's the naked truth. By this time next year, you'll be a complete orphan.

I'm sorry, Justine.

I would have liked to meet you again under more positive circumstances.

There's a journalist I've been talking to, nice young man from back East. We've been working together for the past year, putting together my story. I'm not allowed to profit from the sales, you know. That was part of the court order.

The journalist tells me that my book has bestseller potential. It's not even done yet, and he's already found some publishers who want me to sign on the dotted line. But I'm not going to do that until I get the chance to talk with you first.

You're the only surviving relative of your father's. That means anything I make from the sale of my story will go directly to you. I know you're not worried about finances. That husband of yours has you set for life, and I'm glad to hear it. I don't want to think of you and my little grandson suffering for lack of anything.

I'm not writing my book for the money. It's not for the infamy either. Trust me, I had my share of that during the trial itself. I'm sick of it all. But it's an important story to get out there. Might even help women in situations like mine.

I just want to clear my name.

I don't want you to live your life as the daughter of a murderess.

I want you to know what happened.

It's time for you to hear the truth.

CHAPTER 6

WEST HAD EATEN EVERY single French fry and licked each individual particle of salt from his McDonald's lunch. With nothing but the discarded pickles from his burger left on his tray, he was already asking for dessert.

No surprises there.

If West stayed where he was on his growth chart, he'd be taller than his dad before he graduated high school. Steve had been a football star before a back injury kept him from playing college level. He was proud of the life he'd made as a Boston attorney, but Justine knew he still had hopes that West would follow in his athletic footsteps. Genes were on West's side, and if you could judge by their grocery bill, her son already had the appetite of a teenage athlete.

"Look, Mama." West pointed at a little bakery halfway down the terminal from their gate. "Donuts. Can we get some? I'm hungry."

Of course he was hungry.

Well, their flight wasn't scheduled to take off for another hour and a half. Dumping a ton of sugar into his system was probably easier now than trying to keep all his extra energy corralled at the gate.

Justine picked up her purse, and West gave a preemptive squeal of excitement. "Think they've got sprinkles on them?" he asked while jumping from one foot to the other.

Justine was fumbling through her wallet, trying to decide if it would be easier to just pay with cash than credit. West was so excited he started to dash out of the gate when he bumped into a white-haired woman wheeling her carry-on to a nearby seat.

"Be careful!" Justine snapped at her son. She reached out her arm reflexively to catch the old woman in case she stumbled.

"Oh dear," the stranger exclaimed in a smiling voice. "I'm afraid I wasn't looking where I was going. That could have been trouble."

"No," Justine corrected and gave West an angry glare. "My son should have been more careful and should have remembered not to run when there are so many other people around."

West stared at his feet and mumbled a half-apology. Justine doubted the woman even heard.

"Are you all right?" she asked. The woman looked frail enough that a fall might have resulted in a broken bone or worse.

"I'm fine, thank the dear Lord," she replied, dusting off her pants. "I'm just worried that I hurt your little guy there. Is he all right?"

"Yes." Justine was still upset with West and was debating whether or not she was going to keep him from getting any donuts after all. If he was still so hungry, he could eat a veggie tray or something that wouldn't send him into a sugar craze when he was already too energetic. When she'd convinced herself the stranger was fine and unharmed, she gave one last apology and prepared to leave, but the woman grabbed her by the hand.

"You have a lovely child," she said. Her grip was twice as strong as Justine would have expected.

"Thank you," Justine answered, somewhat flustered.

"Children truly are a gift from the Lord, aren't they?"

Justine didn't know how to respond. It was a saying she'd heard before at church and knew was there somewhere in the Bible, but on days like this, she didn't exactly feel like West was as big a blessing as everyone else made him out to be.

The old woman smiled and let Justine go.

"I'll see you two soon," she said with an air of certainty that struck Justine as slightly creepy.

She offered a noncommittal smile and took her son by the wrist.

"Ow," West complained, straining against her hold.

Justine made him apologize once more, and then she led him down the terminal in search of something to eat.

CHAPTER 7

DENNIS WAS A CRUEL man. A heartless man.

His lawyer did a good job keeping them out of the trial, but there were two exes willing to testify against him. To let the judge know how violent he was.

I was young, Justine. Barely eighteen when your father and I met. In his defense, I told him I was twenty-one. They used that at the trial, trying to prove I was dishonest. A pathological liar. The defense attorney grilled me for a full hour about the details of my age. Too bad he didn't spend a fraction of that time probing into Dennis's past abuses.

I don't mean to speak ill of your father. I've debated whether or not to tell you everything. I don't want you to worry that you've got a monster's DNA making up half of who you are. Because you're different, Justine. I know you are.

I'm not a well-off woman, not anymore, but I have my resources. I hired a female investigator to tell me what she could about you. To keep me posted. Once she even sent me pictures from my grandson's birthday when you took him to the swimming pool with all of his little friends.

I love that child, Justine. I'm sorry if you feel like I've been spying on you, and I hope you know I only did it because I love you so much. Your son is adorable. So sweet. So innocent.

So pure and happy.

I was like that once. At least I think I was. It's hard to remember now. But that's what I'm doing. Remembering so you can finally understand what happened.

Dennis was eighteen years older than I was. My parents didn't like him, but I was raised to be an independent thinker. Strong and ambitious. In a way, I like to think that you inherited these same traits from me, just with a little bit of wisdom to temper that stubborn streak. A woman who's fiercely independent as well as sharp and intelligent, now that's a woman the world has to fear.

Sometimes I wonder who I might have become. What might have happened. I think a person could drive themselves crazy going down that rabbit trail for too long. But not me. I think about the what ifs, wonder how drastically different my life would have turned out, but you know what?

If I hadn't met Dennis, I would have never had you.

You're my gift to the world, Justine. You're my reason for living. You're the only hope I have that somehow, some way, God knew I needed my life to matter. Otherwise, I should have died the same night your father did.

CHAPTER 8

JUSTINE GAVE IN AND let West eat three donuts then bought him two puzzle books and a new headset at the outlandishly expensive airport electronics kiosk. She was probably spending extra money on him just to assuage her guilty conscience. While other happy families meandered by in the terminal to spend Christmas with relatives or embark on exciting vacations, she was traveling to Detroit with her son so she could dump him off at a daycare while she visited a woman she loathed.

Happy stinking holidays.

She didn't want to face Alice. Even now, she realized, she could take West's hand, walk down toward baggage claim, and leave the airport.

Steve might be a little upset, but he's not the one who lived his entire adult life knowing he was the offspring of a felon. Why in the world had Justine let him talk her into a trip like this?

Snow was falling outside. Part of Justine wished that they'd cancel her flight. If it got delayed due to weather, maybe she'd take that as a sign from God she shouldn't go to Detroit after all.

She wasn't a religious woman. Not as religious as her husband, at least. Steve had befriended one of his key witnesses last year, the leader of a big church in Cambridge who'd been shot by a home intruder. The pastor had invited Steve to Bible studies and Sunday sermons, and then all of a sudden Justine's husband was a walking, breathing Bible thumper.

It shouldn't bother Justine all that much. She believed in God, and she didn't argue when Steve wanted to take the family to church on Sundays. It was something she thought would be good for West anyway. But she couldn't help wondering if Steve's encouragement to visit her mom came as part of his newfound faith in this God of forgiveness, grace, and love.

Did her husband expect her to absolve a convicted murderer? There was a reason Justine's mom had spent nearly thirty years behind bars. Alice had deprived Justine of anything resembling a normal childhood. Alice had murdered Justine's father, robbing Justine of both her parents in one fateful blow.

In his spare time, which wasn't much to speak of, Steve had been going over details from Alice's case. In his mind, there was enough doubt regarding the circumstances that he thought Alice should have gotten herself a new trial. As far as Justine was concerned, there was nothing her mother deserved less.

Justine reached the gate over half an hour before her flight was scheduled to take off. There weren't any seats near the window, but West was far more concerned with his handheld games than he was at watching planes departing down the runway.

She found a seat next to two young women, one with her hair dyed a vibrant blue. It wasn't even noon yet, and Justine was exhausted from her day of travel.

You don't have to do this, she told herself once more. West might be disappointed not to go on an actual airplane, but she could always buy him a new game or toy as a concession.

She pulled out her phone, contemplating what might happen if she texted her husband right now. *Changed my mind. Staying home with West where we belong.*

The nice thing about Steve's newfound faith was that he yelled at her less than he had before he met that Cambridge pastor. He might be disappointed, might give her a disapproving glare or two, but in the end he'd realize that the choice was Justine's to make and Justine's alone.

All she had to do was stand up, take West's hand, and explain to her son that their plans had changed. He'd be disappointed for a moment, but the promise of a trip to the water park or a gift of a new video game would melt away any permanent unhappiness.

She should go.

And yet something in her heart was telling her to stay.

Was it possible she actually did want to return to Detroit? Was it possible there was anything Alice could say or do that would change what Justine thought about her mother?

Wishful thinking. That's all it was. The hope that once she saw her mother face to face, she'd realize that everything she'd read about the husband-killing monster was a lie. They'd hug. Embrace. Everything would be forgiven.

No, there was no possible outcome that involved the restoration of Alice and Justine's relationship. Nothing at all.

Justine took her son by the hand. "Come on, West."

He looked up at her. "Where are we going?"

She stood. "We're going back to see Daddy."

"What about the airplane?"

"Some other time," she answered half-heartedly. "Let's go."

CHAPTER 9

YOU MIGHT BE SURPRISED to know that I'm a woman of faith now. I haven't made any big announcements to the press or anything. I told you before, I'm not in this for the publicity.

But my faith is real, and it's carried me through some of the most difficult times here during my sentence.

I hear your husband is also a Christian. I'm glad about that. God knows this life is hard enough even with his Word to cling to in times of trouble.

I don't want to preach at you, Justine. I really don't. But maybe one day you'll read these words and know in your own soul that they're true. I hope so. I pray so.

I don't have anything else in this life to cling to, which is probably why I've accepted my imminent death.

You don't want to have a relationship with me. I get that. I understand. I really do. But maybe once you've heard my side of the story you'll feel a little differently.

Dennis was abusive. I'm sure you're familiar enough with the court case to know that much at least. But it wasn't the physical blows, Justine. That's not what did us in.

I still have nightmares about it. Did you know that? One of the guards here makes fun of me. Tells me if I'm so filled with remorse that I wake up screaming I shouldn't have murdered my husband in the first place.

I tell her I'll pray for her. I think that really gets under her skin.

The screams and the nightmares aren't about the night your father died. Not at all.

The nightmares are about being trapped. Do you know what it's like to be trapped, Justine? Stuck? I can't move. It's like trying to walk through cement that's dried up all around you. You thrash and scream and try to get someone to help you out, but the only one who hears your cries is the man who poured the cement on you in the first place.

And he laughs.

Just throws his head back and laughs in your face, his breath hot, his palpable evil unbearable.

Laughing in your face.

People thought we had a perfect marriage. That's what's so distressing about the entire thing. If he hadn't been a TV personality, if there hadn't been a two-million-dollar life policy in place, if we'd been ugly or poor or from the wrong side of town, nobody would have cared when he got himself killed.

But that wasn't the kind of couple we were.

I knew when I married a newscaster as popular as Dennis that I was subjecting myself to the public eye. I thought I knew what that meant. Thought I was ready. I was expecting some rude remarks, some comments about our differences in age or race.

I was even prepared for words like gold-digger and trophy bride getting thrown around. That's just what happens when a young, attractive woman marries a millionaire who's twice her age, right?

Well, Justine, I have news for you. There's a reason a man like Dennis went through three other exes before settling on me. And there's a reason his first wife attempted suicide (on more than one occasion) and why his second underwent a very public mental-health breakdown.

I should have seen the warning signs, but I was mesmerized. I was nothing but the intern, the minimum-wage employee whose job was to dress smartly and show up with Dennis's coffee just the way he liked it. You probably don't have to use your imagination all that much to picture what it was like when he paid me so much attention. Smothered me with gifts. Paid down my credit cards and set me up in one of the nicest apartment complexes in Detroit.

I was young and stupid, but that's no excuse. I should have known better. I did know better. Right before we got engaged, I even tried to call things off. He tapped my home line. Can you believe it? He'd got it into his head that I was flirting with the weatherman, and he actually paid to get my phone tapped in order to try to prove I was cheating.

I told him we were done, and that's when he showed me his true self. He reminded me about how much debt of mine he'd paid off. He knew lawyers, plenty of lawyers. It was either stay with him or get myself sued.

I should have let him bankrupt my savings account. Instead, I let him destroy my very soul.

Tapping my phone, it turns out, was only the beginning of Dennis's madness. Once we were married, it only got worse. Following me to the store. Hiring his employees to track my whereabouts. He made up stories about crazy stalkers who were sending threatening letters to the news station and told me I couldn't go anywhere without protection.

It wasn't a bodyguard he hired for me. It was a prison guard.

A year into our marriage, I couldn't leave the house. He told all our friends I'd had a nervous breakdown. Told my parents I'd been diagnosed as schizophrenic. Even convinced a doctor to prescribe drugs that kept me foggy, placid. Just the way he liked me.

You were the best thing that ever happened to me, Justine. When I found out I was pregnant, I felt for the first time in years like I had something to live for. A reason to exist. A reason to survive.

Dennis didn't want children. I know it's terrible to tell you this, but you have to know the truth. Dennis had no desire to become a dad. I had to hide the pregnancy from him. Starved myself in hopes I wouldn't show. I couldn't tell the doctor I was expecting, but I was terrified the pills would hurt you, so I'd take them while Dennis watched then force myself to throw them up.

You deserved so much better. You have no idea how terrible I feel when I read scientific studies that talk about prenatal health. I did what I could to take care of you. God knows I tried, but all I could do was keep your existence hidden from your father for as long as I could.

But Dennis found out anyway.

Of course he did.

And that's when everything turned horribly wrong.

CHAPTER 10

"WHY DO WE HAVE to go back home?" West whined.

Justine had to practically drag her son as they made their way toward the airport escalators. "You don't need to worry about that," she answered. "All you need to know is we changed our plans. Sometimes that happens." She was trying to decide whether to offer him more junk food or a trip to the video game store as a concession. Either one should be enough to settle him down and prevent a tantrum here in the airport.

At least she hoped so.

"I thought we were going to visit Grandma." West pulled against her grip with all his strength.

"Alice is not your grandma," Justine snapped, fully aware of the passengers staring at them both. She pulled West toward her and whispered in his ear, "Listen, I'll explain more in the car, okay? But right now, I need you to be a big boy and do what I tell you."

West didn't budge. "I want to go see Grandma!" he screeched.

"Hello there, young man. Did you lose somebody?"

Justine blinked at the stranger, trying to remember why her face looked familiar.

The white-haired woman smiled at Justine. Great. The same little old lady her son had nearly plowed over in the terminal.

"Is everything all right?" the woman asked.

Justine let out her breath. No, everything was not all right, but that didn't make it this stranger's business.

Justine was about to pick up her son and carry him out of the airport kicking and screaming if necessary, but the old woman was rummaging through her ancient-looking purse.

"Does your son have any allergies?" she asked Justine. "I have some farm-fresh goat-milk chocolate here and would be happy to share if that's all right with you."

West's eyes had already widened at the promise of candy. There was no way Justine could deny him now. "That'd be fine," she replied with a resigned sigh.

She hoped the woman would catch from the tone of her voice that she didn't feel like a long, drawn-out conversation.

"I'm Grandma Lucy." The woman shook West's hand then extended hers to Justine.

"Nice to meet you." Justine made a show of glancing at the clock above them. "West, say thank you for the candy, and then we've got to go."

"Where are you flying to today?" Grandma Lucy asked.

West stuck out his lower lip, and Justine knew he was preparing to give this stranger his best impression of a sob story. "We were gonna see my grandma," he began, his voice trembling slightly, "but now my mama says we can't."

Grandma Lucy frowned. "How disappointing." She turned to Justine. "Was your flight cancelled? That snow's really coming down, isn't it?"

So far, Justine hadn't been able to come up with a compelling reason to give West why they were leaving the airport, but she figured the weather was a as good an excuse as any. "Yeah," she responded quickly. "It's really too bad."

"Where does your grandma live?" the old woman asked, bending down to address West as if Justine weren't even there.

"In Detroit," he answered, and Grandma Lucy's face lit up.

"Really? Well, that's where I'm headed too. In fact, they've been calling standbys on my flight for the past half an hour. I bet we can get you on board if you really wanted to."

West's face brightened, and Justine was convinced he would have taken Grandma Lucy's hand right there and gotten onto the plane whether his mother followed them or not. She really had to have more in-depth discussions with him on stranger danger.

"Come on, Mama." He grabbed Justine's sleeve. "Let's go see if they have room for us."

Justine didn't move. She didn't want to give in to her son, didn't want to reward him for throwing a tantrum. She thought about how disappointed her husband would be if she took West home right now, then she looked at Grandma Lucy. There was something calming about her presence. The woman's confidence and familiarity unnerved her, annoyed her to no end, and yet Justine felt somehow drawn toward her.

"Come on, Mama." West wrapped his arms around Justine's waist. "Let's go to our airplane. Please?"

Justine let out her breath. There was something inexplicable about this stranger's presence that felt both inviting and unwelcome. As her eyes moved from Grandma Lucy to West, Justine knew as certainly as she knew that it was snowing outside or that she loved her son more than anything else in this world that she was meant to get on that airplane. Call it destiny, call it whatever you want, but she knew in that instant as this little white-haired lady smiled at her warmly that she and West were supposed to fly to Detroit, and no amount of nerves or fear or protests could get her to change her mind.

CHAPTER 11

AFTER KEEPING MY SECRET for nearly the entire pregnancy, Dennis had finally figured it out. You have no idea how hard your father's lawyers had to fight to keep the jury from hearing this part of the story.

I'll spare you the details. Suffice it to say, your father reacted as deplorably as I thought he would, and about an hour later, I was in the ER getting ready for surgery. I was hemorrhaging. They weren't just worried about your health. You and I both were close to death that night.

You were delivered by emergency C-section. Your father couldn't come in the room, and the OB who delivered you begged me to call the police.

"You don't have to pretend that you fell down the stairs," he told me. "I know what happened. I've seen this kind of thing before."

He was giving me a way out. Telling me he'd call the police for me if I was too scared to do it myself. Promising me they'd help me find a safer life, a better life for me and my daughter.

He didn't know who I was. Didn't know who I was married to. Didn't realize that no matter where on God's green earth I took you, your father would hunt us both down. Dennis didn't want a child, but now that you were here, he wasn't about to let you go. Not without the fight of our lives.

And so I told that nice doctor I really had fallen down the steps. Thanked him for saving your life. Told him there was nothing at all he had to worry about.

He was older, probably in his sixties when he delivered you. Most likely, he's dead by now. I think about him, wonder what might have happened if I'd listened to him. Allowed myself to believe he could actually help the two of us, desperate as we were.

You were in the hospital for several weeks. You had to put on weight and learn how to nurse before we could bring you home. Overnight, Dennis turned into the father of the year. He even got permission to bring in a camera crew to the hospital and introduce you on TV to the greater Detroit area.

"My little miracle baby," he called you. And it was true. Back then, they didn't have as fancy care for babies born too soon. The doctors told us you had a fifty-fifty chance to survive.

And survive you did.

Your father was a monster, but nobody knew it. People sent in gifts from all over the state. That's how much they loved your father. The newspaper wrote you up as the most famous baby in all of Michigan.

Nobody knew your father was the reason you were premature.

Nobody knew it was your father's fault you and I both nearly died the day you were born.

Nobody knew it was going to get even worse before I could find a way to deliver you permanently to safety.

CHAPTER 12

"How old are you, young man?" Grandma Lucy asked West. The old woman hadn't left their side since Justine headed to the gate with her son.

"I'm four," he answered, beaming proudly.

"Four? Wow. You're awful big for your age."

West grinned at the apparent compliment. Justine wondered how it was that adults could make comments like that about children's body size and shape without it coming across as aggressive or rude. She also didn't appreciate how Grandma Lucy was addressing West and not herself, but to be fair, Justine hadn't done much more than answer the old woman's questions with monosyllables.

"And are you a Christian, West?" Grandma Lucy asked, leaning in toward him. "Do you know Jesus as your personal Lord and Savior?"

Good grief. Was this eccentric stranger really about to start preaching to a preschooler?

"We go to church," Justine inserted sharply. She picked up her purse, trying to decide if there was time to get West one more snack from McDonald's before they had to board.

"Not every week," West started to protest, but Grandma Lucy didn't seem to hear him. She was addressing Justine directly.

"Oh, there's so much more to having a personal relationship with Christ than just showing up to church on Sundays."

Justine was finished. It was bad enough Steve had changed so much over the past year, droning on and on about Jesus this and God that. Last summer, his pastor's wife had given Steve a kids' Bible to read with West at bedtime. Justine was certain Steve would let the habit die after the first few nights, but here they were, months later, and Steve was still going at it strong.

Justine didn't mind that West was learning Bible stories and going to church. And she couldn't deny that her husband was infinitely easier to live with now that he had "come to God." But even though he never stepped right up and said so, Justine got the feeling she was a constant disappointment to her husband, that he'd be more in love with her, happier with her if she got into this whole Jesus thing as much as he did.

Maybe he'd prayed this annoying old woman into their lives. Maybe Steve asked God to send them someone persistent who'd pester Justine until she finally got as serious about her faith as Steve wanted her to be.

Justine was spared the need to end the awkward conversation when the flight attendant invited passengers traveling with small children to board. West wasn't a toddler anymore. Justine didn't have a stroller or booster seat or any clunky baggage to take on the plane with them, but she wasn't going to sit here and listen to some stranger proselytize her son anymore, either.

"Come on, West." She took her son's hand and let out her breath. "It's time to get on the plane."

CHAPTER 13

You were a beautiful child. I don't know what happened to them, but I had boxes and boxes of pictures of you when you were a baby. You weren't even six pounds by the time we brought you home, but you were strong. You were a fighter.

I was so proud of you.

You gave me a reason to live, Justine. If it weren't for you, I ... well, you don't need to hear that side of it.

For the first little bit after you came home from the hospital, your father and I got along. He seemed to have changed his mind about not wanting to be a dad. I think part of him just liked the attention he got because of you. But I think there was a part of him, however small, that loved you in his own way.

Your father had demons, Justine. I'm not sure I mean that in the literal sense of the word, but he didn't necessarily want to be a monster. I don't know what went wrong with him, and it's too late now to try to figure out anyway.

You had just started crawling when the beatings started again. Dennis was taking me to different doctors, telling them that I was unstable. Post-partum psychosis, they called it. I'm sure you've heard of it.

I wasn't depressed. I wasn't crazy.

I was a prisoner.

Dennis found a doctor who prescribed me something horrible, something meant for people with severe mental illnesses. It knocked me out. Made me gain fifteen pounds the first two months, and that's on top of all the weight I gained during the pregnancy. I couldn't nurse you anymore. Could hardly function.

He took me to more doctors. Complained about my behavior. Hinted I might not be safe around our child. Hired a cute, perky au pair to move in with us and "help out with the baby," as he put it. Really, he just wanted someone to take to bed since I was so drugged up and overweight by then he'd lost his interest in me.

I'm ashamed to admit it, but I was relieved when he found another focal point for his attentions.

The drugs kept coming. You kept growing. Dennis told the au pair all kinds of terrible things about me, made it sound like I couldn't be trusted alone with my own child. She took you out and about every day, leaving me home alone. Nothing to do but cry and beg God to end my life.

I could have done it, but I held onto the hope that if I managed to get myself healthy, Dennis would let me be your mother again. I did everything he told me to do. Ate nothing but cabbage soup for weeks on end because Dennis told me I was fat. Took my meds, not having a clue that my problem wasn't a mental illness but that my husband was drugging me up to keep me compliant.

I don't know what happened to the au pair, but she disappeared. Dennis told me her mom was sick and she flew back home, but she'd told me she was an orphan. Truth be told, I bet he killed her. They'd gotten into a terrible fight the night before. I heard him yelling at her.

The next day she was gone.

Of course, I can't prove anything. When I mentioned it at the trial, the judge told me to shut up. Said it had nothing to do with the case. I think it had everything to do with the case. I was scared for my life. If Dennis could make an au pair simply disappear, a woman nobody came looking for, a woman with no connections or legal representation, what could he do to me? He'd already gotten multiple doctors in his pocket, men who testified that I was unstable, unfit to be a mother.

Dennis controlled every single aspect of my life. And the nightmare was far from over.

CHAPTER 14

JUSTINE AND WEST WERE seated in the same row as a sharply dressed businesswoman in her forties or fifties. The passenger introduced herself as Meredith then went back to the journal she was writing in. Justine was glad when she saw Grandma Lucy board and find her seat in the very back of the plane. Something about the old lady's pointed questions and intense gaze left Justine feeling terribly uncomfortable.

At least they were on the flight. The more she thought about it, the more Justine couldn't shake the feeling she was meant to be here. Did that mean she was meant to visit Alice as well?

Justine might not be as into church as her husband was, and she certainly wasn't the type of person to go evangelizing in an airport like Grandma Lucy, but she believed in God and wondered if it was his voice telling her to go to Detroit after all. But why? Did she need some kind of closure with her bio mom? What had the woman done for Justine other than give her birth? It was because of Alice's murderous rage that Justine had spent years in the foster system before getting adopted. It was because of Alice's notorious mental illness that Justine had spent years in therapy, paralyzed with fear that the monster that had taken over her biological mother might be lying dormant in her as well.

Why did her husband, God, and the entire universe seem to be conspiring to get Justine to visit this woman?

Alice was unhealthy. Steve had let it slip. Justine had no idea her husband was in communication with that felon. Why in the world hadn't he told her sooner? But Alice was sick. Maybe even dying. She wanted to see Justine.

The trip had made sense when Steve first arranged it. A family trip to Detroit. See some of the area Justine remembered before her adoptive family moved to the East coast. Take West to the Children's Museum and the zoo.

But now with Steve working, there was nothing about this trip that felt like a vacation.

And yet here she was.

You chose this, Justine reminded herself. She and West could have walked out of the airport. They'd been close to doing so when Grandma Lucy grabbed a hold of them. Justine wasn't some prisoner being held hostage on a flight she hadn't agreed to take. She was here because at some point, she and Steve agreed it would be a good idea, and at some point in the past hour, a fluke encounter with a stranger in the airport made Justine change her mind about going back home with West.

She was meant to be on this flight. She knew it.

But that didn't mean she wasn't worried. What would Alice say to her? What if Justine met her mother, saw her infamous insanity up close, and that woke up the dormant demons she'd inherited from that monster?

She wouldn't let West come anywhere near his grandmother, but what if this trip had some kind of negative impact on him anyway? Alice's negative energy seeping into her son.

She was overthinking things. She had to stop. The flight attendant began her safety speech about seat backs and tray tables. Justine checked West's seatbelt to make sure it was buckled snugly, then she shut her eyes, let out a deep breath, and tried to force her anxious body to relax.

CHAPTER 15

He died on a Tuesday.

I remember it was Tuesday because that was the only morning he went into work a little later, not hours before the sun rose.

He couldn't find the cufflinks he wanted. Thought I'd left home and sold them. Accused me of pilfering money away so I could leave him. Even suggested I'd given them as a present to a secret lover.

He was raving around the house, shouting like a lunatic, throwing drawers open, telling me he'd find my stash of cash and kill me.

You were asleep in your room. You poor, sweet angel, you'd learned to sleep through anything.

As hard as life was for us, you were a happy little girl. You were chubby once you started growing as a baby, but as soon as you learned to walk your muscles turned lean. I think you spent one day toddling and after that you took off running. Running through the house, laughing, yelling, giggling.

You had no idea your father was a monster.

You had no idea your mother was insane.

You were blissfully unaware of the danger we were in.

But I wasn't.

The truth was I hadn't sold your father's cufflinks, but I had been making plans. You'd gotten an ear infection right after your birthday. I took you to the doctor. Your father came too. Didn't trust me out of the house with you. He was afraid I'd run off.

But he couldn't follow me into the bathroom at the children's clinic. That's where I saw the poster. A toll-free number to call if you were in an abusive relationship.

I didn't have a pen or paper. Your father didn't let me travel with those. He was too scared I'd write someone a note begging for help, and then the picture-perfect prison he'd created for me and you would collapse and crumble around his feet.

I didn't have a pen, but I had my mind. And I stared at that poster, burned the numbers into my head.

I couldn't use the home phone to call for help, but I knew if I kept that number memorized, I'd make sure that once I got the chance I'd use a pay phone. One day, I was certain, your father would slip up. He'd stop for gas when I was in the car and run in to use the bathroom, and I could jump out and race to a pay phone. Or he'd forget to lock us in the house like he always did when he left for work, and I'd walk nonchalantly over to the neighbor's and ask to borrow their phone.

I knew my fantasies were stupid. Knew your father would never be so careless. But memorizing the number made me feel strong. Made me feel brave.

At night, I'd lie awake holding imaginary phone conversations in my head. Telling the compassionate woman who answered the toll-free number that my husband kept my daughter and me locked in our house. That a year ago he'd killed our au pair and had managed to do so without raising a shred of suspicion. That he kept me placid and compliant by threatening to kill our daughter, this perfect little angel who was the only reason I had to live.

I'd tell her about the drugs. "He says I'm crazy," I whispered in my mind, "but I never had any problems like this before we got together."

And she'd explain to me what deep in my soul I already knew. I wasn't insane. I wasn't psychotic. The drugs were part of my prison. With them, Dennis knew I couldn't think clearly. Couldn't fight back.

"You should stop taking those pills," the imaginary woman would tell me.

And so I did.

Dennis didn't find my stash of cash that morning. He didn't find any love letters linking me to this imaginary lover. He didn't find the cufflinks he was sure I'd stolen.

What he found was much, much worse.

CHAPTER 16

JUSTINE WAS THANKFUL THAT West was on good behavior. He ate a few snacks then settled down to watch an in-flight movie. The relative calm gave Justine the chance to relax.

Unfortunately, it also gave her the chance to be alone with her thoughts.

As each minute brought their plane closer and closer to Detroit, Justine felt the stone in the base of her gut churning, growing sour. She had to consciously focus on her breaths to keep from hyperventilating.

"Just because you share her genes doesn't mean you're going to become anything like her," Steve had told her years ago. Justine was pregnant, terrified that she would turn into the same kind of monster as her mom.

And thankfully, for then at least, Steve had been right. Justine's transition into motherhood was one of the most blissful, delightful surprises that had ever happened to her, as natural and as powerful as falling in love.

As it turned out, she wasn't defined by her genes.

When West was an infant, she held her breath, wondering if her descent into insanity would take her by storm the second her son started crawling or walking or speaking.

And then West turned one and next two. Still no depression, no hint of psychosis. The anxiety was always there, but not to the point where Justine couldn't control it.

By West's third birthday, Justine felt like she could finally let out her breath. She'd made it. Hadn't attacked her child or her husband. Hadn't slipped into a murderous, psychotic rage and tried to destroy the ones she loved most. At that point, she gave herself permission to stop worrying so much. Permission to forget about the woman who brought her into the world.

And then a few months ago, Steve told her Alice had contacted him.

"She's changed," he told her, his eyes and tone begging her to believe him. She couldn't understand. Why in the world did he want her to give this woman any chance to get close to her or her family? Even the fact that Alice had contacted Steve should show she was just as manipulative and conniving as she'd always been. Why hadn't she contacted Justine directly if she really wanted to talk?

In the end, Justine attributed her husband's actions to his newfound faith. Didn't Christians believe in grace and forgiveness at all costs?

It wasn't until she'd had that dream that she even considered making the trip to Detroit like Steve was pushing her.

It was just before Halloween. Justine had volunteered all day for the costume party at West's preschool. She was tired. A little grumpy. The next day was Sunday, and she knew her husband would try to wake them up early to go to church. Couldn't she sleep in just one day of the week?

That night, she dreamed that she saw Alice trapped in some kind of haunted carnival ride. Her mother was screaming for help, begging for Justine to find her. To save her.

Inside the mansion was nothing but mirrors. Each time Justine thought she saw Alice's face, it was her own image staring back at her.

Until she got to the far wall. She saw the door, knew she had to open it, knew she was going to open it, knew that once she did open it, her life would be ruined.

Even as she sat next to her son on the flight to Detroit, she could remember staring at her own hand as it reached out for the doorknob. Slowly turned and pushed it open.

Alice was inside, her clothes covered in blood, her face distorted by both insanity and rage.

The knife in her hand was dripping. Disgusting.

The body at her feet wasn't Justine's father.

It was her son.

She'd woken up screaming for West. Even when Steve tried to calm her down, she couldn't stop hyperventilating until she brought her son into bed with them, held him in her arms. Even once she'd managed to convince her logical brain that West was safe, she still couldn't control her breathing, couldn't stop her arms from trembling, her mind from replaying the sense of foreboding she felt as she pushed open that door.

"I think you need to see her," Steve told her the next morning. She thought he was the crazy one until her therapist repeated the exact same sentiment the following day.

Justine still wasn't convinced. It wasn't until a few weeks later when she had another dream, the one that finally changed her mind.

It was the same haunted castle. The same freaky mirrors.

But there was no door this time, no bloody knife, no stabbed son.

Instead, it was Alice, lying on a bed, holding a little doll and crying. "Where'd she go?" she wailed over and over. She reached out her arms, and for a split second, Justine wanted nothing more than to bury her head against this frightened woman's chest and tell her everything was okay.

"Where'd she go?" Alice repeated, her voice so pitiable Justine woke up with tears on her cheeks.

"I think you need to see her," Steve repeated the following day.

And Justine knew he was right.

Now, she wasn't so sure.

In her early twenties, Justine had poured over every single newspaper article she could find dating back to her father's murder. He'd been a beloved TV reporter, which mean the trial made national news. The story had every ingredient of a good scandal for the time. Her father was white, handsome, somewhat famous, and several decades older than Alice. Alice was black, young, and beautiful, with well-documented mental instabilities and quite a few motives to kill her aging husband. Before their wedding, Alice had fallen into a heap of financial troubles, financial troubles that all went away the moment she signed her marriage license. As far as the public was concerned, Alice had every reason to be profusely grateful to her husband, who gave her every material possession she could desire as well as the best medical care for her mental illness that money and fame could buy.

But she wanted more.

A jury member said that he probably would have acquitted her if it hadn't been for the fact that Alice had taken out three separate life policies on both her husband and their daughter just a week before the killing. That and the fact that the detectives found letters from a secret lover, a lover urging Justine to end her marriage and live with him forever.

Justine read the reports and realized her mother wasn't just greedy and insane.

She was also stupid.

Fringe groups still believed Alice when she upheld her innocence, in spite of all the evidence against her — her well-documented mental disorder, her secret lover, the multiple life insurance policies. Alice's supporters argued that the all-white jury and the racial tensions of the time would have made it nearly impossible for her to get a fair trial. And yet her sentence was upheld after multiple appeals, her requests for parole were repeatedly denied, and Alice was doomed to spend the rest of her life behind bars.

Justine didn't want to admit it to herself, didn't want to sound like an ignorant child unable to look at reason. The facts of the trial could hardly be any clearer. Alice had killed her husband. She had even attacked Justine. The scar on Justine's thigh where the knife blade went into her leg was a daily reminder of her mother's criminal insanity.

And yet Justine had to wonder. It was a question she'd never dared to mention to Steve, to her therapist, even to herself except for when she was at her most open, her most honest, her most raw.

Part of Justine wanted to visit Alice. Part of Justine wanted to hear her mother's side of the story.

Part of Justine was dying to believe her mom was as innocent as she claimed.

CHAPTER 17

I'D HIDDEN THE PILLS in a sewn-in pocket of a purse I never used.

Dennis found them anyway.

I'd been off them for nearly a month. I was finally starting to feel like myself again.

A week or two earlier, and he would have killed me for sure. But not that Tuesday morning. I was thinking more clearly than I had in years. I felt like me, not some zombie toy of his.

And I knew I had to save you.

Save my little girl at all costs.

Your father had never hurt you before, Justine. I want you to know that. In spite of how wicked and evil he was, he never caused you any type of physical injury. Even when he threatened to, it was only to keep me compliant.

Dennis shoved me against the wall. He threatened to force-feed me all the pills at once, spelled out how long and painful my death would be if he did. He tried to shove them down my throat, so I bit his hand.

I knew it was dangerous, Justine. I really did, but he'd never hurt you before. I thought he was just bluffing when he pulled out that knife.

He wanted me to overdose. He'd already called two of my doctors and told them I'd threatened self-harm. A week earlier, he dictated a suicide letter and made me transcribe it. That wasn't the first time. And still, I wasn't nearly as scared as I should have been.

Then he began to tell me all the other steps he'd taken to make sure my death looked deliberate. The phone calls he made from our home line to the suicide prevention number. The type-written diary pages he'd forged to make it look as though I'd been planning my own death for months.

There was a time when I would have welcomed death. But then on that fateful Tuesday morning, you woke up and came plodding down the stairs. You were wearing blue fuzzy pajamas, the kind that cover your feet and zip up the front.

You were so beautiful, Justine, and I knew that I had to live. What kind of life would you have if I let your father kill me? How long would it take before his lust to inflict pain destroyed you as well?

I couldn't let him do that.

He had the knife in his hand. Said he'd kill you if I didn't take the pills. Told me that he'd filled out paperwork in my name, taken out life insurance on our little baby.

"Take those pills, Alice," he said to me, "or I'll kill our little girl and tell the police it was you."

I knew he had the resources to make that happen. I hadn't heard about the life insurance policies until then, but I remember him forcing me to sign some papers a few weeks earlier, when I was still detoxing from the drugs and couldn't think straight.

He had the knife up to your neck. You looked at him and smiled. You thought he was trying to tickle you.

He underestimated how much stronger I was now that the drugs were out of my system. Now that not only my own life but my daughter's was on the line.

You should never underestimate a mother's fury. Her innate instinct to protect.

I did what I thought I had to do, Justine. I'm so sorry you got hurt in the process.

Your father is dead. I killed him that morning. I'm not sorry I did it.

It was the only way to keep us safe.

It was the only way to keep you alive.

CHAPTER 18

THE INCIDENT HAPPENED SO quickly, it was over before Justine realized it had started.

Before she realized how much danger she was in.

"He's got a gun!" a passenger shrieked.

A scuffle. Someone got knocked out. And then a man stood up, waving a gun in the air.

Justine wasn't even sure if she had blinked. What was going on? She was supposed to feel scared. Logic told her it was the opportune time to panic, but she was too stunned to react at all.

"The people of Detroit have failed our kids," the man began. For a second, Justine thought this was some kind of drill. A false alarm. Something staged.

Then the palpable fear that enveloped the entire cabin told her the danger was terribly real.

"What's going on?" she whispered to the woman in the aisle seat.

"I think that's the air marshal." Meredith gestured toward the man who had been knocked out in the preceding scuffle.

Justine clutched her son, hoping to somehow shield him with her body from the terror in the cabin.

"I think it's a hijacking," Meredith whispered.

"But why?" Justine had the feeling her brain should be keeping up, but it simply couldn't. "Who is he? Why is he doing this?"

"He calls himself General," Meredith answered. "Says he's doing this for the kids of Detroit. I really don't understand it either."

West was clinging to Justine's side. She kept his body pressed against hers, hoping she wasn't suffocating him in her attempts to shield him from the danger surrounding them.

Justine didn't react when Meredith took her by the hand. Somehow it felt calming to have another woman by her side. The physical touch was comforting.

"I'm going to help you protect your little boy," Meredith whispered, and Justine felt tears of terror stinging her eyes. Protect her little boy? Did that mean this man might possibly try to hurt her son?

The gun was probably a prop. That was the easiest thing for Justine to believe. A prop so he could get what he wanted, gain some notoriety, and then the air marshals or traffic control or whoever took over in cases like this would find a way to get all the passengers safely on land.

But how? The air marshal was knocked out. Maybe even dead. Who was going to protect them? Who was going to keep any of them safe?

"Mama," West whined, and Justine tried to shush him.

"Not now, buddy. Just be quiet and still." The last thing she wanted was for West to make noise, to alert General to his presence. As long as General was focused on his tirade, as long as he kept talking into the cell phone cameras the passengers were pointing at him, he would ignore her son. She was thankful West was in the window seat, hoping that her body was large enough to keep him hidden from sight.

"He's only four," Justine whispered, her eyes filling with tears. Did God hear her? Did he see? Her little boy was only four. This wasn't something a child his age should ever have to endure.

Meredith squeezed her hand once more. "It's going to be all right," she whispered, but Justine couldn't bring herself to believe it could possibly be true.

CHAPTER 19

THE KNIFE WAS IN my hand. The life was draining out of Dennis's eyes.

"You know you'll pay for this," he hissed. Even as death stood by waiting to escort him to judgment, your father tried to terrorize me. "Those insurance policies weren't just for the girl. You know how bad this will look."

I didn't know how bad it would look. How could I? How could I have guessed that just like he made preparations so that my death would look like a suicide, he also made contingencies so that I'd be the primary suspect if he ended up dead?

Which is exactly what happened.

It wasn't just the new insurance policies, although those certainly didn't help my case.

There were the forged love letters from some anonymous boyfriend. The police found them stashed away behind the liquor cabinet. They immediately began to suspect I was having an affair, even though they never found out who the mysterious man was.

Because there was no other man, Justine.

No other man at all.

Then there was Dennis's journal, which he only kept at work. He'd written in it for over a year, notes about how worried he was about my health, how he kept trying to protect me but was afraid I might one day hurt our daughter. He made up imaginary scenarios about coming home and finding you with bruises on your body, bruises I couldn't adequately explain. The au pair wasn't mentioned at all. I imagine if the police ever found his journal, Dennis didn't want them trying to find her for questioning or digging too deep into her disappearance.

Of course, Dennis had been carrying on with multiple affairs. I wasn't surprised, but his journal spelled out how I'd discovered love notes from his girlfriend two nights before he died. How mad I'd gotten. How I'd threatened to kill him and our daughter both because I was so angry.

The doctors who testified at trial didn't help my case, either. It didn't matter that for every single office visit, Dennis had gone in with me, planted firmly by my side like the all-loving husband. Had told me what kind of symptoms to claim I had. Often, he injected me with something before I met with the physicians. I still don't know what it was, but there were times I couldn't even remember the appointments after I got home.

In the end, the prosecutors didn't need anything else. I was a woman, a minority, a gold-digging trophy bride with a boyfriend on the side, a history of insanity, and a well-documented diagnosis of post-partum psychosis which made me dangerous to my daughter.

I knew I didn't stand a chance at the trial.

I was right.

They even tried to blame me for the cut you got on your leg while your father and I were struggling with the knife. It didn't help that I couldn't tell them how you got hurt, if the knife was in my hand or your father's at the time. You know how it ended. First-degree assault and child abuse for your injury. First-degree murder for your father's death.

Two consecutive life sentences.

I imagine that when you read the news articles about everything that happened, you think I'm a monster for what I did. I don't know what I have to say to get you to believe me, Justine, but there's something else you need to know now.

I'm dying. The doctors doubt I'll see much past New Year's. I've made my peace with my sentence. I've made my peace with God.

The only hope I have left in this world is that you can hear my story, look me in the eye, and tell me you believe me. That's all I ask before the good Lord takes me home.

CHAPTER 20

"THE PEOPLE OF DETROIT have failed our kids."

General's loud voice carried throughout the entire cabin, over the hum of the engine, over the pounding of Justine's pulse raging in her ears.

"They've sold our children's souls to the devil, building their school on toxic land."

That's what this was about? The elementary school with lead in the soil? Justine remembered her husband mentioning the case, but surely it wasn't something to murder over.

Was it?

"Five minutes," General was saying. "The governor has five minutes to call me on my personal cell phone before I'm forced to do something desperate." His gaze swept up and down the cabin. Justine's stomach flopped like a fish out of water when his eyes locked onto hers. It only lasted for a fraction of a second, but it was long enough to freeze the blood in her veins. Her entire body went cold and numb.

"Five minutes," General repeated. "Five minutes before a hostage dies."

Justine held West close. Now instead of using her body as a shield so the shooter couldn't see him, she covered West's face with her hands so he wouldn't try to turn and witness the violence erupting all around them.

Justine couldn't believe it. Surely the God her husband spoke about so lovingly, so reverently wouldn't allow something like this to happen. Not to her. Not to her little boy.

Justine's heart pounded in her ears. For a minute, she was afraid she was going to be sick.

Seconds passed. The wait felt like an eternity. Was this the definition of purgatory?

The air felt thinner. Had the captain done something to the pressure system? Were they going to suffocate before General could kill them all off one by one?

General continued to pace the aisle until a single beep sounded from his phone.

"Time's up."

He walked up to a flight attendant. The woman was visibly shaking. Justine couldn't pull her eyes away. She kept her son shielded as best as she could as General pointed his gun at the flight attendant's head.

They were too far away for Justine to hear what he was saying. In her state of paralyzed shock, Justine convinced herself the entire scene was a giant bluff.

When the reverberating sound of gunfire deafened her ears, she realized how wrong she was.

The flight attendant dropped lifeless to the ground, her body heavy, the sound of its thud sickeningly solid. Final.

West dug his fingers into the flesh of Justine's belly and started to cry. Justine pleaded with God to keep him safe. It didn't matter what happened to her. It didn't matter what happened to anyone else on this doomed flight. Just as long as God protected her son.

"She's dead," a woman screamed, her announcement to the cabin entirely unnecessary. There was no way anybody could have survived a shot to the head at such a close range.

"Five minutes," General repeated. "Five minutes before another hostage dies."

CHAPTER 21

YOU LEARN A LOT serving out a life sentence. Did you know that?

Like not all criminals are evil. Sometimes desperate people do desperate things.

I was safer in prison than I ever had been under Dennis's roof. If it hadn't been for the stress of the trial itself and the knowledge that if the jury found me guilty I'd never see you again, I could have felt perfectly at peace.

I gave my life to Christ right before my sentencing. There was a Bible study for the women prisoners. I started going, desperate to give hope or meaning to the terror I'd lived through.

It was in prison that I learned how to pray. Of course, anybody can pray when their husband's beating them up, but my new kind of prayers were different.

I prayed for all the other people Dennis had hurt. Asked God to heal their wounds and show them grace.

I prayed for the jury that found me guilty, the prosecutors who spread vicious lies about me, the public that devoured the scandal like vultures descending on prey.

But mostly, Justine, I prayed for you. I prayed that God would place you in a good home, that he would help you to feel loved and cherished and safe. When I heard that one of your foster families wanted to adopt you, I was thrilled. I'd already been sentenced by then, and even though I was looking into appeals, I was starting to realize there was no way I'd ever leave my cell. Your father was just too smart. The life insurance policies, the journal he kept at work.

He knew that one of us was going to die, and he made provisions to make me out to be guilty no matter which of us it was.

I'm glad that you inherited that money. I prayed that your new family would use it well. By all accounts, it sounds like you've done well for yourself. I'm really glad about that. And I know it's a lot to ask, Justine, probably too much, but I would certainly love to meet my grandson before the Lord calls me home.

CHAPTER 22

JUSTINE HADN'T EVEN REALIZED she was still clutching Meredith's hand beside her until the muscles in her fingers started to cramp. Five more minutes had passed. General's timer beeped again.

"What's he doing?" West asked. Justine didn't have any answer for her son.

General was still in the back of the plane. It should have been good news. It meant that he was farther away from West. But Justine couldn't keep herself from staring as he waved his gun at another young woman and told her to stand up.

"What's your name?" he demanded.

"Willow," she answered. Her hair was blue. Beautiful in various shades, all the way from teal to azure. She looked a little familiar. Where had Justine seen her before?

"Are you following what's going on at the schools in Detroit, Willow?" General's voice was low. Menacing. Like a snarling dog warning another animal to keep its distance.

"A bit," the young woman answered.

"They're building playgrounds on toxic land." His volume increased, and his voice became more animated as he spoke.

Maybe, Justine thought, just maybe if he kept rambling, it would give the other passengers the chance to figure out some plan of attack. Maybe ...

"They're literally poisoning our children, and they don't care."

The young woman's lip trembled. Even in her seat so many rows away, Justine was convinced she could hear the girl's throat working to swallow.

"I'm sorry that I have to do this." General raised his gun and took aim.

Justine willed her eyes to squeeze shut.

"Let her go." The strong voice echoed throughout the entire cabin. It sounded as if the engines themselves had all shut off to help Grandma Lucy's words carry throughout the airplane.

She was so short, she didn't even come up to General's shoulder, and yet the little old lady stood glaring at him until it felt as if General's body shrunk a full foot and a half.

"What do you want?" he asked, but there was confusion in his voice. Weakness.

"I told you to let that young woman go." Grandma Lucy took a step forward. West finally managed to squirm free and turn around in his seat, but Justine was too engrossed in what was happening in back of the plane to tell him to stay down.

"Why would I do that?" General snarled.

"Because she's young, and you don't want to take another innocent life."

There was a filling, soaring sensation in Justine's chest. Had she been holding he breath this whole time? Now that Grandma Lucy stood to confront the hijacker, Justine felt like she could finally remember how to breathe.

"This is the only way to get anyone to listen to what I have to say." General sounded desperate. Scared. Like he was about to lose control any minute.

If the passengers could just find a way to communicate with each other, all it would take was a few strong bodies to bring him down.

Please, God.

Prayers rushed through Justine's soul in the same hurried, unexpected way her breath had returned to her lungs at the sight of Grandma Lucy's boldness. Her body felt warm. Ready for action. Ready for something to happen.

But what?

Grandma Lucy stepped in front of General's gun. "If you need a victim that badly," she proclaimed, so loudly that her words seemed to echo and reverberate off the walls of the cabin, "you can take me. I'm more than willing to meet my Maker."

General stared at her as if considering, placed his hand on the trigger of his gun, and shrugged. "Fine." The menacing growl was back in his voice, and his stature had regained its former confidence. He took a step forward until his gun was just an inch from Grandma Lucy's forehead. "Have it your way, old woman."

CHAPTER 23

THEY SAY THAT CONFESSION is good for the soul. I'm afraid if I tried to list out every single sin I've ever committed, I'd never finish this letter to you. Early on after my sentencing, I visited with the chaplain quite a bit. He kept asking me if I was sorry for killing my husband.

I'm sorry, Justine, but that's the one thing I can't apologize for.

I've forgiven Dennis. That much I can say.

But I'm not sorry I killed him. If I hadn't, he would have destroyed me and you as well. I've searched my Bible, and I've begged God to change my mind if I'm wrong, but I can't regret the fact that he's dead.

The chaplain said that's a sign of unforgiveness. I told him he's never had to kill anyone to save his little girl.

I don't mean to tell you I've lived a perfect life. I struggle every day with anger at the men on that jury who put me here. But I can't change what's past. I can only try to make amends for the future.

I've already told you I'm dying. I don't know how much longer I have, but sometimes as I'm drifting off to sleep at night, I can hear the heavenly music that soon is going to call me home.

I know you might read my words and decide I'm making it all up. You've read about your father's journal, how manipulative he said I was. I imagine that there's part of you that wants to believe I'm innocent and another part of you that might always harbor doubts.

I can't prove to you that anything I've said here is true. I can't make you believe that killing your father was the only way to save our lives. You've read about me online, I'm sure, and have probably already come to your conclusions about who I am and what my motivations were and how reliable of a witness I am.

Just remember, Justine, that looks can be deceptive. Your father had everyone fooled — the doctors, his coworkers, his friends. The jury. Except I have no proof to offer you. Nothing conclusive to guarantee my innocence. God alone knows what really happened. He is my witness as well as my judge. I'll admit there are times when I wake up from terrifying nightmares. I've just died, and God tells me I can't come into heaven because there's blood on my hands. And I pray and I plead and I ask him to show me grace. I wake up crying.

I believe God will judge me justly when my time finally comes, and I rely on his grace to cover all my mistakes. I know you aren't all-knowing like the Lord, but I couldn't die peacefully thinking that you believe a lie about me, about who I was, about why I did what I had to do.

My conscience, my soul, my eternal destiny are in God's hands now. All I can ask is that before I go home you hear my story and tell me that you understand.

Then I can die and finally be at peace.

CHAPTER 24

GENERAL STARED AT GRANDMA Lucy, aimed his gun at her head, and pulled the trigger.

Click.

Nothing happened.

General's eyes widened.

"His gun doesn't work!" The shout from the back of the plane was followed by confusion. Chaos.

"Get him."

"Grab him."

"Careful."

A skirmish. Loud grunting. Someone punched General in the face.

He fell.

Several more shouts, and then it was over.

"We got him!" someone yelled.

And that was it. General was bound, his gun now pointed at his own chest. Passengers let out a collective sigh of relief. In the seat beside her, Justine heard Meredith offering a short prayer of thanks. The captain made an announcement that they'd be landing in Detroit soon.

"You think you've won?" General shouted with a guffaw. "You're all going to die."

Justine chose to disregard the ominous threat. It was the ravings of a madman. Nothing more.

"Mama?" West asked.

Justine wrapped her arms around her son, ashamed that in her fear and then relief she'd momentarily forgotten how scared he must be.

"It's okay," she whispered, tears streaking down her cheeks. "It's over. They caught the bad guy, and we're all going to be okay."

General's laugh still echoed throughout the cabin. "You're all gonna die."

Justine ignored his words, hugged her son close, and thanked God for keeping them alive.

CHAPTER 25

"I'M GONNA KILL YOU both." That's what Denis told me. That's what I believed.

I've talked with the chaplain about it quite a bit since I've been here. Told him that the only thing I feel guilty about is that I don't feel guilty.

Am I a sociopath? Am I the monster the media made me out to be? The monster I'm sure you believe that I am?

He would have killed you, Justine. As sure as I know you're my daughter, sure as I believe God will usher my soul into heaven to stand in his presence any day now, I knew your father meant to kill us both.

I couldn't let that happen.

If you had never been born, I wouldn't have cared. I would have given up years earlier. But you were so little, so beautiful, so perfect. You loved me. Trusted me.

And you loved him too. Your innocence was completely unaware of the pure evil that lived inside that man.

I took the knife. How could I watch while he slit open your throat? How could I sit by and do nothing?

I took the knife, and in that moment, I knew.

Either I would survive, or Dennis would.

There was no way he and I were both going to come out of this alive.

And since my brain was working for the first time since your father put me on those drugs, since I had the adrenaline surge that comes when a mother watches her child in danger, I did what I had to do.

Your father's attorney and the judge were right. I shouldn't have run away after that. Shouldn't have taken you in the car with me and tried to skip town. I didn't even realize you were bleeding until we were halfway to Toronto. We had to stop, had to get you medical attention.

If it hadn't been for that, I like to think we might have made it across the border.

I used to spend a lot of time thinking about that scenario. An alternate reality created entirely in my mind while I sit here, cold behind these metal bars.

We cross the border. I smile and tell the crossing agent we're going to do some shopping. Smile at him nicely, make small talk about exchange rates.

I don't know a single person in Toronto, but it's a big enough city that we manage to get by. I go to one of those women's shelters, take you there with me, explain that we're in danger. I left my ID, everything I had at home.

Eventually, we learn to start over. I get a job working as a nanny for a rich family. They have a little girl just your age, and the two of you become best friends. We go to church. I teach you about the Lord. We pray before meals and sing songs in the car.

Life is beautiful, Justine.

And we never, ever talk about your father again.

CHAPTER 26

JUSTINE COULDN'T BELIEVE IT was finally over.

The captain announced they were just minutes away from Detroit. The first thing Justine did when they landed would be to cancel her return flight and rent a car to drive back home.

There were a dozen emotions she should be experiencing. Relief that the danger was past. Fear for what her son witnessed. Guilt that she had survived while several others on the flight hadn't been so lucky.

Curiosity and confusion. Why hadn't the gun gone off? Was it the old lady's prayers? Steve would tell her it was some sort of miracle. That God had saved her and West both. As glad as she was to be alive, if it really had been God's hand saving them, why hadn't he protected all the other passengers just the same?

Justine's body was trembling, but she wasn't cold. It wasn't until West reached up to touch her face that she realized she'd been clenching her jaw.

"Mommy?" he asked.

Justine's heart nearly broke in two at the sound of her son's sweet and innocent voice.

"Yeah, baby?"

West started to turn around in his seat. Justine held him so he couldn't look behind and see the signs of violence in the aisles.

"Mommy?" he repeated, squirming in her grip.

Justine didn't let go. "What is it?"

"What's that smell?" West asked.

This time Justine did turn and saw a billow of smoke filling the back of the cabin. An alarm started to blare, deafening her ears.

Please, God, no, Justine begged as the passenger behind her shouted in a shrill panic, "Fire!"

CHAPTER 27

YOUR LEG WAS CUT. To this day, I don't even know how it happened. I'm so sorry about that, Justine.

We had to go to the hospital. I tried to come up with a story. You were standing on a chair. You wanted to chop veggies like you'd seen Mommy doing. You tripped. You fell.

The doctors didn't believe me.

I started shaking uncontrollably when they brought the policeman in. At first, he thought he was questioning me in a case of suspected child abuse. He had no idea I'd just ended your father's life.

But the truth came out.

I suppose it always will. At least, that's what the Bible says. Still, I like to indulge myself in daydreams from time to time, think about that nice lady in Toronto who might have hired me as a nanny, think about her imaginary little girl who would have become your best friend. It's not what actually happened, but I've dreamed out the details so vividly I can tell you the scent of the family's laundry detergent, feel the matted hair of their beloved little puppy, a mutt who's just as endearing as ugly.

I'm sorry that's not the life I could have given you.

I'm sorry I couldn't tell you my story sooner.

I'm just glad that soon you'll be here, that I'll be able to explain to you what really happened, apologize to you for all the mistakes I made.

I can't believe I'm about to look at you face to face. I just pray God gives me a few more days, that my body holds out a little bit longer.

I need you, Justine. I need to tell you the truth. That I didn't murder your father. That I never would have deliberately lifted a hand against you if my life depended on it.

That I loved you so much I would have done anything — yes, even kill — to keep you safe.

CHAPTER 28

SHE HAD TO GET her son away from the smoke. But where could they go?

The Detroit skyline was in view, but all Justine could see was a jumble of chaos as men and women scrambled out of their seats in an attempt to get toward the front of the cabin.

The screams of the passengers melted together with the shrill screech of the siren. Justine held her son close. "Don't leave me," she shouted into West's ear, but even then she wasn't sure he heard her.

They were so close. How could so many things go wrong on a single flight? It didn't make sense. General's last words reverberated in her mind, as well as his horrid laugh. "You're all gonna die," he said. Was he the one who planned this? But how could he have set the entire plane on fire when he was tied up in the back of the cabin?

The question of how the fire started didn't matter. The only thing that mattered was whether or not Justine could save her child. How long until the plane would land? And would Justine survive that long to keep West safe?

Terror and chaos swarmed around the cabin as passengers shoved one another their scramble to get out of their seats. Justine gripped her son's arm even more tightly. She was about to lift him up in her arms when she remembered that you were supposed to get low when there was smoke. But how could they get low without being trampled to their deaths?

"West, be careful," Justine shouted as someone plowed into her from behind. She lost her balance. Tripped. Her breath was stolen away as someone stepped on her back. She couldn't breathe.

Where was her son?

"West!" She reached out her arm, flinging wildly. Someone lifted her up to her feet. The smoke was so thick she couldn't even see the face of her savior.

She shot her arms out, blinded by the smoke, terrorized by the fear. She couldn't even see which way was the front of the cabin anymore. She could only assume that if she followed the swarm of panicked bodies she'd be heading away from the worst of the smoke. Not that she had any choice. Everybody pressed up against her. Even now that she was on her feet, the density of the crowds stole her breath away. Or maybe that was all the smoke.

But where was her son?

"West?" Justine tried to yell, but a coughing fit wracked her entire body. What if he'd fallen? What if he'd gotten himself trampled in the swarm of bodies?

"West!"

Somebody grabbed her arm. Justine couldn't see a thing, but the person was leading her away from the throng, toward the thickest of the smoke. Justine tried to fight them off. She needed to find her son, but she was so weak.

"West?"

She heard a faint cry and dropped to her knees. Tiny arms reached for her and flung around her neck. He was on the floor, crouching beneath a set of seats. Good boy. She felt his body, trying to assure herself he was safe, and in that moment she understood.

In the fire, in the chaos, in the terror she'd experienced on this flight, Justine had only one concern. To protect her son. To make sure that no matter what happened to her, West landed in Detroit alive.

She would have done anything. If General had come at them with the gun, she would have plucked his eyes out with her bare hands if it meant saving her child.

She wrapped her arms around him, her lungs filled with too much smoke to form the sobs that promised sweet release.

“We’re going to be okay,” she told him, begging heaven to hear her prayers. “We’re going to be okay.”

CHAPTER 29

CARRIE STEPPED INTO HER patient's room. "Did you press your call light, Alice?" she asked, making her way toward the woman's bedside.

Alice's oxygen canula was a little crooked, and Carrie instinctively reached out to straighten it up. As she did, Alice reached up and took Carrie's hand, pointing at the TV screen in the room.

"What's going on?" the old woman asked in a rattly voice.

Carrie frowned. She and her colleagues had been watching the news at the nurse's station as it unfolded. "A plane hijacking," she answered, reaching for the remote. Her patient didn't have much time left. From what Carrie suspected, Alice's body should have given up days earlier. The only thing keeping her alive was the hope of seeing her daughter.

It was a tragic story, one the nurses all felt keenly. Alice had been incarcerated for the past thirty years, serving a life sentence for murdering her husband. Carrie had gone online to look up the details of the case. Apparently, the murder had been one of Detroit's greatest scandals of its day, and with good reason. Alice had taken out multiple life policies on her husband, then killed him before trying to flee the country with their child. Alice was a murderer, a felon, and a child kidnapper, and now she was trying to reconnect with the daughter she'd injured in her husband's fatal attack.

"Justine's coming from Boston to visit me," Alice announced each and every time Carrie came into the room. Carrie just hoped that her daughter knew what she was getting into. It was common knowledge on the hospital floor that Alice would say anything to get people to give her what she wanted.

Alice continued to stare at the screen even after Carrie had turned off the news. A flight attendant and two passengers had been killed. It wasn't the kind of story an old woman on palliative care needed to worry about.

"Was that the flight from Boston?" Alice asked, her voice weak.

Carrie's stomach dropped toward the floor. Boston? It couldn't be the same flight Alice's daughter was on, could it?

"I don't think so," Carrie replied, but her uncertainty must have been obvious.

"Turn it back on," her patient demanded. "I need to see this."

"Alice," Carrie began, her voice softening, "I'm not sure it's such a good idea to ..."

"Turn it on," Alice snapped.

Carrie obeyed. In spite of her patient's weakness, she thought she detected a hint of the same rage that so long ago had led the woman to cold-blooded murder.

Now, the news was even worse. A fire on the plane. The video footage panned over a tarmac studded with ambulances and fire trucks.

"See there," Alice announced, pointing at the screen. "Flight 219. From Boston. That's the plane my daughter's on."

Carrie patted the old woman's shoulder. There was no way that Alice could be certain of the exact flight number, could she?

"I'm sure it's something else," Carrie began, then let her voice trail off. The plane was about to land. Fire and smoke billowed from its back half. Carrie wasn't even sure how many passengers the medical crews on standby would find alive once it touched down.

"I don't think we should watch this anymore," she said, her voice low.

Alice didn't respond.

CHAPTER 30

JUSTINE'S BODY HAD REMAINED strong and vigilant. She knew that if they survived their landing, the passengers would be even more in a frenzy to get off the plane. She vowed to shield West with her body even if the crowds ended up trampling her to death.

Anything to save her son.

The landing was awful. At one point, the plane tilted and threw Justine's head against the chair in front of her. Still, she held as steady as she could, promising herself and her son and God that she would protect West to her dying breath.

And then they were on the ground. EMTs and emergency personnel flocked in. "Take my son," Justine shouted at the first worker she saw. For the first time since the terror began, she allowed herself to willingly be separated from West. Her lungs were stained with smoke. She couldn't move a single muscle. The only thing that mattered was West was safe.

Eventually, someone else came and escorted her off the plane. She was so weak she almost had to be carried, and her legs gave out the moment they reached the steady asphalt. Justine scoured the crowds for her son. Then she saw him stretched on a gurney being attended to by two paramedics. One of them leaned over and laughed at something West said. Justine let out her choppy breath.

She had done it.

She had saved her son. Maybe her husband was right. Maybe God really had been protecting the two of them after all.

Everything was going to be all right.

CHAPTER 31

JUSTINE HELD HER HUSBAND'S hand. Ever since he landed in Detroit just a couple hours after she did, he hadn't left her or West's side. Even when the federal agents wanted to question her about the events that took place during the skyjacking, Steve refused to separate from her for even a few minutes.

She was thankful he was here. Glad for his support. Now, two days had passed since she landed in Detroit, but her lungs sometimes still stung from the smoke.

West was running up and down the hospital hallway. Justine had snapped at him once, but Steve reminded her that there were worse things her kid could be doing than expending a little extra energy.

Her husband gave her hand a squeeze. "You sure you're ready to do this?" he asked.

She nodded. Ready or not, this was why she had flown to Detroit in the first place. If she didn't carry through, her and West's traumatic experience would be for nothing at all.

"Do you want us to come with you?" Steve's voice was gentle. They'd had this same conversation multiple times before, and each time Justine's answer was the same.

"This is something I need to do on my own."

Steve gave her hand one last squeeze. "All right. I love you."

"I know." She smiled at him. She and Steve had gone through a lot of changes this past year. Some of them good, some of them terrifying. She didn't even want to think about what it would be like once they drove home and Justine had to settle back into life as normal. What's normal after witnessing your son nearly dying in a plane crash?

She was already replaying all the conversations she'd have with her therapist. She should probably find someone for West to talk to as well. There was no way that kind of fear could be healthy for someone so young to keep bottled up. It wasn't healthy for anyone, as a matter of fact, no matter what age they were. Justine couldn't sleep at night without waking up in cold sweats, her lungs stinging with smoke, her stomach dropping as the plane from her nightmare crashed to the ground.

Well, maybe it was good news. After all, she and her therapist had spent so much time this past year analyzing Justine's mother. Maybe it would be nice to have a change. That was one way to look at it, at least. The other way to look at it was Justine had endured more than any human being should ever have to endure. When would God look down and decide she'd had enough?

"I'm gonna take the kiddo to get donuts from the cafeteria." Steve spoke quietly, but not quietly enough.

"Donuts?" West did a complete about-face and sprinted back toward his parents. "Are we getting donuts, Dad?"

Steve smiled and tussled West's hair. Justine noticed he'd been touching his son a lot more than normal these past two days.

Her husband gave her one last kindly gaze. "You ready?" he asked.

Justine nodded. Ready or not, she was here. She was going to do this.

She reached her hand to knock gently on the door of her mother's hospital room, then quietly let herself in.

CHAPTER 32

"SO SHE'S BEEN ASLEEP for how long?" Justine asked.

"Two days," the nurse answered. She had introduced herself as Carrie, had explained that she'd been Alice's primary nurse since she arrived here for hospice care.

"Is it a coma?" Justine stared at the woman on the hospital bed. She looked so frail and weak. There was nothing to indicate that this woman had once been young, beautiful, and murderous.

Nothing to indicate she'd spent almost the entirely of her adult life behind bars.

"Not a coma," Carrie replied. "But she's very, very tired."

"Is she in pain?" There was an inexplicable lump in Justine's throat, which she did her best to ignore.

"I don't think so. In fact, she was pretty restless yesterday, but today she seems so much more at peace."

As if on cue, Alice let out a faint sigh. Justine looked, trying to decide if that was a smile on her mother's face.

"I think she knows you're here."

Justine had no idea how Carrie could make a presumption like that, but she didn't want to waste time arguing. No matter how well this nurse claimed to know her mother, the stranger's presence felt intrusive.

"Have a seat," Carrie said, pulling a chair up closer to Alice's bedside. "You can talk to her. There's no reason to think she can't hear you. Just press that call button if you need anything."

Justine's legs trembled slightly as she lowered herself into the chair. She hated that she felt so nervous. It wasn't as if Alice was going to wake up from her near-coma and try to stab her in the thigh like she had when Justine was just a toddler.

"One more thing," Carrie said, reaching for a tattered notebook on Alice's bedside table.

She passed the book to Justine, who reached out for it tentatively.

"Your mother wanted me to give this to you when you got here."

"What is it?" Justine asked, uncertain if she wanted to open up the pages.

"I'm not sure," Carrie answered. "But it was very important to her to make sure you read it."

The nurse left, and as soon as she was gone, Justine wished she'd come back. She had no idea what to do, what to say. Should she tell Alice she was here? Try to hold her mother's hand? What good would it do if Alice was already unconscious?

Two days ago, Justine had been terrified of dying and losing her child to terrorists. Now, she was afraid of a little old lady asleep in a hospital bed.

Justine let out her breath. Well, if she didn't know what to say, maybe she'd let her mother's words fill up the silence of her soul. She opened up the notebook, and her hands started to tremble even as she read the first line.

I didn't murder my husband. It's important to explain that from the very beginning.

Justine flipped ahead, trying to guess just how many pages in this notebook Alice had filled. How long had she been working on it? And was it just for Justine?

I didn't murder my husband, Alice repeated on the second line.

Justine settled in her chair then checked the time. This might turn into a very long day.

All That She Saw

Alana Terry

Christian Books Today

CHAPTER 1

I'm not who you think I am. These are the words I rehearse to myself when I board the plane with my husband.

I'm not who you think I am. I hold little Annie's hand. She gazes up at me, her eyes wide and full of blissful adoration. She insisted on wearing glittery make-up to the wedding, and the corners of her eyes still sparkle with the tiny incandescent sprinkles.

I'm not who you think I am. The words catch in my throat. Beat through the four chambers of my heart. Pulse throughout my entire body.

People stare at us as we board the plane. I need to get used to the constant gawking. This is my life now.

Russel holds our boarding passes out like they're a crucifix that's meant to ward off the devil himself. "Here's our seats," he says, indicating two rows.

Two rows. A short courtship (Russel's word, not mine) plus a 25-minute ceremony, and I've gone from being a woman who thrived on personal freedom and independence to this. A wife. A mother. A mother of four young children, to be exact. The kind of woman who wears a head covering and skirt that reaches the floor. The kind of woman with a family that takes up two rows on an airplane.

The kind of woman people gawk at while she boards.

I'm not who you think I am.

I came so close to telling Russel everything the night before our wedding. He could see I was nervous. Thought it had more to do with the fact that his first wife's only been dead for six months, and not only am I inheriting Sarah's marriage bed but her entire way of life. The five-hundred square-foot garden. The two separate chicken coops, one for layers, one for meat birds. Up until my first dinner over at Russel's house, I had no idea there was a difference.

I'm also inheriting Sarah's kitchen utensils, her pottery wheel (not that I have a clue how to use it), and her position of first lady at Gospel Kingdom. Funny really, if you were to have known me before I met Russel, to think that I'm now married to a pastor. Especially at a place like Gospel Kingdom. Where they don't let women wear pants, and skirts must reach past the ankle. I'm not supposed to make much of myself in the sanctuary, but my new husband assures me that if I want to visit with the ladies after the sermon's over, that would probably be seen as a hospitable gesture.

I've also been informed that Sarah hosted a women's luncheon at the parsonage every other Wednesday, although the church ladies are going to be kind enough to not expect me to follow in my predecessor's steps until I've had at least a couple more weeks to settle in.

Of course, after this vacation, the church ladies are planning on throwing me a proper bridal shower. They all want to get to know the woman who stole Pastor Russel's heart after he was bereaved of his darling wife.

I'm not who you think I am.

Russel gestures with his hand, a silent motion telling me to take the seat behind his. He and the two eldest girls will sit in front. I let go of Annie's hand, and she clambers excitedly into the window seat. Andrew, so far the only one of Russel's kids that hasn't seemed to instantaneously warm up to me, eyes me warily when I ask him if he wants the middle seat or aisle.

As it turns out, Andrew only wants the aisle seat if I'm seated in the window. We shuffle everyone around since Annie refuses to sit anywhere that's not next to me. It's musical chairs in a three-foot area. Not that I blame my stepson, mind you. How hospitable can you expect a five-year-old to be in a case like this? This little boy is already expected to call me Mom, adjust to an entirely new way of life, and his poor mother isn't yet cold in her grave. That's a metaphor, by the way. Russel had Sarah cremated.

I should have mentioned her urn in my litany of odds and ends I've inherited as Russel's new wife.

Sarah's remains still sit in the greenhouse where she grew her prize-winning tomatoes. Russel assures me he'll take care of it by spring, but I haven't asked what he plans to do with them. Somehow, it doesn't seem like that's any of my business.

I love Russel, I really do. We're an unlikely pair, even more so if you were to know my entire history. Let's just say that I didn't grow up churning butter and wearing head coverings in public (or anywhere at all for that matter).

You do strange things for love.

I'm not who you think I am, but maybe, just maybe, with a lot of luck and some of those miracles Russel preaches about at church on Sunday mornings, we'll manage to be all right.

I do believe in miracles.

I'm just not sure after everything I've done that God has any left in store for me.

CHAPTER 2

"HOW ARE YOU DOING?" Russel asks, turning around in his seat to stare at me.

I give him a smile. "A little tired," I tell him. I discovered early that Russel likes it when I act a little mopey, a little weak. Heaven knows his departed wife must have been exhausted every minute of the day. I get drained just thinking about all of Sarah's barn chores and homeschool activities. Something else I should have mentioned earlier. Gospel Kingdom, where my husband preaches, acts as if any child who sets foot in a public school setting will be worshipping Satan by the time they reach their first recess.

There are some things I'm totally fine with. If Russel refuses to get his kids their shots, that's on him, not me. He's their father, after all. I'm just the substitute. But seriously, teaching four kids I barely know everything they need for their K-12 education? Just because their dad is afraid of the big bad world corrupting his sweet, impressionable children?

In the back of my mind, I know that if we're going to make this picture-perfect family thing work, I'll have to change my mentality. I'm going to have to stop using words like *his* and *mine* and let everything morph into that nebulous gray area called *ours.*

Until then, we're definitely what would qualify as a work in progress.

I hope Russel is as patient now that we're married as he was when we were courting.

"Miss Anastasia?" Betsy sits in front of me, her blond braids streaming over her shoulders. I may not know how to milk a cow, churn butter, or lead a church ladies' luncheon, but I do a wicked French braid. Actually, six of them, seeing as how I now have three stepdaughters who want nothing more than to twin pigtail braids each and every morning.

It's the one thing I do for them that makes me feel like their mom. That makes me believe this blended family thing might just work.

I do believe in miracles. But I've learned from experience not to hold my breath.

"Miss Anastasia?" Betsy asks again, and I wonder if I'm meant to correct her or if her father will take the lead.

"Betsy," Russel says. His voice is gentle but firm. That sums up my new husband in a nutshell.

Gentle but firm.

Don't tell him so, but I think that's what made me fall in love with him to begin with. I wasn't looking for romance, I hope you understand. I can't tell him that, though, or he'll think I was using him. Manipulating him to get what I wanted. That's not how it happened.

Not really.

I love him. That part isn't a lie. But I'm not who he thinks I am.

My husband is lecturing his nine-year-old daughter — *our* nine-year-old daughter — about family, respect, and titles. She gives me an apologetic smile and starts over. "Mom?"

"Yes, Betsy?" I hope my smile doesn't look as uncomfortable as hers. I'm trying. God knows how hard I'm trying.

"Can I have my fruit salad now, or should I wait?"

Betsy is Russel's oldest, and she looks just like her father. Long face. High cheek bones. Shave off Russel's beard and cut off Betsy's braids, and they'd be indistinguishable.

Almost.

Russel looks pleased that his daughter has caught on to the new routine. That she's calling me Mom and asking me about domestic matters like the proper time to eat. I packed the snacks all by myself, I'm pleased to tell you. Woke up with Russel right at five this morning. While he went out to tend to the animals, there I was in his kitchen, cutting up fruit so his children wouldn't have to stoop so low as to purchase commercial airport food.

I check the time, my smile still glued to my face. "Let's take off," I tell Betsy, "and when the captain turns off the seatbelt light, I'll pull out the fruit. Does that sound okay?"

Russel gives a slight frown at this last part. I forgot I'm not supposed to ask the children about their own preferences and desires. I'm the mother figure after all. It's up to me to tell them when it's time to eat. But I notice the hint of a genuine smile flick across Betsy's face, and I figure I'm doing all right for now.

When Russel proposed to me, he made his high view of marriage absolutely clear. Come hell or high water, nothing but death itself would have the power to dissolve our most holy of unions.

That was all right with me. Sure, I was nervous. What bride isn't? I may be young, but I'm not an idiot. I didn't walk into this marriage blindly and assume that love itself would fuel our lifetime of matrimonial bliss. Come on. The man's been a widower for less than half a year. Don't you think I'm expecting there to be some so-called bumps in the road?

Russel also made it clear on the afternoon of his proposal that he by no means expects to stop having children. He went on to quote some Bible passage about quivers and arrows, old-fashioned stuff I didn't understand and didn't have the heart to ask about.

I'm not who he thinks I am, but I can't tell him the whole truth. Not yet. That's the problem with a courtship as fast as ours.

I hate to think that I'm using my husband. But I'm pretty sure that if you were to dig down deep, the offense runs in both directions. Would I ever advise someone to marry a widower whose wife has only been gone for six short months? Not a chance. I'm no psychologist, but I think it's pretty clear that Russel's using me too. Not in any nefarious kind of way, but in a very practical one. He needs a woman to look after the kids, to water the hens, wash the laundry, pass out bulletins at church. Pastors and farmers are similarly notorious for relying on their women to keep things running smoothly, and my husband happens to be both.

I know the road ahead of us is going to be difficult. I know there will be some shocks coming our way. Like when Russel realizes that my body's unable to give him any more arrows for his quiver, or however the metaphor works. I'm supposed to be far less initiated into the world of fertility and reproductive health than I am, so I can't tell Russel the truth.

Not yet.

I'm not who he thinks I am.

And yet I know he loves me. I see it in his eyes when he smiles approvingly at me before he turns around in his seat. Apparently, he's pleased with the way I've handled his daughter's mealtime question. I know he's looking forward to flying back to Michigan with me. To introducing me to his parents, to the infirm father and the rest of the family that was unable to make our wedding on such short notice. I know he's proud of me. I've only seen one picture of his first wife, and she looks just as tired as you'd expect a homeschooling, homesteading mom of four to be. She isn't ugly. Far from it. But you can tell farm life and the demands of being married to a pastor had drained away a decent amount of her youthful vitality.

Is this why Russel chose me? Am I simply the ten-year newer model? Is that why we're doing this, pretending to play house together? I worry about that sometimes. Worry that in ten years I'll look and act as tired and as drained as good old Sarah must have been before she reached her chapter's end.

But I can't think about ten years in the future right now.

"Mom?" Annie asks from her seat beside me. She's the youngest of Russel's kids and has had the easiest time adjusting to my introduction into their family.

"Yes, sweetie?" I ask, feeling like I'm an understudy reciting someone else's lines.

"Can you read me a book?"

I let out my breath. Yes. That much I can do, at least. When I'm done raising Russel's kids, I really should find myself a job as an audiobook narrator for all the practice I've had.

I grab my bag. Before Russel, whenever I went traveling, I brought one small carry-on suitcase for clothes and essentials. Now, I feel like I've packed for an army just so our kids can look clean and stay entertained on this three-day excursion to meet his folks in Michigan.

The good news is that while I'm reading to Russel's kids, I can turn my mind off. Most of these books I've already memorized.

Part of Russel's parenting philosophy involves a general shunning of the materialistic world. I can't say I love the idea that even books for children are lumped into the category of extemporaneous expenses. Thankfully, I bought the children books as presents when their father and I were still dating. Since technically they were purchased with my money and not ours, Russel hasn't complained.

Besides, the older kids have plenty of books for their assigned reading. There's no reason the younger two shouldn't get the same gift simply because they're not officially school aged yet. I'm about to remind Betsy that she and her sister have homework to finish, but then I realize they've both already pulled out their books.

Good girls.

Now if I can only teach them to act like kids every so often, I'll feel like I've really started to make some progress.

"Mom?" Annie asks, tugging at my sleeve. It's a gesture that would make her father frown, but I don't mind. Aren't mothers supposed to be tugged on every now and then?

"Give me just a second," I tell her. "I've got to find the books I packed." I'm digging through my carry-on. So far I've found enough food to last our family at least two days, extra water (the only expense Russel agreed to purchase at the airport itself), and all the kids' toiletries, including their multivitamins and an entire case of essential oils (which I still don't know how to use properly). I even have Betsy's pajamas, which she forgot to pack into her own bag and which I tossed into mine at the very last minute while Russel was waiting in the driveway, eager to head toward the airport this morning.

"Andrew has the books in his backpack," Annie reminds me.

Right. I'd entirely forgotten. Back when we were getting ready to load the car, I made an exaggerated grunting noise when I picked up my carry-on. Really, I was just trying to get at least one of the kids to crack a smile, but Russel took me seriously and told Andrew to put some of the items in his bag to lighten my load.

Nothing like getting rescued by a five-year-old boy.

"Andrew?" I ask in as kind of a voice as I can. "May I have your backpack, please, so I can pick out some books to read to your sister?"

I'm expecting a scowl, an unkind word, an askew glance, but Andrew just shrugs then grabs his bag from beneath the seat in front of him.

Good boy, I want to tell him, although it sounds more like something you'd say when you're training a puppy. Instead, I just smile and thank him. It's a little ridiculous the degree of relief I'm feeling that I didn't have to get into a fight with my stepson or delve into a lecture on the importance of parental respect.

Trust me, kid, I get it, I want to tell him sometimes. It's not like going from single to married with four kids is a simple transition. But I'm supposed to be more mature than he is, and I'm certainly not allowed the luxury of throwing a tantrum. Instead, I open up the book, take a breath, and start to read.

To onlookers, we're the picture-perfect family. A little stoic, perhaps. I'm sure I look strange in this head covering. People stare at me when I'm out with my family in public, but I don't care what they think.

If they knew the whole truth of who I was, what I've been through, what I've done in the name of survival, their entire opinion of who I am would change in an instant.

I'm not who they think I am. But for right now, I'm doing my best to pretend.

CHAPTER 3

I'M READING ANNIE THE same Dr. Seuss book she's heard five thousand times before. Whenever I pull it out, part of me expects Russel to tell me that he'd prefer it if our kids stuck to children's Bibles or stories with strong moral instruction. Thankfully, he hasn't taken my Seuss books away from us yet. Maybe he remembers they're the first gift I ever purchased for his kids.

Maybe my new husband has a hint of appreciation for the sentimental left in him after all.

I like to do the voices while I read, which is guaranteed to get Annie off on a giggle spree. My end goal is to hear Andrew laugh. One of these days, I know it's going to happen. I already told you I believe in miracles, right?

I've performed these books so many times I let my mind wander off. Back to the first few weeks of my courtship with Gospel Kingdom's recently widowed pastor.

I was new to town. New to a lot of things, truth be told. I'd put on weight, partly due to stress, partly due to the fact that I was still terrified of being recognized. With this head covering, people don't stop me anymore. Don't ask me why I look so familiar.

Don't look at me with a mix of both pity and fear when they realize who I truly am.

I wasn't an obvious candidate for the secretary opening at Gospel Kingdom. I responded to an ad in the paper and showed up to my interview wearing a gray pants suit. That was strike number one.

"Is this a Mennonite church?" I asked Russel when I saw the photo in his office of his congregants posing in front of the spotless, white steeple.

He gave a little chuckle, which led me to believe that this man was always that easy to laugh. "No, not Mennonite, although you certainly wouldn't be the first to jump to that sort of conclusion."

I apologized for wearing trousers, for not having my head covering. I acted as if I had a closet full of floor-length skirts and color-coordinated hair kerchiefs to match, but Russel told me not to worry.

"It's an old-fashioned dress code," he explained, "but we're a family here, and we like our traditional ways." Somehow he managed to speak these words, to sum up the entire personality of his church in a single word — *traditional* — and yet did so without making me feel at all inferior or ashamed of my more contemporary appearance.

"Can you tell me about your spiritual journey?" Russel asked. It wouldn't have boded well for my prospects at landing a job if I were to tell him that honestly, I thought about spirituality as much as I thought about garden slugs or tennis-ball-sized hail. So I offered some sort of noncommittal response like, "Oh, well, I grew up going to church pretty regularly, then kind of fell away ... Still love God, just haven't been connected to an actual congregation for a while."

Before I knew it, Russel had opened up his Bible, set it on the table between us, and was explaining to me truths about Jesus I'd never heard before. Answering questions about the Lord that I never even realized I was wondering.

"Do you want to ask Jesus to forgive your sins? Are you ready to make him Lord of your life?" he prompted.

I told him yes, but it wasn't just to land the job. And it wasn't that strange magnetic force I felt when we were talking together. I think those things may have played a part, but there was more to it than that.

Far more to it.

I've always believed in God. Even during those two years I've never told my husband about, when it seemed like everything had been taken away from me, I had a sense that God was there. That he was with me. That he would somehow see me through the hell on earth where I was trapped.

But when Russel talked about Jesus, I realized this man knew the Lord far more deeply than I ever dreamed possible. So I told him yes, I wanted what he had. Then I prayed with him. Recited this little prayer about getting God to forgive my sins, saving me from hell. Russel looked pleased with me when I was done, and that's when I knew that if I got this job as his secretary, I'd keep on trying to find ways to make him smile at me like that.

No matter what it took.

No matter what I had to give up.

I started working at the church office the very next day. In addition to helping Russel print bulletins, schedule appointments, pay the bills, I sat at his feet (in the metaphorical sense at least), learning daily from him as he led our little office "staff" (consisting only of him and me) in morning Bible study, in closing prayers at the end of the day.

I wasn't deliberately keeping my past from him. But things moved so quickly from there. I was excited about my newfound faith, and it was impossible to distinguish my spiritual awakening with the emotional connection I felt with Russel whenever the two of us were together.

We fell in love. Before we'd even known each other a full season, he introduced me to his children, proposed courtship, then announced our engagement to the entire congregation.

And now here I am. Stepmother of four, struggling to work my way into this family that managed to get along swimmingly on their own before I came around. A grateful bride, thankful for the sense of protection and security that comes from belonging to Russel and his family and his church, even if they are a little strict by worldly standards.

I'm happy to be with Russel. I'm happy to call his children my own. Once we return from meeting his side of the family, Russel wants me to adopt the kids. I'm not one to argue. I'll never be able to bear Russel the quiver full of offspring his heart is set on. The least I can do is formalize my relationship to the four he already has.

I'm not who he thinks I am.

But maybe, with a little luck, a lot of prayer, and some very powerful miracles, things will work out all right in the end.

Maybe, just maybe, I'll look back on these past few months and realize how blessed I really am.

And if Russel finds out the truth ... Well, isn't he the one who said that we're united now? That nothing but death will ever part us?

I keep waiting for the day when I'll wake up and actually feel like Anastasia Strickland, wife of Gospel Kingdom's pastor. When I can look at Russel's kids and not feel the pangs of guilt at my deception when they call me Mom.

And if that day never comes, I just have to remind myself it at least beats where I came from.

The Lord works in mysterious ways. Maybe, just maybe, he brought me to Russel and his kind, albeit quirky little church in order to offer me the stability and protection I needed so many years ago, those days I'm trying so hard to forget.

Is it possible that Russel felt like a safe option for me because of the way he and the others at his church avoid technology as much as they do? I admit, the fact that Russel wouldn't ever think to google my name or stumble across news articles from ten years ago was an added bonus when we started dating.

I'm not who my husband thinks I am. But maybe, just maybe, if I pray hard enough and try hard enough, God will help me turn into the person he wants me to be.

And then everything from the past can stay there in the past. Totally secret.

Totally forgotten.

Just the way it should be.

Just the way it needs to be.

CHAPTER 4

I'M NOT WHO HE thinks I am, but no matter how hard I cry, how fiercely or angrily I protest, he doesn't listen to me. Doesn't believe me.

"Jennifer," he says, "you know how angry I get when you're like this."

"My name isn't Jennifer." It doesn't matter if I scream it at him, if I curse and swear, if I break down into tears and beg him to believe me.

"Come on, Jennifer," he says. "Stop pretending like you don't know your own dad and come here."

I hate him. I hate him. My loathing is the only source of willpower it takes to stay alive down here, trapped in this basement. If I were any weaker, I know I would have died by now.

My survival depends on one thing and one thing only. The hope that one day he'll forget to bind me up the right way. That I'll find some kind of weapon in this horrid cell of his.

And then I'll kill him, screaming in his face as his breath deserts him for the very last time, "My name isn't Jennifer!"

"Mom?"

I jerk myself to attention. "What?"

It's Annie, looking at me with concern in her eyes. Even Andrew has stopped ignoring me in order to gawk a little. Have I done it again? Did I blip out?

I can't let things like this keep happening. Not when the kids are around.

"Mom?"

"What?" I ask, doing my best to shake off this fear, this pulse-quickening panic.

"You stopped reading." Annie points to the book. I don't even remember pulling this one out of Andrew's backpack. The last thing I remember was Dr. Seuss and then ...

And then ...

It must have been Henry. He's been dead these past ten years, and yet he still lives on in my head.

If I had known it would turn out like this ...

No. I can't focus on him. Have to keep reading to the kids. I shouldn't have picked such a familiar book. Too easy for my brain to turn off. To stop paying attention to what's going on right now.

Henry.

Almost nobody survives two full years of captivity. I'm an anomaly, a strange statistic. My story gives hope to parents whose children disappeared decades ago.

If that little Reynolds girl can come back from her ordeal, there's hope for my baby too.

What they don't know, what the news reporters and the family liaisons and the sensationalized docudramas don't tell you is that survival in cases like this can be seen as God's cruelest curse. How many times did I beg Henry to simply kill me? To get it done and over with quickly. How many times did I taunt him, trying my hardest to provoke him to enough rage that he'd finally end it all?

Except he never did. I was too important to him. Too much like his long-lost daughter. Jennifer. The dead child I was meant to replace.

After my escape, I went through a phase where I hated her. Hated Jennifer. She would have been twice my age, but in her father's sick mind she was still the age she was when she was murdered.

Nobody back then was convicted of her death.

And yet I'm the one who paid for it.

Henry and I both paid for it.

"Mom, you read that page already." Andrew's voice is whiny, and I'm too distracted by these daydreams to feel excited about the fact that he's voluntarily called me Mom without having to be reminded. It should be good news. A great step forward in our quest for familial unity.

And yet all I can think about is that we haven't even left the runway yet. A few stray passengers are still boarding, and the kids and I have hours of travel ahead of us. Russel has the easy job. He'll fall asleep with his Bible while the two older girls read quietly in their seats. And here I am with a squirrely little preschooler who can't go two minutes without asking me a dozen questions and her five-year-old brother who wants nothing more than to make my life miserable enough that I abandon his father and leave him alone to miss his mom in uninterrupted solitude.

I feel sorry for Andrew. I really do. My parents split up shortly after I escaped Henry's basement. Dad didn't remarry until a few years ago, and even now it's strange to picture him with someone else.

I need to stop thinking about my past. Need to focus on what those books about trauma say. I survived because I'm tough. I'm a fighter. I'm a warrior. I did what I had to do to survive, and nobody has the power to victimize me ever again.

I think I believe it. I want to believe it.

But sometimes I still wonder.

I think Russel would understand if I told him the first part. If I told him that the reason I don't talk about my high school years is because half of them were spent chained in a crazy man's basement, and after that I never resumed my public education. I could tell him about how Henry dressed me up in his daughter Jennifer's clothes, fashions that hadn't been in style in nearly two decades. Nobody would understand unless they've lived through that kind of torment, and like I said before, I'm the statistical anomaly.

My husband wouldn't understand, but that doesn't mean he wouldn't care. He would listen with those kind, compassionate eyes. It's his empathy that makes him such a good pastor. He's the only reason a church as stuck in its ways and traditional as ours can still flourish and prosper. Gospel Kingdom would only work if the members absolutely love and respect their leader. Which they do.

And with good reason.

Russel would try to empathize with the trauma I've gone through. He's as patient as a saint with me already, and that's without knowing anything I've endured.

I should tell him. I would tell him. Except that would lead to other questions. Like how I got myself out of Henry's basement. How I survived when so many others like me didn't.

And then he'd realize I've lied to him about other things, too. Like how excited I am to start a family with him. He still thinks I'm going to be able to bear him a quiver full of children. How long will I be able to pretend like this before he grows suspicious?

I should never have misled my husband. I should never have agreed to marry him so quickly. It all happened so fast I can hardly remember what life was like before we met. It was as if I woke up single, and in twelve hours I was fumbling around through the world's most painfully awkward wedding night. Now there are kids calling me Mom, kids I'm responsible to clothe and feed and educate. What do I know about homeschooling? Russel's showed me the curriculum Sarah used with the older kids, but I'm serious that you need an advanced degree just to understand the teacher's manual.

It's a good thing I have God on my side now. I'm not convinced the Almighty has forgiven me for lying to my husband, but I hope that he won't take it out on the children. It is not their fault. And Russel's devoted his life to preaching to others. He does it so well too. Just look how he ended up converting me.

I've risen to greater challenges than this. Heaven knows that's true even if my husband doesn't. The way I figure, if God wants to develop my character by throwing me into a scenario where I've adopted four kids who aren't my own and agreed to homeschool them and raise them up in a tech-free, sugar-free, wordly-influence-free environment, well, it won't be the hardest thing I've ever gone through.

Not by a long shot.

I survived two years in Henry's basement.

I survived two years calling him *Daddy*, pretending to be his murdered daughter, wearing clothes that were two decades too old.

I survived the beatings, the assaults, all of it.

More than that. I escaped.

I escaped because I'm tough. I'm a fighter. I'm a warrior. I did what I had to do to survive, and nobody has the power to victimize me again.

I repeat the words to myself. If I can handle myself with a monster like Henry, I'm not going to let a somewhat uppity church and a houseful of kids who aren't sure how they feel about me ruin my chances at happiness.

When I met Russel, I was drawn to his compassion, to his conviction, to the safety and security I felt in his presence. But that's not why I married him. I married him because I love him. And if it's going to take work to make this happily-ever-after thing work, if it means sitting on this airplane for hours with his kids and doing my best to entertain them and keep them quiet and calm so their father can sleep, I can deal with that.

God knows I've fought my way out of worse.

CHAPTER 5

THERE'S SOME KIND OF delay on the runway. Could be the weather. I hear there's snowstorms all over the Midwest right now. Just perfect for flying into Detroit, right? I stop reading long enough to check the time.

Russel turns around in his seat. "Are you all right?" he asks. I'm not sure what prompted him to check up on me like this. Did he hear me stop reading and wonder what was going on? Did he sense the dark thoughts I've been having?

It's like this sometimes. I can go weeks hardly thinking about Henry at all. In fact, until I started having panic attacks a couple years ago, I thought I was over my past entirely.

Shows how naïve I was.

I smile at my husband, worried that his compassionate eyes will see straight through me. That he'll know what I'm keeping from him, the truth about what I did in order to become the survivor I am.

"I'm all right," I answer, "just tired."

That seems to be all he needs to hear. He reaches out for my hand. The gesture is surprisingly gentle. He's usually not one for public displays of affection. I'm glad to see him looking happy and content. I hope this vacation does him good. He's been under a lot of stress. I feel bad, like it's my fault. Like a good wife would anticipate her husband's needs well enough in advance to keep his life running smoothly.

Was Sarah that kind of wife? I wonder. Was she the kind who always had a home-cooked meal ready for him at exactly the same time every evening? Who tucked their children into bed after an elaborate routine that was full of love and attention and care?

Russel doesn't talk about his first wife. Doesn't tell me what it was like as Sarah was dying, how the children reacted to the news of her passing. I don't bring it up. I'm afraid that if I did, I'd see that sadness in his eyes. A sadness that I can't take away no matter how hard I might try to fill the hole in Russel's heart.

The captain makes an announcement. We'll be on our way soon. It's about time. I'd be lying if I said I wasn't nervous about meeting Russel's family, but I also have no desire to sit here in a grounded airplane for the rest of my life. I've never flown with kids before. Wonder what will happen when Andrew needs to use the bathroom. Will he want me to take him or his father? Do I have to go in with him, or do I just wait outside the door?

Again I picture Sarah. Tired, haggered Sarah, aged beyond her years. Did she like wearing her headcoverings? Did she mind the way her long skirts always got bunched up around her ankles? Maybe she grew up that way, so she never knew any differently. I don't even know where she was from or if her mom or dad are still alive. If the kids have grandparents from that side of the family, is it now my job to make sure they stay connected?

There are so many things for me to think about, so many plans I need to make. Russel and I are basically still on our honeymoon, but after this trip to Detroit, it's the start of normal life. There are so many things I need to figure out. How to schedule our homeschool days so that we have some semblance of order. What to do with the younger kids while I'm working with the older ones on their lessons. I haven't mentioned this to Russel yet, but math was never my strong suit. Before too long, Betsy's going to have to ask somebody else for help.

I take a deep breath. Remind myself that nobody's doing any math lessons today. We're all fine. We're here, we're healthy, we're safe.

Safe ...

I sense the change in the cabin before I see anything out of the ordinary. A tension. A kind of electric charge. It would be easy enough to dismiss if I weren't already on edge.

I look around, hunting for the source of my unease. Something's wrong. Something happened ...

Then I see him.

CHAPTER 6

THEY LOOK SO MUCH alike that for a second I forget Henry is dead. I suck in my breath, repeating the truth to myself like a soothing mantra.

Henry Harris is dead, which means the man who just stepped onto this plane isn't my captor.

He can't be.

But he looks so much like him, from his unshaven face to his beer belly to that gaudy Hawaiian shirt.

Henry is dead, I tell myself. *Dead.* He can't hurt me anymore.

He can't reach me at all.

This man isn't Henry.

And then I see the girl traveling with him. The fear that looks so familiar behind her haunted eyes.

She doesn't belong with him.

I stare at the other passengers. Don't they see? Isn't someone going to do something? The flight attendants are cheerily helping people load the overhead bins and reminding folks to buckle up. Travelers are scrolling on their phones or reading books or shutting their eyes for a snooze.

Nobody else sees.

Nobody knows.

You're being paranoid, Anastasia, I tell myself. *Paranoid. That's all.*

Just because I happened to be abducted as a teen, just because a man named Henry who always wore Hawaiian shirts kept me locked up in his basement for two years so I could pretend to be his daughter — none of this means the girl I'm staring at is going through anything remotely similar.

She's wearing shorts and a T-shirt, which make her look even more out of place on this winter flight. Her eyes are puffy, outlined in dark rings. Maybe she's tired from a full day of travel. Or mad because her dad told her she had to break up with some deadbeat boyfriend. Or worried about her grandma who's lying on her deathbed in Detroit, praying that her family gets to see her one last time.

That's what I tell myself. That's what I have to believe if I'm not going to drive myself crazy.

"Miss Anastasia?"

"What is it?" I don't have the energy to remind Andrew to call me Mom. I haven't stopped staring at the girl. Begging God to give me some kind of sign to prove to me that she's okay.

"You stopped reading again," he complains.

"My throat's sore," I tell him. "I'm going to take a break."

My husband turns in his seat. Gives me one of his quiet smiles that always breaks my heart. Always makes me certain he's comparing me to her. Sometimes I want to yell in his face that I'm not his first wife and never will be, but what good would that accomplish?

Maybe we rushed into things too fast. Maybe Russel needed more time to grieve Sarah's death. More time to get himself ready for a new relationship. Looking back at how quickly our courtship progressed, I can't even speculate if he or I was the one who came across as the most desperate.

"You all right?" he asks me. I'm certain he's heard me being short with his son. Certain he's wondering why I can't be more soft-spoken, more tender-hearted, more maternal.

Why I can't be more like her.

I force a smile. "I'm good," I announce with such conviction the whole plane must believe me. "It's just a little loud in here. Makes it hard to read. My voice doesn't carry ..." I let the words die on my lips. I'm staring again. Not at my husband. Not at this instant family I've somehow managed to make for myself.

But at her. This girl. She can't be more than fourteen or fifteen. Still a baby, really. Trusting of others because she hasn't learned yet how terrible life can be, how cruel the world can turn.

Happy because she doesn't know about Henry's basement. She hasn't been there yet. He hasn't taken her.

But he will.

My throat seizes shut. For a second, I picture myself jumping out of my seat and demanding to be let off this plane. Running off, getting lost in the crowded airport. I'll write Russel an apology in a few weeks, once I've decided where I'm going to go, what I'm going to do. I'll apologize to the kids too. Tell them I'm so sorry, but I just can't be the kind of mommy they need.

But I don't. Instead, I sit here trembling in my seat. I'm buckled in, my family surrounding me. I have their snacks in my backpack, Betsy's pajamas thrown in too. There's nowhere for me to go. Nothing I can do except remember.

Remember the nightmare, the trauma, the terror. Remember everything I've tried so hard to run away from.

I've done a good job forgetting. At least, I thought I had. Thought I moved on.

When I didn't tell Russel about those two years in Henry's basement, it wasn't because I wanted to lie or mislead him. It was because in my foolishness, I actually believed I'd gotten over it. That my love for Russel and my newfound faith were enough to counteract my past, erase the trauma.

I felt so happy with Russel. So alive. I thought that meant I was finally healed ...

That I could finally forget.

Except now, I remember. I sit here, trapped in this seat, my hands gripping the arm rests, the flight attendants still bustling back and forth to get everything ready for takeoff, and I remember everything.

CHAPTER 7

HE SAYS HIS NAME is Henry Harris. "But you can call me Dad. Or Daddy. Whichever you prefer."

She tells him she wants to go home, and he lets out a soft chuckle. "This is your home, Jennifer."

She's already learned that she can't correct him. Can't tell him that her name is really Anastasia Reynolds, that she's never heard of Jennifer before and has no idea what happened to this poor daughter of his.

How long has she been here? It's hard to know because all the windows in this basement are boarded up. She's slept on and off, but has she been gone for hours or days? Could it be weeks?

At one point he knocked her unconscious. Her head hasn't felt quite right ever since. "You're lucky," he tells her after she wakes up. "It could have been a lot worse." He bandages a cut on the back of her head and says, his voice full of regret, "You remember what happened last time, don't you?"

She doesn't remember a last time because there never was a last time. Except she's smart enough not to tell Henry this. So instead she nods and lets him pet her blood-stained hair as he starts to cry and tell her how happy he is now that they're together again.

"You forgive me, don't you, Jennifer?" And she tells him that she does.

She learns to lie. As the basement grows colder and colder with the chill of winter, she begins to forget that there ever was a girl named Anastasia Reynolds. That there ever was a world outside of the cement prison, a world of snowflakes and ice skating and steaming hot chocolate fogging up her glasses while she takes dainty sips, careful not to burn her tongue.

She forgets that somewhere is a mother and a father desperate for her safe return, a mother and father who might even assume she's dead by now.

As long as they don't think she ran away ...

The cold that seeps into her soul becomes intolerable. She finds herself thankful for the nights when Henry can't sleep and brings down his blanket and joins her in the basement. Tells her stories about her childhood.

"Remember when Grandpa pitched you that softball and you broke the neighbor's window? He told you to go and apologize to the owners because he knew they couldn't be mad at a girl as cute and sweet as you. Remember that?"

And she tells him she does. Tells him so many times that every once in a while, she dreams about being that same little girl, standing on a doorstep she can recall in vivid detail, explaining to a tired-looking housewife that her grandpa was pitching and she accidentally broke their window.

Anastasia never played softball, but Jennifer did. Sometimes Henry even brings down the photo album and shows her pictures of her childhood. "That's your best friend, Shawna," he says. "She's living in Chicago now, married to some big-time businessman. I saw her dad at the hardware store the other day. Says they're expecting their third kid. Isn't that great?"

And Anastasia feels somehow happy for Shawna, this best friend she never knew, this grown woman whose life has no resemblance to her own, this mother of three.

There are times when she wants to cry for Henry, when she looks at this pitiable old man, so alone, so lost in the past.

And there are times when she hates him. Hates what he's done to her. She's grown so skinny, she can feel her hips stabbing the cold cement floor at night when she tries to sleep. She hates the smell of his body odor but knows that she's even more unkempt than he is.

Some days, she's certain she could kill him.

Other days, she falls asleep crying, her heart aching for this lonely old man.

There's murmuring on the plane. My breath returns to me in a rush. I haven't had a flashback this vivid since ... since ... well, since long before I met Russel. That's why I was so sure I was doing better. So sure it wouldn't matter if I told him or not.

I stare at the middle-aged passenger ahead of me. He's in the aisle fidgeting with an overhead bag, and when he raises his arms his hairy stomach pokes out from beneath his Hawaiian shirt. I wonder for a minute how I could have ever confused him with Henry.

Henry wasn't that heavy for one thing. Not that hairy either. And this passenger is too young.

Besides, I remind myself, Henry is dead.

Henry is dead, so I have no reason to keep on thinking about him. No reason at all.

The children are getting restless. The flight attendant is shutting the last of the overhead compartments. That means we'll be taking off soon. Once we're in the air, I think I'll finally be able to relax.

I'm flying to Detroit. I'm going to meet my in-laws, going to spend a nice, relaxing vacation with them. The kids can't wait to see their grandma and grandpa, and Russel tells me that I'm going to get along just great with his sister. Life is good. I have everything I ever wanted, a husband who loves me, a strong and healthy family, the freedom to travel around and take time off to spend with relatives.

I'm safe. I'm healthy. And I can't let these scars from my past bubble to the surface and threaten everything I've got going for me right now.

CHAPTER 8

"I DON'T WANT TO read that one," Annie says.

"Me either," her brother grumbles.

I put the Grover book away and ask Andrew which one he'd like to choose.

He crosses his arms. "Something new," he says with a pout. "We've read all these before."

"Why don't you tell me a story?" I suggest, wondering if the impatience I'm feeling comes through my voice in spite of how hard I'm working to mask it.

"I don't know any stories," Andrew complains.

I'm at a loss. "Maybe your sister does," I finally suggest.

It's the only nudge little Annie needs, and in a second she's rattling off a tale of princesses and dragons in castles. Even with as sheltered as her father has kept her from contemporary movies and worldly influences, she sounds like any other child with the blessed gift of a fantastic imagination.

I fight my mind's urge to wander back, to take me again to Henry's basement. It's been years since I escaped. There's no way I'm going back. Never again. I'd sooner die.

"And then he tells Jennifer she's going to be his daughter forever and ever and ever."

My eyes widen. I feel the breath suck into my lungs as if a black hole has opened up in the space between my ribs. "What did you say?" I manage to stammer.

Annie gives me an annoyed look. She doesn't like to be interrupted.

"What did you say?" I repeat. I feel the blood emptying from my head, gushing to my extremities. For a minute, I have the terrible feeling that the man in the Hawaiian shirt is going to turn around in his seat and start laughing at me.

"I said that the princess and the prince lived happily ever after." Annie's voice is impatient, her lower lip protruding in an exaggerated pout.

"What did you say her name was?"

She's looking at me like I'm crazy. Am I? How can I know for sure?

"What was the princess's name?" I demand, leaning toward her.

"Jessie," Annie answers. "Weren't you listening?"

"I thought you said her name was Jennifer," I mumble. Suddenly exhausted, I slump back into my seat.

"It's *Jessie*," Annie states with all the authority of a four-year-old who's entirely sure of herself.

"And who was it that wanted to be her dad?"

"What?" Her eyes are wide, and now both Annie and her brother are staring at me as if my hair has just turned green.

"You said the bad guy told the princess she had to be his daughter for ever and ever."

Annie contorts her face. I can't quite gauge her emotion. Is it confusion? Disgust?

"That was the *prince*," she tells me with an exasperated huff. "The prince said, 'You'll be my wife for ever and ever.' Didn't you hear that part?"

"Sorry," I answer distractedly. I feel my throat constrict, sense my hands gripping the arm rests of my seat, feel the seatbelt prodding into my stomach. It's too tight, but I can't loosen it. I shut my eyes, and I'm back in the basement, a scared little girl whose only dream is to go home.

A victim who's rage and quest for vengeance is the only incentive she has left to stay alive.

CHAPTER 9

JENNIFER APPLIED HER ROLL-ON deodorant and frowned at the mirror. Her bangs had been hanging a little limp ever since she got home from school.

Nothing some extra hair spray couldn't solve.

Dad knocked on her door. He was in a hurry, like always, but she wasn't ready yet.

"Jennifer?" he called to her. "You done in there?"

"In a minute." She picked up her brush and pretended it was a microphone and she was on stage belting out the melody with Boyz II Men. She practiced a few dance moves in front of the mirror. Would this be the night Darren would ask her to dance?

She sprayed her bangs again, then spritzed more mousse onto the palm of her hand before scrunching up her curls in hopes of giving them a little extra bounce.

It had taken a lot of pleading to convince her dad to let her go out tonight. She could swear it sometimes felt like her dad's one goal in life was to keep her trapped as a prisoner in her own home. If he could handcuff her and keep her locked up in the basement, she sometimes wondered if he would.

Well, tonight was going to be different. It was her first school dance. Darren would be there. All of her friends. It was just this year that Lisa and some of the other popular girls had started paying attention to her. Tonight was her chance to prove she truly fit into their group. She'd been practicing her moves in front of the mirror, sneaking in snippets of that dance show on MTV every morning, studying the dancers until she knew the right way to move her body.

Darren was going to be so impressed. She hoped he'd ask her to slow dance with him. Especially if a Boyz II Men song came on. He knew she loved Boyz II Men.

Dad pounded on the door again. Jennifer applied one more layer of lipliner, gave herself a last once-over in the mirror, and stepped out of her room.

She felt like a princess about to attend her very first ball. No, that was too childish. She was like those dancers on MTV, the ones who always looked perfect and were always surrounded by admirers. This was her night. Her time to make a lasting impression, not only on Darren but on Lisa and all her friends and their entire freshman class.

This was Jennifer's time to shine.

CHAPTER 10

SHE GOT OUT OF the house without Dad grumbling much about her clothes. She'd already planned out each and every one of her arguments if he said her skirt was too short or her top was too tight, but he was surprisingly quiet when he drove her to the school.

"Drop me off here," she said a block away from the bus stop. Behind them, a car sped by.

"Let me off here," she repeated, more urgently when she started to fear her dad might actually drive her up to the school itself. What if Darren was here? What if he saw her getting dropped off? She had her hand on the door and was willing to roll out of the Chevy before it stopped, but Dad finally slowed down to let her out.

"Don't pick me up until 9:30," she told him, slamming the door shut before he could make any last arguments or change his mind about allowing her out tonight. It wasn't really her dad's fault he was like this. He'd been overly protective of her for years, ever since Mom died. Jennifer understood. It didn't make his behavior any more bearable, but at least she knew he meant well.

"Oh, my gosh, is that you, Jennifer?" She recognized Lisa's voice in an instant, her heart skipping a slight beat to have been noticed. "Look at your hair! It's so curly."

Jennifer beamed and joined the circle of Lisa's friends, who were making their way toward the school. When they stepped into the gym, the girls congealed into one massive, dancing throng in the middle of the crowd. Jennifer scrunched up her curls, hoping they'd keep their volume all night, hoping her deodorant would work, hoping this dance would be just as perfect as she imagined.

A familiar beat came over the speakers, and Lisa grabbed her by the wrist. "Come on!" she shouted. "Macarena!"

And in an instant, Jennifer forgot how worried she'd been about her hair, her deodorant, her dad. She forgot about how desperately she wanted her friends at school to like her, to include her, to treat her like one of them. She forgot everything except for the music. The beat washed over her worries, drowned out her fears. She knew this dance, even though she'd never done it with a group this large before. Everyone moved at the exact same time, following the exact same script, one living being whose parts moved together in perfect unity.

She had never felt so happy before. Never so alive before. Like she'd been made for this moment, to dance here to this song at this precise instant in time. Lisa, the most popular girl in the ninth-grade class, was on her left, and they were surrounded by the coolest, prettiest girls in school. There was only one thing that would make tonight even more perfect.

Jennifer was lightheaded when the song ended. A few boys groaned when a slow song came on. Jennifer held her breath. The DJ was playing Boyz II Men already? It was too soon. Darren wasn't here. At least she hadn't seen him yet ...

Shawna and Kylee, Lisa's two best friends, stared at Jennifer and began to giggle. They leaned over to whisper in one another's ears. What was going on?

And then she felt it. The tap on her shoulder. The electric spark zinging down her arm and throughout her entire body.

Darren.

"Wanna dance?"

It was impossible to remember the exact order of what happened next. Did he put his hands on her waist, or did she say yes to him first? Was she the one who took a step closer, or was that him?

"The thing about slow dancing is it's like you're giving him a five-minute hug." That's what someone had written in to *Teen* magazine for their article on your first school dance. And as it turned out, the author was exactly right.

"You like Boyz II Men, don't you?" Darren asked.

Jennifer could hardly hear his words over the pounding of her heart, the swell of the music. "Yeah," she answered, only then piecing the individual words he spoke to her together to try to form some kind of meaning out of them.

And he pulled her closer. Her feet were touching his. Each time he swayed, she swayed, and the music wrapped them up in a warm cloud of perfect bliss.

It was even more perfect than she'd been dreaming.

"Thanks," Darren said, grinning at her. Why had he stopped moving?

Jennifer's face flushed. She hadn't even heard the song end. She wasn't sure what was supposed to happen next. Was she supposed to say thank you back? Was she supposed to tell him you're welcome? Or maybe she was supposed to grab his hand right there and make sure everyone around them knew that she'd be dancing with Darren and Darren only for the rest of the night.

She was still trying to decide what to do, terrified of saying the wrong thing, thinking back desperately to that article in *Teen* to remember if they'd given any kind of rules. How do you end a slow dance?

"Thank you," she finally managed to stammer, but Darren had already disappeared.

Shawna and Kylee pounced on her an instant later. "Oh, my gosh. Did you seriously just dance with him? You two looked adorable. Are you going out?"

"When did Darren start to notice someone like you?" And then Lisa stepped up to their group, her face not so excited, her smile not so friendly. Shawna and Kylee backed away. Jennifer could feel their eyes on her. Wait, why were they upset? She hadn't done anything wrong, had she?

"Was that Darren you were dancing with?" Lisa's voice had a grainy edge to it that made Jennifer want to cover her ears.

She tried to laugh. "Yeah, crazy, right? He just came up and started dancing." Was that how it happened? Jennifer couldn't even remember. They were playing a rap song now, but it felt like her feet were still swaying slowly, like they were still pressed up against Darren's as their bodies moved together in perfect rhythm.

"Cute, Jennifer." Lisa flipped her hair over her shoulder. She'd straightened it for tonight. Jennifer suddenly felt juvenile and fake with her bouncy curls and took a step back.

"Cute," Lisa repeated.

Jennifer glanced at Shawna and Kylee to see if she could pick up any clues from them. What was going on? They circled around Lisa, giggling, and the trio turned their backs on Jennifer and walked away.

What was that all about?

The very next song was another slow one. Jennifer didn't recognize it. She glanced around the gym, wondering where Darren was, if he'd come up from behind and tap her on the shoulder again like before. Or maybe she'd see him first, smile, and walk straight up to him.

She inched her way toward the walls as couples took over the center of the gym. They looked so awkward together, some of them standing with a full foot of separation between them. Not like Jennifer and Darren, where she'd been pressed so close to him she was certain he could feel her heart thudding against his chest.

Where was he?

And then she saw. Lisa was talking to him, her hand on her hip, her body at an angle. Her two best friends stood on either side of her like guards, their arms crossed, their faces set in scowls. Darren looked helpless. He looked ... Wait, what was going on?

Lisa's posture relaxed. She slunk up toward him, putting her hands on his shoulders. On Darren's shoulders. That's not what was supposed to happen.

Shawna and Kylee grinned when his hands circled around Lisa's tiny waist. Her hair was so long now that it was straight it fell past the small of her back. Somebody bumped into Jennifer. She thought she heard someone asking her a question, but her mind refused to work. Her body refused to move.

What was Darren doing?

Shawna and Kylee turned and looked straight at her. Did they know she'd been here watching them this whole time?

Jennifer wanted to turn and run away, but she couldn't. Not when Darren was there, dancing with the most popular girl in ninth grade. Lisa with her straightened hair. Why had Jennifer decided to scrunch up her curls tonight, anyway? She looked ridiculous. Like a poodle in a dog show.

Shawna and Kylee grinned as they stepped up to her. "Hey, Jennifer, can we talk to you outside?" Shawna asked.

Jennifer still hadn't stopped staring at Darren. There were dozens, maybe hundreds of students in between them, but their eyes locked for a split second.

He gave a shy smile and an embarrassed shrug. Then he rested his cheek on Lisa's gorgeous, straightened hair as he swayed with her in perfect time to the music.

CHAPTER 11

"YEAH, SO HERE'S THE thing." Shawna jutted out her hip, just like Jennifer had seen Lisa do a dozen times a day. Next to her, standing just behind Shawna's shoulder, Kylee twirled her straight hair around her pointer finger and chewed loudly on her bubble gum.

"So, Darren's gonna ask Lisa out tonight," Shawna said, never once taking her eyes off Jennifer. "And, well, we know you like him."

"Yeah," Kylee inserted. "It's totally obvious."

Jennifer ignored the burning in her cheeks. She shouldn't feel embarrassed. She should feel angry. What was this? Some kind of interrogation in the girls' bathroom?

The toilet from one of the stalls flushed, and the three of them were silent as a gangly girl hurried out, not even bothering to wash her hands.

Shawna and Kylee followed her out with their eyes.

"Gross," Shawna hissed.

"I know," Kylee whispered back.

Jennifer was relieved to no longer be the center of their focus. Unfortunately, the reprieve lasted only a second or two.

"So, anyway," Shawna went on, "Lisa asked us to tell you to stop hanging all over Darren, if you know what we mean."

Kylee smacked her gum loudly and added a very emphatic, "Yeah."

"Because you're kind of embarrassing yourself the way you're all over him and everything."

Shawna and Kylee laughed. Jennifer took a step back.

"We don't want to hurt your feelings," Shawna concluded, "but Darren's already told Adam and Russ and Craig that he likes Lisa better. We just wanted you to know so you could stop acting all weird around him. No offense, but people are starting to talk about you."

Kylee gave a little snicker. Jennifer wished that she could conjure up a spell to make the floor open up and swallow her whole.

She didn't hear what Shawna and Kylee said next. She hardly even noticed them walk out and leave her in the bathroom alone. She reached into her pocket, counted out her change. Down the hill from the school was a pay phone. Maybe her dad was right. Maybe these dances were nothing but a big waste of time.

Whatever happened, she wasn't going back into that gym. Not with Darren acting like such a two-timing player, not with Lisa standing there with her arms draped all over him. It was either call her dad, walk home in the dark, or stay here in the bathroom.

Jennifer allowed herself the luxury of a short cry locked inside one of the stalls, then she counted her coins again and made her way down the hill.

It was time to call her dad.

CHAPTER 12

THE FLIGHT ATTENDANT MADE one more announcement, another apology for the few minutes' delay. We're not in the air yet. The door to the gate isn't even closed. I could get off now. Pretend like I need to use the bathroom in the front of the plane, then walk away and never look back ...

Except I know I can't do that. At least, I know I shouldn't do that. When I became a Christian, Russel assured me that God freed me from the sins of my past. That means I don't have to be terrified anymore, do I?

I wonder if Russel would have told me those same comforting platitudes if he knew who I really am.

I stare down the aisle, stare at that open door as if it's my last connection to safety. If those attendants shut that gate, if I just sit here and fly out to Detroit and meet my in-laws and accept all their profuse congratulations for my marriage to Russel, I'm stuck in this life, in this skirt, in this headscarf for good.

I'm not who any of them think I am, but if I allow myself to stay here on this plane, I'm going to wake up one day and realize there's no more me left at all.

I had a dream right after Russel proposed. I was her. Sarah, his first wife. I was wearing her clothes, cooking meals in her kitchen, homeschooling her kids, tending her garden. The children called me Mom. Even Russel called me by her name.

When I looked in the mirror, it wasn't my own face that I saw. It was hers. Pale and tired and wrapped up in that old-fashioned kerchief. I felt like I'd stepped out of an 1860s frontier TV show. Is this what I am? A mail-order bride escaping the dangers of the city to hedge my bets and do what I can to make life work out in the untamed wilderness?

I woke up crying. I hadn't done that in years. My pajamas were drenched in sweat, my cheeks soaked with tears. I don't want to be Sarah. I don't want to pretend. But if Russel knew the truth ...

I can't do that to him. Not after he's trusted me with his love, his kids. He's flying us out to Detroit to introduce me to his parents, for goodness sake. It's because of Russel I have a roof over my head. I have food to eat. It's because of Russel I know who Jesus is. When I ran away from my past, I wasn't looking for spiritual awakening, but God brought it to me anyway.

And he used this man who loves me, the man I pledged to love and honor and cherish until death do us part. Russel has already started the paperwork for me to adopt his kids. It will be my name on their new birth certificates, as if Sarah never even existed.

I'm sweating. I'm shaking. I'm biting my lip until I'm certain I'm about to draw blood.

"Are you ready to hear what happens next?" The tiny voice beside me has grown familiar but still sounds so strange. How can I pretend that this child is my own, that I can ever be a fraction of the mother that she needs?

"What happens next?" I ask, still keeping my eyes on the front of the plane. They haven't shut the doors yet. There's still time ...

"So the prince tells the princess that he wants to be married to her and live together for ever and ever in their great big castle, and he's going to keep her locked up in the basement for the rest of her life."

I snap my focus away from the front of the plane to stare at my stepdaughter. "He did what?" I demand. I hope her father hasn't overheard. If so, he'll think I'm the one filling her head with scary images of kidnappings and torture.

"I said he kept the wicked witch locked in the dungeon." Annie pauses with a pout before finally adding, "That's the end."

I feel the breath return to my lungs, repeat the words I just heard her say. *He kept the wicked witch locked in the dungeon.* I don't remember a wicked witch in the story, but I assume she got what was coming to her all along.

"That sounds like a very good ending," I say, but even I'm not convinced by my own words. I repeat them, more forcefully this time, and the captain gets on to tell the flight attendants to prepare the cabin for departure.

CHAPTER 13

DAD WAS IN A foul mood by the time he rolled in to pick Jennifer up at the bottom of the hill. If she'd known he'd be this late, she would have started walking instead of standing in the cold like an absolute idiot. What was her dad thinking, leaving her out alone like this?

She was glad when they got home. Glad when Dad sauntered into his room and slammed the door shut instead of yelling or telling her how dumb she was for wanting to go to a school dance in the first place.

The truth was humiliating to admit, but Dad had been right all along. Dances were stupid.

The *Teen* magazine she'd been studying all month lay open on her bed. She ripped out the pages about school dances and flung the shreds into the trash. Too bad their home didn't have a fireplace. She would have liked to watch the pieces burn.

Hot tears streamed down her cheeks by the time she saw her eighth-grade yearbook on her nightstand. She yanked the cover open. She hadn't realized it before, but Darren and Lisa's pictures were just one row apart from each other.

She ripped out the entire page, crumbling it to a ball, wishing there was something else she could do to give voice to her rage. She turned to the page where she knew she'd find Shawna's photograph when she heard something at her window. At first she ignored it. The wind had picked up. She couldn't let herself get interrupted by every little sound that made her jump. She had a job to do.

Out with Shawna's smiling face. Another page to crumble up. Maybe Jennifer should have drawn on the picture first. Given Shawna and Lisa and all of them the hideous makeovers they all deserved.

The humiliating conversation from the bathroom ran unchecked through Jennifer's mind.

You're kind of embarrassing yourself the way you're all over him and everything.

Jennifer gave a roar as she ripped Kylee's face out of the yearbook then paused to see if her dad had overheard. Most likely, he'd already fallen asleep, but she didn't want to wake him up with her yelling.

She strained her ears, fearing the sound of her father's door opening down the hallway. Then she heard it again. A tapping outside her window. Either the wind had really picked up or ...

She froze when she saw the flashlight beaming in through the glass. What was going on?

Another rapping. Was it Darren? He knew where she lived, didn't he? They rode the bus together through all of middle school. Even though she thought she'd been totally invisible to him at the time, he could find a way to remember that much, right?

She wiped the tears from her face then yanked up the blinds. It felt just like in the TV shows. Darren at her window, come to apologize.

Except it wasn't Darren.

"Shawna?" Jennifer couldn't remember the last time she'd talked to Shawna without Kylee in arm's reach. It felt strange to see her alone.

"I came to apologize," Shawna said, smoothing out her hair. "I didn't see you at the dance and thought you might be upset. There's a party going on at Kylee's house. I wanted to know if you'd come with me." She paused and lowered her eyes. "I'm really sorry about what we said to you. You know we didn't mean it. Wanna come?"

Jennifer glanced at the clock on her desk then at her closed door. If her dad found her sneaking out like this, he'd kill her. She thought about how silent and withdrawn he'd been since

Mom died. How he could spend weeks hardly leaving his room. How protective he'd gotten of Jennifer. How worried he'd be if he found her gone.

Jennifer was about to fake a sore throat when Shawna laid her hand against the screen. "Come on. Basically everybody's going to be there."

Jennifer held her breath. A real party? And Shawna came all this way to invite her?

Jennifer looked at the clock once more. Kylee's house wasn't too far away. She could go for just a short time and be right back. Her dad would never know.

Shawna gave a sly smile. "Darren'll be there," she added.

Jennifer turned back once more to find her shoes and told Shawna she was ready to go.

CHAPTER 14

DARREN HADN'T LEFT HER side all night. Jennifer had promised herself to leave Kylee's by eleven, but it was nearly midnight, and she was no closer to going home than she'd been when she first arrived.

"Isn't your dad going to get mad if he finds out you're here?" Darren asked. He had a dimple in his right cheek when he smiled.

And he'd been smiling the entire time he and Jennifer had been talking.

Jennifer didn't like the fact that everyone in her school seemed to know how protective her father was, so she gave a convincing laugh and shrugged. "What he doesn't know can't hurt him, right?"

Darren laughed too, a confident, easy laugh. Jennifer wasn't sure she'd ever been as relaxed and happy as he appeared to be right now as they sat side by side in Kylee's living room.

"I looked for you at the dance," he said in a low voice. Jennifer couldn't be certain, but she thought he leaned toward her an inch. His hand was so close to hers, a small twitch and their fingers would be touching.

"I, um, I had to leave early." She hated herself as soon as the words escaped her mouth. Why couldn't she have come up with something else to say? She cleared her throat and forced as massive a smile as she could manage. "What did you think, though? Did you have fun?"

"It was all right," he answered. "I would have had even more fun if you were there the whole time." He inched toward her again.

His leg brushed against hers, or maybe that was just part of his pants. Jennifer was afraid to breathe. What if he could sense how nervous she was? What if she had bad breath? Why hadn't she thought to add more deodorant before she sneaked out of the house and ran off with Shawna?

His pinky finger moved subtly. What was that? Was he trying to hold her hand? Sending her some kind of secret signal? She'd never held hands with a boy before. What if he took her hand now and it was all sweaty? What would he think?

She moved her hand and wiped her palm on the couch cushion. Darren looked down for a minute. Had she hurt his feelings? Did he think she was turning him down? She had to think of something to say, something fast.

"Dad hasn't really been the same since Mom died." And right there, Jennifer wished that she could disappear into the floor. It was as if the magic she'd been pretending to live under — here with Darren, him paying attention to her and only her — was a spell she'd just destroyed by bringing up such a depressing topic. She had to think fast, had to make it right, had to correct her mistake.

"Yeah, that really sucks," he replied before she could say anything else.

She couldn't breathe. Darren was staring into her eyes. He didn't laugh at her. Didn't get up and walk away. Didn't abandon her to go find Lisa, who was so much prettier and cooler than Jennifer could ever hope to be. He didn't do any of those things.

Jennifer gave a half-hearted chuckle. "Yeah. It kinda does."

And they both laughed and started talking about Mr. Green, the science teacher back in middle school who was rumored to smoke marijuana on a daily basis. Half the girls at their school secretly had a crush on him, and there was no end to making fun of the ones who made the biggest fools of themselves to win his attention.

It was past midnight now. Jennifer knew she'd have to go home soon. She hadn't meant to stay nearly this long to begin with. But she'd lost all sense of time with Darren by her side, their legs pressed up against each other, his pinky inching close to hers before pulling away so subtly she sometimes feared she imagined it.

Kylee's stereo had already started to reshuffle its playlist. Only a few kids were left. Kylee wanted them all to come outside so she could show off the new hot tub in the back yard, and for a fragment of an eternity, Jennifer and Darren were in the living room completely alone.

He'd been telling her about what it was like spending summers with his dad when everything stopped. The din of the crowd. The song on the CD player. The pulse of Jennifer's heart.

Their eyes locked. She couldn't have looked away from him if her life depended on it.

And then his hand was on hers. Not just touching and slipping away. He was grasping her hand now, and all of a sudden, she didn't care how sweaty her palms were.

And in that instant she knew. She knew that he would have never told Adam or Russ or Craig that Lisa was prettier. Would have never preferred to dance with Lisa. Jennifer thought back to the scene in the gym. He'd wanted to be with her. That's why he gave her that look, that shrug. Lisa had grabbed him, demanded a slow dance, and he was too kind-hearted to turn her down. Shawna and Kylee and Lisa were all jealous. That was all there was too it. Jealous of Jennifer because Darren liked her.

Darren chose her.

Darren wanted her.

She held her breath, certain that if she opened her mouth just a little her heart would leap up out of her throat. That's exactly when it happened. The tiniest of kisses, the kind that wouldn't have even counted in any other situation. He missed her lips but grazed the corner of her mouth. A quick motion, not quite a peck but definitely something. Something real.

He pulled away. She tried to think of something to say. Anything to say. What do you say at a time like this?

She realized her hand was still in his. He hadn't pulled it away.

She stood up. She had to think of something to do. Had to make it sound like this sort of thing happened to her every single day. Darren could never know that she'd never been kissed before, never held hands before, never been so in love in her entire life before. She just had to act cool. Natural.

Piece of cake.

"Wanna see the hot tub?" Darren's voice gave a little squeak. Jennifer stared at her feet.

"I should get home," she said. "It's … my dad … It's getting late …"

She raised her eyes once, let them flicker up to his face. Was he blushing?

She wiped her palm on the side of her pants. "Thank you," she stammered and hoped that he wouldn't ask what he was thanking her for, because she wouldn't have the slightest clue how to respond.

Darren cleared his throat. "Yeah, um, thanks to you too. I mean, have a good night. I mean, yeah."

Jennifer couldn't suppress her giggle. "Okay. Yeah. Bye."

He scratched at his neck. Shifted his weight from side to side. He called something out after her, but she was already racing toward the front door, her feet flying, her heart soaring into the stratosphere.

She was halfway down the driveway when a low, menacing voice made her stop in her tracks.

"So this is where you've been."

CHAPTER 15

"I HAVE TO GET off," I'm telling my husband. The moment the pilot told the attendants to shut the doors, I knew. Knew there was no way I could go through with this. No way I could continue on to Detroit.

"What's gotten into you?" Russel's voice is firm. I know I'm making a scene, but I can't help it. I haven't felt this trapped in years, not since I found myself in Henry's basement.

I was fifteen, even though he insisted I was a full year younger. I told him my name was Anastasia, I begged him to let me tell my parents I was okay, but he wouldn't listen to me.

"Your name is Jennifer," he said. "You're my sweet little pineapple. We're finally together, just like we were supposed to be."

I tried running away. After the first few weeks of compliance, he finally took the cuffs off. The very next morning I made it halfway up the basement steps before he stopped me, tackled me to the floor. I went days without food as my punishment.

I complain. Tell him how my stomach hurts.

"You've always been worried about being overweight," Henry tells me. "I'm doing you a favor."

I cry then, tell him I'm sorry about whatever it was that happened to his daughter, but I don't know anything about anyone named Jennifer and won't he please let me go.

It's talks like this that earn me starvation rations. More beatings. Endless nights chained up in the basement, an animal in a cage. An animal he insists on calling Jennifer, his daughter.

The weeks wear on. The cold seeps into my bones. I'm ashamed to admit it. Maybe I should have been stronger. I go along with his games. I call him Daddy like he wants. Every time he begs for my forgiveness, I give it to him, even though I have no idea what he's sorry for.

"They came every day, questioning me," Henry says. His voice is so full of sadness I want to cry for him, for his poor little girl, whoever she was, for his loss.

I don't ask him what happened to Jennifer. I'm not sure I want to know.

"Once your mother died, I thought I couldn't go on," he says one night. He's recently cracked one of my ribs, and now he's rubbing some kind of salve on my skin. It stings, but the touch is gentle. His voice is kind but filled with heaviness.

"I begged God to put me out of my misery," he admits. "I didn't want to live anymore, not without her. But I had you. You're the one who kept me going. You're the one who kept me alive." There's a hint of pride in his voice, and I'm so tired and so homesick and so confused that for a minute I wish that I really was this man's daughter. That I really could ease his sorrow, heal the wounds of his past just like he's healing the wounds in my side.

I forget how long I've been here now. Long enough that I don't think of my captor as Henry. I call him Dad, and at night when I dream, I'm his daughter.

Sometimes I ask him what day it is, but I can never keep his answers straight in my head. And sometimes I know he deliberately lies to me, like during that heat wave he told me it was still March. We celebrated my birthday in the fall. Jennifer's birthday, I should say, although these days it's hard for me to remember that there's a difference.

"It's the anniversary of your accident," he tells me one day. I don't like it when he talks about the accident, when he hints to the tragedy that befell his daughter.

When Henry first brought me here, when he kept apologizing to me and telling me I was Jennifer and he was so sickeningly sorry for what happened, I was convinced he'd killed her.

"They kept questioning me after it happened," Henry says to me nearly every day.

At first when he talked like this, I wondered why the police didn't do more than just question him, why they didn't put him in prison to rot for the rest of his miserable existence. I imagined he must have killed her. Strangled her maybe. Or beat her with a bat. But now, it's hard for me to picture him doing anything to Jennifer like that. He has a temper on him, but he acts so gentle. He's old now. Weak. Sometimes he stops in the middle of whatever he's doing to me simply because he's out of breath and needs to rest.

He likes me to soak his feet in salts. The skin on his heels is hardened and cracking all over, and he likes it when I massage them in warm water. When he's done, I pat them dry and rub in lotion.

"You're such a good daughter," he tells me, and my heart aches because somewhere I remember I have a father who used to say the same thing to me, but it's been so long I can hardly recall the sound of his voice. Sometimes I feel like I've been living in Henry's basement for decades, that my whole life has consisted of nothing but his rage, his pity, his love.

He's worn me down. I don't fight anymore. The truth is I don't want to. I'm too tired. When he gets angry, I remember that somewhere is a dead teenager who must have looked and acted at least somewhat like me for Henry to have gotten the two of us so confused. I remember that at some point Henry did something terrible to her, that she's gone, dead, and Henry is a broken man because of it.

I believe he's responsible for Jennifer's murder, and that means he could kill me too. The thought comes to me most often in the middle of the night, when I hear him snoring upstairs. If this man could murder his own daughter and get away with it, why in the world do I think myself safe?

Except what can I do? Everything's locked. Even though he hardly ever uses the handcuffs anymore, there's no place for me to run. Nothing I can do. When he's awake, when he's in one of those fits of rage that overcome him, I'm quite certain that he not only possesses the strength to kill me but the will as well. Sometimes I wonder why he doesn't just get it over with already. I wish for it at times. Intentionally egg him on. There's very little left for me to fight for. I don't want to hurt anymore. That's all I know. And life with Henry is a life of pain. Not the physical so much as the mental. The emotional. The sadness, the regret, the remorse, everything he feels about his daughter — all that grief and anguish — I take it upon myself, just like after I've finished rubbing lotion into his scaly heels my own hands are drenched in oil.

I think we've become inseparable, Henry and me. I think if I were to leave it would kill him. Is that why I stay? Or do I stay because of the chains, the locks, the fear? And in the end, if I'm destined to die here in this cement basement one way or the other, does it really matter?

At night, I dream about my mother. I dream that she's at home praying for my safety. I try to tell her I'm all right, that she can move on, that she doesn't have to worry anymore. I try to promise her that I'll fight harder next time, that one day I'll manage to escape and return to her, heal her broken heart. But she can never hear me, and when I wake up, I realize that I've forgotten the details of her face. I can't recall her smell, the sound of her making breakfast in the kitchen in the morning.

All I see is Henry. All I hear is Henry. He's become my life, just like I've become his.

I forget about the promises I make to my mother in my dreams. I forget about a world outside of this cold basement. And I massage my father's feet and lotion his dry skin and take his pain upon myself because he's old and weak and needs me to ease the intolerable anguish in his soul.

CHAPTER 16

"WHAT DO YOU WANT me to do?" Russel asks. "We're about to take off."

"I'm sorry about your parents," I say. "But I can't do this. I need to get off."

Russel looks at me as if I've started speaking gibberish. I want to make him understand, but how can I? He doesn't know who I am. He doesn't know what I've done. He doesn't realize that I never should have married him in the first place, not with all the secrets I've kept from him. The truth is I can't make this trip with him to Detroit. Can't meet his parents. I can't keep on pretending.

I glance at the man ahead of me, the one in the Hawaiian shirt, the one that for a moment I was convinced was a younger version of Henry. If I keep seeing images of my captor every time I'm out in public, how am I supposed to lead anything resembling a normal life?

I need to get myself back home, back to the quiet of Russel's farm. Actually, I don't care where I go, but I know I can't stay here.

Russel needs an explanation. He's not the sort of person who goes by gut instinct, who lets himself be driven by fear or emotions. I've got to give him an actual reason, something he can accept even if he can't understand.

Even if I have to lie.

"I don't think it's safe," I blurt out. It isn't exactly what I meant to say, but I realize as soon as the words leave my mouth that they'll serve their purpose nicely. “It’s not safe,” I repeat, lowering my voice.

Russel still isn’t ready to let me walk off this flight, so I play the women’s intuition card, hoping it’ll be enough. “I have a really bad feeling about this,” I say, keeping my voice low.

In a flash, I see the next five minutes playing out perfectly in my head. Russel tells me I’m being ridiculous, that we’re totally fine, that his parents are waiting for us in Detroit. Then I get up anyway, tell the flight attendant I’m demanding to get off this plane.

I give Annie a quick hug. Out of all the children, I’ll miss her the most. I don’t look back to see Russel’s pained face, because even though he might not be quite as intuitive as some, he’ll understand, he’ll realize that I’m not just giving up on this flight.

I’m giving up on this dream, this ridiculous notion that with all of our differences and the secrets of my past we can actually make this marriage work.

Except that’s not what happens. I watched wide-eyed as my husband takes a deep breath, looks at his kids, sighs once more, then signals the flight attendant.

“I’m sorry to cause trouble,” he says when she walks up to check on us, “but I need to get my family off this flight. Now.”

CHAPTER 17

I KNOW THAT EVERYONE is staring at us as we walk down the aisle to get off the plane. The children are confused. I have no idea what I'm going to tell them. I have no idea what I'm going to tell Russel.

We pass the man in the Hawaiian shirt. My skin bristles. I feel dirty and exposed just being within arm's reach. I hold my breath, as if the air surrounding him might somehow be contaminated. It was the same way I used to hold my breath when I'd hear Henry coming down the stairs first thing in the morning. I was never certain if he'd be in a good mood or not.

I've read a few articles about women who've survived the kinds of things I have. A lot of them talk about how important it was to get therapy after what they'd been through. I never saw a therapist myself. Couldn't stand the thought of sitting in front of some stranger reliving everything ... everything ...

I actually haven't told anyone the full truth.

I learned to hide the emotion, at times even from myself, but my hatred and loathing for Henry grew with each passing day of my captivity. It's hard to imagine now that I could despise him so much and still ache for his pain. Still mourn his tragic family life. I don't pretend to understand how or why it turned out that way, but that's what happened.

I had no idea two full years had passed since my kidnapping. I'd lost track of time. Didn't know if I'd been in Henry's basement for four months or four decades. It all felt exactly the same to me.

It was the day I finally learned the truth about what happened to Henry's daughter. I'd grown so used to Jennifer's disappearance being such a mystery, I think I actually forgot sometimes that Henry was mourning the loss of a real flesh-and-blood human being and not some phantom he'd created in his mind.

"You snuck out of the house that night," he tells me. There's something strange in his voice. I don't think he's drunk, but there's something not quite right. Sometimes he calls me Jennifer, and other times he talks about her as if we're separate people and always have been.

"I would have let you go if you asked me." His voice is so pained my heart feels like it's going to bleed dry. "I would have driven you to make sure you got there safely."

I know he doesn't really expect me to answer him back, so I simply sit and listen. I'm not thinking about his daughter. I'm not thinking about how strange it is that he's finally decided to talk about what happened to her after all this time I've been with him. I'm thinking about how sad he sounds, about how desperately I'd like to find a way to make him smile. To ease his pain.

"She was stubborn. There was a boy there that she liked." The words jog a distant memory, the vaguest of notions that at one point I also was a teenage girl who had crushes and went out to parties and did things I hoped my parents would never find out about.

"You were beat up pretty bad." He's staring at me now, but there's something strange in his eyes, like he's not really looking at me at all. I feel exposed. Vulnerable. For a second, I want to ask him to stop, but then I think that maybe if he gets the rest of this story off his chest, it'll finally bring him the relief we've been searching for.

"I went out looking for you. I searched everywhere. And there you were, in the woods behind your old school. I swear I didn't lay a finger on you. It wasn't me, but they wouldn't believe me. Police asked me all kinds of questions. Why I went out looking for you myself instead of calling 911. Why two girls said they saw me pick Jennifer up from that party even though I said she ran away. Why I couldn't show them the next day exactly where it was I'd found you so they could test the crime scene themselves. Why I brought you home and didn't think to take you to a hospital right away.

I had no idea the injuries were that bad. She was in bad shape, Jennifer was, but I thought she was drunk. Heaven and everything blessed forgive me, but I thought she was drunk and that's why she was so floppy in my arms. Kids do that, you know. Teens do that. But they did an autopsy and there wasn't a drop of alcohol in your system, my little pineapple. I'm sorry I ever even suspected you. You hadn't been drinking, but I didn't know that. I thought you just needed to come home. I thought you needed to sleep it off."

Henry's voice is cracking, and my heart aches so much it's decided to hold still. I can't erase the words you say next. Can't stop you when you start to cry.

"The next morning, I wanted to let you sleep in. By the time I started to get worried, you were cold. Heaven help me if it's not the blessed truth. You were already cold. I called 911 right away then. Screamed at them to get me an ambulance. Begged them to help you, but they couldn't. It was too late by then. But that wasn't all. It was bad enough losing you. Then everyone thought I'm the one who did it. I was in a bad way after Jennifer's mother died. Lost my job. Didn't function too great. One doctor said I had an illness in my brain, but he was a quack.

"I'd gotten angry with you before. I guess you even told the school counselor you were worried for me. You had every right to tell her those things, by the way, and I've never blamed you, but by heaven that counselor took your words and twisted them and told the police that you were scared of me. Can you believe it? Scared of me. And they couldn't understand how if it happened the way I said it happened that I could have just put you in bed to die. Heaven help me, Jennifer, but I swear I had no idea you were that bad off. You'll never forgive me, but you have to know how sorry I am. I love you so much, pineapple. I've never stopped loving you."

And something clicks in my head right then. Memories of home, of love, of my parents. It's like I've been living under a shadow and the spell is finally broken.

I look at Henry, who's begging me to believe him, whose cries have turned into sobs, and I wake up from a two-year-long hypnosis.

"I believe you," I say, gritting my jaw because I truly want to gag on the words. "I know you didn't mean to do it." Except I'm lying to him. For the first time in Henry's basement, I feel like my brain is working clearly. Call it survival instinct, or maybe it was the answer to all my mother's prayers, but I realize now that I've been duped by a crazy man.

A man who's not only crazy but a murderer.

"I believe you," I repeat, even though I've put the pieces together to know exactly what happened to Henry's daughter so many years ago. The way he talks about it, the way he lets things slip out, this bizarre explanation he's trying to get me to believe, I can read through the lines and finally know what happened.

Jennifer sneaked away from home. That part's true enough. She went to a party, probably flirted with that boy Henry mentioned she liked. And the rest is easy to piece together. Henry realized what she'd done. Either he went looking for her himself or waited until she came home. Where he found her didn't matter as much as what he did next. Beat her to death. Then put her in her bed. Turned off his alarm and waited until she was completely cold before he called the police the next morning and made up an elaborate story about driving all around town and finding her battered body in a field.

I know it's true as clearly as I know my name isn't Jennifer Harris. I don't belong here. This isn't my home. There's a life and a family and a future beyond these cement walls, and somehow I'm going to get myself out of this prison. Henry won't let me leave without a fight, but if it comes down to his life or mine, I'm going to win my freedom no matter how much it costs.

CHAPTER 18

JENNIFER STARED AT HER father in his ugly, beat-up Chevy. She knew she should be afraid, but it took her a half second longer than it should have to wipe that stupid grin off her face, to forget her elation over the absolutely perfect night with Darren. It wasn't until she heard her father's voice that she understood how much trouble she was in.

"I've been looking all over for you." Dad sounded eerily calm. She would have felt far more comfortable if he'd been yelling at her.

"Get in the truck," he growled.

Jennifer hesitated a moment too long. In an instant, her father reached his hand out the window and yanked her by the arm. She hit her head on the side of the door, the dull metallic thump giving way to a high-pitched ringing in her ears.

"Did you go deaf all of a sudden?" Dad growled, his fingernails digging into her flesh. "Get in the truck."

Jennifer heard a noise from the front porch. She glanced over to see Shawna and Kylee standing in front of the house gaping at her.

She scurried over to the passenger side, her head swirling with pain and dizziness.

Her father let out his breath, and Jennifer saw his worried expression, his aged face. "Dad, I'm really ..."

"I don't want to hear a word out of you," he snapped. "Not a word, do you understand me? For years, I've done my best to feed you, to clothe you, to keep you safe. Well, how am I supposed to do that when you're sneaking out at all hours of the night, huh? No, I really want you to tell me. How am I supposed to keep you safe?"

Jennifer bit her lower lip, uncertain if her dad wanted an actual answer or not. The corner of her mouth where Darren had given her that kiss still burned hot. For a second, she worried her dad would look over at her and know everything. Everything she and Darren talked about. Everything they did.

She thought about Darren's hand holding hers. About how earnestly he'd looked at her. Nobody had treated her as kindly and lovingly as Darren had tonight. Her father certainly had never been so warm and attentive.

If Mom were still alive, she'd understand. Jennifer could tell her about Darren, ask her questions. Mom would know what you're supposed to say to a boy when you're done with a slow dance. She'd know if you could call a peck that wasn't even quite on the lips a real kiss or just practice.

Jennifer crossed her arms. It wasn't fair. If anybody should have died, it should have been Dad. The euphoria she felt just a few minutes earlier, the confusion and giddy embarrassment that bubbled to the surface when she thought about Darren, the grief that came crashing over her unexpectedly when she remembered Mom ... it was impossible to give a name to each and every emotion swirling around chaotically in her soul.

Dad was gripping the steering wheel and muttered something under his breath.

"What did you just say?" Jennifer snapped, her anger now rising to the surface of every other conflicting emotion.

"I said if your mother could see you now, she'd be rolling around in her grave."

Jennifer's fists started flying. "How dare you!" she shouted, punching, scratching, pummeling. "I hate you. Hate you, hate you, HATE you."

Dad jerked the Chevy to a standstill at the bus stop near the school. He turned to her, the tired expression on his face replaced with a look of disgust and rage.

"Get out," he snarled, putting the truck into park.

Jennifer stared for a second, trying to catch her breath, trying to replay what had just happened. Had she really punched her own father? He knew she didn't mean it, right? She didn't really hate him.

"Dad, I'm sorry ..."

"Don't give me that." His face was contorted in anger, but his tone was bone-chillingly controlled. "Get out of the truck."

Jennifer hesitated. "I really didn't mean ..."

Dad reached across her and flung open the passenger side door. "Get out of the truck," he repeated with a curse.

Jennifer was crying now, not tears of anger but of fear. She raised her eyes to her father, who glowered at her unblinkingly. "What are you going to do to me?" she asked.

Dad adjusted his belt. "I'm going to teach you some manners, young lady, and you better pray you catch on because one wrong move, and I swear I'll make you regret it for the rest of your life."

CHAPTER 19

I'M SHAKING BY THE time we get off the plane. Shaking to the point where my husband has to support me while I walk.

"Are you going to be all right?" one of the gate attendants asks.

"She's not feeling well," Russel answers for me. "I think we need to get her home."

The worker tells Russel something about our bags, the kids are squirrely around me, Andrew's demanding to know what's happening and poor little Annie is confused and thinks we've already landed in Michigan.

"Where are Grandma and Grandpa?" she asks.

I can't focus on any of this. Can't pay attention to the conversations, the noise. I think about that man in the Hawaiian shirt, about how much he reminded me of Henry. I think about the day I escaped, the same day I discovered what happened to his daughter. I think about Russel, about all the things I should have told him before we got married. I was stupid to think that faith and love alone could erase the memories from my past.

Just like I was stupid to think that I could replace the picture-perfect wife he lost.

We're both broken, Russel and I, but in such different ways. The shattered pieces of our lives in theory might fit together to make something beautiful, but right now we're destroying each other with our lies, our trauma, our grief.

I didn't mean to say it. I should have known better after two years in Henry's basement. But he was so pathetic, sitting there crying, blubbering.

"You're lying," I tell him. I haven't spoken back to him like this since my first few weeks as his prisoner, posing as his daughter, wearing her clothes. I've lost weight, haven't seen the sun in two years. My muscles are weak, but the hatred I feel for him at this exact minute makes me strong and empowered.

This sniveling old man is nothing to be afraid of. He can't hurt me. Can't touch me. Because I know his secret. I've figured it out. When I look back, I'm pretty sure I've always known but haven't wanted to accept the truth until now. At this precise moment.

Everything Henry and I have gone through together has led to here. Like destiny.

"I know what you did to her," I say, my voice calm and even.

His eyes grow wide. He probably forgot I was still a human with the capacity to speak my own mind.

"You got mad at her for sneaking out. You got mad because she hated you, because she knew you were nothing but a pathetic old man, and you killed her. You knew she was growing up. She liked going to parties now. She was interested in boys. You couldn't keep her home, no matter how hard you tried. And you were terrified of losing her. Terrified that she'd wake up one day and realize what a coward you truly are. You saw it happening, saw the end coming. So you killed her. Because you're sick and twisted and pathetic. You killed her, and you managed to keep enough evidence away from the police that they couldn't actually arrest you or anything. You got away with it, but the guilt's been eating you up inside for years. That's why you've made me pretend to be her. Why you've made me say I forgive you. Well, you know something? I don't forgive you. I hate you. I think you're weak. Pathetic. I can't stand another minute in this house with you. And guess what else. I'm not your daughter. I'm not Jennifer. But if she were here, she wouldn't forgive you either. And she'd be saying the exact same things I am. You're weak. You're nothing. You're a terrible father. And you're totally crazy. You killed her. Killed your own flesh and blood and now the guilt's making you even more miserable and pathetic than ever."

Once the words start pouring out of my mouth, I'm certain that nothing can stop them.

"You say you love her, that you're sorry for what you did to her, but you know what? I don't believe you. I know you meant to kill her. I know what a horrible person you are. You're sick in the brain. She wanted to get away from you. You know that, don't you? And the only way to keep her from despising you was to kill her before she learned how wretched you really are, what a miserable old man ..."

And then I stop because Henry's face isn't just contorted in anguish. There's something else there.

"Stop," he gasps. "Help."

I want to keep yelling, telling him that I've finally discovered his secret. I finally know what kind of contemptible human being he truly is, but I can't.

Henry's face is frozen as if carved in stone. He clutches at the collar of his shirt. "Stop," he wheezes. Sweat's dripping down his temples.

My heart quits beating at the sound of his voice. I see his chest make a choppy motion. I don't know what this is. I don't know what's happening.

I jump off the couch and grab a flashlight to see better in the dark. Henry's lips are turning blue, and I realize I'm killing him. Literally killing him.

I reach out for his hand. "What do you need me to do?" I ask. "How can I help?"

I didn't mean to hurt him. Didn't mean to cause him actual physical harm. I just needed to get some things off my chest ...

His chest ...

I place my hand over his heart. Feel how erratically its racing. "What should I do?" I ask.

Henry's face is ashen gray. "Help me," he croaks once more.

I race up the stairs. I try to race up the stairs, is what I should say, but my legs are weak. By the time I'm at the top, I realize I'm about to step into a world I haven't seen in years. I look back down. Is Henry going to stop me? Is he going to yell at me to get back down?

He's bent over himself. I can hear the labored breathing from here. Does he even know I'm at the top of the staircase?

I throw open the door, steel myself for whatever terrors await me on the other side. Monsters. Guard dogs. Soldiers ordered to shoot me on sight. Instead, nothing but blinding daylight streaming in from the windows. I can't see anything. Pain pierces to the back of my skull. I have to help Henry.

I stumble into a messy room, a den or a living room of sorts with trash and molding food strewn everywhere. Is there a phone I can use?

I trip over a takeout box. My hands dart in front of me to break my fall. I scrape my forearm on something. I don't care. Henry is downstairs dying, and it's all my fault. I shouldn't have let my anger take hold of me that way. I should have been more compassionate ...

Why doesn't this man have a stupid phone?

I'm looking everywhere. To my left is a front door with three separate dead bolts protecting me from the outside world. I could run outside, yell for help. I glance out a grimy window. All I see is a looming fence surrounding the house, but beyond that must be something.

Can I get help for Henry fast enough?

I've overturned a small table. A shoebox full of photographs has spilled onto the floor at my feet. I pick up one of the pictures. It's of me. There are dozens of them, all close up, photographs of me when I'm sleeping. My skin is pale. I almost look like I'm dead.

My hands are trembling. I don't have time to stop and stare, but I do. Because there's something wrong about the pictures. Something I didn't notice at first.

I don't own a shirt like that. And the sleeping head I'm staring at is resting on a pillow. A real pillow with a real pillowcase, not the hard couch cushion Henry's given me.

Even more surprising, the sleeping girl in the photograph is in a real bed.

And then I realize I'm not looking at pictures of myself at all. It's Henry's dead daughter. I drop the images, my heart speeding wildly. I tell myself I'm running outside to get help. It's the only way I can justify leaving Henry here like this. I hate him. Despise him. Fear him. But the thought of him down there all alone, feeling so remorseful ... I can't make myself leave unless I lie. I tell myself I'll run and get him help. I tell myself I'll race down the road, find the nearest house or wave down the nearest car and call 911 to get them to send Henry an ambulance. It's the only thing that allows me to unlock the deadbolts. They're heavier than I expected, as if they've rusted in place.

Hurry, I tell myself, *Henry could die any second.*

Except that's not why I'm hurrying. Not really. I know that once I leave this house, I'm going home, and nothing's going to stop me.

The last bolt finally slides out of place.

The sun hits my skin for the first time since my capture. I don't have time to pause and wonder. My only thought is to get away. Do I go right or left? I don't know. All I know is that I need to put one foot in front of the other. I force myself to be strong, to resist the urge to turn back.

I can't do it. Can't leave him here like this. I think I hear him call my name. "Jennifer." Then I think about the pictures I saw. I think about Henry's dead daughter, about how he's kept me prisoner in his basement. I remember the vaguest notion of a mother and father who loved me once upon a time, and I realize I want to see them again.

I desperately want to see them again.

I know they're out there. And I know I don't belong trapped in a basement for the rest of my life.

I have no idea how long I've been walking. It feels like a lifetime. The houses are set back in the woods. All I see are driveways. One road turns to another. I can't keep the directions straight. I might be walking in circles for all I can tell. I think it must have been an hour, maybe more. Maybe whole days have passed since I ran away from Henry, since I abandoned him alone in that basement to die.

The shadows are long, the evening chilly when I spot a woman walking her dog. My eyes want to spill over with tears. How long has it been since I've seen another human being? Seen an animal of any kind?

My legs threaten to collapse beneath me the moment she comes into view. I wave my arms. She raises her hand but then stops.

"Help," I call out, certain now that my legs can't carry me another step.

She jogs toward me. I don't know if it's my stress or my fear or my physical weakness, but I'm only half conscious when her dog comes up, sniffs me once curiously, then licks my face with a warm tongue.

His kiss makes me start to sob.

The woman kneels down. I can't understand the questions she's asking me, but I hear the worry in her voice.

"I need help," I tell her.

"What's your name?" she asks.

I nearly answer "Jennifer" before I remember. That's not me anymore. It never was me. "My name is Anastasia," I answer. "Anastasia Reynolds. I want to go home."

CHAPTER 20

"ANASTASIA," MY HUSBAND SNAPS.

I gasp in a desperate breath of air. "Russel?" My voice is hoarse. Like I've just been strangled and my windpipe has been bruised.

"Anastasia." He repeats my name. It sounds strange coming from him for some reason. "Are you all right?"

The children are looking at me with fearful expressions, even the older ones. I glance around, half expecting to find myself facing a very alive Henry or locked in his basement again.

But that's not what I see. I'm in the airport. My husband and children — my family — are here staring at me worriedly. Two others, an official-looking man and woman, are standing far too close, asking me questions, feeling my wrists, talking to each other in hushed tones.

"I'm all right," I tell them. I don't know if they're EMTs or airport workers or what, but I can't breathe when they're crowding me like this. "I'm all right," I repeat. I'm not sure who I'm most trying to convince, but I do know that none of them believe me.

It's okay. I don't even believe myself.

"We should get you to a doctor or something," Russel says. "Is there someone who can give her a checkup?" he asks.

I don't hear the woman's response. I'm too busy reminding myself that I'm here. I'm alive. I'm safe.

More strangers approach. An old lady asks if Russel needs help watching the kids. My head is spinning, my whole body clammy.

"I think she's coming down with something," Russel tells the concerned onlookers.

I convince my husband in no uncertain terms that I will not be pushed through the airport in a wheelchair. He gives the gate attendants what must be his dozenth apology, then he gathers the children from where they've been seated, watching me fall apart.

"What's wrong with her?" Andrew asks.

"Mom's just a little tired," he says, "that's all." Russel looks over at me, his eyes full of concern. Of fear. Of love.

I shouldn't have kept this from him for so long. I had no reason not to tell him before. Do I have the courage now to make things right? Or will that only make everything so much worse?

Why didn't you tell me sooner? I'm certain that's the question he'll ask when he learns the truth. And then, even once I come clean, how will he believe anything else I tell him from now on? He wouldn't trust me. I wouldn't trust me if I were in his shoes.

The Bible says to tell the truth, right? But it also says that we need to work hard to make our marriages last. So what am I supposed to do?

We're early enough into the relationship. There may be cause for an annulment. I've looked it up. We were both in our right minds getting married. Neither of us were coerced or anything like that. But the state will annul a marriage in the case of fraud. Does lying about my past count as fraud? What about the fact that I never told Russel about my infertility? I was pregnant when I ran away from Henry's. Neither of us knew it at the time. I miscarried the week after my rescue. My mother insists it was the shock. My father believed it was a merciful act of God. Either way, the resulting hemorrhaging and complications have left me unable to bear children.

I was too riddled with guilt over having left Henry to die that I hardly thought about the other life I lost. Never mourned the inability to ever conceive again.

I tried telling the policemen where Henry's house was, but I'd been walking for so long before I found help. I couldn't retrace my steps, no matter how hard I tried.

I told them he was sick. I told them he was old, he was weak, he was having a heart attack or something. I told them I shouldn't have left him all alone. They told me I'd done the right thing, the brave thing, the only thing I could have done to get myself out of a terrible situation.

I still have nightmares that Henry's dying in that basement, begging me for help, pleading with me to save his life.

A week and a half later, the police called my parents to let them know. A man had been discovered dead in his home. The basement was just as I described.

Henry was gone. My mother was ecstatic. My father furious that my captor would never stand trial.

"God himself'll judge that monster," he'd say. "It's the most we can hope for now."

I did what I could to try to adjust to life back home. Mom and Dad had left my room exactly as it had been, but the mattress was too lumpy, the pillow too soft. I woke up every night burning up from the heat. All that winter my parents kept the thermostat set at 62.

I remember that season after my escape like I remember watching documentaries in history class. I study them clinically, wonder if the final bullet that killed my parents' marriage was the stress of my abduction or the turmoil they experienced when they realized the carefree child they lost was gone forever, dead and buried in Henry's basement.

I didn't cry, didn't lash out. Mom was worried for me, begged me to open up and tell her what was wrong. I didn't want to talk.

I just wanted to forget.

CHAPTER 21

"Feeling better now?" my husband asks me.

I try in vain to offer him a smile. "Yeah. I think you're right. I must be coming down with something."

I've lost track of how long we've been here. At least an hour, maybe more. After I calmed down, it took three different agents to help us locate our bags. Now we're waiting near some back office for the airport workers to grab our luggage and wheel it out to us. I forget how many times I've apologized to Russel for ruining his vacation.

"You and the kids should go on without me," I insist, but of course he won't leave me.

He's already called his parents. I have no idea what he told them, nor do I want to. I just want to go home. Get out of here. I feel like every pair of eyes is staring at me.

What was it about that man on the airplane that got me so freaked out? The Hawaiian shirt? The way the girl he was with looked so uncomfortable?

I should tell someone. Maybe.

But tell them what?

Hey, there was this weirdo on the plane traveling with a teen girl and ... I don't know. I just didn't like the way he looked?

It's ridiculous. Just like it's ridiculous for me to even think about telling Russel about why I started to panic. I know my husband. If he knew about Henry, he'd just pity me and worry about me, and I'd feel even more suffocated under his loving care. That's exactly what happened after I escaped Henry's basement and tried to live back home.

I try to remember how long it's been since I called my mom, but I can't. Her birthday was three months ago, but I know I missed it.

"Mommy?" Annie grabs my hand. "I need to go potty."

I'm thankful for something to do. Something that only I can do. I remind myself that I'm an adult. I'm the responsible one. I'm probably just coming down with the flu or something like that. Russel already asked me after we got off the plane if I thought I was pregnant. I wish my outburst could be chalked up to some kind of hormonal imbalance.

I should be so lucky.

I tell Russel I'm taking Annie to the bathroom, and while I wait outside her stall, I have a little time to think. Take a few deep breaths, try to compose myself. I'm not in any danger. Nobody is trying to capture me or force me to wear someone else's clothes and pretend to be their murdered daughter.

I'm safe. I'm here with my family. I'm a grown woman, a wife, a survivor.

Nothing can hurt me here.

Annie starts humming a song to herself, one clue out of many that she's going to take her sweet and precious time. The bathroom isn't crowded, and I pace the length of the stalls. Anything to get my mind off that airplane, that teen girl I saw. The one with scared, haunted eyes.

Suddenly I'm dizzy. I know my mind's about to send me right back to Henry's basement. I've got to get control of myself.

My breath comes in choppy spurts. "I'm going to be in the stall right next to you," I tell Annie, and I shut the door behind me. Something about the enclosed space makes me feel more at ease. Less exposed.

There's a small poster taped above the toilet paper.

It is estimated that at least twenty thousand minors are trafficked in the United States every year.

My stomach flips once. Twice. I press my palm against my abdomen to try to stop the sloshing.

Questions you can ask yourself if you see something suspicious: Does the potential victim in question act confused, submissive, or afraid?

"I can't reach the toilet paper," Annie calls to me. I manage to find the voice to tell her I need a minute.

Do they avoid eye contact?

The image of that girl on the plane flashes again in my mind. I tell myself I'm overreacting. I'm projecting my own experience and trauma onto a situation that's none of my business.

Is the potential victim wearing appropriate attire?

It's this question that literally sucks the breath out of my lungs.

"Mommy!" Annie whines.

"Just a minute." I need to think. Was that what finally gave it away? A T-shirt and shorts? There was no crime in dressing inappropriately for the season.

I squeeze my eyes shut, compose my breathing as best as I can, then unlock the door. I help Annie finish and wash up, and I hold her hand as we make our way back to her father. Russel's standing with our luggage. I can't tell if he looks tired or annoyed or concerned. I'm dizzy. My mind can hardly focus on anything.

"There's a problem," I tell him as soon as I'm at his side. "I need to talk to someone from security."

CHAPTER 22

JENNIFER STARED AT HER father. Was he seriously kicking her out of the truck this late at night?

"Get out," he growled again and made a lunge toward her.

She jumped onto the curb, afraid her father would come after her, afraid he'd slap her right then and there for sneaking out, for talking back, for getting angry and hitting him.

What she didn't expect was for him to slam the Chevy door and drive off.

She stood there on the sidewalk in front of the school, shivering in the cold, waiting for the red glow of his taillights.

Dad sped through a stop sign and disappeared from view.

Jennifer hugged herself to ward off the cold and waited. Ten minutes. Fifteen minutes. Had he already gone home?

When she was finally convinced that he wasn't returning for her, she felt into her pockets for change. She didn't have any coins left, and even if she did, she didn't know who she should call. Shawna? Kylee?

She had Darren's number memorized. Even though she'd never called him before, she'd spent hours staring at his last name in the phone book, wondering if one day she'd ever have the courage to give him a ring.

It couldn't be tonight, though. What she had to ask herself was whose parents would be the most likely to be awake past midnight. That and who would be least likely to get upset if Jennifer woke them up.

She could walk home, but it was totally dark out. Dark and freezing. She wished Darren were here with her. She couldn't believe that such a short time ago she was sitting next to him on Kylee's couch, their legs touching. He'd kissed her, right? What if he'd only been trying to give her a hug and his lips accidentally touched hers? Did that still count?

What if he already regretted spending time with her?

What if he and Lisa were together right now?

She couldn't think like this. It was late, but Kylee must still be awake. Jennifer could call her or just walk over to her place. She could walk to Kylee's and spend the night there. Give her dad time to sleep it off. In the morning, he wouldn't be so upset.

She still couldn't believe he'd driven off like that. For a split second, Jennifer was sickened by a terrifying thought. What if her dad had gotten into a car accident? What if he'd only been planning to scare her, to teach her a lesson, and he had a heart attack behind the wheel or something? Just last week, the doctor had told him he needed to exercise more and lose weight. The tiny aspirin pill he took once a day wasn't enough to keep his heart healthy as he got older.

Was it possible something had happened to her dad? She had to find out.

She took a step off the curb then saw headlights coming down from the school parking lot. Good. Her dad really had just meant to scare her. He probably drove around the neighborhood until he figured she was adequately spooked, then drove through the football field entrance and was coming back now to pick her up.

He'd apologize when she got into the truck, but she wasn't going to let him get off so easily. What had he been thinking?

The car slowed down, but it wasn't until it was just a few feet away from the curb when Jennifer realized it wasn't her father after all.

"Jennifer Harris? Is that you? What in the world are you doing out here? Get in the car."

He leaned over to open the passenger door. Jennifer hadn't realized until now how much she'd been shivering.

She gave him a little smile, hoping he wouldn't ask too many questions. What would she tell him to explain how she ended up out here in the cold?

He locked the doors as she was buckling up. “You must be freezing.” His voice was full of worry. He sounded so concerned for her safety, Jennifer thought she might start crying.

“Let me turn up the heat,” he said, and soon the hot air was blowing on her at full blast.

“First question for you,” he said when Jennifer’s teeth finally stopped chattering. “Are you safe?”

She nodded.

“Are you hurt?”

“No.”

He let out a relieved sigh. “That’s all I wanted to know. Now, tell me where you need to go. Let’s get you out of this cold.”

CHAPTER 23

I EXPECT RUSSEL TO ask me more questions, to demand to know everything that's going on. Maybe he's resigned to the fact that his new wife is a nutcase. Maybe he is just trying to do whatever he can do to appease me.

"Are you sure this girl was in trouble?" is all he asks.

I shake my head. "I can't say. It's just, the guy she was with gave me a really bad feeling ..."

I don't know how else to respond. I'm still surprised that Russel hasn't told me I'm overreacting, that after the scene I've already made on the plane there's no need to conjure up an encore performance here.

Let's just take our bags and go home. That's what I want him to say. Instead, he stops someone wearing an airlines nametag. "Excuse me, is there someone from security I can speak to?"

For the next fifteen minutes, my face burns hot as I sit behind a desk answering a stranger's questions.

"Did you have any interaction with the passenger in question?" "Did the girl you noticed say anything to you or try to signal you in any way?" "Did you overhear any conversation between this girl and the man she was traveling with?"

Now that I'm getting interrogated about two individuals I've never met in my life, I realize what a mistake I made insisting on speaking to security. I've lost track of how many times I've told this officer that I was just overreacting on the plane. It's nothing. I'm sorry for wasting his time.

Russel and the kids are waiting for me outside the cramped office. I can only imagine what's running through my husband's brain right now. Is he wondering what his parents think of me? Is he ashamed of my outburst on the plane? Maybe he's wondering how to tell his kids that their new stepmom is certifiably insane.

I'm shaking by the time we're done. The officer did a good job listening to my concerns, asked all the right questions. The problem is I don't have any actual evidence. Nothing tangible to go on but the fact that a girl was wearing shorts and a T-shirt in the winter. But what does that prove? Maybe her next stop after Detroit was Hawaii for all I know.

My face is burning when I join Russel and the children.

"Everything okay?" he asks me.

I smile. "Yeah, I think ..." I don't know what to tell him. "I'm sorry for ruining the trip." It's the best I can do.

His voice is gentle. "Don't worry about that. I talked to a gate agent while you were having your meeting. They got us on another flight. We leave in three hours."

My stomach sinks. It was stupid for me not to have expected this. Russel's glowing and raving on and on about what a huge blessing it is they were able to squeeze six of us on a flight together, and all I can think is I wish the attendant told him there was room for Russel and the kids but not for me.

I need time. Time to catch my breath. To remind myself that just because a girl's wearing shorts doesn't mean her life's in danger. That just because I was captured and locked away for two years it doesn't mean every other teenager with sad, haunted eyes is going through the same horror. The trauma I went through.

I had only been home for three months after escaping Henry's basement when a policeman knocked on our door. I hated him and that stupid Styrofoam cup of coffee he always carried around with him.

"We've had a new development," he said, stepping into our home without waiting to be invited. "Call your mom in. She'll want to hear this."

And then the officer proceeded to tell me the truth that's going to haunt me until the day I die.

Henry hadn't killed his daughter.

Concerning the murder of Jennifer Harris, Henry was completely innocent.

CHAPTER 24

JENNIFER HADN'T SEEN MR. Green in a while. It had been a full two years since she was a student in his science class. He seemed different now. But maybe that was because she was looking at him through the tears she was desperately trying to blink away.

"So," Mr. Green said as he put his car into gear. "I'm not going to ask what you were doing, but if you wanted someone to talk to about it, I'm all ears." He had a sign for some old band dangling from his rearview mirror. Back in middle school, Jennifer and her friends had spent hours speculating on the rumors that Mr. Green did drugs every night, that he'd been in a rock band in college, that he kept a shrine to the Grateful Dead in his attic. When Kylee's older brother told the girls that Mr. Green was suspected to have dated one of his former students once she came home from college, the rumor mill seemed to have a limitless supply of fodder.

How much of it was true? Jennifer wondered. Mr. Green was strange. There was no denying that, but at least his car heater worked.

"Where am I taking you to, m'lady?" he asked, his voice happy and good-natured.

Jennifer's jaw hurt from clenching it while she stood outside in the cold. She tried to will her body to relax a degree but wasn't sure she was that successful. She sniffed loudly and hoped Mr. Green didn't think she was crying.

"I live over on Belview."

"Belview?" he repeated. "I know right where that is," Mr. Green answered enthusiastically. "It would be my great honor and privilege to take you wherever you need to go."

Jennifer glanced at him out of the corner of her eye. Tried to determine which if any of the rumors about her former teacher were true.

"How are you liking high school?" Mr. Green asked. "You're a sophomore now?"

"Freshman," she answered.

"Really? I could have sworn you were older." Mr. Green glanced over at her. "Are you doing all right? Or does the fact that I found you on the corner alone with your makeup all smeared answer that question for me?" He waited for an answer.

Jennifer stayed silent.

Finally, Mr. Green let out a sigh. "Well, I know it's not any of my business," he finally announced, "but I do tend to worry about my students. Teacher's curse, I'm afraid. I worry about each and every one of you."

"Mm-hmm." Jennifer squirmed in her seat. Something was making her uncomfortable. Maybe she shouldn't have gotten in the car with Mr. Green after all. Maybe she should have just asked him for some change so she could call her dad, beg him to come pick her up.

It wasn't until then that she realized they were driving the wrong way. She tried to remember. She'd told him Belview, right?

"I think my home's the other way." She kept her voice low, didn't want him to think she was ungrateful for his help.

"Oh." Mr. Green gave the steering wheel a small slap and let out a chuckle. "I'm sorry, I must have been driving on auto-pilot. I'm taking you straight to my house."

Jennifer glanced at the time on his dashboard. Wondered why she hadn't thought to ask what Mr. Green was doing driving around town this late in the first place.

"Hey, I've got to pick something up at the middle school. You okay if we take a quick detour?"

Jennifer couldn't guess what he had to do at the school this late, but Mr. Green was already going way out of his way to get her home. She couldn't be rude. "No problem." She tried to make her voice sound at ease. Tried to mask the growing discomfort she felt. Tried to tell herself that in a few more minutes, she'd be back home in her warm bed and the stress of the night would be nothing but a distant memory.

CHAPTER 25

GIVEN THE STATUS OF what remains in my backpack, I grossly underestimated how many snacks I'd need to pack to keep four children and two adults from growing hungry. Our newly booked flight doesn't start boarding for another hour, but I know better than to ask Russel to spend money on airport food.

I'm feeling much better now. Finally got over whatever shock I had. In fact, I'm actually glad Russel was able to get our family on this other plane. I would hate to think that I've ruined this vacation for everyone. Yes, I'm still anxious about meeting the in-laws. Still terrified that every single thing I do, every word I say will be compared to Sarah. Russel's parents loved his first wife like a daughter. He hasn't told me this, but his sister has. Their whole family saw her as one of their own.

They're all still mourning her death.

Which is exactly why I was dreading this trip.

But there's nothing like a massive panic attack on a crowded airplane to put things into perspective. I'm a survivor. I can't even guess how many times I've reminded myself of that fact since I finished talking with airport security. The man was attentive enough, but he realized as soon as we started talking that there was nothing to go on. I have no idea why I got so upset in the first place. What did I expect him to do? Order the captain to turn the plane around so they could arrest a man simply because his teenage daughter wore shorts and a surly expression?

As humiliated as I am by the experience, I think in the end it's all for the best. I've forgotten how much energy it takes me to keep everything that happened with Henry hidden, secret, and forgotten. My trauma is a trapped animal, expending all its effort trying to get out of its cage. It's a full-time job keeping my demons in check.

I've promised myself I'll tell Russel everything. But not right now. Not here in the airport, not until we're home after this vacation. But he deserves to know. I won't tell him in a way that makes him feel sorry for me or worried about my mental health. I'll just bring it up casually. *Hey, there's something I didn't feel totally comfortable telling you earlier, but now that we're married, I think it's important for you to know.*

That's the kind of conversation two rational adults can have, right?

Picturing this future encounter holds my guilt at bay, the guilt I feel for not exposing my secrets earlier. Eventually I'll tell Russel everything. When the time is right. Might be next month, might be in a year ... The longer I wait, the more awkward it'll be, but then again, by that point our marriage will be stronger. More resilient.

Who am I kidding?

This is a secret I might as well carry with me to my grave.

"We should have packed more sandwiches," Russel announces factually. I love how he uses the pronoun *we*, as if he had any part in packing for this trip for six. But who am I to complain? It's my fault we're here and not on our way to his parents' already. If I hadn't overreacted like I did, we'd be landing in Detroit any minute.

"Look, Daddy," Andrew says, pointing at a TV screen. "It's an airplane."

Russel glances up. I'm still rummaging through my carry-on, looking for more food to pass around, when I hear my husband suck in his breath.

My eyes follow his gaze. The ticker at the bottom of the screen reads *Flight hijacked. Missing Detroit teen identified as one of the passengers.* A school photo accompanies the text. Blood drains from my brain. I'm glad I'm sitting because the room has tilted onto its axis.

Russel grabs my hand. "Is that ...?" He doesn't complete his sentence. He doesn't have the chance.

Three men and one woman in very professional-looking suits walk directly up to me, brandishing official badges. "Are you Anastasia Strickland? You talked earlier with one of our security officers?"

I give a faint nod and try to tell them yes. I can't even hear my own voice, but that doesn't seem to matter to these agents.

"Come with us, please. We have some questions for you."

CHAPTER 26

RUSSEL REFUSES TO LET me go anywhere without him. It's sweet, actually. A little protective.

It takes a few minutes, but the airlines agents call in someone to keep an eye on the kids in the adjoining room and take my husband and me to another small office. Through the cracks in the door, I hear Andrew whining about how hungry he is.

"Mrs. Strickland, are you aware of what's occurring aboard Flight 219?"

"I saw something on the news," I answer, uncertain if this is what I'm supposed to say or not. "I don't really understand ..."

"Flight 219 has been hijacked," the man interrupts. "And as part of the attack, the perpetrators have kidnapped the daughter of Detroit's school district superintendent."

I don't understand what a school district has to do with hijacked planes or acts of terrorism. A small portion of my brain worries that I've misheard everything this man is telling me.

I'm thankful when Russel leans forward in his seat and takes the lead. "That's the same girl my wife mentioned. The one she talked to the security officer about." I don't know how to describe what I hear in his voice. Is he angry they didn't listen to me in the first place? Scared to think that his entire family was supposed to be aboard that plane? The only name I can give to his tone is intense.

The officer nods his head. "Yes. We took your wife's concerns very seriously when she brought them to our attention, and in the end, it seems she was right to sound the alarm."

"What's happening to those people right now?" my husband asks.

"I assure you we have every available law enforcement agency and officer involved to ensure they don't harm anyone else in their ..."

"I mean the passengers," Russel interrupts. "What's happening to them? Are they all right?"

"News is just coming in," the agent answers. "I'm afraid that's all I can tell you right now."

I'm trembling. I'm afraid I'm going to throw up my peanut butter and jelly sandwich and granola bar. So I wasn't wrong. I wasn't crazy. I wasn't making things up.

Which means that girl really was stolen from her parents. That she really was as terrified as she appeared.

I should have done more. Asked her for her name, found a way to talk to her alone. What was I thinking? I just left her there, left her alone her with her abductor ... And now the plane's been hijacked.

She must be so scared.

I want to know everything about her. Her age. Her favorite color. What kind of music she listens to. The name of her crush. I want to know where she sleeps at night, in a bed safe and warm or in a freezing cold basement, her hands cuffed behind her back.

And the man with her, who is he? Has he just abducted her, or has she been trapped with him for weeks? Months? Has she gotten to the point where she's forgotten her age? Where she's certain at least one birthday has passed but all she can do is wonder what her parents did to commemorate the day ...

An agent who's been silently standing in the corner speaks up. His partner turns around, and they have a small huddle in hushed tones, using words and phrases that cascade over me.

I squeeze my eyes shut. Russel puts his arm around me. Draws me close.

"I'm so glad you got us off that plane," he whispers. "That must have been God guiding you."

There's nothing but awe in Russel's voice, except I can't share his sense of grateful relief. Because that girl is still on that plane with her captor. And the other passengers ... I can't even imagine what's happening to them.

"... demanding to speak to the superintendent," one of the agents is saying, and they continue talking about some elementary playground. I can't believe that an abduction and hijacking all revolve around school politics, but what do I know? After I escaped Henry's basement, I never even returned to school. I got my degree from a correspondence program, which meant my mother didn't need to let me out of her sight. Which meant I never had to leave the house.

If you were to ask Mom the details, I was in shock when I first returned home. Then came the miscarriage. The hemorrhaging. The surgery. A few months later, once my body healed and I realized I didn't have to simply exist in survival mode anymore, I broke down and fell into an unbreakable depression.

The real depression was because I had discovered the truth. I'm the reason Henry died. I killed him. His heart gave out when I accused him of murdering his daughter. I was so sure of it at the time. But I'd been wrong. Dead wrong. The cop who came to our house that day told me that they reopened Jennifer's case, that they found a DNA match.

Henry hadn't killed Jennifer after all.

Which meant I broke Henry's heart when I accused him. I'm the one who killed him.

Mom couldn't understand. "Whether or not he murdered his daughter, he was a monster. He kept you trapped in a basement for two full years." She stated the words so factually, as if she expected them to break through my despair and get me to see reason.

Henry hadn't killed Jennifer. How many times had he begged me to tell him I believed him? That I knew he'd never lift a hand to hurt me?

And then one day I snapped. I yelled those terrible things at him, accused him of those monstrous acts.

I killed him with my words.

I'm a survivor. Some would say I did what I had to do. I escaped with my life, didn't I? Do you know how rare it is to survive two years of captivity?

Going strictly by the numbers, I should have been dead within the first 48 hours.

I'm a statistical anomaly.

I survived. I got myself out of there.

Now I'm free.

Free from Henry's basement. Free from his handcuffs. Free from his delusions. Free from his oppressive grief.

Free from everything. Everything except the overwhelming guilt I felt that I accused a weak, sad man of a crime he didn't commit, then I ran away when he needed my help the most and left him to die, terrified and alone.

CHAPTER 27

"ARE YOU CRYING?" RUSSEL asks me.

His voice is so gentle. So pained to think I might be in any sort of turmoil or anguish.

"I don't want to answer any more questions." I choke on the words. I didn't expect to break so easily.

The agents turn and look at me.

"We need to go," Russel tells them. "My wife is unwell."

He doesn't wait for their permission but stands me up, holding onto my elbow. My legs nearly collapse under me.

"Are you all right?" he asks, worried. "Do you need a doctor? Is there a doctor she can see? I think it's the stress. She isn't well ..."

I hear the hint of panic in his voice, and that's when I crack. I let the pieces of my soul that I've tried so desperately to hold together all these years crumble to shards around me.

"She's in shock or something," my husband insists, and still it takes the men in the room several seconds staring at us before one of them says, "I'll see what I can do."

Russel is trying to support my weight, trying to keep me from falling to the ground. I can't stand the feel of his fingers clenching my arm, can't stand the memory of Henry's grip on my body.

"Let me go," I shriek, only half aware that I'm yelling at my own husband and not a man who's been dead for ten years. "I don't want to stay here. I want to leave."

A childlike voice from the doorway carries over the sound of my hyperventilating. "What's wrong with Mommy? Is she all right?"

I don't process the child's words or Russel's answer. Someone's hurrying toward me. Seconds later an oxygen monitor is clasped to my finger, a blood pressure gauge wrapped around my arm.

"Has she had anything to eat or drink lately?" a voice asks my husband.

"Here, someone take my wallet and go get her something from McDonalds," he says, and I want to laugh at the thought of Russel ordering me fast food.

My breath returns to me in short, choppy gulps. I want to pass out. I want to ignore the faces around me, the worried expressions, the shouted questions.

"She's unwell." I've lost track of how many times Russel has repeated himself. *Unwell, unwell, unwell ...*

My wife is unwell.

The man has no idea.

No idea whatsoever.

CHAPTER 28

JENNIFER FELT SILLY FOR getting herself so worked up. Just because it was dark out, just because there was nobody out on any of the roads this late at night, she didn't have to create all kinds of spooky stories about her teacher. She blamed Shawna and Kylee and all their silly rumors about Mr. Green from all the way back in middle school.

He'd kept the car running while he ran into the school to get whatever it was he'd left. Jennifer was glad the heater was on. First of all, she was still freezing cold. Second of all, it made her certain that whatever Mr. Green was here to do, it wouldn't take long.

For a minute, she wished she'd asked if she could go inside with him, but she didn't want to make it seem like she was afraid to stay out here alone. She wasn't the same little pre-teen she'd been when she was a student in his science class so long ago. She was older now, far more mature.

Now that her body had started to warm and her mind was no longer fixating on the problem of how to get herself home, she found herself remembering her evening at the party with Darren. She couldn't wait to see him at school on Monday. Maybe she'd even see him sooner than that. Her heart gave a little leap to her throat at the thought, and she immersed herself in playing out the various scenarios. Maybe she'd go to the mall tomorrow with Lisa and Shawna and Kylee, and he'd be there with his older brother, and they'd see each other and smile and break off from their respective groups and go ice skating together.

Maybe Lisa would decide that she didn't want to be outdone by Kylee's party, so she'd throw a party of her own tomorrow night, and Jennifer and Darren would meet up again there.

Maybe it'd be a total fluke where you knew it had to be God making things work out, and she'd run into him while she went to the grocery store with her dad to pick up something for dinner.

For the first time in her recent memory, she felt truly happy. She was so lost in her thoughts she gasped when someone flung open the passenger side door of the car.

She gave a little jump, then let out her breath when she realized who it was. "You scared me," she said with a giggle, a giggle that died on her lips the moment she saw his face. Something wasn't right. Something was terribly wrong.

"Get out of the car," he told her, and that's when she saw the knife in his hand. It was one of those dissecting tools she remembered from that frog lab that made her and Shawna both feel sick.

"Get out," Mr. Green repeated.

Jennifer glanced once more at his scalpel and did what he said.

CHAPTER 29

IT'S ALMOST NIGHTTIME BEFORE we load the car to drive home, our bags in the trunk and our flight plans forgotten. The kids are disappointed their vacation's ruined. Russel's decided not to tell them the specifics of the hijacked airplane. They know there was a problem with one of the airplanes, and that's why we're not going to see Grandma and Grandpa after all.

What they don't know is that the same airplane that crash landed in Detroit was the airplane we were seated on earlier today. That we were hours away from what could have been our deaths.

Russel's mom insisted on talking to me when he called. She tells me I'm a prophetess, that I have the gift of discernment, that God saved our family by giving me divine insight into what was about transpire on that plane.

I didn't have the heart to tell her otherwise.

Russel still thinks my emotional reactions today are all related to the hunch I got that something wasn't right with our flight. News reports have been filing in all evening. Apparently, the Detroit school district ordered an elementary school to be built on toxic wasteland. A few parents were upset enough they got up in arms, literally. Kidnapping the superintendent's daughter to use her as a bargaining chip. Tampering with the electric wiring in the airplane lavatory to cause a fire. I still don't know all the facts. Not sure how many people died.

The truth is I don't want to know any more details than I already do.

The kidnapped girl is safe now. I didn't realize how much tension I'd been holding in my body until I saw the news coverage showing her reunited with her parents. Does she know about me, I wonder? Will the federal agents who are debriefing her right now let her know that some unnamed passenger got off the plane and sounded the alarm?

I'm not sure it really matters. I might have been right about her being a victim, but that didn't stop the plane from getting hijacked.

"Look, Daddy! It's Chuck E. Cheese! Just like the one Grandma and Grandpa take us to!"

I certainly can't imagine Russel being the type of father who'd let his children into a venue like Chuck E. Cheese. It makes me wonder if his parents are more lenient than he is. Or maybe Annie's referring to her mother's parents.

Regardless, I'm shocked when Russel turns on his blinker and pulls into the parking lot. "What are you doing?" I ask.

He shrugs. "The kids are hungry."

Squeals erupt from the back seats. Russel grins at me sheepishly. I wonder if I'm supposed to keep our family excursion to Chuck E. Cheese a secret from the congregation. Or maybe I'm reading too much into it.

The children don't seem nearly as out of place as I feel. When they get inside, they hold their arms out expertly so the workers can mark their hands. I don't realize until Russel follows suit that adults are given the same kind of stamp. Indisputable proof that our family belongs together, I suppose.

Russel pulls out two twenty-dollar bills and tells Betsy to get tokens and divide them evenly. "Stay together," he gives as a final ultimatum, and the children race off.

I blink, wondering if my husband's mind is simply reacting to the stress and shock of the day. Never in our entire engagement did I picture our family hanging out in Chuck E. Cheese. I want to ask him what the members of Gospel Kingdom would think, but he looks so happy I don't bring it up.

"Are you hungry?" he asks then shocks me again by ordering two large pepperoni pizzas. We wait for our food at an empty table, and he takes me by the hand.

"I'm so glad you were with us today. I'm so glad God gave you that warning and that you heeded it and got our family off that flight."

I take a deep breath. On the wall behind my husband, robotic rodents dance on stage. The strobing lights are distracting enough I'm surprised we're not all suffering seizures yet.

Russel gives my hand a squeeze. "You really are amazing, you know that? You probably saved our family's life today."

I'm about to tell him. I'm about to tell him everything, but he isn't giving me the chance.

"That took a lot of courage," he continues. "And I'll admit, I was worried at first. I thought maybe you were having second thoughts about meeting my parents. The last couple days have felt a little ..." He leaves the thought unfinished.

"It's been kind of stressful," I admit.

He nods, as if I've just confirmed what he'd been wanting to say but couldn't. He squeezes my hand again and lets out a chuckle. "For a minute, I thought you wanted off the plane to get away from me."

I smile back at him, but I can't force myself to feel any joy or relief. There's so much he doesn't know.

Betsy comes running up. Andrew's got a scrape on his knee and needs a bandage. Good thing I've got half a dozen in my purse.

I may not be the world's most experienced mother, but I'm a fast learner.

I hand Betsy the Band-Aid, tell her to wash her hands before and after putting it on, and the entire time my husband stares at me as if in shock.

"You're amazing," he says. "You really are. I see you with the kids, I see how much you love them, what a great mom you are, and I realize just how blessed I am. I thank God so much for bringing you into my life."

I want to ask him about Sarah. Want to ask if he thinks I'll ever come close to being the wife or mother she was. I want to ask if he sometimes has doubts too, if he wonders whether or not we should have waited before getting married so quickly.

I want to ask if he has second thoughts.

But I don't.

I'm thinking about that girl from the airplane, wondering what it will be like now that she's been returned to her parents. The good news, if you can call it that, was she was missing for less than 48 hours from the time of her abduction.

She beat the statistical odds.

Lucky her.

"What are you thinking about?" Russel asks.

I picture myself telling him everything. Just opening up my mouth and vomiting out the truth. *I'm thinking about the man who kidnapped me. He held me trapped in his basement for two years and then I caused him to have a heart attack when I accused him of murdering his daughter. Oh, he didn't murder her, by the way. She was killed by a schoolteacher who beat her and drugged her and left her on a football field for dead, but the police figured that part out later.*

By then, Henry was already gone. And I'm the one who killed him.

The words are so close to the tip of my tongue I can nearly taste them. "Can I tell you something?" Immediately I'm interrupted by the worker who comes with our food. Our children must have pizza radar. They're swarming the table in seconds, and it seems almost as quick until they're gone again, leaving half-eaten slices and tomato-stained napkins in their wake.

"I should warn you they have monstrous appetites," Russel says with a grin.

This time I manage to laugh, but the sound is hollow and unconvincing.

He holds my hand gingerly in his. I wonder if Sarah took the kids to Chuck E. Cheese like this. If they ate pizza like this. If he held her hand like this.

"You're so beautiful," Russel breathes. "Have I ever told you how blessed I am to have you in my life?"

He sounds so sincere. I can feel the love he's pouring into my soul at this exact moment. Our relationship might not be the most conventional, but the love we have for each other is real. I'm not sure I ever realized that until this very moment.

I think about Russel on the airplane, how he didn't question or complain when I told him I needed off. How he stayed by my side when the agents were asking me questions, how he did everything in his power to try to comfort me when I was falling apart piece by piece in front of him.

"I'm blessed to you have you in my life too," I assure him then clear my throat.

The setting is far from idyllic. The music is way too loud. The stage rodents are still dancing just a few feet away from us. Any second one of our children will come running up and interrupt our conversation.

But if I wait for the perfect time to get it all out, it will never happen.

There are two things I know right now. That I love Russel more than anything.

And I trust him.

It's time for me to make things right.

"There's something I've been meaning to tell you." I test the words, noting how they taste in my mouth. I admit that I have no idea how our conversation is going to go after this. I don't know if Russel's going to be hurt that I didn't tell him sooner or if he'll jump into fix-it mode like he did at the airport and try to figure out what he could possibly do to take away the pain of my past.

He might be angry. Might yell at me, demand to know why I kept something so huge a secret from him. But I do know his love for me will never change, and that conviction gives me the courage to grab hold of his hand and look him in the eyes. My gaze doesn't waver.

"Something happened to me when I was younger I never told you about," I begin.

He looks startled. Surprised. Perhaps even a little nervous.

But the love and protectiveness I saw earlier is still there, shining even more brightly as flashing lights and deafening music surround us and blast our senses.

I take a deep breath, wondering if he can feel the way my hand shakes.

Russel thinks I have some sort of divine intuition. His mother calls it the gift of discernment. I certainly don't claim to be a prophet, but I suppose there are certain things I just know even though I can't explain why.

What I know right now is that even though what I'm about to tell Russel will surprise him, even though it will be incredibly hard for him to hear, God is going to use this conversation to make our relationship stronger than it's ever been before.

"The reason I reacted like I did at the airport, the reason I could spot that girl and why I was so upset afterward wasn't because I've got some magical gift from the Lord. It's because I was kidnapped as a teenager." The truth pours out from my mouth. There's no more lights, no more noise. Even the children have been infused with the miraculous ability to entertain themselves without coming to interrupt us.

It's just me and Russel. Us and the painful secrets of my past.

I tell him about everything. Henry's basement. The night he died. His daughter's murder that went unsolved for so long.

"I'm sorry," I conclude, and for what feels like a lifetime, my husband remains completely stone-faced and silent.

"Why are you apologizing?" he finally asks.

"For not telling you sooner. I wanted to. I just ... I couldn't talk about it. I thought I was over it. I thought I'd moved on. I just ..." I take in a choppy breath. "I'm so sorry I lied to you." I nearly choke on the words. "But you deserve to know the truth."

Russel gets out of his seat then. Comes over to my side of the table and kneels down just like he did the night he proposed.

"You're the woman I love," he says. "You're the woman I chose to marry. You're everything to me."

I shake my head and pull my hand free to wipe away my tears. "I'm not who you think I am," I say, choking a little on the words.

He reaches his arms out toward me. Wraps me in a strong, protective hug. "You're everything I've ever needed or wanted," he whispers.

"You're everything to me too," I answer back.

And I realize then that that's the perfect truth.

Tears of Terror

Alana Terry

Christian Books Today

CHAPTER 1

CHELSEA KNEW FROM THE moment she stepped onto the airplane that she was in over her head.

Imposter syndrome. That's what her life coach called this feeling. The sense that no matter how far Chelsea advanced in her field, she still lived each and every day in constant fear of being discovered.

What would her colleagues do when they realized she was a fraud?

Chelsea had begged and schmoozed and pleaded in order to get this assignment. And now that she was on her way to Detroit, the nerves threatened to make her throw up.

Great. That's all she needed to start her three-hour flight.

Chelsea was one of the first passengers to board. A few men in stuffy business suits glared at her first-class seat, no doubt wondering why a 23-year-old who barely topped five feet tall needed that much extra leg room.

The truth was Chelsea didn't need the extra leg room. She'd splurged for the upgrade because her life coach told her to. If Chelsea wanted other people to take her and her career seriously, she had to take herself and her career seriously.

Starting with first-class seats.

She shouldn't feel guilty, right? After all, it was Clark's idea, not hers. She was just doing what her life coach told her to do.

Now that she was sitting here, with twice the space she actually needed, Chelsea couldn't remember why this frivolous luxury had seemed like such a good idea.

Tired of questioning herself, her career choices, and her right to be sitting here in first class, Chelsea did her best to silence that inner critic she hated so much. Instead, she did what came most naturally to her as a writer. She stared at the travelers as they boarded the plane, trying to come up with backstories for each and every one of them.

There were two girls, college aged by the looks of them, giggling as they lugged their mismatched carry-ons down the aisle. "You're gonna love Alaska," said one with bright blue highlights in her hair. "It's wicked awesome."

Alaska. Chelsea tried to picture what that might be like, but all her mind could conjure up were images of sled dogs and igloos. Somehow, she doubted that's how this cosmopolitan young passenger lived.

A scowling man with an SVSU sweatshirt boarded soon after. Chelsea thought through all of the local colleges and universities in the Boston area, trying to figure out if she could place the acronym. He wasn't dressed like a typical businessman. Maybe a divorcé on the way to visit his kids? He didn't strike Chelsea as the type to be racing off toward an illicit affair. More likely he was flying to Detroit to visit his beloved granny.

Chelsea sat back in her seat, ignoring the initial pangs of what was likely to turn into a piercing headache. When she'd graduated with her journalism degree, Chelsea had been so excited. So eager. A stereotype, really. Journalism major about to make a name for herself while simultaneously changing the world one perfectly constructed paragraph at a time.

And here she was, just a few years later, already turning into another trope — the jaded, lonely single woman wondering what she was doing chasing scoops and investigating scandals when the very next week the public would forget everything she wrote about in the first place.

Chelsea had begged her editor for the chance to cover the Brown Elementary controversy. A primary school in Detroit had been built on land that had once been the illegal dumping grounds for a pharmaceutical company. Tiny kindergartners were landing in the ER with respiratory problems and horrific fevers and rashes, but the school district claimed it had nothing to do with the school's location. Chelsea didn't understand why the entire country hadn't already shown up to march on the superintendent's home. Most people on the East Coast hadn't even heard of Brown Elementary School.

It was the kind of story that propelled Chelsea into reporting in the first place. Immigrant parents, many who could barely speak English, weren't given a voice. The children served by Brown Elementary were among Detroit's poorest, which is why the superintendent assumed he could get away with poisoning each and every one of them.

At her most zealous, Chelsea would have considered this the perfect assignment. Brown Elementary was news on a national scale. It was also the entire reason she dove into journalism as a wide-eyed first-year college student in the first place. To give a voice to the voiceless. To speak up for the downtrodden, shine the light on oppression, and just about any other cliché you could come up with.

But now she knew what to expect. She'd show up in Detroit, interview some of the parents whose kids had fallen ill, talk to the few key players who were trying to stand up for this underrepresented community. Then she'd fly back to Boston, type up her story, maybe even get choked up as she did her best to represent the frustration these parents felt. If she did her job well, she might even get a little nod from her editor, a pat on the back or a "Nice article" from one of her colleagues.

And then nothing.

No marches on Detroit. No public outcry. No real justice for the kids of Brown Elementary.

In short, no change.

So why did she keep doing it?

At her most jaded, she'd probably answer because it paid the bills. A journalism degree wasn't cheap, and at the rate she was going she'd have to keep writing until she was eighty to pay off all her debt.

But there was still something inside her, something that hadn't yet been completely hardened. The idealistic, trusting, impossible hope that this time would be different. Her upcoming article would be the one that made that lasting impact. That effected positive change. That united citizens from across the political spectrum, that inspired the general public to rise up and support the children of Detroit.

She could always hope, right?

Chelsea opened the lid of her water bottle and took a big drink.

Working on this story was a dream come true for her, and she didn't want to reach such a pessimistic state that she refused to see it for the incredible opportunity it was.

As men, women, and children continued to file past her first-class seat, Chelsea took a deep breath, reminded herself that this trip represented the entire reason she'd gotten into journalism in the first place, and allowed her mind to hope and dream.

CHAPTER 2

Flights coming into Boston had been delayed due to weather, and Chelsea's plane was late to take off. They should be in the air by now, but they hadn't even shut the doors.

Chelsea had spent the past twenty minutes watching more and more passengers board, trying to dream up life stories for each and every one of them.

There was a Middle Eastern man traveling with his aged father. A man in a Hawaiian shirt, followed by a surly looking teen. Moms with babies, parents traveling with toddlers. A woman boarded whom Chelsea recognized as a well-known Bible study teacher. Chelsea's mom had been reading Meredith Crowley's books and watching her videos for over a decade. It had been a few years since Chelsea had regularly attended church with her parents, but every so often her mom would send her a link to one of Meredith Crowley's podcast episodes. Chelsea was surprised when Meredith continued past the first-class seats and headed toward economy.

An eccentric old woman with shockingly white hair boarded. She was even shorter than Chelsea, but there was something fiery in the old woman's face. Chelsea tried to think up an appropriate backstory. A doctor? Teacher? Maybe a flight nurse. There was something confident, something piercing in the woman's expression. It reminded Chelsea of an interview she'd done a few months ago with an old woman who had the distinction of being the very first female detective on Boston's police force. Whoever this passenger on the airplane was, Chelsea could sense she had the spirit of an adventurer. A pioneer.

Chelsea liked to think of herself in the same way. At least at one point she had. Female journalists weren't oddities anymore, but there were still obvious roadblocks she faced on her way to success. Any time one of the men she was sent to interview called her "Sweetie," any time a colleague or a lead tried to flirt with her, Chelsea was reminded of the inherent setbacks of her position. Unfortunately the environment was hostile enough that women were suspicious and jealous of each other instead of joining forces and standing up for themselves. Chelsea knew for a fact that some of her colleagues talked behind her back, complaining and gossiping that the only reason she'd progressed as far as she had in her career was because she was a pretty face. As hard as Chelsea tried to keep her reputation squeaky clean and her work relationships free from drama, there were still people who thought she was advancing in her career by sleeping with her bosses.

As if.

Chelsea's coach told her that the only way to prove these gossips wrong was to become an even better journalist. The problem with Clark's advice was that with each new step Chelsea took up the ladder of acclaim, there were over a dozen of her colleagues who hated Chelsea for her advancement and made up horrible lies about her success.

Chelsea was storing up all these experiences. One day she planned to write a memoir exposing the rampant sexism and harassment female journalists still faced in the twenty-first century. Until then, she had to do exactly what Clark told her to do in those coaching calls she was paying so much for. Focus on advancing her career, silencing the inner voice that told her she wasn't making any difference.

"Ladies and gentlemen, I'm Tracy, one of your flight attendants today." The voice pulled Chelsea out of her pity party. While the flight attendant recited her safety speech, Chelsea sat back in her seat and tried to relax. She'd been working insanely long hours, preparing for her Detroit trip, finishing up work on a story about police brutality in a city as purportedly progressive and forward-thinking as Boston. If anything, Chelsea deserved a few hours of uninterrupted rest. She'd already made herself a promise that on the way to Detroit she wouldn't pull out any writing. Her cell was prepped with dozens of podcast episodes she'd been meaning to catch up on. Nothing overtly work related. Mostly true crime shows she liked to follow. And if she felt guilty being that frivolous with her time, she had several workbook assignments due to Clark before their coaching call next week.

"The captain has closed the doors," Tracy announced to the cabin, "and we'll be taking off shortly. Welcome aboard Flight 219, offering you nonstop service to Detroit."

CHAPTER 3

WHILE THE PASSENGER SEATED beside her slept, Chelsea pulled out the workbook assignments Clark had emailed her last week. Typically, she wouldn't want to write anything so personal with strangers looking over her shoulder, but her neighbor was dead to the world, the aisle was twice as wide as the ones in coach, so Chelsea had all the privacy she could want.

She'd met Clark last year, covering a story about the digital nomad lifestyle. Clark was based in Boston, but he'd set up his online coaching practice so he could travel the world. After their interview, she'd been intrigued by him and the raving testimonials of his clients, so she signed up for an initial coaching consult. She'd been his student for only about six months, and already Clark had called her for their coaching sessions from too many different exotic locations for Chelsea to remember.

There were aspects of the nomadic lifestyle Chelsea found alluring. Like never having to live in an area with snow if she didn't want to. Last month, Clark had set up his laptop in a little coworking space in New Zealand. He said he would have liked to stay there longer, but the time difference made it difficult for him to connect with his clients on the East Coast. Now, if Chelsea remembered correctly, he was temporarily settled in Costa Rica, in a little village where the average temperatures never dipped below 65 or above 72.

Yes, that was something Chelsea could definitely get used to.

Still, she wondered if Clark ever got lonely. Chelsea had been born and raised in Worcester. Her parents and grandparents and she all lived within five miles of each other. Her older brother was the odd one out, having settled with his new wife in Delaware, which may as well have been the deep south as far as the rest of the family was concerned.

Chelsea's family was close, relationally and not just geographically. She ate dinner with her parents at least once a week, more often than that when her apartment's hot water heater acted up or the coin-op washing machines downstairs stopped working. She'd specifically planned her trip to Detroit so that she could have her article researched, written, and on her editor's desk with time to spare before Christmas.

Chelsea stared at her notebook page, thinking about her schedule for the next few days. The Detroit superintendent was impossible to reach by phone, but that didn't mean Chelsea wouldn't try to get a quote from him in person. She had an interview lined up with a medical doctor who'd treated some of the elementary students who'd fallen ill. In two days, a group of parents were meeting at a local YMCA to discuss the situation.

Chelsea tapped her pen on her tray table, reminding herself she wasn't supposed to be thinking about work right now. That's something she and Clark had talked about extensively in their coaching calls. Chelsea needed to develop better boundaries to ensure that her entire life didn't get overrun by journalism. So far, she hadn't found too much success in that nebulous quest for work-life balance. She'd joined a gym but stopped going after that creepy janitor kept ogling her during spin class. She went online a week later and read that two years ago another employee had been fired and faced legal charges for hiding in a closet in the women's locker room. Next time, Chelsea wouldn't join a gym without reading the reviews first. Except now she was locked into a year-long contract.

Well, nobody could claim she hadn't tried.

Chelsea's best friend from high school was working as a youth leader at a large church in the Cambridge area. It was the perfect job for Brie, really. Even as teens, Brie had been the most serious about her faith, and Chelsea was happy her friend had found a calling that was not only rewarding but offered her a regular paycheck.

It seemed as if everyone Chelsea knew when she was younger was now settled into real life. Brie had church. Her brother had his wife and new job out in Delaware, as well as something like a dozen nieces and nephews he saw on an almost daily basis.

Chelsea knew she should be thankful for her job and the opportunities God had given her. Heaven knew finding steady work as a journalist straight out of college was on the same level as stumbling across a winning lottery ticket while picking up litter in a parking lot. So why did she feel like she was still searching for her life's meaning?

Clark told her it was a normal stage of young adulthood. Brie said it was because Chelsea still hadn't surrendered her life totally over to God, whatever that meant.

Mom thought this sense of unrest came because Chelsea had such miserable luck in the dating world.

Whatever the reason, Chelsea couldn't shake the feeling that something was missing from her life, and that unease only made her feel guilty. She had every reason to be thankful. Her sense of dissatisfaction with her personal status quo was the reason she'd hired Clark to be her life coach in the first place. That and the fact that when she interviewed him, he seemed to light up every time he talked about helping people discover their life's deeper meaning. Well, if he could help Chelsea find even a tenth of the motivation and passion she saw in him, he was well worth his monthly retainer.

That was why she was so disciplined about completing each and every task he assigned her. That was why she'd printed up these dozen workbook pages and was committed to knocking some of them out before she put in her ear buds and tuned out the world with something light and funny to listen to.

She took a deep breath, tried to get her mind into a state of gentle awareness like Clark taught her, and began the process of filling out her first worksheet.

The problem with Clark's coaching method was that Chelsea still hadn't learned to turn off her inner editor. She read each and every word of her answer through Clark's eyes, wondering what he'd think of her, what he'd say to her.

Sometimes, hearing his gentle encouragement in the back of her head was immensely helpful. Like the time she wrote about how stupid she felt for stumbling over her words at a meeting with mostly male colleagues. *I hate it when I make myself sound like a fool*, she'd written, and immediately heard Clark's encouraging words.

Would you tell a five-year-old that she was stupid and you hated her if she pronounced a word wrong or got a little flustered with public speaking?

No, of course she wouldn't.

This coaching process was taking longer than Chelsea hoped, but at least she was learning how to be gentle with herself.

Chelsea's mom didn't approve. According to her, it wasn't right for a female to get counseling from a male. It also didn't help that Mom didn't understand the difference between a life coach and a licensed therapist to begin with. She assumed that the fact that Chelsea was talking to anybody about her deep personal issues meant she was somehow psychologically scarred.

"I didn't think we did that bad of a job raising you," she'd say, as if all Chelsea and Clark talked about were the lowest points in Chelsea's childhood.

Brie was a better listener, but even though she never said so, Chelsea got the sense that her best friend would approve more if Chelsea went to a pastor or Christian counselor.

Chelsea wasn't against church or Christianity. She still attended services with her parents if she was home for the weekend, and she couldn't remember missing an Easter sunrise or Christmas Eve service in her entire life. Sometimes it bothered her the way Christians she loved acted as though she was selfish or somehow less of a believer because she wasn't working for the church like Brie or attending Bible studies or prayer meetings three or four days a week like her mom. Chelsea loved the Lord but had other interests and hobbies outside of church. What was so wrong with that?

The worksheet she'd been journaling on had questions about her past achievements. When Chelsea saw all the accomplishments she'd made in the past two years written out on paper, she felt even more guilty for being so dissatisfied. If Chelsea could have seen this list during her first year of college, if she could have known where all that hard work would one day take her, she probably would have started squealing with giddy excitement.

So where was the joy, the spark?

Clark's worksheet — his ta-da list as opposed to a to-do list — was meant to help Chelsea realize all that she did have to be thankful for, but instead it just reinforced her fear that there was something intrinsically wrong with her.

Imagine you're receiving an award for all the hard work you've done. Your friends, loved ones, and colleagues are all there cheering for you. How do you feel?

Chelsea stared at the question, wondering if she'd answer it truthfully or the way Clark expected.

She poised her pen above the lines. *Honestly*, she wrote, *I'd feel like a total fraud. Like any minute whoever gave me the award would turn on the lights and stop the applause halfway through and tell everyone that it was all some giant mistake.*

She let out her breath. Her answer wasn't going to make her life coach happy.

Is that what you'd tell a little five-year-old girl if she was about to accept an award she'd earned by her hard work? Clark's voice in her mind was gentle but firm.

Of course she wouldn't tell that to a proud little kid on the happiest day of her life. So why did she say it to herself? What was wrong with her?

Maybe Clark gave her these assignments to prove how messed up she was. Maybe it was all some giant ploy so she'd keep on paying him for coaching.

Chelsea's negative thoughts were interrupted when a passenger tapped her on the shoulder. It was the same white-haired woman Chelsea had been studying during the boarding process.

"Excuse me," the old woman said, her wrinkles breaking out into tiny streams when she smiled.

Chelsea shut her notebook so the old woman couldn't read what she'd written.

"The bathroom in the back of the plane is full," the traveler explained, "so I came up here to use this one. As soon as I saw you here, I knew I had to stop and say something. I don't usually do this type of thing, but I just had to introduce myself."

She reached out a hand, which Chelsea took automatically.

"My name is Lucy Jean," the passenger said, "but I insist on being called Grandma Lucy. And I believe the Lord has a message for you."

CHAPTER 4

CHELSEA BLINKED UP AT the stranger. A message from God? It sounded like something her mom would arrange. Hire some weirdo on Craigslist to stalk Chelsea on her flight and make small talk about Jesus, remind Chelsea that there were about a million ways she could become a better Christian if she just set her mind to it.

Chelsea stared and didn't know what to say.

Despite her obvious age, Grandma Lucy showed no signs of pain or stiffness when she squatted down in the aisle to bring herself to Chelsea's eye level.

"I wasn't supposed to be on this flight," she began. "But the airlines changed my itinerary, and wouldn't you know it, I told the Lord that if he wanted to disrupt my plans, he's more than welcome to. I figure that if he put me on a different flight, it's because there's someone on this plane who needs to hear about his love."

Chelsea realized that she'd rather fill out a hundred of Clark's journaling pages, no matter how bad they made her feel about herself, than sit here and get preached at. Both her mom and best friend wanted Chelsea to take her faith more seriously, but they certainly wouldn't start lecturing her in the aisle on an airplane full of strangers.

"I think the bathroom looks unoccupied," Chelsea said in a quiet voice. Too quiet.

Grandma Lucy didn't even appear to have heard.

"There's something I sensed in my spirit the moment I saw you," she went on. "God has called you to something amazing and profound. Tell me, do you have children?"

Of course this fanatic woman would assume that the only way Chelsea could make God happy was to pop out a bunch of kids. "No," she answered.

Grandma Lucy didn't look surprised. "Well then, tell me what you do for a living. Are you a teacher, maybe?"

"No, a journalist."

The old woman's eyes lit up. "Journalist? My grandson is a journalist. Have you read anything by Ian McCallister?"

"The name sounds familiar," Chelsea answered.

"Well, let me tell you, the world needs more Christian journalists, that's for sure. With all the terrible things going on today, every reporter with a slanted agenda ..." Her voice trailed off, and Chelsea dared hope it meant she'd run out of things to say, but apparently that wasn't the case.

"I just want to tell you that I think it's amazing, the work that you're doing."

Chelsea stared at the stranger in surprise. What did this little old lady know about her work? She hadn't even given Grandma Lucy her name.

Before Chelsea could do or say anything in protest, Grandma Lucy grabbed Chelsea's hand, seized it in hers, and started to pray.

"Dear Lord, great and merciful Savior, you are so good to us, and you are so gracious to look past our shortcomings and use us for your kingdom as you see fit. I pray for my dear sister today, Lord. I believe that you've anointed this young woman. I believe you have unbelievable plans for her, plans to prosper her and not to harm her. I believe that you will walk with her through whatever trials she might have to face, and that you will use these storms in her life to draw her closer to you. Teach her to rely on you, Lord. Teach her that without you, she can do absolutely nothing. Teach her that you are the way and the truth and the life, and that it is such a wonderous and glorious honor to be able to worship you as our Lord and Savior.

"May you guide her in every step she takes. Keep her as the apple of your eye. I believe you've poured out on her an incredible gift, a gift that she wants to use for you and for your glory."

Grandma Lucy's eyes were open and staring overtly at her notebook. Chelsea was glad she'd thought to close it before this strange encounter.

She was trying to form the words to explain that the old woman's actions were making her uncomfortable when Grandma Lucy stood up, straightened her blouse, and let go of Chelsea's hand. "Well then," she said, as if they'd been chatting about something as innocuous as the weather, "it looks like the bathroom's open now. We'll talk more later."

And she walked down the aisle, leaving Chelsea's brain reeling.

CHAPTER 5

AN HOUR AFTER HER encounter with the outspoken stranger, Chelsea still hadn't been able to shake off the old woman's words. What did it all mean? Pieces and fragments of Grandma Lucy's prayer floated chaotically through her brain.

I believe that you will walk with her through whatever trials she might have to face, and that you will use these storms in her life to draw her closer to you. In a way, Chelsea knew that these words were meant to somehow encourage and inspire her, but they sounded more ominous than anything else. Was this eccentric old lady seriously wishing bad things to happen in Chelsea's life just so she could get right with the Lord again?

What kind of sense did that make?

Teach her that without you, she can do absolutely nothing. Chelsea thought about her list of accomplishments, what Clark called her ta-da list. Well, that was something, wasn't it? In addition to feeling guilty for not appreciating her life more than she did, was Chelsea supposed to do penance because she hadn't acknowledged God enough for all that she'd achieved?

Teach her that you are the way and the truth and the life, and that it is such a wonderous and glorious honor to be able to worship you as our Lord and Savior. Never had a prayer sounded so preachy to Chelsea's ears. Never had she felt so condemned, so unworthy.

Clark would tell her she was giving this stranger too much authority. Nobody could make Chelsea feel sad or glad or guilty but herself. This stranger had no bearing on Chelsea's life. Her words shouldn't matter.

And yet somehow they did.

Such a wonderous and glorious honor to be able to worship you as our Lord and Savior... That last part of Grandma Lucy's prayer stuck out the most. When had Chelsea ever thought of worshiping God as a privilege or honor? Church was something she attended to keep her mom placated. God and the Bible were things Chelsea talked about with her best friend because faith was important to Brie, just like journalism and politics were important to Chelsea.

Such a wonderous and glorious honor... Was it possible that this was the thing that had been missing from Chelsea's life? Was that why she'd felt so dissatisfied for so long?

She tried to imagine what Clark would tell her if he were sitting next to her, if they could talk about this bizarre encounter with a stranger on the plane.

"She didn't even ask if I wanted her to pray for me," Chelsea would whine.

"And how did that make you feel?" he would prompt.

How did it make her feel? She knew how it should make her feel.

That part was easy.

It should make her feel completely annoyed. Grandma Lucy didn't even know if Chelsea was a Christian. What if she was a Muslim or a Jew and found Grandma Lucy's prayer to Jesus totally offensive?

What if Chelsea was just an introverted and somewhat shy young woman who didn't appreciate having that much attention drawn to herself? Who wanted a stranger prying into her personal life like that?

Chelsea should be annoyed. Put off. It'd be well within her rights to complain to the flight attendant, force them to tell Grandma Lucy not to bother her anymore. Maybe she'd even write a blog post about her experience. Something that could serve as a warning to other religious fanatics to be careful not to shove their beliefs down people's throats on an airplane, where it was literally impossible to get up and leave to end an awkward conversation.

But Chelsea didn't feel annoyed. She didn't feel put off.

Something had happened to her during the old woman's prayer, something that made her wish for a quiet place to sit and think. Think and maybe cry.

There was no mistaking that Grandma Lucy had been out of place. You can't just walk up to a stranger and ignore all semblance of personal space and privacy. That's not how life works. Not how a civilized society works.

And yet ...

Lord, I believe that you've anointed this young woman. Anointed. It was a word Chelsea had heard. A word she could define. But what was this strange old woman trying to say to her? Chelsea was anointed ... What did that even mean?

I believe you have unbelievable plans for her, plans to prosper her and not to harm her. One of Chelsea's biggest frustrations with herself was that she had no spark of joy when she thought about the future. Sure, she planned on advancing in her career. She planned on covering bigger, more impressive stories. More bylines. Better job offers. Bigger benefit packages.

But what for?

Plans to prosper her and not to harm her ... Chelsea tried to imagine the future that this old woman was envisioning. Was it possible that Chelsea's destiny included more than growing a name for herself, working her fingers raw at her laptop, and giving herself eyestrain and migraine headaches from staring at her screen for ten hours a day?

Of course there was something more to life. Isn't that why Chelsea had hired Clark in the first place? It wasn't like she wasn't trying to better herself, improve her outlook. Carve out that glorious future Grandma Lucy seemed to believe was in store for her.

And yet here she was, still filling out the same workbook pages, still asking herself the same questions. Had she and Clark made any real progress at all since they'd met?

Teach her to rely on you, Lord ... Guide her in every step she takes. The way Grandma Lucy talked about it, you would think that Chelsea could jump online and schedule an appointment with the Almighty himself just like she did when she needed to talk to her life coach. Wouldn't that make things simpler? Not to mention the fact that she wouldn't have to pay God for his time.

But life didn't work like that. God gave people the Bible. He gave people consciences. He gave people good teachers. And the rest was up to them to figure out, right?

Or maybe there was something more to it. Chelsea didn't know exactly what the Lord was trying to tell her right now, but she desperately wanted to find out.

CHAPTER 6

THE PLANE HIT A patch of turbulence, and Chelsea realized she'd been staring at Clark's worksheet page but hadn't written anything since her unexpected conversation with Grandma Lucy. Even now the old woman's words from her prayer still rang in Chelsea's ears. A siren song. Calling her somewhere.

But where?

It was impossible to give a name to the ennui, the unrest. All Chelsea knew was that she wanted to figure out what her soul was trying to tell her. She needed something more out of life. She'd known that for years. That was why she hired a life coach in the first place.

But there was something else. Something still missing after all these months of intense journaling and dozens of hours of reflection. Her mom would say that what Chelsea was missing was an intimate connection with the Lord. Even Brie, who wasn't nearly as tactless as her mother could be, felt the same way.

But Chelsea was scared. She'd met too many obnoxious Christians. Heard too many horrible stories from her colleagues about the bigotry and chauvinism and hatred that infected the church.

Chelsea didn't want to be like that. Didn't want to breathe Bible verses down people's necks like her mom. Didn't want to devote her life to church ministry like Brie. More than anything, Chelsea didn't want to turn into the kind of Christian who'd make a scene of herself on a crowded airplane to kneel down in the aisle and pray for a complete stranger.

She wanted to be herself. Chelsea. The journalist. The writer. The career woman.

She just wanted to be a happier version of herself.

Was that so much to ask?

For a couple years now, Chelsea had wondered if what she was really dealing with was some sort of clinical depression. It had gotten to the point last winter that if she hadn't been worried about insurance coverage, she probably would have made an appointment to talk to her family doctor. She hadn't brought it up to her parents. Thankfully, she was still managing just fine, but maybe all the mental unrest she was experiencing was nothing more than a chemical unbalance. How could she really know unless she talked about it with an expert, right?

Chelsea squeezed her eyes shut. She was tired of being so mopey, so down all the time. She had a great life. Hadn't that ta-da list she wrote for Clark proved that? Chelsea deserved to be happy. Deserved a brain that could truly experience a deep sense of appreciation for all that she'd accomplished.

Maybe once she got back from Detroit she'd call the doctor ...

"Help!" The desperate scream from several rows behind her made Chelsea jump in her seat. She bumped her thigh on the tray, hurtling her notebook to the ground, as a young woman struggled in the aisle with a middle-aged man in a Hawaiian shirt.

"Help me!" the girl screamed again.

A flight attendant raced ahead. Chelsea didn't know if she was supposed to stare or join the screaming or simply mind her own business.

She overheard someone shout the word *kidnapped*, and her heart froze for an instant. What was going on?

"Let her go." There were several passengers in the aisle now, and everyone was trying to pry a teenaged girl away from the man in the Hawaiian shirt. Chelsea didn't feel right staring, but what choice did she have? One of her colleagues had recently written an article about human trafficking in the US and how airlines were now training all their personnel to spot potential victims. Is that what was going on?

A muscular man planted himself squarely in the aisle. "Air marshal," he announced authoritatively, pulling out his sidearm. "Freeze."

For a moment, Chelsea allowed herself to experience relief. If there was an air marshal on board, everything would be under control. This girl would be saved. Her assailant would get the full punishment allowed under federal law. Life would go on as normal. Chelsea was already thinking about a pitch for a new story about air marshals, airline safety, and human trafficking.

The captain's voice sounded over the PA, but before he could get out a complete sentence, his announcement was cut short by the screams of another terrified passenger. Chelsea instinctively jerked her body around to see what was happening behind her. Two men were now attacking the air marshal. One of them grabbed the officer's gun. This time it was Chelsea who screamed as the man brought the butt of the gun down on the air marshal's skull. He crumpled to the ground and lay in a grotesque heap in the aisle.

A man Chelsea hadn't noticed before raised the air marshal's gun above his head. "I'm in charge of this airplane now," he declared. "My name is Bradley Strong, and I suggest you all do exactly as I say."

CHAPTER 7

CHELSEA'S HEART COULDN'T HANDLE the stress. Any instant, it was going to give out entirely.

Her head was light. Was she even breathing?

"Listen up," Bradley bellowed. His voice carried and echoed through every crevice and cranny of the cabin. "Let me tell you how it's gonna go."

Behind him, the man in the Hawaiian shirt was binding the air marshal and dragging his unconscious body to the back of the cabin. Chelsea thought she saw him make eye contact and give a silent nod to another passenger as well. How many men were in on this plot to take over their plane?

"You have to let us go," a woman pleaded. "Please, you don't want to do this."

"No." Bradley's voice was level and eerily controlled. He continued to aim the air marshal's gun overhead. "The truth is I don't want to do this, but the Detroit mayor and his crony superintendent have failed our kids. All year, we've been complaining about the health hazards of the Brown Elementary School playground. All year, we've been calling, petitioning, and demanding that the superintendent move our children to a safer location. And you know what? Nobody's listened. Until now."

Chelsea's brain was struggling to keep up with his rant. It didn't make sense. What did any of these passengers on board have to do with Brown Elementary School or the Detroit school system?

Another pocket of turbulence shook the cabin. Several passengers screamed. Chelsea was so shocked she couldn't even be certain if she'd been one of them, but the raw soreness of her throat suggested she was.

A man from the back of the cabin took advantage of the chaos and raced at Bradley. While the plane jerked yet again, the two men grappled, grunting loudly. Chelsea was about to be sick, maybe from the fear or the turbulence. Maybe both.

A single shot rang out. Everything happened so quickly, Chelsea didn't even realize it was the gun that had fired until she saw the man who attacked Bradley lying in the aisle, a pool of blood forming around him.

Bradley used his foot to push the man to the side, stepped over his body, and addressed the passengers in an eerie monotone.

"Anybody else feel like questioning my authority?"

Chelsea didn't know what to say or what to do. It was one thing to be a bystander on a flight where a kidnapped girl was rescued from her abductor. Her brain still hadn't processed that event, and now she was supposed to take in the fact that she was on a hijacked plane, the terrorist had a gun, and one passenger had been shot. She wasn't sure if the air marshal had survived his attack or not, but he was now bound in the back of the cabin. Even if he wasn't tied up and unconscious, what could he do now to help them?

The man in the aisle was most definitely dead, however. Chelsea could tell.

When she was a little girl, Chelsea and her parents once stumbled across the scene of an accident. A drunk man had smashed his car straight into a telephone pole on a deserted stretch of road in the middle of the day.

He was still alive when her family pulled up to see if they could offer any help.

"Don't get out of the car," Dad ordered. "And keep your eyes shut no matter what."

Of course, that kind of rule was next to impossible for an inquisitive seven-year-old to follow. Chelsea had stared, her eyes both wide and dry, as her dad pulled the man out of the car and her mom attempted CPR. The entire scene lasted only a few minutes, and her parents insisted the man didn't die until he was en route to the hospital, but Chelsea knew what she saw. Knew that the life had already left him.

And she immediately understood why her parents had ordered her not to look.

Chelsea mentioned the story to Clark as an aside one day. He wanted to explore the possibility that the helplessness and hopelessness Chelsea experienced as a little girl, forced to stay in her parents' car while a man literally died in front of her eyes, sparked the passion she now had to speak up for the downtrodden, to use her words to give voice to the voiceless.

She had never thought about the incident in those terms before, but his hypothesis seemed logical.

Since then, Chelsea had been to one funeral wake and avoided looking at the body. Until now, she'd never seen another dead person.

Until now ...

The hijacker had ordered the passengers to take out their cell phones and record his tirade.

"My name is Bradley Strong," he repeated to the cameras. "I reside at 324 Trenton Street in Detroit, Michigan. My children attend Brown Elementary School. If you've been paying attention to the news at all, you'll know what that means."

Chelsea's heart was pounding all the way up in her throat, not just because she was on a plane with a murderous terrorist and at least one dead body already, but also because she was so familiar with the controversy at the school Bradley was talking about. For a sickening moment, she feared he must know. Must know that she was a journalist covering the story. Maybe he'd blame her and people like her for not exposing the situation earlier. Plans for the building started over a year ago. Now here it was nearly Christmas, and the poor kids had been attending classes on this toxic wasteland since the fall.

Chelsea understood his frustration. If she had children of her own, she'd rather move to a different state than send them to a place like Brown. Unfortunately, the families served by that school generally lacked the funds to move even to a different neighborhood. The town hall meetings where they could have voiced their complaints were held during working hours when most of them were on the clock, and a significant portion of them didn't feel comfortable communicating in English, which is how their children's school ended up being built on a former pharmaceutical sludge pile in the first place.

Chelsea had never experienced anything like what the families at Brown Elementary had, at least not firsthand. Growing up in Worcester, she'd been smack dab in the center of middle class. Comfortable suburbs. Involved parents. Quiet cul de sac. Sometimes she felt guilty. What right did she have trying to speak up for the oppressed when her entire life had been so comfortable?

Clark told her that instead of resenting her privileged existence, she should leverage her position as a relatively attractive, reasonably articulate white female college graduate in order to raise awareness for those who were more easily overlooked. His words even coincided with a Bible verse Brie liked to quote: *From everyone who has been given much, much will be demanded; and from the one who has been entrusted with much, much more will be asked.*

Chelsea sometimes wondered why matters of faith came so much simpler to her friend. Brie had grown up with an alcoholic father and an enabling mother. Her older brother had been in and out of jail on multiple drug charges, and her family had always struggled to make ends meet. Even now, Brie was living in a studio apartment in a neighborhood rough enough that Chelsea begged her to get a smart security system, or at least a second deadbolt for the door that she could fasten from the inside.

As a minority, as a young adult from a not-so-idyllic family background, Brie had every reason to be anxious, depressed, and maladjusted. But she was the most put-together person Chelsea knew, which only made Chelsea feel even more guilty for the personal struggles she'd been wrestling with since her early teens.

Bradley continued his tirade against the state of Michigan, the Detroit mayor, the nation who sat back and did nothing while helpless children were being poisoned day in and day out. The majority of his rant was directed at the superintendent of the Detroit school district.

"Charles Weston has failed our kids," he spat out. It was a name Chelsea was quite familiar with. In her preliminary research on the Brown scandal, Charles Weston stood out as the primary culprit, which was why she'd been working so hard to try to get a hold of him before she'd made this trip.

The fact that the terrorist holding her plane hostage was protesting the very story Chelsea was flying out to Detroit to cover was unnerving. It was bad enough sitting here with an armed gunman who'd already killed at least one passenger. But the fact that she and Bradley were somehow both concerned about the same travesty impacting the kids of Detroit made her feel squeamish and alarmed. Airplane hijackers were supposed to be greedy, monstrous villains. Was it possible that Bradley was nothing more than a desperate father, doing anything and everything in his power to make it so his kids didn't get lead and arsenic poisoning when they played four-square outside after lunch?

No, that didn't make sense. Chelsea cared about the students at Brown Elementary School, which was why she was on this plane. Never in her wildest dreams would she consider hijacking one.

Maybe there was something deeper to it than this. Maybe Brown was just a smokescreen. Maybe Bradley would have turned toward murder and terrorism no matter what school his children went to, and his frustration with the mayor of the Detroit and the school district superintendent was simply an easy excuse.

It certainly was an easier explanation to accept.

"By the way," Bradley was saying. "If Charles Weston is looking for his precious little girl, I want you to know I've been keeping Selena in good hands." He grabbed the wide-eyed teenager the air marshal had been trying to protect. Lifting her up by the collar of her T-shirt, he shoved her in front of a passenger's phone.

"Say hello to your daddy," Bradley told her, his voice taunting and full of spite.

Selena Weston was shaking so hard she could barely stand. Overcome with compassion and pity, Chelsea resisted the urge to jump out of her seat and race to the girl's side.

Just stay calm, Chelsea told herself. *Stay calm, stay quiet, and you just might get through this ordeal alive.*

CHAPTER 8

CHELSEA HAD NEVER CONSIDERED herself that gifted in prayer. Her mom could sit for hours with her Bible and a cup of coffee and pour out her heart to God while highlighting passages of Scripture and jotting down notes in the margins. Chelsea, on the other hand, found her mind wandering when her dad said grace before the evening meal.

Even now, Chelsea realized, she was no better at praying than when she wasn't being held hostage thirty-thousand feet above ground by an insane murderer intent on kidnapping, hijacking, and terrorism.

Her mind wanted to pray, but she couldn't slow down the racing of her heart long enough to focus on anything. There was nothing in her soul, no pleas for protection, no comforting passages of Scripture brought to mind at just the right time.

There was only uncertainty and fear.

Bradley was pacing up and down the aisle. Each and every time he came close to first class, Chelsea willed herself to grow even smaller. When his steps receded and he headed toward the back of the cabin, Chelsea experienced a surge of relief that left her head light and her body cold. A surge of relief that also left her feeling incredibly guilty, because it just meant his attentions were focused on some other helpless, terrorized passenger.

"I'm going to give Charles Weston five minutes to call me," Bradley declared. "Five minutes for a little heart-to-heart with the city's good old superintendent. We can talk about anything you like. About the elementary school you built on poison, about the grown men on the construction crew who landed in the hospital. Or maybe you'd like to talk about something else. Your daughter, maybe? I don't want to hurt her, but I assure you I will."

Chelsea couldn't bring herself to look at the kidnapped teen who'd returned to her seat after being paraded in front of the cameras. From somewhere behind her, Chelsea heard muffled whimpering, but she had no idea if it was from Selena Weston or any of the other hundreds of passengers on the flight. They were all here, all captive. They had all seen Bradley shoot his first victim. And yet Chelsea felt incredibly alone in the horror of it, as if nobody else in the world could imagine the terror she was experiencing at this exact moment in time.

She tried to think of what Clark might tell her in a situation like this, but her coach's voice in her mind was silent.

She tried to guess what her mother would do if she were stuck here on this flight. Pray. That was probably it. Mom and Dad always talked about heaven, and they were both certain about their future in the afterlife. Chelsea believed the exact same things they did, but that didn't mean she was anywhere near ready to die.

Please, God. Chelsea couldn't think of anything else even remotely appropriate to say.

"Five minutes," Bradley repeated, making a show of checking on the time. "Five minutes before another hostage dies."

Please, God. It was the only prayer Chelsea could muster.

She just hoped it would be enough.

CHAPTER 9

BRADLEY'S TIMER BEEPED. HE pulled his phone out of his pocket and turned off the alarm.

The silence was terrifying.

"That's five minutes," he declared in a monotone. "Time's up."

Chelsea held her breath. Any doubts she had about Bradley's willingness to use the air marshal's gun had already vanished when he shot the first passenger. Now it wasn't a question of whether or not he was going to kill. The only question was who would end up in the aisle next, collapsed in a puddle of blood.

For a brief stint during her tenth-grade year, Chelsea had entertained thoughts of going into the medical field. Nursing, maybe labor and delivery, she wasn't sure. Plans changed one night in youth group when they were playing a raucous game of sardines in the dark. Brie tripped over a stair on the sanctuary platform, cracking her forehead open on the baptistry. While they waited for Brie's mother to pick her up and take her to the ER, Chelsea sat beside her best friend, terrified that Brie was about to bleed to death by her side.

It was that night when Chelsea realized she could never handle blood or trauma or basically any type of emergency.

Brie was fine. She didn't even need stitches. It didn't matter how many adults and experts assured Chelsea that the amount of blood from head injuries almost always made them appear worse than they were. She'd spent ten terrible minutes convinced her best friend was going to die, just like the man in that car accident when she was a kid, and given how her body still shook the next morning when she woke up, Chelsea realized she just wasn't built to handle emergency situations.

A lot changed that night.

Brie now had a permanent scar above her left eyebrow. The teens from youth group weren't allowed to run in the sanctuary anymore. And Chelsea gave up her plans for nursing.

Maybe if Chelsea had continued down that career path, things would be different right now. She'd have no reason to be on this flight to Detroit, for one thing.

There was a verse Chelsea and Brie had memorized when they were on the Bible quiz team together in middle school. Chelsea still remembered it verbatim: *And we know that in all things God works for the good of those who love him, who have been called according to his purpose.* It was the kind of passage meant to encourage Christians to persevere during hard times, knowing that good would eventually come from their trials.

But how would you tell that to the man Bradley had just killed? How would you tell that to the next victim he shot?

"Mr. Weston," Bradley boomed. He spoke into the cameras that were pointed at him as if he'd hosted his own YouTube talk show for decades. Chelsea couldn't help but wonder what might have happened if he'd put this same amount of energy that he spent on hijacking this airplane into actually campaigning or raising awareness for the students of Brown Elementary.

"I've been patient with you, Mr. Weston," Bradley announced. "I've given you five minutes to call me. More than five minutes, actually. And you know what I've gotten from you? Nothing. Nada. I thought that if I made this personal, if I actually had your daughter on board this flight with me, that you'd be willing to negotiate. I guess I was wrong."

He paused, stared at the camera, and glowered. "You've had ample time," he said, "and plenty of warning. I just want you to rest assured that everything that happens from this moment forward is entirely your fault."

Chelsea turned around in her seat as Bradley's resumed pacing brought him closer to the front of the plane. She couldn't look at him, didn't dare to breathe for fear of drawing attention to herself. Was it fair? Was it right? If she made herself little, if she hoped that

Bradley would pass her by, did that mean she was actively wishing for someone else to die?

She tried to picture Clark's face. Tried to guess what her coach would tell her now to help her calm down. Help her regain her composure.

But when she pictured Clark here on this plane with her, he was just as terrified as she was.

God, help us.

There was no way over the roar of the airplane engines that Chelsea should be able to hear Bradley's boots as he stomped up and down the aisle, but her senses were heightened exponentially, and each step he took sent shivers of panic and terror racing up her spine.

"This is your fault, Mr. Weston," Bradley repeated then reached out and grabbed a flight attendant by the elbow.

"Get over here," he growled at her.

Chelsea hated herself for feeling even a hint of relief. Is this what terrorism did to you? It made you happy when somebody else was about to get killed because at least you yourself had the chance to survive. Chelsea already carried around enough guilt in her life. Guilt for not being happier, more thankful. Guilt for being depressed when she'd been blessed with such a privileged upbringing. And now she was supposed to live with survivor's guilt on top of that?

She hated herself. Hated how she'd never appreciated life until this exact moment. How sick and twisted was it that it took an act of terrorism for her to finally feel thankful for everything she'd been given?

God, I'm so sorry.

Her prayer sounded pathetic. Ridiculous. And yet she held onto what her parents and pastor and youth group leader always told her growing up. *You can be a thousand steps away from the Lord, but it's only one step back.*

She knew she was a trope. Knew she was only praying this hard because it felt as if her life literally depended on it. But that didn't change the fact that it was the sincerest offering she'd ever lifted up to heaven.

God, I'm so sorry for not taking my relationship with you more seriously. I'm so sorry that I haven't been living for you like I should. I'm so sorry for not being more thankful and loving and kind.

I'm just sorry all around.

She held her breath and waited. She'd never prayed that earnestly before in her life. Shouldn't something happen now? The air marshal should wake up, break free, and overcome the hijacker. God could send an entire legion of angels to protect the innocent passengers. Or just strike Bradley down dead. Didn't he do that once for one of the wicked kings in the Old Testament?

Something.

Anything.

Instead, silence.

Silence until Bradley snarled at the trembling flight attendant, aimed his gun, and stared at the cameras.

"Remember, Mr. Weston, this is entirely your fault."

The shot sounded through the cabin, ringing over the screams of the terrified passengers, then the flight attendant fell to the floor.

Chelsea turned around in her seat so she didn't have to watch the blood pool.

"That's another soul on Charles Weston's conscience," Bradley declared. "Five more minutes, and if I don't hear from you by then, another hostage dies."

CHAPTER 10

CHELSEA HAD COVERED A fair number of disturbing stories in the past. A Kenyan college student attacked brutally and without provocation by a white police officer. A murdered Boston politician, a Medford pastor shot in his own home. All around Massachusetts, children went missing, spouses got beat up, victims were abused repeatedly every single day.

For most of her career, Chelsea found ways to separate herself from the trauma she covered. It was the only way she could keep on doing what she did. That didn't mean she was without compassion or empathy. It was just that because she was so compassionate and empathetic, she had to come up with coping mechanisms to protect herself from the terror and crimes she reported about on a daily basis.

Now, Chelsea wasn't even thinking about herself as a journalist. It didn't matter that her editor continued to give her bigger and more high-profile cases to cover. It didn't matter that this trip to Detroit meant Chelsea was breaking out of her local sphere and into the world of national reporting.

Who cared?

And what was it all for if Chelsea was going to be the next person to die when Bradley's timer went off anyway?

He was continuing to pace the aisles when his phone rang. He pulled it out of his pocket and answered with a smirk.

"This is Bradley." He wasn't what she would have expected a terrorist to sound like. When she looked at him, it felt as if she were staring at a man who could have been her third-grade teacher or the guy working on his laptop beside her at the corner café.

Bradley's phone was set on speaker, and Chelsea strained her ears to hear the lifeline whose voice rang out from the other side.

"This is Frank," the man said. "Brad, is that you? May I call you Brad?"

Chelsea watched as the hijacker's face and expression grew even more angry and irritated. "What do you want?" he growled. "I want to talk to the superintendent."

"I know, Brad. I know."

Chelsea tried to picture Frank on the other end of the line, tried to imagine who this man was, how he managed to get through to a cell phone on an airplane flying thirty thousand feet in the air. It wasn't until she started to get lightheaded that she realized she was holding her breath. Would this Frank person, whoever he was, manage to convince Bradley to put down his gun and let them all go?

Chelsea had never covered a real-life hostage situation before. Of course, she was familiar with the most famous cases. The Stockholm bank heist gone wrong. The Patty Hearst ordeal, where the victim ended up shocking the police and FBI by siding with her captors. Chelsea recalled details from a true-crime podcast she listened to where a rich young heiress was kidnapped, held for ransom, and ended up falling in love with her abductor.

Of course, not every hostage developed feelings of dependency on their captors. Sitting where she was, cowering in fear and drenched in sweat, Chelsea wondered how anybody could sympathize with someone like this madman in their cabin.

It certainly wasn't the first time that Chelsea had felt scared during a job. There was that riot that broke out when she was covering what should have been a peaceful prayer vigil. In another instance, Chelsea had gotten threatening letters, strongly urging her in no uncertain terms to drop a case she was covering about a senator's daughter who got kidnapped a few years ago.

In each and every one of those situations, Chelsea had been able to convince herself she wasn't in any real danger. People faced hazards at work no matter what career they chose. Chelsea's job as a journalist was tame when you compared it to the risks that firefighters and soldiers and policeman, sometimes even public schoolteachers, took each and every day.

The man on the other end of Bradley's cell phone identified himself as a hostage negotiator, but Bradley refused to talk to anybody but the Detroit superintendent. Chelsea wondered how Selena felt, the superintendent's daughter who had been kidnapped.

Chelsea had never heard of any parent threatening anybody just because they were unhappy with school district policies. Of course, the scandal at Brown Elementary and its location on toxic soil was far more serious than whose child did or didn't make it into honors band or whether or not high school seniors should be allowed to drive themselves off campus during lunch.

If her editor realized she was here on this hijacked flight, he'd expect her to be taking notes, documenting the terror second by second. As Bradley got more and more agitated, arguing with the professional negotiator, Chelsea couldn't think about work at all.

She couldn't think about the story she could write as a first-hand witness to Bradley's murderous rampage. Couldn't think about how much time and effort he and his men must have put into planning this takeover.

In the grips of her terror and fear, Chelsea could hardly find the strength to pray.

She wondered if her mom was watching the news, if her parents had any idea what Chelsea was experiencing right here on Flight 219. Were they praying for her? Did they even know? Maybe they were just going about their normal, everyday lives, completely unaware that their daughter's plane had been hijacked. Chelsea thought about her friends. Of course, everybody at work would be seeing these events and covering them in real time, but had any of them put the puzzle pieces together to realize that one of their own was aboard this flight? What about Brie? Chelsea's best friend was notoriously bad at keeping up with current events unless she stumbled across them in her Facebook feed. Brie was probably the last person to guess what was happening on this plane.

Chelsea had lost the flow of Bradley's conversation with the hostage negotiator, but his yelling snapped her attention back to the phone call.

"You tell Weston that he calls me in two minutes," Bradley snarled, "or another hostage dies."

CHAPTER 11

SECONDS PASSED. CHELSEA TRIED to mentally calculate how much time was left, but in her terror, her mind could never count past five before she lost track of where she was.

When Bradley's timer beeped, shivers of panic cascaded down Chelsea's spine, then circled around to her gut, where they sat like a monument to fear and terror.

It wasn't supposed to happen like this. She was supposed to land in Detroit in half an hour. Get off the plane, check into her room, and prepare for the next few days of interviews and investigation.

None of which she could do if she was dead.

Bradley was marching to the back of the cabin.

"Get up," he ordered.

Chelsea twisted in her seat and stared as a young woman with bright blue streaks in her hair stood up, her entire body trembling. It was the passenger from Alaska. She looked even younger than Chelsea.

This wasn't right.

But there wasn't anything Chelsea could do. Nothing but sit and stare.

"What's your name?" Bradley demanded.

"Willow," she answered.

Chelsea wanted to turn around. Wanted to shut her eyes and pretend like none of this was really happening. But she couldn't.

"Willow," Bradley repeated. His voice was disturbingly pleasant, almost charming. "Tell me something about yourself, Willow. Do you have a boyfriend?"

She gave her head a slight shake.

"Family, then? Parents?"

The young woman nodded, and a grin spread across Bradley's face.

"Is there something you'd like to say to your parents, Willow? Any last words you'd like to leave them with?"

Chelsea's body was shaking in tandem with the victim's. She tried to squeeze her eyes shut, unable to watch another passenger killed.

"Put that gun away, young man."

Chelsea recognized the strong, bold voice even before the old woman stood up in her seat and stepped in front of Willow.

"Put that gun away," Grandma Lucy repeated.

"And why should I?" Bradley snarled.

"Because," the old woman answered boldly, "if you're going to kill anyone, it should be somebody who has lived a full and vibrant life and who is ready to meet her Maker."

Bradley stared at the tiny old woman and scoffed. "You must be out of your mind."

Grandma Lucy shook her head. She barely reached up to Bradley's chest, and yet it somehow looked like she was the one staring down at him.

"I'm not out of my mind," she stated. Her voice was so calm and fearless that Chelsea found herself straining to hear better, as if the old woman's words themselves could give courage to Chelsea's soul.

Grandma Lucy was standing between the young woman and her assailant. Willow took a few steps back until it was just Bradley and Grandma Lucy staring at one another in the aisle.

Bradley had his gun aimed at Grandma Lucy's head. "You must be crazy," he snarled. "Either that or you've got some kind of a death wish."

Chelsea squinted, preparing to shut her eyes in case Bradley shot the old woman right there.

Grandma Lucy's voice didn't falter. "It's not a wish to die per se," she told him, her eyes never leaving his. "But if you shoot me, I know that the moment my soul leaves this frail, old body that I'll find myself in the presence of the Lord, where I'll go on to worship Him eternally. In all honesty, I can't think of a better way to end my life than to save this innocent girl here." She gestured toward Willow, who was hugging her knees and shaking in her seat.

Bradley stared at Grandma Lucy in bewilderment. In the silence, Chelsea could hear the pounding of her heart. For a split second, she was almost convinced that the old woman's faithful conviction would change the hijacker's mind. Chelsea held her breath. Was he going to lower that gun?

Chelsea cast a furtive glance around the cabin. While Bradley was distracted, mesmerized by the spiritual force emanating from this little old lady, it was the perfect time for the other passengers to act. There were hundreds of them and only a few of the terrorists. If the passengers found a way to coordinate their efforts, they could regain control of the plane in a matter of minutes. But how many bullets did Bradley have left in that gun, and how many more lives would be lost in the effort?

Chelsea had been a too young to understand the terrorist attacks of 9/11, but years later, she learned the story about the brave men and women who took down the plane heading for the White House. As far as Chelsea knew, Bradley and his men had no desire to crash their flight at all, but she imagined how much courage and determination it must have taken for the passengers on Flight 93 to do what they did. For the first time, she found herself wondering if everyone on board that day had agreed to the plan, or if some would have preferred to take their chances with the terrorists.

Bradley's apparent moment of wavering passed, and Chelsea watched in horror as he set his jaw and took a step closer to Grandma Lucy. He pressed his gun against her forehead. "Let's see if this God you worship is powerful enough to stop me."

Chelsea scrunched down in her seat, trying to make herself as tiny as she could, her hands ready to cover her ears at the sound of a gunshot that never came.

Bradley stared at his weapon and cursed.

"The gun's jammed," someone shouted. At this declaration, the fear that had paralyzed every single passenger on Flight 219 dissipated in an instant. Several travelers jumped out of their seats, rushing Bradley and his assistant in the Hawaiian shirt.

"We've got them," a man announced victoriously.

It all happened so quickly Chelsea hardly noticed that she had unbuckled her own seat belt and jumped into the aisle. The other passengers had Bradley subdued before Chelsea could do anything to intervene, and she felt somewhat embarrassed for thinking that with her tiny stature she could have done much of anything to help. Still, the passengers had won. The terrorists were caught and bound. The air marshal was awake now and trying to keep the passengers and criminals under control.

Everything was going to be okay.

"Well, folks." The captain's voice over the PA system was comforting and familiar. "It looks like the danger has passed, and we'll be landing in Detroit in just a few minutes. Emergency personnel are already standing by, so once we land, let's let them get on board to do their jobs as quickly as possible. I'd like to thank all of you for remaining calm in a very frightening situation," he concluded, "and lastly, I'd like to thank God who allowed us to arrive in Detroit safe."

Bradley had been dragged to the back of the plane, where two passengers and a flight attendant guarded him with the gun.

"Safe?" he spat, his voice carrying throughout the cabin. "You don't know anything. You're all about to die."

CHAPTER 12

ONCE THEIR PLANE LANDED, it was nearly impossible for Chelsea to recall the exact order of events. Weeks later, as she sat at her favorite café, trying to type out a single sentence to describe what she went through, she couldn't even write one word.

There were those few minutes of relief. The sense that the worst was behind them.

Then Bradley's dire warnings ringing and echoing throughout the cabin as he promised they were all about to die.

At the time, Chelsea attributed his words to the ravings of a madman.

That was before she smelled the smoke.

After the ordeal, Clark told her it was understandable why she couldn't stand the fireworks on New Year's Eve that year. Why even the little poppers her nephew threw on the sidewalk made her cringe.

Chelsea was scarred. That much was for sure. Weeks after that emergency landing at the Detroit airport, she was still having nightmares. Nightmares about smoke and fire alarms. Nightmares about watching innocent people shot in front of her.

In most of her dreams, Bradley was pointing the gun at her, and it was Grandma Lucy who stood between Chelsea and her would-be murderer. After they landed in Detroit, while EMTs rushed to attend to the injured passengers and men in SWAT suits swarmed to arrest Bradley's men, Chelsea had searched for Grandma Lucy in the ensuing chaos.

The old woman was never found.

"Maybe you could ask Google to find her," Mom suggested.

But Chelsea never did.

She talked about Grandma Lucy so much during her coaching calls with Clark that she was sometimes self-conscious.

"She obviously made a big impact on you," Clark told her gently when Chelsea expressed her embarrassment. "There's nothing strange or weird about that. It could be that this little old lady you met saved not only that young woman but the rest of you as well. Who knows how far Bradley would have gone if she hadn't stood up to him?"

Chelsea didn't like to think about all the other what ifs. She was trying hard to move on. She'd written her article on the Brown Elementary School scandal. It wasn't her best work, not by a longshot, but her editor went easy on her after all the trauma she'd gone through.

Clark was willing to bump her up to three coaching sessions a week, stating that an anonymous donor was footing the bill. In all honesty, Chelsea thought he was just gifting his time to her.

She wasn't going to complain.

In the aftermath of the hijacking, Chelsea had made it a point to start going to church more regularly with her parents. When she wasn't spending Sunday mornings with them, she'd visit the church where Brie worked, and they'd go out for lunch afterward. Out of everybody she knew, Brie was the one who seemed the most comfortable letting Chelsea absorb the terror and fear she'd experienced in her own time and in her own way. They talked about Flight 219 every so often. Chelsea found herself particularly upset about the flight attendant who was killed, especially after news stories came out about the two little kids she'd left behind. Sometimes Chelsea felt guilty, as if there was something she could have done to help the passengers who never made it off Flight 219.

But other times, she enjoyed sitting across the café table from her best friend, laughing about a silly Facebook meme or retelling a joke Brie's pastor shared that morning in his sermon.

There were days when Chelsea felt like her despair was getting the best of her, but she was learning to accept that even if she did have lots to be thankful for, there was no shame in feeling down. If anything, Chelsea would have thought that her near-death experience would give her a deeper appreciation for living, but that wasn't always the case. The same inexplicable sense of sadness still impacted her. Not all the time, but enough that she was thankful for the extra sessions with her life coach, thankful for the new antidepressants her mom had encouraged her to talk to the doctor about.

The trauma Chelsea experienced on board Flight 219 would be enough to fill up a hundred therapy sessions, and even the strongest drugs in the world might not take all the fear completely away. But Chelsea was excited to start a new chapter in her life, a chapter where she learned to accept herself exactly where she was instead of always wishing to be something different or someone else.

A chapter where she appreciated her friends and family and recognized how blessed she was to be surrounded by such an inspiring and encouraging support system.

A chapter where her soul could experience God's love in the midst of trials, joy in the midst of terror, and peace and happiness regardless of her circumstances.

You Raise Me Up

Alana Terry

Christian Books Today

CHAPTER 1

My name is Lucy Jean, but I insist on being called Grandma Lucy.

I should warn you starting out that my mind isn't quite as sharp as it once was. I hope that's all right with you. What I'm saying is that I've got a story to tell you, except I can't always be sure that I'm getting things down exactly the same way as they really happened. Comes from getting older, I suppose.

I've lived a long life on God's beautiful earth, and I'm tremendously thankful to say that the good Lord has sustained me for all these years, and I have no doubt he'll continue to do so until the day he calls me heavenward.

I make my home in Washington. We've got a little farm in a small town named Orchard Grove. Maybe you've heard of it. Kind people. Small community. My niece and I raise goats there. Well, Connie tends the goats, but I declare she's getting up there in years too and really needs to hire help.

If my own niece is a senior citizen, I wonder what that says about me and my age!

We do serve a wonderful Lord, don't we? He's so good to us in all his ways. I was just telling my grandson about it the other day. Let him know that it's high time he realizes all the things he's going through in life are God's way of getting his attention. That's the problem with young people. When something bad happens or things don't go their way, they automatically assume God's out to get them.

If they even believe in God at all, I should add.

Ian doesn't. Not yet. But he will. I know it's going to happen.

He's had a sad life, my grandson. Mother killed by a drunk driver, and him so little. He and his sister both. Alayna's doing well these days. Married to a pastor so far out in the country in Alaska those poor folks are hauling their own water. But they're doing God's work, Alayna and her little family.

Ian's the one I worry about most. He's got such a compassionate streak, my grandson does. Always talking about this injustice or that oppressed people group. And I love him for it, believe me. Some Christians stick up their noses at that type of thing, which I just consider hogwash. All you've got to do is flip open to any passage in the Old Testament, and you'll see that God is a warrior for justice. Yes, he is.

Well, my grandson makes his living traveling the world. He's a reporter, by the way, in case I hadn't mentioned that earlier. He's building a pretty big name for himself, too. Recently helped make a full documentary about that terrible tragedy in Detroit. You've heard of it by now, I'm sure. After what happened on Flight 219, everybody in the world's heard about it, no doubt.

Short story is there's a school for little kids in Detroit that never should have been built. You'd have to ask my grandson to give you all the details because as a journalist he's better with the facts. But kids were getting sick. Parents were worried about long-term damage just because the particular spot where this school was built used to be a pharmacy factory, making all those pills, and that was before there were better safety regulations, so they didn't handle their waste properly at all.

I feel so sorry for those poor kids and sorry for their parents too. But that certainly doesn't excuse what General and his batch of criminals did to my flight when I was only trying to get home last December.

I'd gone to see Ian, the grandson I was just telling you about. He travels all over the world, like I mentioned, and was about to take off on another trip. He's been working on a documentary about North Korean refugees, and I told him the day he started it several years ago I had a bad feeling about that place. The North Korean government really doesn't take kindly to Americans poking around in their business, if you know what I mean, and I worry for my grandson, which may surprise you, seeing as how I've developed something of a reputation as a prayer warrior. Truth be told, I'm a worrywart, and that's the perfect truth, especially when it comes to my grandchildren. It'd be different if Ian was saved already, but he hasn't accepted Christ as his personal Lord and Savior. Not yet. So I told him, "Ian, it's one thing if you go to North Korea and get yourself captured there after I'm perfectly convinced that your soul's made its peace with God. It's totally different if you're still walking in rebellion to him. I'm worried for you."

And he always says the same thing to me. That he's not going into North Korea, he's just interviewing refugees who've made it out to China. He promises me he'll be safe, but I'm not so sure. Call it a premonition if you will. I just don't like him going over there all by himself.

You'd think with him spending so much time in Asia, I'd be thrilled. That's where I grew up, actually. My parents were missionaries in Shanghai. In fact, my father owned and operated one of China's first bookstores and printing companies for Bibles and Christian literature. You can't do that type of thing now, not unless you have special government permission, but back then things were a little different.

Of course, the political climate at the time was pretty unstable, but we managed. Even saw ourselves through the bombings of Shanghai, but that's a story for another day.

I was telling you about Ian, wasn't I? That's where I was. So, my grandson lives out near Boston, even though, like I told you earlier, he's traveling all the time. I really do pray that one day God sends him a nice young woman to help ease that restless burden in his soul. I sure would love to see that boy settled down before the good Lord calls me home to glory.

Anyway, I was on Flight 219 because I'd been out East to visit my grandson. See him off before another one of his trips around the world. I wanted him to hear the gospel one last time as well, so we went out to dinner, and I spelled it out to him plainly. He's a sinner, just like we all are, and unless he repents and asks God to forgive him, he'll remain lost.

Ian's a smart boy. Graduated from Harvard, even. But he doesn't like to be told that he's wrong. Thank the good Lord, we have a good relationship, and he knows I'm only telling him these things because I love him so much.

What I did was plant some seeds. It's up to God now to water them and make them grow.

That's why I pray for Ian as hard as I do. For Ian and all my other grandkids and great-grandkids who aren't walking with the Lord. Not yet. I pray that God would open their eyes to the glorious truths of his Word, that he'd send them conviction when they need it, that he'd make them so unmistakably aware of his love for them and his presence in their lives.

It's one thing to know about God. It's quite another thing to know him personally.

I went decades not understanding the difference, squandered years of my life before the good Lord showed me some sense. But that's a story for another day.

CHAPTER 2

I WASN'T SUPPOSED TO be on that particular flight, not originally.

I'd visited my grandson, I'd told him what I flew out there to say, and then it was time to leave Ian's soul in God's hands and fly myself home. Connie doesn't like me traveling alone. Says I'm too old for that. I suppose one day I might need to slow down, but I don't think that day's here.

Not yet.

There were snowstorms in the Midwest. Lots of flights were getting cancelled or delayed. If I'm remembering correctly, originally I was meant to fly from Boston to Chicago, and from Chicago on home. I was looking forward to it too because last year when I was flying through Chicago, I met a woman who served me tea at a little restaurant, and she looked so sad, and I asked her what was wrong, and she told me a tragic story about how the foster father she loved like her daddy had just gotten shot, and more than anything she wanted to be there to spend her Christmas with him, except she didn't have any money and was desperately worried about her father.

Well, I prayed with her, and I ended up sharing the gospel with her too. I figure if God's granted me the chance to travel and hasn't decided to take me home yet, that's just because there's more people here on this earth like that worried waitress he wants me to witness to.

Fine by me. I know my marching orders.

Anyway, I gave that young woman my phone number, and she promised to be in touch, but I haven't heard from her since. I don't know if her father survived his injuries, if she made it to be with her family that Christmas or not. More than anything, I want to know if she took anything that I said to her that day to heart. She told me she grew up in a Christian foster home. Her father was actually a pastor out East. But you can have a saint for a parent and still not be saved. Just look at me. My parents were missionaries during some of the most dangerous periods in China's history. And even then I didn't come to know the Lord personally until well into my adulthood.

But that's a story for another day.

Well, I'd been looking forward to reconnecting with that waitress in Chicago. Then my flight got cancelled, and the airlines decided to fly me out to Detroit instead to catch my next plane from there. Well I told God that was fine with me. I figured the Almighty had that nice young waitress taken care of, and instead there must be somebody in Detroit I was meant to minister to. Either that or maybe somebody on the airplane.

I could tell even while I was waiting for my flight that the Lord was working mightily behind the scenes. Some days I travel and use the waiting periods to pray and think about all the blessings God's poured out on me during my long life on his beautiful earth. Other times, he just seems to send one person after another my way, people I can share the gospel with or give a little word of encouragement to.

That's what happened in the airport while I was waiting for Flight 219.

First it was a young mother traveling alone with her little boy. He was a real sweetie too. Perfect manners. Absolute gentleman.

Turns out they were headed to Detroit, but the flight they were on was cancelled, and this little tyke was so sad he wasn't going to be able to see his grandma for Christmas. Well, the good news was I'd been at my gate by then for a little while and knew they were calling standbys, so I told them they should see about getting on my plane.

I had a real heart to pray for that young woman. She struck me as anxious. Sad. When her son said they were visiting their grandma, I could tell his mom wasn't nearly as excited as he was.

And so I prayed for her.

Prayed that God would be working behind the scenes to restore her relationships. To bless her little boy. To show them both just how incredibly he loves them and wants what's best in their lives.

I still pray for her, by the way. I don't know her name, but I've added her and that darling little boy of hers to my prayer list. When I first started praying for them each afternoon from my prayer room, I got such a heavy sense of sadness, but now my prayers feel lighter. I hope that means this young mother has finally found some peace. When I talk to Jesus about that little boy, my heart's just filled with joy. I'm convinced he's going to grow up to change the world for Christ. I just know it. Sometimes I get a sense about these things. And I might be wrong sometimes, but in this case I have no doubts.

Well, I kept on waiting for my flight, kept on running into other passengers. And it's interesting. It really is when you sit back and realize just how intertwined our lives all are. It's like a novel, where each of the characters comes in and out of the story, and you realize there's somebody at work behind the scenes. There just has to be. These things don't happen by chance.

But I suppose you didn't come here to chat with me about the people I met and prayed with before we boarded Flight 219, did you? It's interesting though, isn't it? How we're in a spiritual war each and every day. And yet it's things that happen in this temporal world that make the news. A plane getting hijacked. A young girl being kidnapped. That's the only danger most people see. They have no idea about the spiritual battle raging on around us each and every day. I suppose the devil likes to keep us blind like that. If we spend our whole lives scared of terrorists and kidnappers and murderers, we almost forget that the real battle is for our souls.

Flight 219 was a war zone, both in the physical and spiritual senses. God gifted me a premonition of the attack before it started. I was at the gate praying with another passenger when he gave me the vision. Maybe you want to know why I didn't sound the alarm, let somebody know. Well it doesn't quite work like that. See, I didn't know if God was giving me a picture of my own flight or someone else's. I didn't know if the danger was going to happen today or five years from now.

All I saw was a plane going down in smoke. I could hear the screams of the passengers. And there I was in the back of the cabin, my hands outstretched just like Moses while the Israelites fought in the valley below him, and I was praying for God to uphold that plane.

That's what I saw.

It could have meant almost anything.

It could have meant that God was showing me what he was protecting me from.

It could have meant that God was prompting me to pray for my grandson and his flight to China.

It could have meant that I'm an old, old woman with an active imagination, and sometimes when I let my mind wander during my prayers, I see pictures that don't mean a single thing.

Like that time God gave me a dream about a goat in labor, and I was so sure it meant our little doe was in trouble, and I made Connie get out of bed and her husband too, and we all went to check, and everything was fine.

But that's a story for another day.

At the airport, when I was praying with another passenger before we were supposed to board, I saw an image of fire and smoke and a cabin full of terrified passengers.

It wasn't until that man knocked out the air marshal that I realized exactly what my vision meant.

And by then, it was too late.

CHAPTER 3

I'VE BEEN IN SCARY situations before. You don't get to be my age without going through your fair share of fear and trauma. That's the way life works, isn't it?

I'm certainly not afraid to die. I figure that statistically speaking, it's going to happen soon. And since I'm not really keen on the idea of weeks or months in a hospital bed, drifting in and out of consciousness, it's not that frightening to picture myself getting shot in the head.

People who know me, people who've read about that flight ask me about it quite a lot. Did I know what was going to happen when I stood up to General? Did I know his gun was going to misfire?

No, I didn't.

But that doesn't make me a hero. Not in the least.

I'm getting ahead of myself, though. I suppose if I'm going to tell this story, I should try to stick to things in the order they happened. That's harder to do than it sounds, you know. Sometimes I wonder how people like Ian manage who make their living from writing words all day.

On the airplane, I was seated toward the back. There was a family who got on then got off again before they closed the doors. I think it was God giving the mother a feeling, warning her that something was about to go terribly wrong.

I've added that family to my prayer list as well. They looked so nice, all dressed up for their flight. I remember when that was the thing to do. You'd never travel anywhere without putting on your Sunday best. Now, people show up at the airport in sweats or flannels. Look like they're still in their pajamas. I suppose if that's how they feel the most comfortable, that's fine with me, but it's one thing that made this family stand out to me all the more.

The mother wore a long denim skirt. So did her daughters. The father was young but had a long beard. Made me wonder if the man had ever seen a razor in his life. They were quiet. Sweet. But there was something in the mother's eyes that caught my attention. A fear she was trying to hide.

I've been praying for her quite a bit these days. I'm afraid I can't recall just how many kids she had and how many of them were boys and how many were girls, so I focus on praying for her. She's the one I remember most.

And in my prayers, I ask God to ease that fear she's been carrying around for so long. He sure is an amazing Lord, isn't he? Big enough to bear our burdens, even the ones that feel like they're going to drown us in despair.

I think about that young mother, and I think about Psalm 91. Are you familiar with that one? It's such a beautiful blessing to pray over anyone who's frightened.

Whoever dwells in the shelter of the Most High will rest in the shadow of the Almighty. I will say of the Lord, "He is my refuge and my fortress, my God, in whom I trust."

Such a beautiful promise, isn't it? And how encouraging to picture ourselves resting in the shadow of the Almighty. So many times we think of shadows as places of fear and uncertainty, of darkness. Like the shadow of death.

Except this verse is different. It's talking about the shadow of the Almighty and the rest we find ourselves in when we're safe within his protective care.

Surely he will save you from the fowler's snare and from the deadly pestilence.

God brought this verse to mind a few decades ago when I was going to return to China on a missionary trip. I don't live there anymore, obviously, but I've never forgotten my second home where I grew up. I've lost track of how many times I've returned there since I've given my life entirely over to Christ. Maybe six or seven? I go carrying Scripture. They call me a Bible donkey. The idea of it sure makes me laugh. Well I was all set to go on one of my Bible smuggling trips when the bird flu epidemic broke out. Do you remember that?

My family didn't want me traveling to Asia. Said it was too dangerous. So I just reminded them of Psalm 91. Told them that God promised to save me from the fowler's snare and from the deadly pestilence. If that isn't a reference to divine protection from bird flu, then my name isn't Lucy Jean.

I used to have that entire chapter memorized, all of Psalm 91, I mean. Now, it's harder to recall the verses all at once, but I trust that God will bring the right ones to mind when I need them most.

I'm afraid I've been rambling so much I forgot what I'd started telling you about in the first place.

But when I'm rocking in my prayer chair, those are the verses that come to mind when I pray for the young mother who God used to get her family off that plane.

To safety.

CHAPTER 4

I DON'T KEEP UP with the news all that much. I figure that if there's something happening in the world God wants me to pray for, he's going to let me know about it whether or not I pick up a paper. I guess lots of people have written about me in articles and things like that. Say I saved the whole plane for what I did, standing between the gunman and his victim.

Well, that's not how I see it, and if you want to know the full truth, I think most of those stories are blowing things out of proportion. General was holding a gun, about to shoot a young girl barely past her teens. I told him if he wanted to kill someone that badly, it may as well be me. I've already explained to you before my philosophy on death. If it's a bang from a bullet and then I'm in heaven, don't you think that sounds more bearable than languishing for years in a nursing home?

Now, if I were younger, if I still had kids to look after for example, we wouldn't be having this discussion at all. But the death of an old lady who's already raised her kids and grandkids and has lived to see multiple great-grands is far less distressing than the death of a young girl who's not even lived a quarter of her life yet. Even an evolutionist who doesn't believe an ounce of Scripture would agree with me on that one.

The young woman I allegedly saved is named Willow. I know that because I was chatting for a while with her roommate on the plane. Kennedy and Willow. Two college girls traveling home to visit Alaska.

They weren't what you'd expect at first in best friends. Kennedy was quiet and studious. We got to talking, and I learned that she grew up on the mission field in China as well. I don't believe in coincidences, but this was most certainly a wink from the Almighty if I've ever experienced one.

She was a sweet girl, that Kennedy. A little bit timid, still unaware of the amazing power of the Holy Spirit residing in her. But she's learning. I get the sense when I pray for her that God has amazing and dramatic plans for Kennedy's life. The kind of story you'd like to see made into a movie or listen to as one of those old-fashioned radio dramas.

I also get the sense that Flight 219 wasn't the last time I'll be crossing paths with this sweet, young daughter of God. But maybe that's just the wishful thinking of an old woman like me.

Well, inasmuch as Kennedy was quiet and sweet and kind, her best friend Willow was quite the opposite. Not in a bad way, mind you. It wasn't like she was brash or rude. Just louder. More vibrant. The first thing you'd notice about Willow if you met her was her hair. Dyed bright blue. Don't ask me why someone would take such gorgeous locks and style them that way. I guess that's just what some young people like to do these days. I'll never understand it, but that doesn't mean I should judge.

Willow was sitting with a young man on the flight, which gave me the chance to get to know Kennedy more. And we talked about it. How Willow isn't a believer. Not yet, I should say. How Kennedy wanted to share the gospel with her friend but still hadn't figured out how.

I sensed a lot of fear in Kennedy. She's another one that when I pray for her, Psalm 91 comes to mind. *If you say, "The Lord is my refuge," and you make the Most High your dwelling, no harm will overtake you, no disaster will come near your tent. For he will command his angels concerning you to guard you in all your ways; they will lift you up in their hands, so that you will not strike your foot against a stone.*

I guess it's a meaningful verse when you're talking about a stranger you meet on a hijacked flight.

For he will command his angels concerning you to guard you in all your ways. I can't say for sure that I've met a real angel before, but I have my suspicions. Like that time when I was a kid and

Shanghai was getting bombed and my mother and I were trying to reach home. There was a man who claimed to be a French diplomat who just showed up to our aid, but that's a story for another day.

I absolutely believe that angels are surrounding us, protecting us from harm. And yet there are so many believers just like Kennedy who still feel scared of sharing the gospel.

My prayer for her is that God will fill her up with incredible boldness, that the fear of man will no longer have a hold on her, and that she'll finally learn how to tap into that amazing power she has as an anointed child of God.

I'm trying to think if there was anything else to tell you about what happened before the flight got taken over. I'm sure I talked to other passengers, but like I said, I'm afraid I don't recall details quite as clearly as I used to. There was a young woman in first class I prayed with while I was waiting to use the bathrooms. I would have added her to my prayer list as well, but I'm embarrassed to admit I can't recall what it was we prayed about or why God prompted me to stop and talk with her in the first place.

I'm sure at this point you want to hear all about the hijacking itself, but I'm afraid I have bad news for you there, too.

I slept right through it.

I'm telling you the gospel truth. After I talked with Kennedy a while and we prayed for her friend Willow's salvation, I went to use the bathroom and stopped and prayed with someone else (although like I said, I can't seem to remember who). Then I headed to the back of the plane and took a little nap. When I woke up, a man was waving a gun at Willow, the young woman I'd been praying for just an hour or so earlier.

So that's when I stood up and did what any other believer in my situation would do.

CHAPTER 5

WHEN THE FAMILY CAME over for dinner a few weeks ago, everyone wanted to hear that part of the story.

What I was feeling. Wasn't I scared. Did I have any idea the gun wouldn't go off. How did I ever get to be so brave.

Really, the answer to all those questions is simple.

I knew Willow wasn't saved, which meant that I couldn't stand by and watch her die. Not while I had the chance to do something to help her.

The news articles and blog posts tell me I preached for five or ten minutes with the hijacker's gun pointed at my head. I'm afraid I don't remember that part either, so I can't give you many details about what I said.

But I know people have read about me in the news. At one point there was even speculation that I might be an angel because apparently nobody could find me when the airport security folks were conducting their interviews after we landed. There's actually a really good reason for that.

Nobody told me I needed to stick around, and I wasn't injured at all, so I decided that what I really needed was a good night's rest. I got off the plane and found myself a quiet gate in the airport, and I napped until the next morning. Then I woke myself up and talked with a sweet young man serving coffee at a little donut shop whose wife is expecting their very first baby, a tiny boy with Down's syndrome, but that's a story for another day.

I don't like the fact that my actions on Flight 219 have been turned into something spectacular. It wasn't that at all. But I do know people want to hear my side of the story, and since I can't remember at all what I said or felt while I was trying to talk the gunman down, let me tell you about my prayers for him since then.

I don't believe in praying for the dead. That's just superstitious mumbo-jumbo. General died in the fire. I know some people are upset he won't face the American justice system, but I'm certain that God's justice is quite a bit more powerful and to be feared.

So I don't bother praying for General, not because I don't care about him or the state of his soul when he passed, but because he's already gone. He had his chance on earth to get right with God. And who knows? Maybe he did right before he drew his last breath. We won't know about that until we reach heaven.

But I do pray for General's kids. They're so young still. It's not their fault their father took over an airplane and murdered those innocent people. Unfortunately, I worry that General's children will blame themselves since after all it was their school General was so upset about.

I guess if anything good has come from this, it's that the Detroit school district has closed down Brown Elementary. The students enrolled there are currently being taught in trailers at nearby schools, but plans are underway for a new building, funded mostly by private donations.

I'm thankful for that much at least. But it's such a shame the way it all came about, isn't it?

So I've added General's children to my daily prayer list. I pray that God would give them maturity beyond their years to see and understand that their father loved them, but he needed help. Like I said, I don't pay much attention to news reports, but there've been quite a bit of rumblings about General's mental health. Who knows? With the right doctors and a lot of prayer, maybe he could have run for mayor of Detroit or gotten himself elected superintendent himself and brought about change for his children in a much more positive way.

It's too late for anything like that to happen now, though.

And so I pray. Day in, day out. When I can't sleep, I make my way down to my prayer room. Sit in my rocking chair, talking to God.

I talk to him about the passengers I met on that flight. The mother in the long skirt who took her children off the plane. The mom traveling with that sweet little boy. That studious college student Kennedy and her blue-haired best friend.

I pray for them all.

I pray for God to cover over the fear and the trauma they endured on that flight.

I pray for the Almighty to wash over them with his peace that surpasses all understanding.

I read Psalm 91 and I pray the verses over them. Pray that God would protect them, that he would be with them in trouble, that he will deliver them and show them his salvation.

And I pray for you too, my sweet and faithful reader. I pray that your heart and soul today would be filled with the riches and fulness of God's grace. I pray that he would open the eyes of your heart so that you might grasp and understand how wide and how long and how high and how deep is his amazing love for you.

I pray that he will sustain you through sadness and sickness and trials, and that when you reach the last chapter of your life on God's beautiful earth, you'll be able to say with confidence along with the Apostle Paul, "I have fought the good fight, I have finished the race, I have kept the faith."

That is my prayer for you, and that's what I ask God on your behalf each and every time I talk with him.

But that's a story for another day.

From Alana: Thanks so much for joining me on this journey.

The idea for the Turbulent Skies Christian Thriller novellas came to me over three years ago, when I was flying to California to visit my grandparents.

I was people-watching on the plane (as authors tend to do), trying to come up with backstories for each of the passengers. It was both awe-inspiring and a little overwhelming to realize that God knew every single person on that plane (and their stories) so intimately.

I tucked the idea for a thriller series set on a hijacked airplane in the back of my head and focused on other novels.

Grandma Lucy was first introduced in the book *Turbulence*, which is book 5 in the Kennedy Stern Christian suspense series, my most popular collection of novels to date. This book gives the story of Flight 219 from Kennedy's perspective as she's traveling to Alaska with her best friend Willow.

Grandma Lucy's character is based in large part on my own grandmother, who was raised as a missionary kid in Shanghai and who returned to China multiple times to smuggle Bibles. My grandmother died the week before I started writing *Turbulence*. I thought that basing a character on this prayer warrior would be a neat way to commemorate her, and I know if she were still alive, she'd get a kick out of reading about herself in my books.

I'm so thankful for the legacy of prayer and evangelism and missions my Grandma not only lived but passed down the generations, and I know my life has been irrevocably blessed by all her prayers for me and my family. The world lost a tremendous prayer warrior the day my grandma died, which is one reason why it's always so special for me whenever I get the chance to write about her in some of my novels.

Grandma Lucy also plays a large part in the Orchard Grove books. These are different than my typical Christian suspense novels and fall more into the women's fiction category. In the Orchard Grove series, three young women attend a church service where Grandma Lucy offers the closing prayer. Each one of these women is impacted by her words in a significant yet different way.

If you haven't read the Kennedy Stern Christian suspense series yet, where Grandma Lucy is first introduced and where Kennedy and her roommate Willow experience dangerous encounters that test their faith and keep readers turning pages WAY past their bedtime, dive headfirst into the the Kennedy Stern series on sale now.

Save up to 50% off the entire 9-book mystery series when you order directly from our publisher, Christian Books Today at mystery.christianbooks.today/sale ... Or keep reading for a sneak peek from *Turbulence*, the Kennedy Stern novel where Kennedy and Willow first meet Grandma Lucy on Flight 219.

Turbulence

T MINUS 1 HOUR 43 minutes

"Gladys Aylward? What a remarkable woman."

Kennedy was startled by the interruption to her reading.

A white-haired woman with thin-rimmed spectacles and a blouse that might have been ordered from a 1970s Sears catalog smiled at her. "I'm sorry, the restroom up front was occupied, so I came back here and couldn't help but notice your book. Are you enjoying the story?"

Kennedy didn't feel up to chatting, but since the back lavatory was occupied as well, she didn't think she had much choice. "Yeah. It's pretty interesting."

"They made a movie about her life. Did you know that?"

Kennedy shook her head.

"Well, it's quite an old one. The actress who starred in it — oh, I wish I could remember her name just now, but that's what happens when your brain gets as old as mine. Anyway, the story goes this woman became a Christian after playing the role. I assume then that you're a born-again believer?"

That phrase always struck Kennedy as strange. A *born-again believer*, as if there were any other kind. "Yeah. I am." No use getting into a theological debate on an airplane with an eighty-year-old grandmother.

A flight attendant tapped the woman on the shoulder. "Excuse me, can I squeeze past you, please?"

The old lady sat down in the Mennonite mother's empty spot and glanced at the bathroom. "Looks like I might be here a while." She smiled warmly. "My name is Lucy Jean, but I insist on being called Grandma Lucy."

"I'm Kennedy," she replied automatically, wondering how long the bathroom occupant would take.

"Kennedy. What a lovely name. You know, I still wish my parents had come up with something more creative than Lucy Jean. You don't get much plainer than that."

Kennedy was about to protest that it was an attractive name when Grandma Lucy asked, "Are you going to Detroit today?"

"No, I'm on my way to Seattle and then Anchorage to spend Christmas with my friend's family."

"How lovely. I have a granddaughter in Alaska."

"Is that where you're going?" Kennedy asked.

"No, I'm getting off in Seattle. Going home to Washington. I was just in Boston to see off my grandson. He's on his way to ..." She stopped herself to finger Kennedy's necklace from across the aisle. "What in the world is this? It looks New Age."

All Kennedy wanted to do was get back to her reading, but she gave her best impression of a smile. "It's an air purifier. You wear it around your neck, and it filters out germs and dust. My roommate got them for us for the flight." She nodded toward Willow, who was watching some violent movie on her portable screen.

Grandma Lucy frowned at the gruesome image. "And your roommate?" she asked. "Is she born-again, too?"

Kennedy was spared the chore of stammering an awkward reply when the math teacher Willow had been flirting with came up to their row.

"Bathroom full?" he asked.

Willow plucked out her earbuds and offered her most winsome grin. "Hey, Ray. I was hoping we'd bump into each other during the flight."

Kennedy unbuckled her safety belt. "It looks like there's a line, so why don't you take my seat and I'll come over here." She stepped across the aisle and sat in the window seat beside Grandma Lucy. Her contacts were getting dry anyway, so now was probably as good a time as any to take a break from reading.

Grandma Lucy took Kennedy's hand in hers. Her skin was surprisingly soft for someone with so many wrinkles. "That was sweet of you, dear. Now let me take a look at you." She stared for several seconds before she gave her hand a squeeze. "You don't have to tell me. Let me guess. You're studying to be a missionary, aren't you?"

Kennedy slipped her hand away, surprised at how warm it felt. "A doctor, actually."

Grandma Lucy nodded, as if she had known that all along. "Medical missions, then?"

Kennedy didn't know what to say. Did Grandma Lucy's version of a *born-again believer* require some sort of ministry focus to prove your devotion?

"I'm not sure. I'm still doing my undergrad studies, so I guess I have plenty of time to figure that out." She let out an uncomfortable laugh.

Grandma Lucy chuckled too, tentatively as if she weren't sure what was so funny. "It's just that when I first looked at you, something in my spirit said *missionary*. I'm sure that's what I heard." She frowned and looked around her, as if her train of thought had derailed and she had to visibly track it down.

Kennedy had an unsettled feeling in the base of her spine. Why did it seem as though every other Christian on this flight was getting direct messages from the Lord except for her? Had God ever spoken to her that way before? Or maybe he had tried, and Kennedy just didn't know what to listen for.

"You're sure you're not a missionary?" Grandma Lucy pressed.

"No, but my parents are."

Grandma Lucy's face lit up before Kennedy could continue. "That's what it was. I knew you had a missions call on your life the moment I saw you with that book. My family was good friends with Gladys, you know. She came to visit us on more than one occasion when we lived in Shanghai."

"Really?" Kennedy's interest was piqued, and since Willow was busy laughing with her new travel partner, Kennedy figured she may as well try to enjoy her conversation.

"My parents were missionaries in China. I was born over there, in fact, and my father had a little Christian store he ran for decades before the Communists shut it down. When war broke out with

Japan, we ran into Gladys on more than one occasion. She was taking care of so many kids!"

Lost in thought, Grandma Lucy continued to speak of her time in Shanghai during the Sino-Japanese War. Stories of bombings, narrow escapes from death, heroic ventures her father undertook to help the injured, the selfless sacrifices her mother made to assist the war orphans.

"Of course, she never took in as many as Gladys," Grandma Lucy remarked with a smile that lit up her whole face and pushed her spectacles up on her cheeks. "But she did what God called her to, which is all he expects from each one of us, isn't it?"

Kennedy nodded, even though her mind was still back in war-torn Shanghai where Grandma Lucy had recounted stories of fires and destruction as readily as if she were talking about Sunday picnics in Central Park.

"And what about you?" she finally asked. "You say you're in medical school?"

"Pre-med," Kennedy corrected and spent the next few minutes answering questions about life as an undergrad student at Harvard.

"And are you part of a good church body over there?"

"Yeah." Kennedy didn't admit that she only made it to St. Margaret's once or twice a month, fearing it might make Grandma Lucy rethink Kennedy's previous claim of being a true *born-again* believer.

"That's good." Grandma Lucy nodded sagely. "I ask because that grandson of mine I just visited, he graduated from Harvard a few years ago, and it filled him with so many idolatrous, liberal views of God and religion and the world." She sighed. "He's a great boy, don't get me wrong. Has a heart bigger than most Christians who fill the churches across this country. Gets worked up over injustice and actually does something about it. Just to give you an example, before he left for work in Asia, he was in Detroit of all places, interviewing parents about this issue they're having in the education system there. The schools, they're falling apart. Not just the system, I mean the actual buildings are falling apart. One school's pipes were so bad, they were leaking lead into the drinking fountains. Had been going on for years before anyone fixed it. Just terrible. And then this whole big mess over the Brown

Elementary School. You heard about that whole controversy, I'm sure."

"Actually, no." Kennedy tried not to sound embarrassed at the confession. She'd been so busy with her studies that if her dad didn't send her a link from one of his conservative news sites or Pastor Carl didn't say anything about it from the pulpit, she'd never hear about a particular current event. Especially not one from as far away as Detroit.

Grandma Lucy shook her head. "Terrible thing. I don't have all the facts. You'd have to talk to Ian about that. But it has something to do with them closing down one elementary school and merging it with another. Well, that was the plan. But the school they needed to shut down was mostly minorities, and the one they were going to merge with was more upper-class, and those parents got themselves all worked up. Made such a stink that the school district decided to build a new school for the poor kids instead, except the site they were planning to build on was in a bad part of town. I'm not talking crime. That's bad just about everywhere in Detroit from what I hear.

"But where they planned the new building, the land itself was no good. All kind of contaminants in the soil, toxic waste from chemical factories. Except the parents of these students, they weren't like the upper-class folks. They're working families, lots of single parents who are at their jobs during the day and can't attend meetings and forums. Even the ones who have time, a lot of them don't speak English well and they're too intimidated to stand up for themselves. So my grandson, he went and documented everything, got some statements from the families and a few other community members to show just how bad things had gotten.

"He sold it to one of the major networks, had it all lined up to air on national television, but then that night some big breaking story took its spot. Something about a murdered politician if I remember right, and that hogged the news for the next week or two until it was past back-to-school season and his network contact said nobody wanted to think about the education system anymore.

"He was pretty upset, obviously, not because of the money or anything, but because he believed in what these parents were going through. Really felt for them, I mean. He told me what he hated most was seeing how the school district gave in to intimidation when it came from the upper-class folks. The rich ones had the clout they needed to make the right kind of noise, but these minority families — the ones whose kids are going to suffer most in this new school they're building — they don't get a say at all. He thought he was giving them a voice with his camera, but it never even aired." She sighed. "He's got such a sensitive soul, I know God can use him for mighty things if he only gives his life to the Lord."

"It sounds like God's already using him," Kennedy suggested, but Grandma Lucy wasn't listening.

"I pray every day for that boy to come back to Christ. And now he's off travelling around Asia. Same thing. Human rights abuses, refugee crises. Always ready to speak up for the downtrodden and oppressed. So he's off to China with his camera but without the Holy Spirit to guide him. I gave him a Bible, and I told him I'd be praying for him. You know, that's all any of us can do in these situations, right? What about that roommate of yours? Is she born again?"

Kennedy kept her voice low, glad that Willow was sufficiently distracted. "I don't think so."

Grandma Lucy stared over her spectacles. "I take it you've witnessed to her by now?"

Kennedy glanced at Willow, who was snuggled up by Ray so they could share the same screen. "Well, I ..."

"You can't ever be ashamed of the gospel," Grandma Lucy interrupted. "Your roommate ... I can tell by the way she carries herself, that blue hair, those long earrings, that she's looking for something."

Kennedy wasn't sure you could discern that much about the state of a stranger's soul at first glance, but she didn't say anything. Something in Grandma Lucy's words had snuck past Kennedy's conversational barriers and found its mark in a conscience already ridden with guilt.

A year and a half sharing the same three-hundred square feet, and what had she done with that time? How many opportunities had she lost, opportunities to share the gospel with Willow, who was hurting, longing for more out of life whether or not her hair color had anything to do with her spiritual condition?

On the one hand, Kennedy was certain that if she were to bring up God or salvation, Willow would go off on one of her tirades against religion. So what was the point? Willow said once that Kennedy was the only Christian she could stand to be around because she never tried to convert anyone. If Kennedy started preaching the gospel every minute of the day, telling Willow she was a sinner in danger of the fires of hell, that would only confirm her assumption that all Christians are judgmental jerks.

But even though her silence on the subject kept the peace between them, was that in Willow's best interest? Kennedy thought about the missionaries she'd been reading about in those biographies: Hudson Taylor, David Livingstone, Amy Carmichael. The Chinese called Gladys Aylward a foreign devil and threw mud at her the first day she stepped foot on foreign soil. But she had remained faithful to God's call and ended up leading hundreds to Christ.

Kennedy had never had mud thrown at her, had never been called horrid names, but maybe that was because she'd kept her faith so hidden. She thought about the refugees her parents trained to send back to North Korea as underground missionaries. How many of them would suffer imprisonment or death as a result of their witness? And here was Kennedy, scared of mentioning God because she didn't want to annoy her roommate.

Were her priorities that askew? Or was she just doing what God wanted her to do? What was it that Grandma Lucy had said earlier, something about nobody having to do more than God asked them to. Maybe Kennedy's job was to prove to Willow that not all Christians are out solely to win more converts or smugly judge sinful behavior. Maybe that's all God expected of her.

But how would Willow ever get saved if she never heard the gospel? Kennedy didn't like the guilt trip, Grandma Lucy's insinuation that if she really was a *born-again* believer she should have converted her roommate by now or else died trying like the martyrs of old.

Grandma Lucy laid her hand on Kennedy's forearm. "Now, you tell me your roommate's name, and I'm going to add her to my prayer list. Then I'll give you my phone number and you can let me know when she's been born again, all right?"

Kennedy sighed. "Her name's Willow."

Grandma Lucy pulled a tattered notebook out of her purse. "Willow," she repeated. "Oh, dear. She'll be one of the last ones, I'm afraid." She smiled and explained, "I keep my list alphabetized, so when I'm going to sleep I don't forget who's next on the list. I always start with my granddaughter Alayna and make my way down from there. The good news is by the time I get to the Ws, I'll be nice and warmed up. If I haven't fallen asleep, that is."

Grandma Lucy's eyes twinkled, but Kennedy couldn't tell if she were making a joke or not. She didn't have time to wonder long before the bearded man in the turban jumped out of his chair with a startling shout.

"What's he think he's doing?" muttered the Seahawks fan with the BO. Several other passengers turned their heads as well.

The traveler pounded his fist into his seatback and yelled something frantic in Arabic.

The man in Carhartts stepped out of the bathroom and stood frozen in the aisle. Another man lowered his head onto his tray table and covered it with his hands as if he were a first-grader in an earthquake drill.

The man in the turban yelled aggressively, waving his hands in the air as if to emphasize a point.

"Get down," a man hissed to Kennedy. "That maniac is about to take over the plane."

www.ingramcontent.com/pod-product-compliance
Lightning Source LLC
Jackson TN
JSHW020811030325
79783JS00002B/10
9798348547592